"ROUSING."
—*Kirkus Reviews*

"COMPELLING."
—*Booklist*

"FOR READERS OF MILITARY FICTION
WHO WANT SOME BRAINS WITH THEIR BOOM."
—*The Baltimore Sun*

"SUSPENSE, DRAMA, AND ACTION
AS HOT AS A FIGHTER JET'S AFTERBURNER."
—*Publishers Weekly*

"EXCITING."
—*Library Journal*

Praise for *Punk's War*

"Suspense, drama, and action as hot as a fighter jet's afterburner, Carroll's account of modern naval aviation reads like *Top Gun* on steroids. . . . Will delight the military-techno audience . . . Loaded with testosterone . . . Speaks volumes about military careerism, aviation technology, naval operations in harm's way, and the men who fly and fight for a living."   —*Publishers Weekly*

"Tom Clancy meets Joseph Heller in this riveting, irreverent portrait of the fighter pilots of today's Navy. At last somebody got it right. I couldn't put it down."
                    —Stephen Coonts

"An exciting tale of a young lieutenant's tour of duty as a fighter pilot on an aircraft carrier stationed near Iraq . . . An intriguing look at the modern military, this novel honors the men and women who serve while helping to explain why so many decline to reenlist."
                    —*Library Journal*

"A thoughtful rumination on the ethics of war fighters and the notions of duty, loyalty, and honor . . . This is a compelling picture of the harsh realities of professional life for some of the most intelligent, able, and courageous young people in our society."   —*Booklist*

"This is a fine tale of today's post–Cold War military, where pilots patrol no-fly zones, watch their exploits on CNN, and then send e-mails to buddies complaining about careerist superior officers. If you want to know what life is like in the U.S. Navy today, this would be a good place to start."   —Thomas E. Ricks, author of
        Making the Corps and *A Soldier's Duty*

continued . . .

PUNK'S WAR

....

WARD CARROLL

A SIGNET BOOK

SIGNET
Published by New American Library, a division of
Penguin Putnam Inc., 375 Hudson Street,
New York, New York 10014, U.S.A.
Penguin Books Ltd, 80 Strand,
London WC2R 0RL, England
Penguin Books Australia Ltd, Ringwood,
Victoria, Australia
Penguin Books Canada Ltd, 10 Alcorn Avenue,
Toronto, Ontario, Canada M4V 3B2
Penguin Books (N.Z.) Ltd, 182–190 Wairau Road,
Auckland 10, New Zealand

Penguin Books Ltd, Registered Offices:
Harmondsworth, Middlesex, England

Published by Signet, an imprint of New American Library,
a division of Penguin Putnam Inc.
This is an authorized reprint of a hardcover edition published
by Naval Institute Press.

First Signet Printing, May 2002
10 9 8 7 6 5 4 3 2 1

 REGISTERED TRADEMARK—MARCA REGISTRADA

Printed in the United States of America

PUBLISHER'S NOTE
This is a work of fiction. Names, characters, places, and incidents either are the
products of the author's imagination or are used fictitiously, and any
resemblance to actual persons, living or dead, business establishments, events, or
locales, is entirely coincidental.

BOOKS ARE AVAILABLE AT QUANTITY DISCOUNTS WHEN USED TO PROMOTE
PRODUCTS OR SERVICES. FOR INFORMATION PLEASE WRITE TO PREMIUM
MARKETING DIVISION, PENGUIN PUTNAM INC., 375 HUDSON STREET, NEW YORK,
NEW YORK 10014.

For those on the Boat right now. Never forget what motivated you to walk through the front door of naval aviation, and never allow your squadronmates to forget either.

ACKNOWLEDGMENTS

Thanks are in order for the following people who answered the call for thoughtful feedback or whatever else I asked for: Vice Adm. A. A. Less, USN (Ret.); Capt. James A. Barber, USN (Ret.), Ph.D.; Stephen Coonts; Derek Nelson; H. Gelfand; Tim O'Brien, Ph.D.; Brad Johnson, Ph.D.; Shannon French, Ph.D.; Cdr. C. C. Felker, USN; Lt. Col. Bryan Riegel, USMC; Lt. Cdr. "Ice" Gamberg, USN; and Lt. "Nose" Dickerson, USNR.

Special thanks to Tom Cutler of the Naval Institute Press for his help throughout the process of writing and publishing this book, and thanks to Chris Findlay for his copyediting. Thanks to Giles Roblyer, associate editor of *Proceedings* magazine, for taking a great deal of time to slug it out and for sharing a literary vision with me. Thanks to Fred Rainbow, editor in chief of *Proceedings* magazine, for his friendship and support. And thanks to Ron Chambers, Naval Institute Press director, for hearing me out and for making the experience around producing this novel entirely enjoyable and rewarding.

My sincere gratitude goes to Lt. "Indy" Culler, USN, fighter pilot, for her sanity checking from the front lines of this effort.

Many thanks to my agent, Ethan Ellenberg, for listening to me for the last decade, for his hard work, and for keeping my dignity intact.

Special thanks and love to Col. Ned Carroll, USMC (Ret.), for his sage input, to my wife, Carrie, who spent countless hours providing constructive criticism, and to my boys, Hunton and Reid, for patience and wisdom well beyond their years.

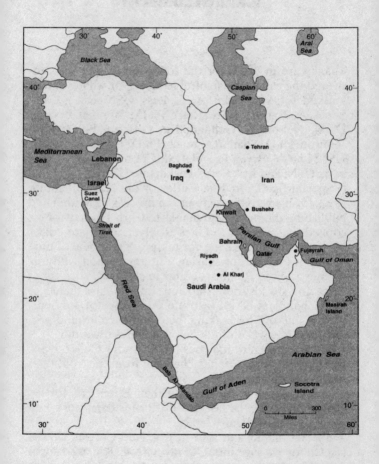

ONE

"Punk, wake up, goddam it!"

No. Not now. He wasn't up for the hostility right now. In spite of the noise of the phone constantly ringing at the duty desk and the maintainers doing full-power engine runs above his head and the incessant switching between red and white lighting and the blaring soundtrack and flash of the movie on the screen just feet in front of him and the angle of his ready room chair, he'd slipped into the most desirable of all worlds: *Not here.*

His body mustered a strong resistance toward the transition back to *here.* He attempted to counter the hostility with some fleet-savvy witticism, but all he could think to mutter through his pasty dream-world mouth was, "Help me, Mr. Wizard. I don't want to be on the Boat any more."

The Boat, the three-billion-dollar instrument of American foreign policy, was inseparable from its hostility—not the hostility that might be unleashed by a flurry of bomb-laden jets following failed diplomatic efforts, but the hostility resident inside the hull, the hostility of wake-ups punctuated by "goddam it." Though the majestic pace of the huge ship on the dark, calm seas of the Northern Arabian Gulf may have projected a certain tranquility to the dhows and freighters that passed in the distance, all was not quiet aboard the aircraft carrier. In fact, all was never quiet aboard the carrier. Somewhere between the ambitious goal of protecting the rights of the free world and simple job preservation was the buzz of the Boat—that *hostility.* Regardless of the time of day or the carrier's location, there was always some load being sweated, inane or legit, and some commander running around frying a circuit about the latest tasker from any of the seven numbered fleet staffs, or railing with a handset to each ear because of the admiral's "concerns."

"Punk, get up, you lazy, pampered nose gunner."

He thought of Duty, the pie-in-the-sky higher calling admirals and statesmen claimed would make the hostility tolerable at times like this. They said a sense of Duty would put the whole thing in perspective. And while he was busy buying the program, he might just arc around the Naval Academy grounds and carve a few monuments and get all teary-eyed. Duty, honor, country; honor, courage, commitment—boilerplate, designed to motivate him from place to place all day long. The actual words weren't important, just their rhythmic cadence: bhoomp, bhoomp, bhoomp.

"C'mon, Punk. We have to get on the roof and relieve the Alert 5 crew."

Sensing the battle lost, he allowed himself the luxury of another quick mental excursion: It had been so damn long since he'd felt the warm softness of the inside of Jordan's upper thigh, or brushed his nose across her.

"Yo, Punky . . . wake up, sleepy time . . ."

What else really mattered? Nothing. Not a thing. And the great thinkers definitely didn't develop their theories on cruise because if they'd tried they would have come up with only one finding: Sex is the only thing that matters. Life flashes at the point of imminent demise? He wanted his highlight reel to be a collection of women he'd known caught on their backs in the beautiful act of arching up and hauling their panties down across their gorgeous rumps.

"I see you smiling, Punk. I know you can hear me. You'd better wake up, asshole, or I'm going to go *oops* upside your head with my helmet."

The lieutenant finally gave a reaction to the hostility with a full stretch of his lanky six-foot-one-inch frame, and then he brought his long arms down from above his head and grabbed the scuffed toes of his flight boots. "Then who would you get to fly your ass around the beautiful Arabian Gulf, Spud?" he asked. He sensed he was perhaps semi-aroused after his brief but enjoyable repose so he chose to wait out the situation in the sitting position for a few moments. "Punk" was demeaning enough; he didn't need his call sign modified to "Woody," or the less-subtle but oft-assigned "Boner." And his backseater's caustic tone made it that much harder to relieve himself of the relative warmth of his faux-leather ready room chair.

Actually, the chair he'd fallen asleep in wasn't his; it belonged to the squadron's executive officer, the second in command. As Punk was only a lowly first-tour lieutenant, his chair was located more in the middle of the thirty-seven identical chairs in the ready room, but when you stood the 0200–0400 Alert 15, there weren't too many people around to care which chair you occupied. The XO's chair was in the front row and came complete with a leg-stretching ottoman fashioned from an old hydraulic fluid can covered in red naugahyde, the material the parachute riggers used to cover everything.

He ran his hand through his sandy blond hair, too long for anyone claiming the modern standard for military bearing, and glanced at the line-up on the white dry-erase board behind the duty officer. Who were they swapping with? Oh yeah, Bill Thompson and Biff. Punk figured he'd better get himself up to the flight deck in short order. He could see Biff checking his watch every few seconds and impatiently craning around in the ejection seat to see if his relief had made it to the airplane yet. Biff, the Big Fat Fighter guy, was basically a good man, one of his seven roommates, but he was not a stoic. And Punk didn't feel like receiving the business end of a whine right now. It was too early, or late, or whatever the hell it was.

He finally rose and felt the price for dozing in the sitting position. He winced, bent over to stretch out his lower back and glanced at his everything-proof watch: *Big hand on seven after, little hand on four.* A saying popped into his head, something admirals used when counseling groups of sailors about their conduct on liberty: *Nothing good happens after midnight and before breakfast.*

The crew grabbed their helmets along with nav bags full of charts and kneeboard cards and headed out of the ready room, but not before Spud paused to verify the film's best boy and gaffer line-up during the credit roll. "Those two are the best team in the business," he announced to no one in particular.

They continued outboard, down the passageway toward the ladder that led to the flight deck. The two aviators walked with the grace of football players coming out of the stadium tunnel before a game: cool, but encumbered. The narrow space they traveled darkened from red lit to completely black as they reached the final bulkhead. Punk extended his hand to work the hatch that opened to the outside, but he felt nothing. The hatch was already open. The blackness outside was merged with the blackness of the unlit passageway. *God, it's dark,* Punk thought. *If we have to launch let's at least wait until the sun comes up, please.*

The two aviators obediently followed the cones of light emanating from their flashlights as they climbed the short way to the flight deck. They moved slowly and deliberately so they wouldn't get nailed by the nocturnal predators on the Boat: open deck hatches, ankle-high fuel hoses, razor-sharp edged composite wings at eyebrow level, decks without railing, and hanging fins that were just as effective at slicing through skin as they were at guiding missiles toward enemy fighters. Punk's last flight instructor in Meridian liked to tell of the brand-new pilot in a Vietnam-era fighter squadron who'd disappeared into oblivion by walking over the edge of the carrier one night while engaged in the seemingly innocuous act of pre-flighting his jet.

The F-14 they were about to strap themselves into was spotted on catapult three, located about the middle of the ship toward the port side, which made the jet easy to find. Punk caught sight of their airplane once through the tangle of aircraft and support tractors around the edge of the deck and noted, that as the jet stood framed in the yellow tint of limited floodlighting from the carrier's island, it looked appropriately like a lone animal watching out for the rest of the sleeping herd.

In spite of his fatigue, he allowed himself to reflect on and be moved by the lines of the Tomcat, evidence of a fighter pilot's learned narcissistic sense as much as anything else. Where did gloved hands end and sticks and throttles begin? The question was moot.

Christ, boy, how cliché. The thing Punk feared as

much as a dual-engine flameout right after takeoff was becoming one of *them,* the twerps who showed up at the front door of flight school with a blank slate of a personality and slowly allowed the business of naval aviation to define every facet of their existence—guys who constantly used expressions like "the wife must've rolled in hot on you over that one" and "check six." He chided himself for his entry into the arena of the dorks. Who did fighter pilots impress? Boy Scouts and other fighter pilots.

Punk remembered that first squadron party, where Jordan had demonstrated her disgust with the self-centered, one-dimensional aspect of it all, amidst the Wings of Gold needlepoint and aviation line art that seemed to dominate career fighter pilots' homes. She spent the night asking all the wives wearing miniature Wings of Gold pins how they had performed during flight school, and whether they found flying jets to be a challenge. There was no scene. None of the handful of well groomed, if not attractive, wives had demonstrated the sense to be offended by his girlfriend's get-a-life jab. Punk saw the women differently after that. Only Jordan had a way of reorienting Punk, at times changing his long-held opinions with a simple statement or a gesture. She would dismiss his favorite song as bubble gum or sneer her distaste for a movie and everything would change in his head. And where the wives had originally seemed full of charm and grace, they came to reek of need and servitude.

And maybe that's what career fighter pilots wanted out of their mates. As the crews had worked to solve the world's problems during a deployment's worth of meal conversations, the topic had once landed on "the most desirable trait in a wife." While the junior officers had idealistically agreed upon "garners respect" (which barely topped "decent ass") as their platform from which to launch a lifetime of companionship, the lieutenant commanders and commanders across the table snickered and countered with "loyalty," which Punk found sadly curious, but congruous.

He was different, or at least he wanted to be different. Loyalty was a trait one sought in a dog, not a wife. Not that he would be at peace with his wife running around on him, but why would she? He was going to be the most tolerant, understanding husband ever. And she would be married to *him,* the catch formerly known as world's most eligible bachelor.

After knowing Jordan, Punk felt he could never be attracted to a woman who didn't try to stake her own claim. She had her own goals and aspirations, her own career, her own circle of friends. She was cocky like he was cocky—cocky in a good way. She was capable of changing his opinions, for crying out loud.

He needed just two days with her now. Two hours. Two minutes.

Spud didn't make it out of the catwalk as cleanly as Punk had. The backseater tripped on a tie-down chain several steps after his arrival on the non-skid; the unmistakable sound and expletive that followed caused Punk to chuckle and yell sarcastically back, "Watch out for those chains, Spud." Punk looked around and saw that Spud's flashlight had spun in his hand as he fell and was now illuminating his bald pate. Spud continued to curse as he picked himself up off the flight deck and, once fully upright, he used his flashlight to illuminate his left hand and gestured an "Okay," which slowly morphed into the bird.

Punk made it to the catapult track, stepping gingerly on its greasy surface. He crossed under the jet and stood at the base of the ladder on the left side of the nose. "Hey, fat boy!" he shouted up to the pilot seated in the front cockpit of the fighter. "Time for the first-string team to come in." In response the pilot in the jet redirected his flashlight from the paperback he was reading toward Punk's face. "Christ, Biff, so much for night vision."

"You're late."

"No, I'm not."

"Yes, you are. My watch is set to GPS time and it shows you're exactly nine minutes and thirty-eight seconds late . . . and counting." Biff threw his meaty hands above his head. "I'm still sitting in this jet, aren't I?"

"Well, you can blame Spud," Punk shot back as he ascended the ladder. "He woke me up late. I think he lost track of time watching *Cheers for Reggie*."

"Spud's flick addictions do not relieve you of your military duties, Punk," Biff said as he strained to undo the Koch fittings near each shoulder. He was a big fellow, somewhere between fat and husky (a word Punk's mom had always been fond of). Punk watched Biff deftly torque himself out of the jet and noted that the big pilot was actually kind of nimble. Biff was very self-conscious about his genetic plight and waged a constant battle with the Navy's weight standards. His peers rode him hard on the issue, but that battle ultimately earned him respect in the squadron's otherwise insensitive world. He ate like a rabbit and worked out like a professional athlete, never scoring less than "outstanding" on the semiannual physical readiness test. Nevertheless, he remained the Big Fat Fighter guy.

As they passed while making the switch into the front cockpit, Punk caught how Biff's face squished out of the front of his helmet. In fact, he stared a beat too long at the visage before him. Biff sensed the judgment and said, "Screw you, Punk."

"What?"

"I love this. Show up late and give me shit. I've lost twenty pounds already this cruise. It's not easy, you know."

"Biff, Biff, relax." Punk patted him on the right shoulder. "Spud and I were just talking about how good you look."

"I'll bet you were. Speaking of Spud, where is that old fart? My man Bill back there is as eager to get into the rack as I am."

"Now that I seriously doubt," Punk answered as he worked himself into the ejection seat. "Nobody has logged as much rack time as you this cruise." He fished near his left hip for the connection to his oxygen mask, and once the two halves were mated, he tested the system for good airflow. He then synched down his considerably loosened lap belts and asked, "How's this jet?"

"The oil pressure gauge was inop when we turned the jet about two hours ago so I had the ATs stick in a new—*aaahh.*" Spud made his presence known by smacking the back of Biff's helmet as he passed on his way toward the backseat. "You're funny as shit, asshole. Glad you found us. What does that make? Four hundred-plus viewings of *Cheers for Reggie*?"

"No, Biff. You're confused with the four hundred-plus times I've had to kick your ass since you joined the squadron," Spud said with an exaggerated flex of his runner's-frame forearm. "And I hope you're not complaining to my pilot about our being slightly, and I emphasize *slightly*, tardy."

"You guys are late, and the day your skinny bag of bones has the ability to kick my ass is the same day that Punk beats me in a dogfight."

"Well," Punk said, "that day was yesterday." Biff remained crouched down for a second on the front step and pondered Punk's words. Recent aviation history clicked in, and he shook his head in disgust and dismounted the airplane without another word. In turn, Spud climbed into the rear cockpit and reviewed the jet's backseat status with Bill Thompson. After a short time, lanky Bill followed husky Biff back down below to attempt whatever sleep he might be afforded before the daily grind kicked in again.

Punk removed his helmet and perched it on the forward canopy bow. He surveyed the cockpit and the area around the jet to ensure everything was in order: electrical power unit hooked up, air starter in place, fire fighters positioned, plane captain present. Although other cogs in the machine were charged with cognizance of their function within its workings, aviators knew the bottom-line responsibility of successfully getting the fighter airborne rested with them. The higher-ups would never point an accusatory finger at a tractor driver if an alert didn't get airborne in time because the jet's starting equipment had wandered off. The crew in the plane would be at fault; or more specifically, the pilot in the plane would be at fault.

Satisfied things were in order, Punk assumed his standard alert posture: book out and tunes on. He rummaged through his helmet bag and found the six-disc holder that was as much a part of his alert gear as his oxygen mask or G-suit. He decided that something instrumental would be the perfect soundtrack for a dark Arabian Gulf night. He laid the player down on the cockpit's right-hand console. He then trained his flashlight on the paperback and began splitting his attention between the novel and deciphering the movements outside his peripheral vision. Notification to launch came as often from a frantic, arm-waving flight deck chief as it did from the ship's P.A. system.

After a few minutes he craned around to see what Spud

was doing. Spud had also assumed his standard alert posture: He was fast asleep. *How the hell does he do that?* Punk had found an ejection seat to be the one place on an aircraft carrier where he could not fall asleep. He figured it was the combination of the upright angle of the seat and the fact that deep down he feared it might inadvertently go off, and he wanted to be awake if that ever happened. Unlike Spud, Punk was still naive enough to believe he had control of his mortality. In Punk's world, people didn't just crash. They fucked things away and then crashed.

Punk further pondered the wonder of Spud. Spud had entered the Navy as an enlisted man during the early seventies to avoid the draft. He spent two cruises in the Gulf of Tonkin aboard destroyers, mostly in the wake of aircraft carriers, and that exposure piqued his interest in naval aviation. Then, as he put it, his need for achievement eclipsed common sense and he was accepted into the Navy's enlisted commissioning program, sent back to college, and made an ensign after receiving his bachelor's degree.

During the initial medical evaluation prior to flight training, the flight surgeons discovered his vision was worse than 20/20 and he was declared ineligible to be a pilot. He was not left without a flying option, however. At the time of his commissioning, the Navy had moved toward multi-seat fighters and multi-place airplanes in general, and the guys in seats other than the pilot's could wear glasses as long as their vision was correctable to 20/20. So rather than return to the ship-driving force, Spud opted for the naval flight officer program and took the leap of faith that allowed him to ride along at either side of the speed of sound while someone else drove the aircraft.

But shortly after they were introduced, Punk realized Spud's hands-off-the-controls role in the airplane did not translate into a type-B personality. Spud was about eight years older than most lieutenant commanders by virtue of his prior enlisted experience, and he was now an old-world fighter guy. He came from the days before the ruling elite had changed everything in the names of "tolerance" and "equality," the days when a man could act like a man, or even a caveman, and no one would think to charge him with "conduct unbecoming an officer" as a result.

Spud often described himself to Punk as a "politically incorrect Cold Warrior," further explaining, "We *won* the Cold War." During the five deployments he'd made in his time as an officer, he'd survived a brand-new pilot's removing the bottom half of a jet on the back end of an aircraft carrier, ejecting at 400 knots, one divorce and his current wife's constant threat of a second one, and the back bar at the Cubi Point Officers Club.

He'd also come to love his job. He challenged common pilot perceptions about a backseater's second-class status in the fighter community. He often referred to Tomcat pilots as "nose gunners" and liked to point out how all the classified gear in the jet, "the important stuff," was in the rear cockpit. "This is a two-man fighter," Spud would pronounce. "If you don't like it, go fly Hornets."

Much to the delight of the more junior radar intercept officers in the squadron, Spud's assertion was that it was, in fact, harder to be a good RIO than a good pilot because the RIO had to be even farther ahead of the airplane in terms of decision making. RIOs, Spud claimed, were in the business of predicting pilot moves and preventing pilot errors. While those sentiments were tough for headstrong pilots to swallow, those who had ever flown with him knew he possessed the talent of which he spoke. Punk had lost count of how many times Spud had saved the day with a timely input from the backseat.

In spite of his advanced age, Spud had still been born about twenty years too late. Although the act of taking airplanes on deployment and flying them on and off of aircraft carriers was inherently rife with challenges and danger, Spud's time in the barrel had not been characterized by shots fired in anger, so he was measured by a different yardstick than those tested during protracted conflicts. And historically he'd been a little sloppy with the administrative side of an officer's duties—the kiss of death in the peacetime Navy. "Airmanship" was only one small block on an officer's fitness report. Spud's chances of getting his own squadron or even attaining the rank of commander were very slim, which gave him an attitudinal peace-of-mind that ironically made him one of the *Arrowslingers'* more influential lieutenant commanders. He realized this tour in Fighter Squadron 104 would be his last flying job and he wanted to finish on the same tenor that had sustained him throughout his career. No hidden agendas. No need for ready room politics. No traits that might ally the squadron's junior officers against him.

Punk shifted his gaze through the bulletproof glass in front of him and worked his eyes down the catapult track. He savored this spot on the flight deck. It made him feel like he truly was in a launch-in-five-minutes status. They'd also be airborne before the alert Hornet, which was always good in the world of bragging rights and competition at every level over every little thing. He had stood Alert 5s parked in ridiculous positions: pointed the wrong way behind the carrier's island and, in one instance, below the flight deck on the hangar bay. The aviators joked that on the Boat Alert 5 didn't mean launch in five minutes, but rather five jets had to be moved out of the way to get to the alert bird.

And why were they standing the alert? Satellites provided twenty-four-hour cable news coverage to the ship's crew, but that medium didn't give them any real understanding of their present situation. The heavies at the Pentagon called it being "on the tip of the spear," but the average aviator knew more about NFL team standings than any immediate impact the carrier's presence was having on the Middle Eastern dynamic. There hadn't been any media coverage of the area since the last cruise missile had knifed over the Tigris months ago. The place was dead. Punk could just hear the admiral saying, "It's dead because we're here."

Okay, he imagined his reply. *But that's lame and boring and it sucks.*

A few crews had intercepted some Iranian P-3s when the Boat had first arrived in the Gulf, but no one had seen anything but commercial airliners since. They could also forget about Iraq. The daily enforcement of the no-fly zone south of the thirty-third parallel was now about as exciting as an instrument round robin over the east coast of the United States. A crew would have to troll over downtown Baghdad at fifty feet to get any response out of those guys.

The Boat's mere presence drove the hostility and mandated the spool-up, so there he sat, a prisoner of bhoomp, bhoomp, bhoomp . . .

Time passed with Punk in the company of only his thoughts. His mind wandered back to his girlfriend. Five A.M. in the Gulf, nine P.M. on the East Coast—what was she doing now? That would depend on the day of the week. What day of the week was it? He honestly didn't know. He fished for some event that might give him a clue, but came up empty. One day pretty much resembled another on the Boat, except Tuesday was laundry day and Friday was pizza dinner day. He couldn't remember sticking his laundry bag out and they hadn't had pizza for dinner. It was time for an experiment. He pulled the disc player headset off and yelled down to his plane captain. "Sanders! Sanders, are you down there?"

"Yessir," the grease-covered airman returned as he scrambled out from under the jet. "Is something wrong?"

"What day of the week is it?"

The youngster scratched the matted black hair under his protective helmet and replied, "You know, sir, I don't have any idea. I'll go ask the chief." Before Punk could object, the airman bounded off to find the flight deck coordinator. Punk grimaced. His subject had escaped from the castle and now the angry villagers would certainly be returning with torches lit.

Chief Wixler showed up at the side of the jet a few minutes later with Airman Sanders in tow. "Lieutenant," he said up to the cockpit with his thick Louisiana drawl, "I understand you've got a question for Airman Sanders here?"

"No, not really, Chief," Punk replied sheepishly. Chief Wixler was not going to let him off the hook that easily. They'd had words a few weeks before when the chief downed Punk's jet on the cat just prior to launch for tire pressure. *Tire pressure.* Punk prided himself on being ever mindful of the role of the maintainers in the mission, but that particular call had seemed a bit self-important. Moreover, it had caused him to miss the best Saudi Arabian low-level hop to date. He hadn't stayed up half the night planning the damned thing to get pulled for tire pressure. The wheels were basically round . . .

"Sir," Chief Wixler began with the studied inflection of a senior enlisted man capable of meting out criticism under the blanket of respect, "I can't have an officer task-

ing an airman to hunt down a trivial fact when that airman should be vigilantly standing his post by the jet.
What if the alert got called away? You wouldn't want the
squadron to look bad, now would you?"

Punk winced. "Of course not, Chief, but . . ." He
thought about putting the situation in perspective,
about explaining the context of his simple question—
a lark—but he knew that would probably just cause
an argument, and he definitely didn't feel like getting
into another argument with Chief Wixler. The flight
deck chief was a man to have on your side, not gun-
ning for you. "I apologize, Chief," Punk finished with
a let's-all-relax chuckle as he rendered an informal
salute.

"You should get yourself a good watch, lieutenant,"
the chief said.

"Actually, I've got a Breitling," Punk replied, displaying
to the chief the monster on his left wrist. In the darkness,
the chief could tell the pilot had his arm raised, but
couldn't see the detail of Punk's reference. And he
wasn't about to buy into any rich-boy brand name bullshit.

"A what?"

"A Breitling. It's a very good watch."

"Does it do days of the week?"

Punk looked at the face of his watch as if he wasn't
quite sure of its features. "Well . . . no."

"Then how good could it be?" the chief cracked as he
slapped Airman Sanders on the back as if to say, "That's
how you handle these young officers, shipmate." With
that the chief returned into the darkness from which
he'd emerged seconds before.

Punk lamely called after him with, "It *is* very accurate," but there was no response. Punk imagined Chief
Wixler would go to some dark corner of the flight deck
and have a good laugh over his radio's in-house fre-

quency with the rest of the union labor on night check down in VF-104's maintenance control.

The lines were not as well drawn as Punk had come to believe they were during his years at the Naval Academy. Back then the world of military theory and leadership class was straightforward: the rank above you was to you what you were to the rank below you. Sure, they'd had discussions about informal chains of command and respecting subject matter expertise as a way to supervise and avoid micro management, but no one had captured the extremes of informal power in the fleet. No one had looked him in the eye and said, "You wanna go flying, officer boy? Well, the Chief Wixlers of the Navy are going to own your ass."

No, as he thought about it now, the irony of his "development" at the exalted United States Naval Academy was that it had done very little to prepare him for life in the United States Navy. He had walked into the Yard on Induction Day one hot July morning armed with above average SAT scores and without any better ideas, and he'd left four years later with a bachelor's degree, ensign's bars, and some really funny stories. Surviving the Naval Academy taught you about one thing: surviving the Naval Academy. For the average eighteen-to-twenty-year-old midshipman, the Academy was not about character and core values and professional military acumen infused into the marrow; it was about making the noise stop. What was the minimum effort required not to lose the privilege of getting away for a few hours on a weekend? A 2.0 grade point average, something even the worst crisis managers could manage. The conduct and honor systems? Hey, you rated what you got away with and only the stupid got caught. And how did you know you'd really arrived your senior year?

You were sometimes allowed to wear civilian clothes and *drive a car!*

But the Academy had defined him, and he knew he'd be foolish to deny it. Plus, he had loved his simple existence then, full of friends, girls, and pageantry. Hell, every day was a dress parade; every weekend was a gala ball. He even signed autographs for tourists on the way to class. America loved them because they were better than other college students, or so the Academy's leadership told them, although nobody ever really questioned what *better* meant. They had to be better, right? The broad-brush application of better was the only thing that grounded the frustration and angst of post-adolescent rites of passage squandered in the name of bhoomp, bhoomp, bhoomp. That and the fact that midshipmen were paid to go to college and had a guaranteed job after graduation. Who wouldn't put up with a little bullshit for that? Social retardation be damned!

Punk scanned the horizon off the port side of the ship. The fire in the distance from an oil platform's burn-off stack had faded as the friendly orange hue of sunrise grew to the east and gradually defined the end of sea and the beginning of sky.

The weather didn't give the aviators anything to complain about. Winters in the Gulf were generally mild: daytime highs often crept into the seventies and the sea was like glass most of the time, which meant no pitching decks for pilots to contend with while trying to land on the Boat.

Punk's first deployment had been a storm-tossed Mediterranean Sea event. The Med in winter was a place of good liberty ports, yes, but cold, swollen seas and ice-laden skies also. The air wing had lost four aviators that cruise, not to hostile fire over the former Yugoslavia, but to Mother Nature's effects on visibility and her sometimes-unannounced burden on an airplane's flying qualities.

Punk noticed movement off to his right. Although the ambient light was still limited in the early morning, the purposeful stride and gold-tinted visor perched on the helmet could only belong to one man on the Boat: Commander "Soup" Campbell, VF-104's commanding officer. Soup Campbell, former Topgun instructor, former Blue Angel, current pain in everybody's ass. *What the hell?* They weren't supposed to be relieved for another thirty minutes, and Punk didn't remember seeing the skipper's name on the schedule. Were they in trouble? Was *he* in trouble? Where was Chief Wixler?

"What's up, skipper?" he asked once the CO got close enough to the right side of the Tomcat to hear conversational tones.

"Oh, I couldn't sleep so I figured I'd be nice and spell you guys," the skipper said back up as he patted the nose of the jet. "Why don't you two head down to the wardroom and grab some breakfast and then get some more sleep?"

Unbelievable. This man—who defined "rank has its privileges" with his old-money scion, private high school, University of Virginia pedigree, his Lexus with FTR PLT vanity plates, and his greasy she's-with-you-only-because-I-don't-want-her aura—was now here sucking up a bad deal?

The gold visor said it all to Punk: the guy was about form over function. Commander Campbell was the only aviator in the air wing—probably the whole seagoing fleet—with a gold visor, and he never even wore it down over his eyes. It didn't function as a visor; it functioned as a crown. He was a Fighter Pilot, capital *F,* capital *P,* and he was *the* commanding officer now. His time had come. Prince Soup had become King Soup. *He* was going to pick the nightly movie in the ready room. *He* was going to decide on the topic of conversation in informal settings, and that conversation would always be about flying fighters so he could use his two trump cards at will: his Topgun experience ("Well, when I was at *The School* . . .") and his Blue Angel experience ("Well, when I was on *The Team* . . .").

Most important to the career-minded, he alone was going to decide for the Navy who was in and who was out among his charges, and he was quick to lord that power over all with the veiled threat: "Don't bite the hand that feeds you." The skipper had plenty of staff duty experience up his sleeve and had served on enough promotions boards to know how to write a fitness report that could make or break an officer's record. And unlike the other two commanding officers Punk had served under, Soup never asked for lieutenant commander input when writing fitness reports on junior officers.

Commander Campbell was not without redeeming qualities. If you caught him in his coveting phase he was downright enchanting. He could be fascinating with his cocksure swagger and worldly, crowd-dominating, name-dropping anecdotes ("So Senator Glenn says to his aides, 'We're not getting on this airplane until Soup gets here!'"), coupled with his gunmetal-blue eyes, thick, gray-flecked mass of hair, and permanent tan. At first, Jordan was even taken with him . . . before she was put off by his need to kiss the squadron wives and girlfriends on the lips at every chance meeting *and* parting.

Maybe Punk was a bit over-critical of the skipper, but he was growing tired of always playing the game on Soup's field with Soup's ball. Actually, they were all getting to that point in a cruise where everybody bugs everybody else. Five months down; at least one to go.

There may have been a light at the end of the tunnel for them, but it was yet too faint to make out. They'd been at sea for twenty-seven days now and had another week to go before pulling into Bahrain for a port call, their last before beginning the three-week transit back to Norfolk. The lab rats needed to get out of the maze for a few days.

Without giving the commander time to change his mind about his charity, Punk unstrapped and went through the off-going routine that Biff had performed with him hours before. Heading down the boarding ladder, he noticed that Spud was still slumping forward, asleep.

"Wake up, sleepy time."

Spud grumbled, gathered his things, and got out of the plane. He helped the skipper's RIO, Lieutenant (junior grade) Paul Francis, strap into the rear cockpit. Paul had only been in the squadron a few days and had not stepped on his crank in any fashion during that time, and therefore he still went by his Christian name. He came from the F-14 training squadron with Top Scope honors and seemed like an okay guy to the first-tour cabal, which was the strongest endorsement they ever gave to new aviators. The skipper had toyed with the idea of allowing Paul to remain stateside and join them upon their return, but the department heads had convinced the CO it would be a good idea to get the new RIO some hands-on fleet experience, even if that meant just teaching the new officer how to get from ready room to stateroom, or how to stand the duty.

"Well, I broke the seat in for you," Spud said, attempting to put the new backseater at ease as he manned his first alert. "Seriously, just relax. I don't want to burst your bubble, but I doubt you'll launch. I've stood twelve of these in the last month and I haven't done anything but sleep during every one of them." The young RIO nodded and smiled politely.

Spud joined Punk at the base of the ladder and they headed up the flight deck toward the bow and then below to Wardroom One. Breakfast awaited, the meal even the Navy couldn't screw up, as Spud often remarked. Punk started to salivate as he wrestled with the decision between pancakes and an omelet.

Once into the wardroom they were greeted by the warm, woody redolence of bacon frying. After stepping out of their harnesses, hanging them on chair backs, and placing their helmets and nav bags on adjacent shelves, the aviators backtracked through the dining area, shuffled by the scullery and made their way along the narrow passage and around two bends to the vacant food line.

Wardroom One, known as "the dirty shirt" because flight suits and deck jerseys were permitted, was the air wing's wardroom, as opposed to Wardroom Two four decks below, which was a stuffy place that demanded pressed khakis and table manners and was frequented by ship's company officers. The dirty shirt was conveniently located on the same level as all nine of the squadron ready rooms. The pace was slow at this early hour as most aviators didn't get out of bed until lunchtime because the flight schedule usually didn't end until after midnight.

Punk yielded to Spud's seniority and Spud grabbed a plastic tray from the stack and placed it on the aluminum railing in front of the glass-covered food bins. "Well, lookie here, my favorite cook is in the house," Spud said to the sailor at the grill. "Good morning, Petty Officer Byrne."

"Good morning, sir," the petty officer answered as he scraped the gristle from his latest effort off the otherwise shiny cooking surface and into a collection bin at the front of the appliance. "Not used to seeing you around this early."

"Well, I don't generally like to be around this early, if you know what I mean."

The mess specialist laughed and asked, "Is anything going on out there?"

"Just the standard stuff of making the world safe for democracy, the same thing you're doing down here."

Petty Officer Byrne smiled as if he'd heard exactly what he'd needed to hear. He turned from the grill and moved toward the two aviators. "In that case, I'll bet you could use an omelet with all the fixings." He proudly held his tray of chopped red and green peppers, mushrooms, and onions up for Spud to inspect.

"You're a surgeon, Petty Officer Byrne, nothing but a goddam surgeon," Spud said. "Give me the works, my friend. You know I'll eat whatever you're serving."

Punk admired Spud's genuine manner with the troops. His sincerity was born of having been in their shoes. Most enlisted guys had a sensitive B.S. meter—they resented officers who went through motions just to make themselves feel as if they were reaching in and getting their hands dirty for the drill of it. Spud suffered no such problems in his dealings with the crew.

As Spud's omelet sizzled to life, the mess cook turned his attention to Punk. "How 'bout you, sir?"

Recognizing Spud was a tough act to follow in terms of grassroots congeniality, Punk made no attempt to mirror his RIO's folksy vibe as he requested a tall-stack of pancakes. Both meals were served up in short order, complete with bacon and toast, and the aviators headed back into the dining room with their trays.

"I guess the skipper must've gotten a good letter from home or something, maybe an X-rated e-mail from the wife," Punk said as he pulled a glass out of the

top of a stack of eight-glass-by-eight-glass green plastic
holders. "That was wild of him to relieve us early." He
scooped some ice out of the nearby metal bin and
moved the glass under one of the soda machine nozzles.

"Yeah, wild all right," Spud replied.

"I never thought of him as the giving type," Punk
said.

"Giving? You'd better wake up and smell the Coke,
buddy boy," Spud said. "There's only one place we got it
and that's where the sun don't shine."

"What do you mean?" Punk asked.

Spud removed the articles from his tray and placed
them on the table at his setting, and then handed the
tray to an undertasked wardroom attendant who seemed
happy to have something to do. "I mean if the skipper
got his ass out of bed this early without being scheduled,
and went to the trouble of waking up young Paul to join
him, then he was in the possession of some information
that you and I did not have." Spud scooted his chair in
and reached for a paper napkin from the holder at the
center of the round table. "The intel geeks must've told
him something." He spread a napkin on his lap, focused
on his plate and voraciously crunched down on the first
of the nine pieces of bacon he had drawn.

Intel geeks: the intelligence officers who worked out
of CVIC, the carrier's information center. They weren't
aviators, although a number of them had washed out of
flight school. Aircrew viewed them as officers who had
access to volumes of information, but seldom knew anything useful to the war fighters. The intelligence officer's
job was mostly administrative although most of them
viewed themselves as high-tech spies right out of a Tom
Clancy novel. They wore flight jackets (which they'd
either procured surreptitiously or had "forgotten" to
return as they were banished from the halls of Pen-

sacola) to ward off the constant equipment-directed cold of CVIC, and on them they'd sewn a patch that read, "In God we trust, all others we monitor." They conducted general information briefs over the ship's closed circuit TV system before each flight, droning on with clunky monotones and jerky intonations that made it obvious to the aircrew the intel officers had no idea what they were talking about as they wrestled with the acronym-rich lexicon of naval aviation. They also debriefed crews after hops, but the questions weren't on the order of, "Did you see anything the President needs to know about ASAP?" They were more like, "How much gas did you take from the tanker during in-flight refueling?"

Each squadron typically had one intelligence officer, although VF-104, also tasked with the mission of tactical reconnaissance, had two: one male, one female, both androgynous in a more mannish than neutral way, and hard to differentiate to the degree that it was a little bit creepy. They were the same height and build, and both wore Navy-issue glasses with thick brown plastic frames. The female, Ensign Holly Dunbar, had further contributed to the illusion by styling her hair very short—not a feminine pixie look, but a regulation Navy male, complete-with-part, hairdo. Her male twin, Ensign Steven (*not* Steve) Grimes, had been in the squadron four months longer than Holly. He had quickly made a name for himself by throwing a fit because the operations officer had refused to install Dungeons and Dragons on the ready room's computer. "So how are we supposed to have any fun?" he'd raged, a response that had unintentionally become the rallying cry for the squadron's junior officers and was already the front-runner in the contest for the deployment's theme.

"So what did the Pats tell the skipper?" Punk asked.

Collectively the VF-104 intel officers were known as the
Pats, a reference to an old recurring skit on *Saturday
Night Live*. "And why didn't they tell us about it in-
stead?"

"Well, say what you will about them, they're not
without survival instincts," Spud said. "They wanted to
shake the hand that feeds." At that moment the sound
of the retracting catapult shuttle could be heard overhead. The distinctive clack, clack, clack meant only one
thing: the Boat was about to launch airplanes.

Punk jumped up from the table and turned the nearest television on and switched to the PLAT (Pilot
Landing Assistance Television), the channel that displayed what was happening topside. The PLAT camera
showed Slinger 102's stabilizers, spoilers, and rudders
deflecting in the dance that always preceded takeoff as
the pilot cycled the stick in the cockpit during his final
check of authority over the machine. At the same time,
the exhaust nozzles puckered as both General Electric
F-110 engines roared to full military power. Once he
was satisfied the dog would hunt, the skipper snapped
a salute at the catapult officer who returned the gesture
in kind. The cat officer crouched down and touched the
flight deck and then extended his left arm dramatically
forward, signaling the enlisted operator in the port catwalk to push the button that activated the launch se-
quence. A second later, sixty-seven thousand pounds of
F-14 went screaming across the deck, and 2.2 seconds
after that the fighter was thrown into the sky. The camera followed the jet through a left-hand clearing turn,
watched the landing gear retract, and then returned to
the deck to show an F/A-18 Hornet taxiing forward to
the catapult.

"Those bastards," Punk muttered. "They knew they
were going to launch all along, didn't they?"

"Bingo," Spud sang like a retiree at a church bazaar. "No wonder that new guy gave me his cat-with-the-mouse grin."

"Well, you've gotta like that," Punk said with resignation. "We sit in the ready room for two hours in our flight gear and then up there for ninety minutes in the dark, doing nothing, and then the skipper cruises in and takes the gouge daytime hop . . ." His voice trailed off.

"What good is power if you don't abuse it?" Spud asked paternally.

"I practically jumped out of the airplane for him," Punk said with an air of self-deprecation. "I'll tell you what: the skipper has a convincing poker face. He should go into politics." He fast-balled the last half-slice of toast to the plate and rose to head back to his stateroom.

"Actually, he's already in politics, or haven't you noticed?" Spud replied before pausing to allow the cacophony of the Hornet's launching overhead to pass. "Don't worry about it too much, though. They'll probably just drill holes through the clouds for a while. The Pats are wrong more often than they're right."

The Tomcat Punk and Spud had been seated in just minutes before was now fifteen nautical miles from the carrier and climbing through twenty-five thousand feet. The skipper and Paul went through their weapon systems' checks and sharpened the Tomcat's claws.

Their jet was loaded with a variety of long- and medium-range radar-guided Phoenix and Sparrow missiles, and two heat-seeking short-range Sidewinder missiles. The Tomcat was also armed with a nose cannon. While the notion of downing an opponent with bullets was somewhat dated, crews felt comforted knowing they still had offensive capability once they ran out of missiles.

Paul had the backseat UHF radio on preset button one, the primary control frequency labeled Strike. Strike was monitored by the E-2 Hawkeye control aircraft, the battle group's northernmost cruiser and the admiral's rep, the battle watch captain.

"Slinger 102, say your state," the controller in the E-2 requested.

"One-oh-two's state is sixteen-point-zero," Paul answered, indicating sixteen thousand pounds of fuel remaining, which would keep them airborne for a while, depending on how much the skipper selected afterburner.

"Do you have a station for us?" the skipper asked, his thick, salty radio voice in stark contrast to Paul's nascent utterances. Although most of the radio communication was performed by the RIO, the skipper had a habit of jumping on the frequency himself. Soup's RIO worked for Soup, and was not an equal-voting member of the crew. Paul was allowed to handle the administrative or routine communications.

The controller answered the skipper's question, "Slinger, your station is Mother's zero-nine-zero for thirty miles." They needed to position themselves thirty miles east of the Boat. "Report when on station." The skipper wondered why they wanted him to report on station when they had a planeload of black boxes to track him to within a foot. He felt good in light of the launch, so he had Paul comply with the request instead of righting the wrong in the name of professional semantics.

They uneventfully held on station for a time, scribing five-nautical-mile-long racetrack patterns through the sky, although in execution the shape looked more like an oval than a racetrack. The length of the legs was less than ideal due to the navigational constraints of the Northern Gulf, and didn't afford Paul much time to build a radar picture in any direction. The Boat was navigating Carrier Operating Area Four (CVOA 4), which wedged it and its airplanes between Kharg Island twenty-five miles to the north-northeast and the one-mile-square Farsi Island twenty miles to the south. Iran claimed both small tracts as sovereign territory, and the act of inadvertently flying over them was a diplomatic hot button, not really with the Iranians, but with the United States, which did not want to give the hostile Gulf states any grounds for lodging an international complaint against the carrier's operations in the region.

The center of CVOA 4 was also only about sixty miles west of the air base at Bushehr on Iran's upper Gulf coast. Fifth Fleet had imposed a twenty-mile standoff distance from the mainland, and Slinger 102's current station pushed them right against that limit. And they couldn't very well defend the ship by orbiting on the far, or western, side of the carrier—that would've been like defending a basketball goal by standing next to the sports photographers and cheerleaders behind the baseline.

The airborne Hornet occupied the northern station and was able to fly a more relaxed pattern over the more open waters, but if the Pats were correct, the skipper was on the better of the two stations in terms of intercept potential. Good photos of Iranian aircraft always translated into good visibility with the admiral, and that spoke to the skipper. As he thought about it, a wave of paranoia washed over him.

"Hey Francis, you brought a camera, right?"

"Roger that, skipper," Paul answered over the intercom. "Got it right here on the console next to my nav bag."

"Put it on around your neck," the skipper shot back. "It ain't gonna do us any good sitting next to your nav bag. C'mon, now. Stay up with the situation. I can't do everything."

Paul fumbled to throw the camera's strap over his helmet and flight gear as he struggled to remain resilient in the face of the skipper's sudden acrimonious shift. This was only their third flight together, and although Paul had experienced the skipper's quick temper over seemingly minor issues in the jet before, he hoped the CO would begin to calm down as they became more familiar with each other. He had felt quite the skipper's confidant as the CO had revealed his insider information on the way to the jet, but how many flights would it take to gain his complete trust? Well, obviously more than three.

Paul had graduated from Annapolis three years behind Punk, but his school had been a much different place than the dodge-the-bullet institution Punk had attended. Like his father and grandfather before him, young Francis strode up Stribling Walk and achieved and achieved and achieved—academically, athletically, and militarily. He was the über-mid: Brigade Commander, 3.6 GPA, and three-year varsity letter winner on the crew team. And unlike many of his classmates who'd walked into service selection with either an apathetic or lesser-of-all-evils mind set, Paul's desire to "Fly Navy" had the strength of the Fly Navy sticker's bond to the rear bumper of his Honda Accord, even with his poor eyesight. No, he wouldn't be a pilot like his Corsair-driving grandfather or his Crusader-flying father, but he was going to wade in amongst 'em catapulting off the front end of the Boat. Hell, the day his father had pinned his NFO wings on him had been the greatest day of his life, even better than graduation day at Annapolis when the President of the United States had awarded him his diploma and commission. Just thinking about those moments gave him clenched-fist motivation. If the Punks of the Navy accused him of believing the hype, Paul would counter with something his father had told him long ago: "If you can make a living doing what you love, you don't have much choice."

But he knew he had arrived the first time he talked to Spud in the ready room and watched his fellow fleet RIOs in action at sea. There was so much he hadn't been exposed to before his arrival in VF-104: targeting pods for precision-guided bombs, jam-resistant auto-frequency hopping radios, hand-held global positioning systems. He'd even drawn a pistol and a blood chit (a message written in Cyrillic that promised payment for his repatriation in the event he fell into the hands of apolitical locals) for his second flight in the squadron, an Operation Southern Watch hop patrolling the no-fly zone over Iraq. Now here he was on his first alert launch.

But even with his unlimited supply of idealistic, bright-eyed can-do, Paul had to admit to himself that the skipper's irascibility had started to mute the overall level of excitement. Why did he get so angry? *Is it something I'm doing,* the young RIO wondered, *or is he always hair-trigger in the jet?* Paul had already proudly e-mailed his dad to let him know he was crewed with the CO, in theory a coveted role for any backseater, not to mention a brand-new guy. Paul had only known success in his short life and wanted to make the pairing work. If the task required enduring some abuse then he'd just have to muster up a thicker skin. He was sure that in time the skipper would see how good he was.

He focused on the tactical display before him and

crosschecked their position with the jet's inertial navigational system and the hand-held GPS strapped to his left thigh. Nav was tight. He'd deftly used the limited number of waypoints available in the F-14's mission computer and oriented the display to a god's-eye view that he hoped would keep the skipper happy in spite of their precarious station.

"How's the nav?" Commander Campbell asked. "The admiral will rip my face off if we fly somewhere we're not supposed to, and if he rips my face off then I'll rip yours off."

"No, we're fine, skipper," Paul replied with feelings mixed between pride for anticipating his pilot's immediate concern and frustration because he had absorbed another draconian barb.

Too much time had passed. The skipper began to think the Pats had given him a bum scoop with their "possible tripwire player" leak, and that this flight was going to turn out to be another in a series of dull flights he had endured during this cruise. *The operations officer is going to pay for this,* he thought, ignoring the fact he wasn't actually scheduled for the alert. *I've got too much going on to waste time up here doing nothing.*

"Are we having fun yet?" the skipper thought out loud, interrupting an all-source silence that had lasted at least five minutes.

"I'm just happy to be here, skipper," Paul returned enthusiastically. A nice word? Dare he call it a breakthrough in crew relations?

The harmony was short-lived. The AEGIS cruiser's enlisted controller jumped on Strike with, "Hawkeye, are you going to do something about that track?"

"I've got it," the E-2 controller said. "Slinger 102, snap 180."

In the back end of the Hawkeye, the controller had been monitoring this particular track for almost twenty minutes, a track that had been the only activity in the E-2's three-hour flight so far. The track had started from Bushehr and worked its way east over a mountain range and into Iranian exercise airspace. It had flown in circles for a while and was now headed back to the west . . . and quickly. Whereas most of the tracks the E-2 crews had observed turned north as soon as they hit the water, well inside the territorial limit, this one kept going west at more than five hundred knots. *This ain't good,* the controller thought. *At this rate he'll be over the Boat in a few minutes.*

"One-zero-two copies the vector," the skipper said. "Say weapons' status."

"Red One," another voice answered on Strike. The skipper recognized the midwestern nasal twang as the admiral's. Obviously this track had grabbed the battle watch captain's interest to such a degree that he'd quickly brought the boss into the loop. The admiral, a ship driver by trade, didn't want anybody lobbing missiles yet. He had stated during the battle group's preparation phase that his greatest concern was trigger-happy U.S. Navy fighter pilots starting wars.

"What do you think, skipper? Commair?" Paul found it impossible to suppress the excitement in his voice. They were actually going to intercept something. Even an airliner would be something to e-mail home about.

"I dunno, goddam it," the skipper replied. "We're not going to see anything if you don't get a radar contact." The CO keyed the radio. "Bogey dope for 102."

"One-nine-zero now for twenty-five miles," the controller responded.

One-nine-zero? He's already behind us.

"Say bogey's angels," the skipper demanded, trying to figure out where to direct Paul to point the radar antenna.

"Negative altitude readout, Slinger," the controller replied. "Estimate angels medium."

Angels medium? Paul ciphered as he ratcheted the antenna up and down, desperately trying to get radar contact with anything at all. *That could be any altitude between ten thousand and twenty-five thousand feet . . .*

The scripted warning came over the military distress frequency, generated by the back-up controller on the cruiser: "Unknown aircraft, unknown aircraft, you are steering toward United States naval forces conducting routine training. Alter your course to the east or you will be subject to defensive measures."

"Alpha Whiskey's showing angels low," the AEGIS cruiser's tactical action officer (TAO) interjected onto Strike. "Look two-zero-zero, twenty miles, two hundred feet." Although the AEGIS cruiser was thirty miles north of the aircraft carrier in the battle group's "shotgun" position, the ship's phased array radar system and digital tactical information processing gave it an impressive look at the air picture over the entire northern half of the Gulf.

"Alpha Whiskey, what are you showing for his IFF?" the admiral asked.

"Non-squawker, sir. No ID at all," the TAO replied. "Alpha Whiskey can take with birds, if required."

"Sit on your hands, damn it," the admiral sharply directed toward all, but mostly at the overly aggressive initiative demonstrated by the cruiser's TAO. Airliners sometimes had faulty transponders, and the battle group commander was in no hurry to have another accidental shoot down of innocent civilians splashed all over the world's airwaves. *All we need is for the AEGIS to go robo-cruiser on us,* he thought.

The admiral assessed their options. The Hornet was too far to the north. "Slinger, can you make the ID?"

"Need bogey dope, sir," the skipper answered, his voice showing increasing irritation over their invisible opponent. It was now personally and professionally embarrassing, and Soup hated being embarrassed more than anything else. "Paul," he pleaded with his last bit of civility, "we need to find this guy on the radar . . . please. I'm saying 'please' and I never say 'please' in the jet."

"Skipper . . . I'm . . ." Paul fished for the contact while performing a full suite of mental gymnastics. He mashed the radar mode buttons before him and switched from the Doppler mode he'd been using to pulse search. *Contact!* "There he is. Two-four-zero for thirteen miles." He looked at the range and bearing to the Boat. "He's flying right over the carrier!"

"Alpha Bravo, we have radar contact," the skipper said on Strike. "Show him over your posit at this time."

"Yeah, thanks a *lot*," the admiral replied dryly. "We just made the ID using the PLAT camera." The faint roar of a jet flying by could be heard in the background of the transmission as the admiral spoke.

"What kind of airplane was it?" the cruiser's TAO thought to ask.

The admiral keyed the radio before he was prepared to answer and the flurry of surface warfare officers trying to identify the aircraft in question could be heard by all monitoring Strike.

"What was it . . . no, no, the jet . . . the one that just flew over . . . no, it's not one of ours. What kind was it? That jet on the TV there . . . I need to know what kind it is . . . an F-4 . . . an Iranian F-4 . . ."

The warning was given again by the cruiser: "Unknown aircraft, unknown aircraft, you are steering toward United States naval forces conducting routine training. Alter your course to the east or you will be subject to defensive measures."

Things didn't get much worse in the world of fleet defense. A fox was loose in the hen house and the farmer was looking at his dog wondering how it had happened. Soup ran both throttles against their forward limits and resolved to get close enough to the Iranian jet to snap photos in which the Pats could count the whiskers in the pilot's mustache, or to flame out trying.

"Don't lose the lock or you're dead meat," the skipper said to Paul.

"Show your bogey north for ten miles, angels low, estimating one hundred feet," the E-2 added.

"Oh, now the clairvoyance," the skipper muttered over the intercom, more thinking out loud than talking to his RIO. He keyed Strike: "Cease chatter. We've got him on radar." All controllers could kiss his ass about now.

Paul noted the range to and closure on the contact: Eight miles away and 100 knots of overtake. He switched his display, from the puzzle of lines and digits that was the tactical presentation to the view of the television camera set under the nose of the Tomcat, and watched an object pass through the picture as the system worked to obtain a contrast lock. Paul looked to the left console to verify that he had the mission recorder working and the television camera slaved along the axis of the Tomcat's radar lock. As he looked back at the display a second later, the distinctive shape of the F-4 Phantom appeared. It appeared that the Iranian was in a turn, although the view through the TV was

sometimes deceptive in terms of actual angular difference between the Tomcat and another aircraft.

"Is he turning?" Paul asked the skipper.

Vanity prevented him from ever admitting it, but his
aging-fighter-pilot eyes weren't what they used to be.
"I can't really tell," the skipper said.

Paul continued to watch the television view. "He
looks to be nose-on now, heading right for us," he reported. The young RIO stared at the screen with the
calm curiosity of disbelief as a cloud formed under the
opposing jet and an object fell away from it.

"He shot at us!" the skipper screamed on Strike. He
wrapped the Tomcat into a hard right turn in an attempt to avoid the Iranian missile. The CO repeatedly
depressed the expendable button on the stick, which
rifled a series of flares and chaff bundles out of the underside of the F-14 in an effort to decoy the incoming
weapon. He continued the turn, pulling for all the G
his airspeed would allow.

Before the G forces had surprised him and pinned
his head to his knees, Paul had looked out the right
side and noticed they were right over the Boat. Now
all he could do was study his thighs at close range. He accidentally keyed the radio and transmitted to the fleet a
loud gag followed by a series of grunts as he fought to sit
upright once again.

The noise of human suffering caused the admiral to
look around at the officers gathered in his command
center and ask, "What the hell was that?"

"E-2 is showing merged plot," the controller offered
matter-of-factly, but the skipper was now ahead of the
rest of the battle group. Although he had watched the
Iranian missile fall harmlessly below them, Commander Campbell still had the Tomcat in a right-hand turn.
He realized he had turned too far. He had almost

solved the Iranian pilot's problem and rolled out in front of the F-4. The skipper reversed back into his opponent, reefing his jet into a left-hand turn. The momentary return to one-G flight during the reversal allowed Paul to sit up and brace against the next onset of gravity-plus.

"One-zero-two, what is going on?" The crew was far too busy to answer the admiral's query. The Phantom shot by them 180 degrees out in a nose-low, left-hand turn.

"Let's blow the tanks," the skipper said over the intercom. Paul felt two distinctive thumps as he flipped the proper jettison switches in his cockpit and the skipper did the same.

Reduce the drag, Paul thought. *Good call.*

"I own you now, Abdul," the skipper declared over Strike with an eye to the Classic Quote. Years of personal sacrifice and administrative gamesmanship and finally his name would be where it belonged: among those of the great air warriors. Rickenbacher, Bong, Olds, Cunningham, and Campbell.

The skipper's excitement and desire for the kill caused him to bleed airspeed during the last two hundred degrees of the turn. As they rolled out of their series of hard turns, the Iranian was headed east toward home in full afterburner, and the skipper noted the two bright orange circles going away from them.

"What's the range?" the skipper asked Paul.

"Two miles, two hundred knots, opening." *Opening?* The skipper looked at his airspeed indicator. Two hundred knots. *Damn.* In spite of forty-four thousand pounds of thrust pushing out of the back of the jet, he'd ham-fisted the turns and bled off too much energy. Now they couldn't use the Sparrow or Phoenix missiles. Those weapons needed closure and lots of it.

"One time, babe! One time!" the skipper shouted through his oxygen mask without keying the intercom. He was a raging madman now, not at all the cold, steely-eyed killer. He jammed the toggle switch on the stick down in an attempt to switch from Sparrow to Sidewinder and pulled the trigger.

The bbwwwwwoooopppp of the gun mocked them like laughter from the streets of Tehran and the hundred rounds of 20-millimeter ammunition fell about two miles short of their intended target and into the Gulf. In his near-hysteria the skipper had overshot the Sidewinder detent and selected Guns.

"I think he's too far away for guns, skipper," Paul suggested.

"No goddam shit, Einstein!" the skipper screamed in return. After overshooting the Sidewinder selection one more time going the other way, he finally zeroed in on it. He fired, but it was too late. The Phantom had used the time to get out of the Tomcat's range for good, and in a matter of minutes the Iranian crew would be safely on deck at Bushehr enjoying lamb's meat shavings on pita and flat cola. The Sidewinder followed the bullets into the sea.

"One-zero-two, I ask again . . . what is going on?"

"Unknown aircraft, unknown aircraft, you are steering toward United States naval forces conducting routine training. Alter your course to the east or you will be subject to defensive measures . . ."

TWO

The personal call sign: a fighter aviator's *nom de guerre*. Often painful or embarrassing, sometimes flashy or predictable, the nickname not only served a tactical function during communications between jets, it frequently acted as a guide to human frailty in olive drab packaging or served as the title to an anecdote.

Within the world of call signs there existed an unspoken hierarchy. At the bottom were aviators without one. Some were never given call signs simply because their existence was too neutral to earn them. Bill Thompson was in this group. Several names had been thrown at him during his also-ran days in VF-104, but neither B.T. nor Butter nor T-Dog nor B-Man stuck for the length of time it took to get a nametag made. He remained just plain Bill over the long haul, which was as strong a statement to insiders as the most colorful call sign. "Bill" spoke of an aviator who'd found the squadron's collective blind spot and stayed there—without the flair and popularity of the charismatic, the faculties of the well-timed, good-natured buffoons, or the talent of the naturally blessed—and of a man who'd also avoided dubious and spiteful appellations reserved for the infamous among them: the Snakes and the Darths. A Bill, whether or not actually average, was guilty of exuding the dull, ineffectual resonance of average, and that, in some sense, was a greater crime than being a flaming asshole. The punishment awarded was the scarlet letter of a real name.

Just above the Bills were aviators whose call signs were formed by mindlessly placing a *y* at the end of their last names, like Jonesy and Smitty. At the same level were the what-else-are-you-gonna-call-'em guys like Soup Campbell, Mac McManus, Pink Floyd and Taco Bell.

All hosannas were reserved for those who practiced the art of commission, those iconoclasts who brightly forged a path through the jungle of the mundane and across the tundra of textbook etiquette, who reached out for what they knew in their hearts to be rightfully theirs: the call sign earned by a quirk, a habit pattern or a single stupid, perhaps compromising, and most likely embarrassing act—the call sign that begged the tale, that demanded the answer to "why?"—a call sign like Punk.

Punk had dutifully served the *Arrowslingers* for a few weeks under the name of Rick Reichert, the same name that he'd used for the first twenty-five years of his life. One fateful night during his first deployment, as the Boat transited across the Atlantic toward the Med, hours after taps had been called over the 1MC by the bosun's mate of the watch, the junior aviators worked to deaden the initial sting of family separation and the ennui of six straight no-fly days. The mouthwash bottles circulated, the movies rolled on the VCR, and the stereo volume rose to keep pace with the din of animated chatter among the eight officers who would call the stateroom home for the next six months. At some point, the door to the room opened and a silver-haired figure with gold-framed aviator glasses peered in. He stood there for a time, unnoticed by the denizens within.

Ignorance turned to curiosity followed by recognition. Somebody screamed, "Attention on deck!" In one fluid motion, Punk rose to his feet, reached above his locker and shut the CD player off. The Boat's captain acknowledged the demonstration with a wave of his hand as he took a half step into the stateroom without relinquishing his grip on the life ring that was the doorknob.

"What the hell are you listening to?" the captain asked, eyes working the room in strokes of either disgust because of the mess or nostalgia because of the apparent bonding in progress. "Is that some of that new punk rock?" He chuckled at his own quip and followed with, "Anybody in here got their hair parted down the middle?"—a dated reference to the seventies-coined adage that certain hairstyles were synonymous with illicit drug use.

"It's actually the Beatles, sir," Punk replied with a hint of sarcasm to the captain's original question.

The captain missed it. "Whatever. There's nothing wrong with blowing off a little steam, gents. Let's just keep it down, okay?" He performed a rapid-fire eight-beat roll with the fingers of his right hand on the doorframe, and then he was gone.

They stood for several seconds after the captain disappeared, stunned by the unorthodox intrusion and wondering whether the captain had noticed their ample and very illegal at-sea caches of oral hygienic supplies. Punk finally broke the silence.

"I can't believe the captain didn't recognize the *White Album*. I mean, we're not talking about some obscure band here. We're talking about the Beatles."

"Face it," Biff replied, only a few weeks older in the squadron than Punk, but already permanently labeled nonetheless, "the man has scaled the ladder. He knows punk rock when he hears it." He trained a finger on his roommate. "And he knows a punk rocker when he sees one."

"Hey, I may be a lot of things," Punk replied, "but I am definitely not a punk." He was quickly schooled on the folly of self-serving declarative statements in informal settings around the squadron when the rest of the seven in the room formed a circle around him and began chanting, "Punk! Punk! Punk!" At that moment, Rick died; Punk was born.

That had been almost two years and one ship's captain ago, and he'd worn Punk ever since. "Rick" actually sounded foreign in the unlikely event someone in the business used it to address him; it became a name reserved for parents, a girlfriend, and normal people.

And Spud? Those who felt John Wayne's roles accurately illustrated the military experience might assume that the lieutenant commander hailed from Idaho. Naval history buffs, on the other hand, might connect Spud's ramp strike with the fact that the back of an aircraft carrier was traditionally called the spud locker because produce was stored in that general area during World War II.

Actually, Spud earned the call sign in the Philippines. Although he never told the story himself, accounts said he was "forced" to attend a live sex show at a club in the town just outside of the old naval station at Subic Bay. At one point during the evening's entertainment, the drill was for audience members to throw things at the stage. The nude actress would hide these items in one of two places inside her body before shooting them back at the crowd in an amazing display of pelvic-area muscle control. This was not a new act and fleet veterans came armed with baseballs, taped stacks of coins, and even military-issue flashlights.

Spud had not been pre-briefed on the program and began to feel a bit left out. Just then, he sensed something against his foot. He looked down at the dirty cement floor and saw a large potato, presumably a refugee from the kitchen a few feet away. Without a second thought, he chucked the tuber over the seven rows in front of him and onto the stage.

The actress caught sight of it and waggled her finger in the direction from which it had arrived, a gesture that seemed to say, "You . . . bad . . . boys." But she accepted the challenge nonetheless. She chose Option B and the potato was made to disappear for a time. She moved to the front of the stage, right in the center, and turned her back to the crowd, kicking her hips to the beat of the accompanying loud rock music. She extended her arms over her head, like a swan stretching its wings, then brought them to her side, inhaled deeply and bore down while bending quickly at the waist. The front row was treated to the potato at considerable velocity and more—too much more.

Ringside delight turned to horror and waste-soiled sailors scattered. The chief in the most direct line of fire immediately began to vomit. The sound of a turntable needle being dragged across vinyl announced the abrupt end of the act, and the actress shrugged and ambled off the stage. Those out of the frag pattern rose in an ovation that, under similar circumstances, only a group of true connoisseurs would have been able to muster.

And the fighter aviators said it was good. They knew of a Turd in another squadron, so they hailed the new RIO as Spud.

Still lamenting the stolen flight, Punk opened the door to his stateroom and was greeted by a pornographic video on the twenty-five-inch monitor across from him. The stateroom was completely dark, save the tube's glow, which highlighted one of his seven roommates sitting immediately in front of the screen where no fleshy detail could escape. The roommate, Trash, was wearing nothing but a towel draped across his lap, and Punk quickly noted that both of his hands were in plain view. The starlet's moans were barely audible, as the ever-considerate Trash had no desire to disturb those asleep at the early hour. He turned his head toward Punk as the door shut and quietly said, "Money shot coming up. You've gotta love it," before redirecting his attention to the feature.

God, this place is a shithole, Punk thought as he picked his way the few feet from the door to his desk. Flight suits, running shorts, and T-shirts hung from any device that would support them, giving the impression that the room was constructed of Nomex and cotton. Boots and sneakers were strewn about the floor, none in immediate pairs, and damp towels decorated the backs of chairs. The room was always warm because it was located directly below the midway point of the steam-powered waist catapults, and it had a smell just short of offensive—the kind of smell that could've easily gone totally south with a missed laundry day. Spud had once asked, "What are you guys doing, making cheese in there?" and the eight residents had fondly referred to their at-sea home as the Cheesequarters from that moment on.

Punk's concerns about the mess did nothing to stop

him from adding to the entropy of the space. He stripped down to his skivvies and made ready for the rack, setting off his own little uniform bomb while undressing in the area he'd come to regard as his: the near corner of the stateroom along the wall with the room's only phone hanging on it.

The lines of demarcation weren't drawn into the design of the place; they were understood and honored. Each man had a desk that folded down from the middle of a metal wall unit that included a cabinet above, a full-length closet beside, and two drawers below. The units were in two opposing rows of three, and the other two were at the end of the room toward the sleeping area. The racks, arranged in four groups of bunk beds, made up the back half of the stateroom, and a cloth curtain separated the two areas.

To make the room more livable, the junior officers had covered the floor with five unmatched carpet remnants joined with generous chunks of duct tape and applied self-adhering wood-grain-patterned shelf liner to the outer surfaces of their wall units so that the lockers might appear to be made of oak instead of metal. The effect of both efforts to make the space seem less like a ship and more like a den or finished basement had been mitigated over the months by the stains on the carpet, the weakness of the duct tape, and the tears in the contact paper. All that the accouterments did now, despite their creation in a mood of optimism toward the adventure ahead, was add to the Cheesequarters's clutter.

Punk padded back to the sleep chamber and vaulted into his rack, the one above Scooter, careful not to trod upon the Most Handsome Man in Naval Aviation during the studied move up to the top bunk: the step, thrust, and twist. He flopped on his back and looking up at the labyrinth of pipes and wires that lined the ceiling waited for sleep to come.

He heard the catapult shuttle retract again, the same noise he'd heard in the wardroom fifteen minutes before. The Boat was launching more jets. Punk jumped down from his bed and hurried back around to the desk area of the stateroom where Trash remained engrossed in the video. Punk pushed by him and switched the monitor to the PLAT channel.

"Hey, man! What the hell?" Trash asked indignantly.

"Chill. I've got to check something out." Punk looked at the screen and saw that a Hornet was about to go flying. He looked back at his seminude roommate. "Aren't you at all curious about why we're conducting flight ops right now, Trash?"

Trash was unmoved by the professional challenge and replied, "Boats launch jets," as he adjusted the towel covering him. "Jets launch; jets land. So what?" He held his right index finger aloft—Patrick Henry at the Second Virginia Convention—"Porn endures."

Punk just shook his head as he reset the media center to Trash's specifications. *Another launch?* he wondered as he walked back to his rack. *There must be something going on up there. I guess the Pats did have the gouge.*

Again he performed the step, thrust, and twist, and again he contemplated the array of cabling and machinery above his head. He glanced at the Breitling: *six-thirty here, ten-thirty there.* Jordan lived in a world so far away. Did she think of him as much as he did of her?

They had met three summers ago at a chamber of commerce reception on the resort strip of Virginia Beach. Punk had been invited to the get-together by a neighbor from his condo complex after a poolside conversation about the rut into which his love life had fallen. Jordan was working for a telecommunications firm based in nearby Norfolk, and her boss had ruled attendance at the weekly business mixer mandatory for the company's marketing and sales forces. The guy who had invited Punk in the first place—a guy, he discovered later, who'd been shot down several times by Jordan in his attempts to get something going with her—introduced them.

Jordan had not been exposed to the military during her high school and college years in Champaign, Illinois. Punk's fighter pilot status was the spark that extended the conversation beyond "are you from around here?" and won the first date, but because Jordan was not a fighter pilot or a Boy Scout, his professional standing alone was not going to carry the day—a new one for Punk in the world of girlfriends. His class ring had been the magnet of attraction for the girls he'd been with at the Academy, and his Wings of Gold had served the same function in recent years. With those ornaments as companions he'd always called the shots, sometimes obnoxiously so, and the first midnight request for company one of them had honored had been followed by many more. The boomerang girls, who hung out at the officers club Friday night after Friday night, were a sad joke because of their habit of returning to the spot they'd been thrown from the week before, but when the months wore on and he knew only them, he feared the joke might be on him.

That fueled his attraction to Jordan, and as the relationship slowly progressed, Punk also began to fear a grand conspiracy by the spurned boomerang girls to create Jordan and turn him into the boomerang boy. He wanted things to happen quickly; she kept a cool head and controlled their pairing on her terms. But Punk's hard fought battle made the occasional victories worth it all. But that footage was getting old now. The yearning welled up inside of him again.

Punk thought about what impact the cruise might have on their future. Had the e-mails cooled over the months at sea, or had the innuendoes simply become subtler? Had she finally thrown her hands up in frustration with the abnormality of Navy separations and vowed to keep her life more predictable? He sighed to himself about how the one thing he wanted to control most in his life, a life characterized by his hands on the reins of it, was completely out of his control. The glee the boomerang girls must've derived out of this sort of payback—the same boomerang girls condemned to their own reputations and lives of the pathetic chase to become a Navy wife, a chase that normally had no end for them. Weren't they all laughing at him now?

The phone rang—never a good sign on the Boat. In the real world, the sound of the telephone ringing was most often associated with optimism. Mom and dad called to say hello. Buddies called to pass on a late-breaking party opportunity. A girlfriend called to say her plans had changed and she was free after all.

On the Boat, however, a phone call meant one thing: senior officers looking for junior officers.

"Is somebody going to answer that damned thing?" Punk asked as the phone rang for the sixth time. "Trash, how 'bout it?"

"I'm not getting it," Trash replied. "I'm busy."

Suddenly, six variations on "answer it, goddam it," issued in terse tones by lieutenants who had either been asleep or been near sleep moments before, convinced Trash to get out of his chair and answer the phone.

As Trash lifted the receiver off the hook following the ninth ring, Punk longed for the sleep he'd hoped to get, and the answering machine they'd once had. A few of the roommates had smugly wired the device with the idea that the phone would never ring, and that they could check messages from time-to-time at their leisure. That didn't fly. The first time Beads, the squadron's operations officer, had been unsuccessful in an attempt to speak with one of the officers in the eight-man stateroom, he'd marched down to the Cheesequarters and summarily yanked the machine off its mount and thrown it over the side of the carrier.

Following his clipped blatting of a pained "dammit," the symbolic way of shooting the messenger, Trash hung up and walked back to the racks.

"Reveille, reveille," he called, banging on each metal bed frame as he passed down the line. "Wake up, gentlemen. Emergency all officers meeting in the ready room, right now."

"What?" Biff asked, as the upper half of his ample and unclothed pink body pushed out from behind his rack curtains. His head featured what appeared to be two small tumbleweeds of hair headed in opposite directions. "Why?"

"The duty officer didn't say, and I didn't ask," Trash answered as he dropped his towel and went in search of some clean boxer shorts.

The room slowly came to life. Officers grumbled and climbed out of their racks. In short time, stretches and yawns gave way to the buzzing of electric razors and the running of water.

There were two sinks located side by side, immediately to the left upon entry into the stateroom, but just now only the right one was in use. The sink on the left was commonly known as the "general quarters sink" because it was employed as a urinal during simulated battle stations, and therefore it had ceased to function as a device for human cleansing. Aviators had no official station during general quar-

ters drills; in theory, they would be airborne fighting
off the aggressors if the ship was under attack. So,
the enterprising aircrew unofficially used the hours
of general quarters drills to get some additional rest.
But even the sleepiest of rack hounds reached a
point where matters of nature could no longer be
ignored.

During GQ it was a bad idea for bed-scarred officers to roam the passageways searching for an opportunity to relieve themselves, as sailors lugged fire
hoses and puffed under gas masks while fighting mock
disasters. That sort of officer presence would not go
unnoticed and certainly would not help to build esprit
de corps between the troops and the aviators. There
existed an unspoken agreement between the captain
and CAG, the air wing commander, that the wing's
junior officers would simply "seek deep shelter" once
GQ was called away, and also that any violation of
that agreement would lead to an aviator's detailed understanding of halon and nozzles, the prospect of
which was more frightening than the lieutenants' most
traumatic nightmares.

Compliance was easily obtained. The junior officers'
code implied the avoidance of activities that could impact on sleep opportunities. The rule: "Don't leave the
stateroom during GQ; piss in the left sink if required—
just run about forty parts water to one part urine during
the process." That was probably why naval architects put
two sinks in the room in the first place.

Little by little, the shrapnel from the last sets of uniform bombs was gathered and the temporary Nomex
and cotton structures were brought down as the roommates dressed for the unscheduled meeting. Biff was the
first one ready, mostly by virtue of the fact that each of
his flight boots, although laced, had rugged, custom-

installed zippers up the inner side that allowed him to quickly slip them on and make them snug without going through the lengthy process of lacing them.

As Biff waited for his bunkies to go through the old-fashioned process of unimaginatively tightening their boots using black nylon shoestrings, he did a head count to ensure nobody was left asleep.

Seven. Somebody was missing.

"Where's Paul?" Biff asked.

"He answered the phone about an hour ago, put his bag on and then left," Trash said.

"Geez, Trash," Punk returned, "how long have you been up watching porn?"

Trash smiled demurely and said, "Time holds no meaning for me in the company of my muse."

Punk shifted his attention to Biff's question and replied, "He's airborne with the skipper."

"Airborne with the skipper?" Biff repeated with an animated look of great confusion. He was the squadron's schedules officer and few things upset him as much as deviations from the plan, and since the plan was seldom adhered to on the Boat, Biff always had plenty to get upset about. He looked at a sheet taped to the side of his desk. "The flight schedule doesn't start until 1300 today."

"He launched on the alert," Punk explained.

Biff referenced the schedule again. "The skipper wasn't supposed to have the alert."

"He jumped in behind me," Punk said. "Look, I'll bet this is what the AOM is about. We'd better get going or we'll be even later than we already are." He queued himself in the doorway and waited for the well-groomed-but-ever-sluggish Scooter to finish his last double knot. "I'm sure all things will be cleared up once we get to the ready room."

"He wasn't scheduled for the alert," Biff muttered as he fell in behind Punk.

Passing through the door to the Cheesequarters like paratroopers bailing out of a transport, the seven junior officers formed into a tight column once in the passageway and began to negotiate the obstacle course that was the 0-3 level. The passageway was divided about every twenty feet by hatch-like openings formed by the frames of the ship, known as kneeknockers because of the damage potential they posed to the human leg. Clearing kneeknockers required a deliberate, semi-athletic effort to pass over them, and during a trip along the length of the carrier, the average male gait took the meter of stride, stride, stride, *step;* stride, stride, stride, *step.*

The VF-104 ready room was the aft-most of the nine ready rooms on the 0-3 level and, like all of them, was oriented across the ship with the front of the room toward the port side. It was a relatively large space, running nearly the entire beam of the carrier. The room featured a red and black checkerboard linoleum floor, an acoustic tile drop ceiling, and a single metal door at each end. The walls were thick with plaques, trophies, and historical command photographs. Across the top of the front of the room was a huge gold-painted arrow mounted in a velour-lined box and above that was a wooden sign with the word *Arrowslinger* carved into it.

The origins of the arrow were not a matter of official squadron history, and the associated tales ranged from its being pulled out of the back of Eric the Red by his loving and faithful men at the end of his last Viking conquest, to its being presented in passing to the squadron by a couple of retired farts nobody knew a few years ago.

The seven junior officers accurately assessed that they had been the last to be informed of the AOM, so they opted to enter the gathering via the back door to try and slide in unnoticed. To their mild relief, they walked into a gaggle of officers filling coffee mugs, checking their e-mail accounts one-by-one on the sole desktop computer in the ready room, and otherwise chatting informally—a scene that indicated to the latecomers that the skipper was not yet present.

"What's the meeting for?" Punk asked Beads as the operations officer poured some coffee into his mug.

Beads shook a packet of sugar and ripped it open and answered Punk without making eye contact. "I'll let the skipper tell you. Why don't you grab a seat?"

The ops officer moved away, and Punk shot him a disapproving glance and quickly removed his mug from its hook on a large arrow-shaped piece of mahogany mounted on the wall behind the coffee maker and charged it full. He then finished the trip to his assigned chair, the final stretch of which was across the legs of his squadronmates already seated.

"One of the ordies told Weezer the skipper came back minus tanks and a 'winder," Biff whispered as Punk sat down next to him.

"You're shitting me," Punk said.

"I'll do you better than that," Scooter added from the other side. "Smoke was up on the flight deck checking on the maintenance effort and he said there was a full-blown dogfight between the skipper and some rag head F-4 right over the ship."

"Holy shit," Punk said. "Did the skipper bag somebody?"

"I dunno," Scooter replied. "I think Smoke was afraid the skipper was going to walk in and didn't want to say too much." Scooter also felt a bit uncomfortable with the incendiary nature of the topic and he looked around to ensure the CO had still not entered the ready room. "Needless to say, this is going to be an interesting little get-together."

"Boy," Punk said, "Soup's head won't be able to fit through the door if he got a kill. He'll be even harder to live with."

"I'm more worried about the possibility he didn't get a kill," Biff replied.

As the *Arrowslingers* officers gathered in the ready room, Commander Campbell and Paul were a hundred kneeknockers forward of them in Flag Briefing and Analysis trying to piece together for the admiral the events of their twenty-minute flight. Actually, they were talking to two admirals since the battle group commander aboard the carrier had called his immediate superior, the Fifth Fleet commander in Bahrain, and put him on the speakerphone to hear the explanation for himself.

The room on the ship was packed with staffers, all looking on with knitted brows, some taking notes, others simply nodding or shaking their heads in response to whatever comments were thrown about. Also present was a large contingent of intel geeks, including the Pats.

The speakerphone cracked with the three-star's voice from Bahrain: "I guess I'm trying to figure out if we're now at war with Iran."

"Well, Admiral," the sea-based one-star returned, aiming his voice directly into the box, "I'm assuming we are until you tell me otherwise. I have two alerts airborne right now and I'm moving the cruiser forty miles southeast of her current position."

"That's probably a good idea, Admiral," the Fifth Fleet commander replied. "Be advised I've got SecNav on the speaker phone in my office. Mr. Secretary, what do you think? Are we at war with Iran?"

The secretary of the Navy's response from the Pentagon came through to the carrier as nothing but sentence-structured static. Once he was finished, the fleet commander asked, "Did you copy that, Admiral?"

"Negative, Admiral, can you relay?"

"The Secretary said he's been unable to speak with SecDef or any of the Joint Chiefs on this one yet. They're all over on the Hill testifying—about what, he's not really sure, but he knows it's not this thing—and he wants you to keep your guard up."

"Roger that," the admiral replied.

"Got that, Mr. Secretary?" the fleet commander inquired. There were more beats of static on the carrier's end. "He said, 'Roger that,'" the three-star relayed, indicating that the secretary had not heard the battle group commander's initial response.

The throng in Flag Briefing and Analysis, all standing except for the admiral seated at the center of the long end of the big rectangular "situation table" that dominated the room and his chief of staff seated to his right, listened for several minutes to an exchange between Fifth Fleet and SecNav that consisted mostly of the secretary's unintelligible white noise syncopation. The only English they could make out was the fleet commander answering, "Yes sir," when the static occasionally stopped.

"SecNav wants to hear the details of the engagement," the fleet commander finally passed. "Admiral, I understand you've got the pilots in the room with you?"

"That's correct, Admiral," the battle group commander replied. "Commander Campbell, why don't you walk us through the mission tape?"

"Certainly, Admiral," the skipper responded. He was still covered in the bulk of his flight gear and tilled a wider than normal line as he pushed his way to the front of the crowd that had formed along the wall near the only door to the space. "But before we review the tape, I'd like to set up the incident, if I may, sir." The admiral nodded his concurrence.

The skipper stood for a time trying to figure out where to begin. He'd been yanked out of the jet immediately following shutdown and routed to the admiral's spaces without a chance to organize his thoughts. He rubbed his hands together briskly and sniffed once deeply. Paul stood in his flight gear at the back of the crowd at a modified position of parade rest, nervously waiting for the skipper to tell him what to do and when to talk.

"We launched on the alert and were assigned to the eastern station," the skipper began. "I thought we might be given a hot vector right off the cat, but we just held on station for ten minutes or more."

The admiral interrupted. "Admiral," he said, once again leaning into the speakerphone, "can you hear Commander Campbell when he talks?"

"Yeah, I can hear him. SecNav, can you hear the pilot talking?" There was no response. "SecNav, are you there, sir?"

The silence that followed told that the secretary of the Navy had either directed his attention to another matter and hung up or been cut off. The Fifth Fleet commander assumed the latter.

"Admiral, it looks like we've lost SecNav here," he passed to those on the carrier. "Hold on for a second and I'll have my aide try to get us reconnected with the Pentagon."

As the ball of technology rolled between Manama and Washington, the mood in Flag Briefing and Analysis relaxed a bit, and the ambient noise of conversation grew. Commander Campbell used the break in the action to mentally develop a game plan, a plausible explanation for what had happened. He quickly scanned the room to factor in the local level of aviation subject matter expertise—as much to assess what he might pass as fact in his presentation as to what level of detail to shape his brief.

The bursts of static started up again from the speakerphone and an expectant hush fell over the space.

"Admiral, I think we're ready now," the fleet commander said.

The battle group commander looked to Soup and gave a circular wave that roughly directed the skipper to pick up where he'd left off. "All right, we were on the eastern station when—"

The one-star motioned for the skipper to stop. "Can you hear that, Admiral?"

"Yeah, I've got him. Mr. Secretary, can you hear everything?"

Some static was emitted in return.

"All right, I'll relay . . . the jet was on the eastern station. Go ahead . . ."

"When we got the first vector from the E-2."

"When they got the first vector from the E-2 . . ."

"And . . . well, why don't we roll the mission tape?"

"And why don't they roll the mission tape . . . oh, they're going to roll the mission tape, Mr. Secretary."

More static.

"The secretary says go ahead."

The skipper gestured across the room to one of the Pats poised to hit play on the VCR and said, "Holly, if you please . . ."

"It's Steven, sir," the ensign said.

"What? Oh, whatever. Start the tape."

The tape began to roll and the monitors at the near and far corners of the room showed the view through the pilot's heads up display (HUD). There was nothing for the untrained eye to make out at first. On the screens, digits jumped and symbols tracked against a background of nothing but the early morning cloudless sky.

"Now, Admiral," the skipper said as the tape continued to play, "you'll hear the first call we get is actually almost behind us." Commander Campbell adjusted the volume of the closest monitor between asides. In the background, the Fifth Fleet commander continued to parrot the narrative for the secretary of the Navy.

"Is the E-2 controller here?" the battle group commander asked.

"That E-2 is still airborne," somebody said from the crowd.

"That's fine," Soup replied in an effort to wrestle the floor back. The less other people talked, the more he could mold the facts. "Anyway, we got a very late heads up, and as you'll see in the tape, the intercept wound up being a tail chase."

The skipper allowed the tape to play for a while longer without interrupting. Unsure of what he'd said over the intercom in the airplane, but sensing that the admiral didn't need to hear it, the skipper continued to lower the volume on the monitor he had within his reach.

The view switched from the HUD camera to the magnified TV picture of the F-4 turning back toward the Tomcat. The room filled with expressions of amazement and disbelief as the monitors showed the missile coming off the Iranian jet.

"Hold it," the battle group commander ordered as he leaned back over the speakerphone. "Admiral, what the tape shows at this point is a missile fired by the Iranian jet at the F-14. There has been no provocation on our part up to this point other than to attempt an escort."

After relaying the words to the Pentagon, the fleet commander listened to the secretary of the Navy and then asked the battle group commander, "So in terms of rules of engagement, we're justified at this point in shooting back?"

"That's affirmative," the at-sea admiral answered. "It's down to basic self defense."

Following another wave from the admiral, the skipper continued. "I maneuvered to defeat the missile and then managed to get into a semi-offensive position, although I had to turn a long way to get there." *Semi*-offensive. Nothing too definitive. "And, long story short, by the time I had the first shot opportunity the Phantom was out of range. Steven, you can turn the tape off."

"Wait," said the chief of staff seated next to the admiral. "Don't stop the tape. I want to see something. And turn the volume up so we can hear it."

The skipper's heart stopped for a time as he watched the admiral's right-hand man analyze the images on the screen before him. The chief of staff, who wore the rank of captain, had flown Tomcats for many years before being put out to staff pasture, and he enjoyed the idea that he might still have a bit of tactical thought left in him.

"Freeze it there," he commanded before looking over toward Commander Campbell. "Why do you have Guns selected here?" He studied the scale down the right vertical axis of the view. "The guy is about two-and-a-half miles away. Why would you select Guns at this point?"

The skipper stood nonplused at the ethical crossroads. After a few seconds of looking at the screen and mustering up some feigned confusion of his own he said, "I don't remember selecting Guns, Chief of Staff."

"That little G at the bottom of the HUD does still indicate that Guns is selected, right?" the chief of staff asked with a dusting of sarcasm. "It's been a few years since I've flown the Tomcat, but they didn't change that recently, did they?" The chief of staff looked back at the ensign and said, "Unfreeze the tape and let it play."

At that moment and for the following minutes, the skipper had never felt so vulnerable in his professional life. He stood alone on what was quickly becoming the wrong side of the situation table, growing more and more naked with each frame of tape. Time compression set in; for him, the presentation seemed to move at a painfully slow pace.

As the Fifth Fleet commander's play-by-play for Sec-Nav continued over the speakerphone, sounding a lot like a radio talk show in the background that nobody was paying attention to, the mission tape reached the skipper's first trigger squeeze during the flight. The HUD camera vibrated slightly as the F-14's nose cannon cooked off rounds doomed from the start to hit nothing but the waters of the Gulf.

"Stop the tape again," the chief of staff commanded. He turned toward Soup and asked, "Did you just fire the gun at almost three miles away?" as he referenced the symbology on the screen.

Again, the skipper struggled for the best answer considering the circumstantial evidence before the body that had transformed, in his mind, into an ad hoc court. *An electrical short, maybe,* he thought. *Any precedent for that sort of malfunction in the community?*

Before the skipper could formulate a counter to the chief of staff's question, a new voice jumped into the discussion. "The gun did fire."

"Who said that?" the admiral asked the crowd behind him and to his right.

"I did, sir," a short, young-looking lieutenant with

freckles and bright red hair replied. He emerged from
the crowd waving a VCR tape of his own. He quickly
moved over to the machine and relieved Steven of his
position while asking the admiral, "If I may, sir?"

"Please, go ahead," the admiral answered. "It doesn't
seem like Commander Campbell has any answers for
us."

Paul watched the skipper's normally tan complexion
deepen from a crimson hue to near violet as the carrier's public affairs officer removed the mission tape
and inserted the new mystery tape.

"Admiral," the skipper protested, "I'm not sure
what—"

The admiral silenced him with another wave of his
hand while looking at the monitor nearest to him. The
tape rolled for a few seconds and showed an upper
torso shot of two sailors, dressed in their Crackerjack
dress uniforms, looking down at the flight deck from
Vultures' Row on the carrier's island.

The PAO paused the tape. "We were shooting a
hometown news release with some of our sailors this
morning," he explained, "and we wanted an early morning sunrise shot, so we were out there kind of . . . early."
He smiled but then continued as the admiral passed on
changing his own expression in any way.

"Anyway, as you'll see, our ranking photographer's
mate managed to capture the entire event on videotape." He hit Play and then stepped aside to allow the
performance to speak for itself.

"Hello, Akron," one of the sailors on the island said
with a sweeping wave after a few seconds of waiting for
his cue from someone behind the camera.

"Hello, Jacksonville," the other sailor said with the
same gesture, performed with the opposite arm.

"We're here to say . . ." The roar of a jet eclipsed the

dialog and the camera left the faces of the sailors and fished around the sky to find the cause of the noise. The camera found the F-4 and followed it over the stern of the carrier and into the distance. The argument between the two sailors over the jet's ID served as narrative while the sound of the Phantom's engines faded. About ten seconds later, a second roar revealed the skipper's passing and once again the cameraman worked the skies to find the source.

Cued by the flares flying out of the underside of the Tomcat, the camera captured and stuck with the skipper's jet through the missile-evading hard right turn. The straight-line white plume of the Iranian missile was briefly featured in the foreground as the tape continued with the F-14 in the hard left-hand turn that followed the first move. The chief of staff noted the tanks blowing off and how the jet's variable geometry wings swept from almost fully aft at the beginning of the turn to completely forward by the end of it, a detail that indicated to him a significant loss of airspeed by the aircraft.

Almost as soon as the turn was complete, a wisp of smoke trailed from the left side of the nose of the jet, followed immediately by the distinctive "pops" of bullets breaking the sound barrier.

The PAO turned to the skipper, and innocently enough for a non-aviator asked, "That was the gun going off, right Commander?"

The skipper stood unfocused and motionless. Any compelling argument he'd planned on forwarding was smashed to bits now, not so much by the facts, but by the unorthodox and unplanned presentation of the facts. The admiral, the chief of staff, the PAO—damn, where did *he* come from? They were all growing horns in the skipper's eyes as the inquisition dragged on.

"Of course that was the gun going off," the chief of staff laughed as he slapped the table with his big paws and scanned the room with a turn of his white-frosted head. A number of the gathered officers joined him with closed-lip smiles, and a handful actually clucked quiet noises of acknowledgment, but sounds not well defined or loud enough to be labeled as laughter.

The PAO's tape finished with the Sidewinder coming off the Tomcat, which, with the range from the carrier by this point, appeared on the monitors as a small dot coming off a bigger blob. To his technical credit, in spite of the distance away and the speed of the missile, the cameraman tracked the weapon for the duration of its travel until it hit the water some six miles abeam of the Boat. The small splash blossomed and the view was enlarged to the camera's full zoom capability, effecting the high art of cinematic punctuation.

The PAO stopped the tape and removed it from the player. He slinked in front of Commander Campbell, his body noticeably tensed while within arms reach of the skipper as if he was ready to absorb a blow to the gut. The skipper could've sworn he saw the lieutenant bow slightly toward the admiral as he made his way back across the front of the situation table and into the standing crowd—not the traditional show of respect, but more of a smug ta-da move.

"Put the other tape back in—the HUD tape," the chief of staff commanded the ensign. "I want to check the range of that Sidewinder shot." As Steven hurriedly worked to comply with the order, the skipper attempted to regain control of the floor.

"Admiral, I'd like to—"

"Hold it, Commander," the chief of staff snapped. "We don't need any damage control from you—"

The admiral interrupted his senior staffer with an-

other wave. "Admiral, are you still with us?" he asked
into the speakerphone.

"Yes, I am, Admiral," the fleet commander replied. "I've
actually been having a bit of a sidebar conversation with
the secretary, who's been on the phone the last few minutes with the National Security Council chairman." Flag
Briefing and Analysis grew silent. "The Iranian Ambassador to the U.N. has stated to the chairman that although
Iran is opposed to the American presence in the Gulf, this
incident is not consistent with the will of the leadership in
Tehran. It appears this pilot was acting alone, although we
don't have any real details about why."

"So how should we proceed?" the battle group commander asked.

"Well . . . with caution, I guess . . ." The fleet commander stopped and the sound of whispering could be
heard. "Gentlemen, I think SecNav and I know what we
need to know. Press on and we'll be in touch." The
speakerphone fell silent.

Flag Briefing and Analysis housed a hundred different conversations until the admiral silenced the room
by raising both hands over his head. He looked back to
the skipper.

"Is there anything else we need to know, in your opinion, commander?"

"Well, Admiral, just—"

"I want to see the rest of the HUD tape," the chief of
staff interrupted. "I want to know whether to attribute
the Iranian's survival to mechanical failure . . ." He
shifted his gaze toward the skipper. "Or pilot error."

A loud "whoosh" filled the room for several seconds
and the other officers watched with morbid curiosity as
the skipper grew a rubber ring around his neck and
waist. In the course of the discussion, Commander
Campbell had gradually developed an inadvertent

death grip on the beaded rings that were pulled to in-
flate the bladders of his life preserver, and the chief of
staff's last comment caused him to tense up enough to
unseat both waist-level handles. As the four quadrants
of the survival assembly ballooned to their full capacity,
giving him the appearance of a campy team mascot during a seventh inning stretch, the skipper forfeited the
balance of any dignity he had left.

Buried under the crowd's wheeze of suppressed
laughter and fighting the urge to run from the room,
Commander Campbell reached into one of the pockets of his vest, located a large hunting knife, removed
it, and began calmly and methodically piercing the
lobes of the preserver. A rush of stale air and a hail of
white powder through the wound accompanied each
muted pop of the knife as it found a mark. After the
fourth stabbing, Flag Briefing and Analysis began to
look as if it was filling with smoke.

"Look," the admiral said with a cough as he patted
the dust from the front of his khakis, "you two flyboy
bucks can lock horns some other time." He stood up.
"We're manning CAP stations around the clock until
further notice. Concentrate on the eastern threat sec-
tor. This meeting is over."

The crowd disbursed, and the chief of staff, caked
lightly in white dust, caught the skipper's attention one
last time and mouthed, "You fucked up," from across
the room before following the admiral into the adjoin-
ing Flag Quarters.

Paul followed directly behind the skipper as they
made their way out of Flag Briefing and Analysis and
aft to the ready room, happy he hadn't been made to
testify and not knowing what to make of the beating his
boss had just taken.

"Let that be a lesson to you, if you manage to survive

this little incident," Commander Campbell said over his shoulder festooned with flaccid black rubber while they continued down the starboard side of the ship. "Don't ever piss off people above you, ever. The Navy isn't as big as you might think it is."

Paul didn't know what the skipper expected in response, if anything, so he simply let out an upbeat hum of concurrence.

"That goddam chief of staff wanted to be CO of the Blue Angels when I was Opposing Solo on the team," the skipper continued, "and he didn't get it. He was convinced that I'd personally torpedoed his rush effort."

Again Paul responded with a nonspecific noise that politely signaled the skipper to continue with his story.

"I was a lieutenant, like I had any power. Plus, everybody hated the guy." As Paul tried to figure out if the last statement had been an admission of guilt, the skipper stopped and looked him squarely in the eye. "There are a lot of assholes in this business. Get used to it."

The officers in the ready room had grown tired of waiting for the skipper, so when Commander Campbell finally walked in through the back door, they were caught off guard. The coffee and e-mail lines quickly unformed and all idle conversation stopped as officers scurried back to their chairs like cockroaches scrambling for cover after the lights are switched on.

After dropping his spent and assaulted life preserver and torso harness to the floor immediately inside the door, the skipper walked the center aisle—Moses through a Red Sea of complete silence. Once at the front of the room, he looked to the duty officer for a muster report.

"Everybody's here, sir," Chum passed from behind

the desk on a slightly elevated platform in the front corner of the space, "except for the alert crew topside."

The skipper nodded stoically in response while he reached toward his left biceps and the zipped pocket beneath the pencil holder on the sleeve of his flight suit. He pulled out a sheet of perforated computer paper and held it over his head like a tennis player might display a trophy for photographers following a tournament.

"Does everyone know what I'm holding?" he asked. The answer to the question seemed ridiculously obvious, so nobody spoke. The skipper panned the room and took in the silence. "Let me try again," he said, voice louder and sterner in tone. "Does everyone know what I'm holding?"

The response the second time was many nods and a few halfhearted chimings of "Yes sir."

The skipper shifted his focus from the group at large to the individual. "Punk, what am I holding?" Punk stammered for a few seconds before the skipper interrupted him. "He doesn't even know." The commander redirected his attention toward one of the department heads. "How 'bout you, maintenance officer?"

"It's a Maintenance Action Form," Smoke replied directly.

"No shit," the skipper shot back. "What's it used for?"

"To document airplane problems so the maintenance effort can fix them," Smoke said matter-of-factly, confused by the elementary line of questioning. He ran close to Spud in terms of popularity with the junior officers. Both more apt to walk the walk, it was no coincidence that Smoke and Spud were roommates. Few pilots knew the Tomcat as well as Smoke did, and none was able to describe the jet's complicated systems in poets' terms as he could.

Smoke and the skipper had never enjoyed any chemistry since the moment Smoke arrived at VF-104 from the Naval Postgraduate School in Monterey. Commander Campbell didn't think much of pilots who acted like eggheads instead of aviators. Why would a fighter pilot waste time trying for a master's degree in aerospace engineering when he could be building flight hours in a shore-based squadron? More than once Soup had jabbed Smoke with, "I may not know how to build a watch, but I can tell time."

But if the two pilots' flight time differed by five hundred hours, it was no matter to those who might end up as their wingmen. Smoke was the flight lead of choice—always calm, always ahead, always right. He cut the classic figure of the naval aviator: tall, lean, and mustachioed. His gaunt, chiseled face looked like a coconut nearly sliced in two when he smiled his big-toothed overbite of a smile, an expression that could warm the entire ready room.

Commander Campbell responded to Smoke's answer to the original query. "Let me let you guys in on a little something: Our mission is the defense of this ship, and ultimately, our nation. That is why we're here, gentlemen. Everything we do is to support that mission." For the second time within the hour, Paul watched the skipper's face make a sanguine metamorphosis before a crowd, only this time the commander was in control of the situation.

Punk glanced casually to either side, wondering if he was the only guy in the room with no idea of where the skipper was headed with his diatribe. Obviously he hadn't downed the Iranian or this meeting would've had a more festive slant—a cake with "Way to go, Soup!" frosting and a ship's photographer to document the jubilation for the annals of naval history, at the very least. Punk caught Biff's eye, and the big man subtly shrugged his shoulders in a sign of "don't ask me."

The skipper reached for a large black binder labeled 102, perched on the one corner of the podium next to him, opened it, and began to rummage through the MAFs inside. Each of the ten F-14s in the squadron was represented by such a binder. The aircraft data book (ADB) was full of loose-leaf computer printouts that documented problems normally discovered by aircrew and solved by maintainers. The MAFs were placed to the left or the right of the binder, depending on whether they were completed jobs or unfinished work, respectively. Before each flight, aviators reviewed the ADB for the jet they were assigned as a way of anticipating how the machine might act up.

The skipper maniacally flipped through 102's ADB sheets until he stopped and dramatically ripped one from the binder. He held the sheet aloft and fired off another question.

"Gucci, do you recognize this?"

For all his fashion sense and each perfect brown hair on his head, Gucci was nearly blind, even by RIO standards. From the back row of chairs, he was unable to make out any detail of the item in the skipper's possession, so he answered, "Ah, no sir."

"This is the gripe you wrote after your flight last night," the skipper said. "Let me refresh your memory." Commander Campbell's sarcastic tone intensified with the increased volume of his voice. "On this particular gripe you write: 'Radar won't lock contacts in the pulse mode outside of twenty miles.' And then you indicate the jet is still in an 'up' status." Each MAF had two opposing arrows at the bottom of the form that forced the originator of the gripe to identify whether or not the jet could be assigned by maintenance control for follow-on flights before the corrective maintenance was completed. "So what you're telling me here with this MAF," the commander continued, "is that an F-14 doesn't need a radar outside of twenty miles? Is that it?"

"Ah, no sir . . ." Gucci replied as he pushed the thin tortoiseshell frames of his eyeglasses up the bridge of his sharp-lined nose.

"Well? What's the story then?" the skipper asked. "Why would you possibly make this an 'up' gripe?"

Gucci paused, wondering if the skipper really wanted him to answer. After a few seconds of awkward silence it became obvious he did.

"Maintenance control said one-zero-two was the only jet we had for the alert," Gucci said with confidence, convinced he could clear up the skipper's misconception. "The radar worked well in all the other modes so I figured . . ."

Like a cop directing traffic, the skipper signaled Gucci to stop speaking. He jabbed his finger toward the back of the room and addressed all but the target.

"You see? This is exactly what I'm talking about," the skipper said. "This is the attitude that will kill us." The skipper stopped pointing at Gucci and took the ADB in both hands, studying the binder for a few seconds. He then slammed the book shut and threw it to the linoleum floor directly in front of him. The startling smack of the tiles when the ADB hit caused many to jump in their seats, even after watching the skipper go through the motions of throwing it.

"You call the shots, not maintenance," the skipper railed, upping the decibel level another few notches as he continued. "There's a reason we sit in here on our privileged asses, goddam it. Sometimes we have to make the hard calls. If you don't have the guts to stare down the master chief and tell him you think a jet needs some work before it goes flying, then maybe you ought to turn in your wings."

It was a valid point, although unfair in the context of Gucci's situation. No reasonable flyer would have split hairs over a relatively minor radar issue, not when one-zero-two was the last jet available to stand the alert. If a junior officer wanted to see the skipper really go high order, he'd tell him the admiral was just briefed that VF-104 was unable to muster up a single jet for the alert.

After twenty-seven days on the line, all nine of the squadrons in the wing were having trouble making ends meet maintenance-wise. The supply chain was over-taxed and the sailors were overworked. At some point during operational cycles, idealistic standards and theories of full mission readiness take the fork in the road away from reality, and getting sorties completed becomes an exercise in priorities. The maintenance master chief had looked at young Gucci last night, and in a state of total exasperation asked, "You want a pulse lock outside of twenty miles, or do you want a transmitter? You can't have both, sir, and without the transmitter you won't have a radar at all."

Commander Campbell let Gucci up off the mat as he turned his attention toward one of the young pilots. "Biff, you flew one-oh-two last night, right?" he asked.

Biff's head defensively jerked back a little when the skipper addressed him unexpectedly. "Yes, skipper. I flew one-oh-two on the last event last night," he replied after a second of mustering his composure.

"Did you gripe the electrical short in the weapons select toggle on the stick?"

Biff made the same face of confusion he'd made

thirty minutes ago when Punk had told him the skipper was airborne. "I didn't have any indication of a short on the stick," Biff said.

"Did you check?"

"We ran the normal series—"

"See?" the skipper interrupted. "Once again, that's exactly what I'm talking about here." He tossed his right thumb over his left shoulder and continued. "These jets are only going to be as good as *we* make them, not them out there in maintenance control." He swept the room with both hands. "*Us* in here, we're the ones who set the standard."

The skipper was really starting to feel his oats, and the rush of adrenaline was cathartic after the trouncing he'd endured in Flag Briefing and Analysis. The AOM was just what the doctor ordered: go somewhere and be adamant about something—angry and adamant.

He shifted the topic. "If I may," he mused, strolling across the front of the room, stroking his chin in an exaggerated fashion while using his other hand to move part of his thick hair back up off his forehead, "I'd like to know how many guys debrief with the E-2 controllers following a hop?"

No hands were raised, nor did any of the officers scan the room to see the results of the poll. They all continued to stare holes in the chairs in front of them, afraid that eye contact with the skipper would result in a run through the humiliation grinder. Besides, he had a point to make; there was no use diluting it with facts now.

"Look at this," the skipper said. "Not one guy has given any feedback to the Hawkeyes. No wonder they're clueless." The CO stopped and slowly shook his head from side to side. He started to speak again but checked himself with an exaggerated cleansing breath—a dramatic and contrived show of self-control. He reached down, picked the ADB off the floor in front of him and placed it back on the podium.

He finished the meeting with a final decree: "The next twenty-four to forty-eight hours are varsity time. Ops, I only want those crews with more than five hundred hours in the Tomcat to be on the flight schedule. New guys can suck up the administrative workload and stand the duty." After one more pass of his regal scan across the frozen faces of the crews, the skipper walked back down the center aisle, stepping over his own flight gear pile before disappearing through the back door.

The metallic click of the latch as it shut was the starting gun for a bunkhouse rumble of conversations, and as they went along it became apparent that if the skipper had intended to induce a level of confusion associated with the situation, he'd succeeded.

"What the hell was that?" Punk asked as he rose from his chair and stretched.

"I have no clue," Biff replied with a shrug. "I guess an explanation would've been too much to ask for."

The executive officer, second in command of VF-104, stood and motioned for everyone to be quiet. The skipper had left the raw goods of subject matter scattered at the door of the rumor mill, and now it was the XO's job to oversee the quality assurance of the production run that would surely follow.

In the junior officers' minds, Beamer was a good XO in the clinical sense; he didn't seem to assert any influence counter to the commanding officer's. While lieutenants realized they weren't privy to all discussions between the skipper and the XO, they found it hard to relate to the concept that dissension didn't involve some level of showmanship. What good was an argument if it didn't take place in front of other people?

The Cheesequarters' conventional wisdom gave below average marks to the XO's shepherding of empirical truth to date. To be fair, the junior officers' idea of a nominally effective truth shepherd was someone who was willing to prostrate himself on the altar of his career over even the most trivial bitch, and any officer with the vinegar to do that would have long since been labeled by the Machine as a shortsighted loudmouth and never been promoted beyond the rank of lieutenant. In spite of any perceived company man foibles, Beamer commanded professional respect for his backseat savvy and for the fact that he had bagged an Iraqi helicopter with a Sparrow missile during Desert Storm.

"For your own health and well-being, I recommend you not discuss this incident in the skipper's presence," Beamer said after the room had calmed back down. He reached for a HUD tape that was on the duty desk and held it up before the squadron. "This tape is off-limits until further notice, by direction of the commanding officer. And it should go without saying that nobody needs to write home about any of this."

The XO sat down and the operations officer took the floor. "We're going to have to rewrite the flight schedule based on the skipper's guidance. Standby to jump through your asses." With that, the AOM was officially over.

The questions they had were not going to get answered in the ready room. Punk looked at Biff and they simultaneously said, "To quarters."

THREE

Before he could make it out of the ready room after
the AOM, Biff was tagged by ops to put on his collat-
eral duty hat and rewrite the flight schedule. He sat at
the computer in the back of the ready room trying to
figure out equitable combinations of available aircrews to meet the new air plan, a plan that now had
them flying through the night. He repeatedly mumbled
things like, "This won't work," and, "We're going to kill
somebody."

   After fifty-four minutes and eleven "just shut up and
write" responses to Biff's complaints, even Beads realized it was more than varsity time. There was no way to
write a flight schedule without violating the squadron's
standard operating procedures for the maximum number of flights—two—per crew in a twenty-four-hour pe-
riod. VF-104 had eight pilots and six RIOs with more
than five hundred hours in the F-14, and those aviators
could not fly twenty-two sorties without some of them
flying more than twice. The operations officer became
so frustrated with the machinations he and Biff were

having to go through, with only half the squadron's line-up at their disposal, that he marched down to the skipper's stateroom and attempted to question the wisdom of restricting who was eligible to fly.

"What?" the skipper asked angrily from behind his closed door in response to the knock.

"Skipper, it's Beads. I need to talk to you about the rewrite of the flight schedule."

The door remained closed. "What about it?"

"We're having trouble not flying the experienced guys more than two times to make it work."

There was a slight pause, and then the skipper responded, "So . . ."

"Well, sir, as you know, that's against our SOP . . . your SOP. I'll need your waiver."

"So?"

"I just wanted you to know, ah, in case you might be concerned about the length of crew days and whatnot."

The door opened slightly and the skipper wedged his face into the crack he'd created. "Are you saying I don't care about the safety of the aviators in this squadron, ops officer?"

"Ah, no sir . . . I . . ."

"Safety is why I'm doing this," the CO continued. "That and the fact the admiral didn't seem too impressed by our new RIO's radar work . . . but that's just between you and me."

Beads nodded. He'd been Soup's only by-name call to the bureau for assignment to the *Arrowslingers* as a result of their developed synergy at Topgun. Then–Lieutenant Commander Campbell had been very impressed by then–Lieutenant Beads' ability to ask complicated, yet easy-to-answer questions during lectures. And Mrs. Beads had also left a lasting impression on Soup by sporting a cleavage-featuring, upper thigh–revealing mini dress at the

NAS Miramar Officers Club. One heart-stopping glance and the future skipper knew he had to have the Beads family team in his command, one doing his bidding and the other attending the monthly hot tub parties he'd decided were going to be part of the squadron's social program. The skipper had always called attention to his efforts on Beads' behalf, as ill-defined as they were, and the lieutenant commander felt obliged to support his self-appointed mentor.

"So, I have your permission to fly guys three times? You're granting an SOP waiver?" Beads asked.

"I say again, it's varsity time. We're at war with Iran, for gawdsakes. If dance school graduates don't want to attend the dance, then have them come talk to me."

"What about manning spares for each event?"

"We won't have manned spares, but tell Smoke if we miss a sortie because a jet goes down it's his ass."

Beads sighed and nodded again. He started to walk back toward the ready room until the skipper stopped him.

"How many times am I flying?" the skipper asked.

"I dunno, sir. We haven't finished writing the schedule yet. That's why I came down here to talk to you."

"Don't schedule me more than once. I'm sure the admiral is going to have some meetings for me to attend or something, and I've already flown once today." His face disappeared into the darkness as he withdrew into his stateroom.

As Beads moved a few more steps down the passageway, the skipper reappeared and said, "Oh, and one more thing: I need to catch up on some sleep so I'm turning the phone off. Let the duty officer know."

"What if the admiral wants to have a meeting?"

"I doubt he will . . . oh . . . yeah, well, just have Chum come down and knock on my door like you did. And I'll probably be asleep by the time you finish writing the schedule so go ahead and sign your name in my approval block. I trust you. Just don't fly me more than once or I'm going to be really pissed." And then the stateroom door shut for good.

Biff entered the Cheesequarters with copies of revision one in hand and was confronted with six pairs of outstretched arms before he could make it through the doorway. He wearily handed the sheets to his roommates and braced himself for their reactions.

The lieutenants quickly reviewed the bidding: eleven hour-and-a-half-long events, two planes each, first launch at 1300 and the final recovery the following morning at 0530. The missions were the same for all flights: combat air patrol.

Punk didn't have to search too hard for his name. He was on the first event, the fifth event, and the ninth event. His flying day was going to start with his first brief at 1100 and go straight through until his last debrief following his 0230 recovery. Between events he'd barely have time to make it to the next brief.

He looked up at Biff, who stood ready to fend off his roommates' verbal blows. Pissing people off was a scheduling officer's lot in life, and since he'd been the skeds officer for nine months now, he had long ago given up on the idea that he might be able to keep the squadron happy with creativity and equitability.

"I'm flying three times, twice at night," Punk said with disbelief. He'd heard the skipper's proclamation, but it hadn't hit home until its spawn appeared on paper before him. "And when am I supposed to eat or sleep?"

"There was no way around it, Punk," Biff defended. "I've only got so many guys with more than five hundred hours. I'll be on the event after you all three times."

"I'm flying three times too," Fuzzy said. "And the worst part is I'm on Punk's wing every time." He looked at Biff. "I'm a flight lead, Biff, not a wingman."

"Fuzzy, I didn't have enough guys to even comply with SOP, not to mention stick with the normal combinations of flight leads and wingmen," Biff returned. "Gimme a break."

Seven of them were there: Punk, Biff, Trash, Scooter, Fuzzy, Weezer, and Monk. As they spoke, the desk chairs started moving to the center of the room and forming the circle.

As the last one positioned his chair and sat down, Monk leaned slightly forward in his seat with eyes closed in silent prayer. "What are you doing?" Trash asked.

Monk's eyes shot open. "Nothing," he replied.

Trash shook his head. "No, you're not doing 'nothing.' You know damned well what you're doing."

"What am I doing then?" Monk said.

"You're trying to take the high ground. I hate when you do that."

"I'm sorry, Trash," Monk said, scratching at the semi-circle of jet-black hair that ran around the sides of his head. Although he piously fancied himself a man of strong religious conviction, Monk earned his call sign by the Trappist hairstyle nature had given him, not by his devotion to the Good Book. His embarrassment turned to irritation as he continued. "I like to clear my head before these sorts of discussions with a little reflection. It's personal. I'm not trying to make a big deal out of it."

"Yeah, sure," Trash said. "We don't need a chaplain in the Cheesequarters."

"Actually, *you* do, but that's another matter," Monk retorted.

"Okay, everybody, Monk's the room chaplain," Trash declared. "So, what's my job?"

"You're the minister of social decay," Punk said. "Look, to get to the business at hand, I'm still confused about what that AOM was for. What the hell happened to the skipper during the alert flight?"

"If my detective work serves me correctly," Scooter said, "the skipper launched on the alert because of Iranian air activity, most likely out of Bushehr, and . . ." He paused and his face contorted in frustration as whatever watertight line of facts he thought he had vaporized. "Anyway, something happened and the skipper shot at the guy and missed somehow . . ."

"Oh, that clears it right up," Punk said.

There was a knock at the door and the group hushed, guilty of nothing but feeling conspiratorial all the same.

Monk was closest, so he cautiously opened it. The knob was barely turned when the Pats pushed in and then quickly slammed the door behind them. They both looked about the room with wide-eyes, breathing heavily under their flight jackets with zippers two-blocked to their throats. One of them reached into his or her flight jacket and produced a videotape.

"I do this at great risk to my professional standing," Steven said. "Viewing this tape outside of official channels borders on sedition."

"Whatever that means, I'm not even sure that's still a crime," Biff said.

"No, it is," Punk said. "If found guilty, offenders have to walk the plank."

"You can tease us all you want," Holly said defiantly. "We're not here as friends."

"No, we're not," Steven added. "We're here in search of the truth. We knew we'd get abused coming down here, but this room is the only place we had to turn. So, fire away with your jokes. We don't care. We have a higher calling."

"What's on that tape," Punk asked, "behind-the-scenes footage from the National Star Trek Convention?"

Steven held the tape over his head. "This is the tape!"

"*The* tape?" they all asked in unison.

"The *skipper's* tape," Steven said.

The room sprang to life. In a flurry the Pats were ushered into chairs while Steven was relieved of the tape and it was inserted into the VCR.

"Hold it," Punk said before starting the machine. "Where's Paul? It wouldn't be fair to watch it without him here. Also, we need him to narrate for us."

"He was moping around the ready room a few minutes ago," Biff said.

Punk pointed Scooter toward the phone. "Call the duty officer and have him send Paul back here, ASAP."

As the circle and the Pats waited for the star witness, Trash used the pause to get undressed and into, as he put it, "his comfy mode." He paced the room nude asking, "Has anybody seen a blue beach towel," either forgetting or ignoring Holly's presence.

"Aha, here it is." As Trash bent over to pick up the towel that had fallen off the back of his chair, his eyes met Holly's. Holly stood stoically still in response and Trash was left to cease the exercise and simply wrap the towel around his waist.

Presently, Paul ambled into the Cheesequarters looking like a young man with the weight of the world on his now-slumped shoulders. He'd only been awake for just more than three hours, but it had already been a very long day for the nugget backseater. He caught sight of the circle and felt grossly out of place.

"Somebody called for me?" Paul asked quietly, avoiding eye contact.

"Yeah, we need you to tell us what the hell the skipper did," Trash said brusquely.

Punk saw that the new RIO was uncomfortable in his own stateroom, a violation of the most basic junior officer right at sea, and he moved across the space and put his arm around Paul's neck. "Hey, you're among friends here." He sat him down and massaged his shoulders in an exaggerated and playful fashion. "Don't feel bad about what happened. Although I still have no idea what did happen, I'm sure any of us in this room have done much worse."

Paul puffed a short laugh and said, "I doubt it. I think I've set a new record for time from check-in to skipper's shit list." He looked up from staring at his feet and said with poise and conviction, "And I have no idea how I got there."

Paul's change in demeanor gave Punk a slight opening. "Paul, we have a tape here, courtesy of our friendly intelligence officers." Punk gestured toward Steven and said, "You know Holly here," and then pointed toward Holly and continued, "and Steve . . ." The Pats just took it and nodded in the interest of the mission of truth. Paul gave them a nod in return.

"Well, they've brought us this tape . . . your tape, but I won't play it without your permission," Punk said as he moved toward the media center. "We have a lot of questions—important tactical questions—that probably only you can answer."

"Whatever. Things couldn't get much worse as far as this little incident goes, so go for it," Paul said.

"You've still got your health," Weezer cracked through his Bostonian bucked teeth.

"Unfortunately, I think you're right," Paul said while managing a reluctant smile.

"All right," Punk said, "that's the sarcasm we like out here in the fleet. You'll be salty in no time." He pushed Play and then sat down, scooting his chair across the bunched remnant a bit to see the screen. The rest of the circle temporarily unformed as the video began to roll.

"Would it be too much to ask Paul for an explanation of the events leading up to where we are now on the tape?" Biff asked. "I mean, without that I still have no understanding of exactly what I'm watching."

Paul got out of his chair and stopped the tape. "There's not a lot to say beyond watching and listening to the tape, really."

"Well if there were something to say," Punk offered, "this is a good place to say it."

Paul stood in front of the circle, suddenly feeling like the guest speaker at a business luncheon, and wrestled with where to start. He wanted to launch into an emotional laundry list of grievances against the skipper, but remembered another of his father's wise sayings: "Candid thoughts spoken are the sign of weak character." At the same time he wondered if his father had ever worked closely to a Commander Campbell in the nascent phase of his flying career. He might have come up with "get it off your chest; you'll feel better" instead.

"First, let me say with all due respect and consideration for my inexperience: the skipper and I have not gelled as a crew yet."

"And you never will," Trash said. "The skipper's terrible to fly with, and that's no secret. The senior RIOs have a standing request with ops not to fly with him, and the junior guys treat it as a bad-deal rotating duty. You were just lucky enough to show up at the right time."

"Trash, that's not exactly true. Melon flew with him for a year, and he seemed to like it," Punk said.

"Melon was a kiss ass who deserves every bit of pain he's going to get as an admiral's aide," Trash replied caustically. "Working sixteen hours a day and weekends is not my idea of shore duty."

"They told us during training that flying with the skipper was a good deal," Paul defended.

"Does it feel like a good deal now?" Trash asked pedantically back.

"Well, no," Paul admitted, "but that's probably my fault as much as the skipper's."

"Remember what Punk said about you being salty?" Trash said. "Forget it." He pointed his left index finger at the overhead. "Rule number one for fighter guys: You're never fucked up, the other guy always is."

"While we're on the subject, does he know the Three Lieutenant Rule?" Fuzzy asked.

"The Three Lieutenant Rule?"

"Yes, the Three Lieutenant Rule," Trash said while gesturing the floor over to Fuzzy.

"The Three Lieutenant Rule holds that if three lieutenants congregate, the topic of a fourth lieutenant will always come up," Fuzzy continued. "Two of them will say the fourth lieutenant is a good guy and the third will say he's an asshole. It's simple natural law, as true as rain."

"As *right* as rain," Monk corrected.

"Hey, you two," Fuzzy said to Scooter and Weezer. "Don't you think Monk's an asshole?"

"Back to the subject at hand," Punk said curtly. "Paul, you were explaining how you and the skipper came to find yourselves stealing my alert."

"Yeah, anyway, the skipper calls me here at I don't know what time . . . early . . . and I put on my flight suit and go to the ready room where I meet him. We don't brief at all and just walk into the PR shop, put our flight gear on, and walk up to the jet to relieve you."

"You mean rob us," Punk said.

"Okay, fair enough, I guess," Paul said. "The skipper

told me on the way to the jet that he knew we'd launch because of what the intelligence officers had told him."

Punk looked over at the Pats, comfortably seated and perturbed the video wasn't playing yet. "What did you guys tell the skipper?"

"The skipper has standing orders with *his* intelligence support to let him know of any items of interest," Holly said. "What we told him is privileged information."

Punk could stand the attitude no longer. "Look, you two. You're not spies; you're information managers." He pointed at himself, and then swept his arm around the room. "We're your customers, the war fighters, remember? We have good reason to know what the skipper knew. Otherwise you two come off as a couple of opportunists."

"VF-104 only has one commanding officer," Steven counseled.

"You mean only one guy who signs your fitness reports," Punk said.

Holly moved to the VCR and yanked the tape out of the player. "I knew this was a bad idea. Let's get out of here." With that, the two of them briskly marched toward the door.

"Hey, before you leave mad, let me tell you the truth," Biff offered, stopping both of them dead in their tracks. "The skipper—your idol—screwed up."

"Yeah, but don't say that outside of this room," Punk added. "You might be charged with sedition."

The Pats both stammered a couple of incoherencies through clenched teeth in response and then exited the Cheesequarters with a slam of the door.

"Man, I'll bet you guys used to pick on kids getting off the short bus, too," Trash said as he moved to retrieve the mini basketball hoop jarred off the back of the door by the Pats' exit.

"Yeah, real nice, you two," Fuzzy added. "We were so close to having the gouge."

Paul casually reached into the right leg pocket of his flight suit and produced a tape of his own. "Copies don't compare to the original," he said as he threw the tape into the machine. "Shall we continue?" The gathering gave him a polite golf clap for his forethought, risk-taking, and verve.

"Again, the skipper and I manned the alert," Paul continued with growing confidence. "I think intel told the CO we had activity out of Bushehr significant enough to trigger the tripwire of us launching. They didn't know it was an F-4, but they knew it was a military aircraft.

"So when we launched, we thought we'd be given a hot vector right off the cat, but we weren't, and that started to piss the skipper off a bit." Paul turned toward the VCR and started the tape. "I started the mission recorder with our first bit of bogey dope from the E-2, and I think tape speaks for itself."

The video rolled and the crowd leaned forward and watched intently, listening to the calls and trying to figure the geometry of the encounter.

"Hold it," Biff said quizzically. "The first call has the contact due south of you and the second call has him 190? That's already between you and the carrier. There's no way you're going to make that intercept."

"What radar mode were you in?" Trash asked.

"I started in Track-While-Scan, but once I realized we were looking at him in the beam, I switched to Pulse Search," Paul said.

"So, you're looking down in Pulse Search from fifteen thousand feet at a bogey at two hundred feet and in the beam?" Trash continued. "That's a tough problem for any RIO." All nodded in agreement as the tape continued.

The gasps at the Iranian missile shot were similar to those noises Paul had heard in Flag Briefing and Analysis, then not another word was said until the tape was over. Unlike the chief of staff, those proficient in the art of reading HUD symbology knew instantly why the F-4 had managed to escape. No words needed to be spoken, and no review was required. A few seconds of silence was broken when Punk asked, "Was that really, 'No goddam shit, Einstein'?"

"That's what I heard," Biff said. The roommates looked at each other, and then, all apparently thinking the same thing, at Paul.

"Gentlemen," Punk said, "we have a call sign." He rose and grasped the new RIO on each shoulder and directed him to take a knee at the center of the group. Punk stiffened his right arm, and, as with a sword, tapped Paul alternately on each shoulder, while Monk chanted, "Bless this knight, your servant, from now on known as 'Einstein.'"

"Einstein, huh?" Einstein muttered as he stood up.

"You don't like it?" Trash asked. "That's good."

"Yeah," Fuzzy followed, "if you liked it, we'd have to give you another one."

They formed an impromptu reception line, seven men long; and each roommate passed and shook Einstein's hand in official welcome. Then the circle was reformed.

"So what's the big deal with the tape?" Biff asked as he retook his seat. "So the skipper had a switchology problem in the heat of battle. So he's human. Is that why I went through so much pain with the schedule rewrite? Is that why we had the AOM?"

"It seems that way, doesn't it?" Fuzzy replied. "And the five-hundred-hour thing kind of left me with the feeling that Paul, er, Einstein, was the one who gooned it. This wasn't a new-guy thing at all. From what I could see on the tape, it seems like he did the best he could have given the shit sandwich he was handed."

"I'll tell you what this is about," Biff said. "This is about the difference between theory and reality." He leaned forward in his chair toward the center of the group as he continued. "Think about it. The skipper made a lot of professional money, if you will, at air shows with the Blues and in the schoolhouses of Topgun. Neither of those really involves the man in the arena."

"Hold it," Punk interjected. "Are you telling me that the flying the Blue Angels do is easy stuff?"

"No," Biff returned. "I'm telling you they practice those moves for three months straight at El Centro before they ever perform at an air show. The skills he drew on as opposing solo for the Blue Angels are not the same skills that a pilot needs in combat. He got the Blues gig because he looked good in a flight suit, was a smooth stick and a good formation flyer, not because he was a killing machine."

"So being a Blue Angel doesn't involve any amount of stress?"

"What are you, a Blue Angels groupie? You're missing my point, Punk. There is nothing spontaneous about a Blue Angels air show."

"And combat is all spontaneous?"

"More than a bunch of canned moves are spontaneous, yes. I'm not saying I couldn't make the same mistake. Hopefully, I wouldn't. I'm saying I don't represent myself to be better than anybody else."

"So you're not a better pilot than, say, Fuzzy?"

"I didn't say I wasn't better, I just said I didn't represent myself to be better."

"Do you really think you're a better pilot than I am?" Fuzzy asked.

"I don't think I'm better, Fuzzy," Biff said. "I *am* better. There's a big difference."

Following the few seconds Fuzzy wrestled with the semantics of Biff's retort, he asked, "Why am I always the victim in here? Whatever we talk about, I always wind up taking the hit."

"Stop complaining," Biff commanded. "You get your hits the old-fashioned way: you earn them."

"This whole thing is one of those things you never know," Trash threw out philosophically. "You never know how you'll react until you're faced with the situation. Talk is cheap."

"That's what I'm saying," Biff agreed. "So are we allowed to learn from the skipper's mistake? Hell, no. There's no learning going on. He's too busy covering his ass with all the shingles on his wall to let us know how we might avoid this sort of thing in the future. That's leadership?"

"He's just embarrassed," Punk said.

"You're really turning into a careerist, Punk," Biff said sharply, squaring off with his roommate.

"I'm not even sure what that means, but I'll deny that I am one," Punk said, quickly defusing the tension Biff had sought to explode.

"The bar lives here," Biff said, running his meaty hands along an imaginary ledge slightly above the level of his head. "It doesn't live with the personalities of those in charge."

"So you have an authority complex," Punk observed. "I'd rather be a careerist."

"Does it not bug anybody else here that the Iranian got away a couple of hours ago without so much as a mild scare?" Biff asked. "So he goes back to home base and tells his buddies, 'Hey, I flew right over those guys and nothing happened to me at all. I think the whole thing's a bluff.' So little by little, the Arab world starts to get enough confidence to ignore our presence in the region. And then where are we?"

"Here, I guess," Punk answered.

"No, we're not *here*," Biff retorted. "*Here* is a place where Iranians and Iraqis run scared when we launch." He pointed to the other end of the room. "*There* is a place where they figure out we can't back up our words, or at least not for very long. Look what happened to the Marines in Beirut. They study us. They probe our defenses, looking for a weakness, and then—*wham*—Pearl fucking Harbor.

"It's about readiness, gentlemen," Biff announced with finality. "Today one of us wasn't ready. That's serious, and we all need to assess where we are in terms of readiness. But, hey, we're not even allowed to talk about it."

The circle sat in silence for a few seconds pondering Biff's truth until Punk declared, "That does it. I'm quitting."

"Yes, you are, and so are many like you," Biff said, rising out of his chair and picking up a pace around the room, his pink face growing a deeper shade as he spoke. "The Navy wonders, or appears to wonder, why retention is so bad, and why morale is so low. They blame the Tailhook scandal, they blame MTV, and they blame video games. 'We don't understand these young officers,' they say." He motioned toward the general direction of the ready room. "Look no further. There's the problem. In fact, I'm going to document this whole series of events on my web site."

"Biffsroom.com?" Punk asked. "That'll certainly guarantee nobody sees them."

"Not true," Biff defended. "I've had hits. I have had hits."

Silence followed as Biff's vitriol was eclipsed by a

sense that they needed some down time. Today was
going to be a long one. As the circle began to disband,
Einstein came out of the shadows of the conversation
and said, "I feel much better. Do we talk like this a lot
in here?"

"Only when required," Punk said as he got himself
ready for as much sleep as he could get before his first
brief, "or when Biff needs to vent."

"This was awesome. I'll be a fleet guy in no time,
huh?" With that he moved to the left sink, ran some
water, and splashed it on his sweat-streaked face.

FOUR

Life itself passed through Punk for the third time that day, right through his stomach. That was how he'd come to describe a catapult shot: life passing through him, perpendicular to his spine. All the "accelerated roller coaster" and "car crash and orgasm mixed into one" analogies did not do the feeling justice. For two seconds he was along for the ride, no more in control of the jet than Spud in the backseat, as flesh and steel were joined in the short trip to flying speed.

He tried to anticipate the shot by watching the cat officer, or his flashlight, but that first compression of the nose strut always seemed to happen when Punk least expected it. And then all he could do was gasp, lock his left arm so the throttles didn't creep from the military power stops, attempt to set the jet's correct 10-degree attitude once airborne, and hang on until all the parts caught up to one another several hundred yards in front of the carrier and several hundred feet above the water.

His faith was in the gauges and video screens before him; there was no other reference available on moonless nights like the one into which they'd just been thrown. The altimeter started to wind upward, confirming the jet was in a climb, and after a *one po- tato, two potato,* Punk was reasonably sure they'd sur- vived another takeoff. He gathered his thoughts enough to reach for and raise the gear handle as he programmed the stick slightly aft and increased their rate of ascent.

"One-zero-three's airborne," Spud reported on De- parture.

"Roger, one-zero-three *aaaiiirrr borne,*" a voice sang back cheerily.

Hurtling into the darkness, Punk found the perky tenor of the Departure controller irritating. He pictured the controller hunkered over his coffee mug, seated in a comfortable chair, occasionally taking a break from his scope to comment to the controller next to him how fly- ing wasn't that hard and he could've done it but he just didn't want to.

After several minutes in a climb, Punk eased the nose back to the horizon at twenty thousand feet and banked the Tomcat in the direction of Waypoint 1 on his tactical display, a repeat of Spud's primary scope in the back seat. The efficiency and maturity of their pairing were evident in the silence as the airplane was groomed to fighting trim. The navigation plan, missile selection, radar modes and range scales, and multi-radio frequency selection all happened tacitly.

Spud switched his radio from Departure to Strike and checked in. They touched their station and Punk picked up an arc, similar to the one that the skipper had scribed nineteen hours earlier and dozens of crews from VF-104 had scribed throughout the day, and waited for Fuzzy and Turtle to join up. Punk looked around the blackness that was punctuated only by the red flashing lights of American aircraft, and tried to pick up the ones that might be rendezvousing with him.

"It's quiet out here," Spud said, the first words passing between them since they performed the takeoff checklist on the flight deck.

"What do you want?" Punk responded. "It's one in the morning."

"I want some action," Spud said.

"You've come to the wrong place, my friend," Punk said. "There's nothing but anti-action here."

Their radar warning receiver blinked and hummed with an air-to-air indication, signaling that Fuzzy was most likely in the final phase of his rendezvous. Punk looked out to his nine o'clock and picked up a couple of red and green glows closing on them.

"Is that you, Fuzz?" Punk asked over the front cockpit radio, dialed into the squadron's discrete tactical frequency.

"That's a roger, Big Daddy. I think I finally have this night rendezvous stuff down."

"At least somebody's getting something out of being out here," Punk said. "Position yourself wherever you want. Just don't hit us."

Punk did his best not to overfly Kharg Island, and Spud played the part of the diligent radar intercept officer, painting the skies over Bushehr and the rest of northwestern Iran. He stared intently at the radar display, willing out of sheer boredom the appearance of a contact. But, like all who'd plied the skies that day, he came up empty. The Great Iranian War had come and gone with a hundred and two shots fired (including all the bullets), no casualties, and in most forward-deployed minds, no closure.

The quiet continued and Punk's mind wandered

back to the e-mail he'd downloaded before the skipper walked in for the AOM. The message was only two lines long, and the salutation was strange: "Yikes, Jordan."

Yikes? What happened to "I love you" and other such sentiments? *Yikes?* What the hell did that mean? He didn't like the pattern emerging before him. What people did with their time was a matter of priorities, and it seemed like he was headed for Jordan's B list. Significant others didn't normally reside on the B list. And if a love interest gets bumped down, then someone else has usually moved up, and if so, who was it? The same yearning that had kept him awake all morning burned in his gut again, but he couldn't afford to feel that way now.

Damn, there was that attitude again. Was the fact that he flew jets the only thing he had going for him, his only emotional leverage over the rest of the nation's suitors? Typical fighter pilot . . .

"How do you feel?" Spud asked over the intercom.

"What?" Punk asked, coming out of the robotic daze in which he'd placed himself with his love-life musings. With their level of fatigue, the silence bathed in red cockpit lighting was perhaps a bit too conducive to excursions of the mind.

"Are you tired? I'm really starting to drag back here," Spud said.

"Yeah, I think I'm hitting the wall," Punk returned. "My eyes are burning. I'm having trouble focusing on anything."

"That's not good," Spud said. "You've still gotta dig deep for one more landing, amigo."

"We'll be fine. One no-grade is as good as another."

"Hey, remember our deal," Spud retorted. "You don't kill me; my kids don't sue your estate."

"My estate . . . yeah, they can split my CD collection between them."

"So, what did the LSOs give you on the last pass?"

"A fair."

"Well, it didn't look like a fair pass from where I was sitting. I can't account for gifts."

"It wasn't a gift. It should have been an okay. The ball never moved."

"Exactly. The ball never moved from a cell low."

"Whatever. I'm done caring about landing grades. They're more subjective than a beauty pageant."

"That's fine as long as you stay out of the running for Miss Ramp Strike."

Punk checked the time, looked at his fuel gauge, and then scanned the fuel matrix he'd scribbled onto his kneeboard card. The community rule-of-thumb was twelve hundred pounds of fuel burned every fifteen minutes on a lazy profile like the one they were on tonight. They should be fat.

Fuzzy was also feeling the effects of a long day. "Punk, I'm having trouble concentrating here," he passed over the squadron's common frequency. "I'm going to fall into trail."

"Roger. Just stay safe. I don't think war is going to break out in the next twenty minutes."

Ever mindful of the tactical concerns, Spud added, "You guys will have to check your own six back there."

"Roger that," Fuzzy sang back sardonically, "although I agree with Punk."

Whatever adrenaline had kept Punk operating for the day was almost completely depleted now; normally smooth movements of his head, arms, and fingers were jerky and awkwardly deliberate. His eyes alternately and involuntarily locked onto and jumped between the altimeter, airspeed, RPM, and fuel flow gauges, and it took much longer than normal to register their readings. He felt the ache of lactic acid in his left forearm as he moved the throttles, and in his right hand as he adjusted his grip on the stick. The dull pain made him angry—angry about the crappy e-mail, angry about how dark it was, and angry about the effort they'd been forced to put into the last twelve hours of flying and twenty-four of being awake.

Earlier in the day, about noon, in order to focus all efforts on the real threat to the east, the admiral begged the air wing out of their Operation Southern Watch commitment over southern Iraq, much to the rescheduling heartache of the Air Force–led Joint Task Force–Southwest Asia in Saudi Arabia. Minutes later, the battle group commander also lost points in the NATO arena by canceling a war-at-sea exercise against a British destroyer.

Then at 1300, Punk and Spud took to the air with thirty-four of their fellow aviators, including the helicopter crews. Throughout the day the CAP stations were manned and re-manned in a tag team process called "relief on station." The off-going fighters were not permitted to leave station and return back to the Boat until the oncoming jets checked in on Strike.

But the pace of each mission was such that as soon as the flight was established on station, pilots looked at watches as much as anywhere else, wondering when they could go back and land. They would drive in circles for an hour and a half and then be rewarded for their efforts with a night trap, generally considered by pilots as naval aviation's most consistently terrifying task.

At 0230, launch time for the follow-on event, Spud pogo'd between Departure and Strike, trying to verify that their reliefs were airborne and that soon they'd be able to head back. It wasn't outside of the realm of possibilities that if somebody didn't make it for the next event, Punk and Spud would have to hit the tanker and stay up for another hour and a half, a prospect that Punk feared would, with its lack of stimulation, lower his IQ so much that he might not retain the mental faculties required to control the jet to a safe night landing. All he could think of now was arriving back on deck with all the big pieces still attached to the jet, climbing into bed, and getting some sleep.

Bill Thompson and Biff reported airborne in Slinger 112 over Departure. *One down, one to go.* Minutes passed and the second jet didn't check in, so Spud asked over base frequency, "Biff, where's your wingman?"

"You mean my flight lead? I dunno," Biff answered. "XO, are you and Beads still on deck?"

"That's affirmative," Beads responded. "We don't even have the starboard engine running yet. The power plants guys are troubleshooting a fuel leak from the right nacelle. They're telling me it doesn't look good."

Awww shhhiiiitttt . . . If it wasn't Murphy's goddam law in action. Punk froze in disbelief.

"Gents, we're hard down," the XO passed over squadron common. "We're shutting down. Be safe out there."

"You know what we've gotta do," Spud said over the intercom.

"Yes, dammit," Punk snapped back. "Let's make sure, just in case."

"Hawkeye, Slinger one-oh-three," Spud said over Strike.

"Go ahead, Slinger," the controller returned.

"Assume Alpha Whiskey wants two-jet coverage at all times?"

"Stand by . . . Alpha Whiskey, do you copy the question?"

"That's correct," a new voice said, presumably that of the TAO on the cruiser or even Alpha Whiskey himself, the cruiser's captain. "Two-jet coverage."

"One-zero-three's relief went down on deck," Spud explained. "We can double cycle, if required, but we're going to need about eight thousand pounds of give to make it for another cycle."

"Hawkeye copies. We'll coordinate. Stand by."

"One-twelve's checking in and proceeding to station," Bill Thompson said on Strike.

"Fuzzy, you're cleared to detach and head to Marshal," Punk instructed on squadron common.

"I'll stay out here if you want, buddy," Fuzzy offered halfheartedly.

"Shut up and go get your night trap," Punk said. Fuzzy couldn't even fly loose defensive combat spread right now. He was in no better shape than Punk to suck up more flight time, and he certainly didn't voice any strong counter to his flight lead's direction.

Fuzzy accelerated from behind them, positioned himself directly abeam, flicked his external lights twice and then began a lazy descent back toward the Boat. Punk watched his wingman disappear behind the canopy rail. Fuzzy and Turtle would be in their racks before him.

His needs were meager now, he thought. He didn't want riches, power, or fame, just a few hours of sleep.

Punk drew a big breath and moved around a bit in an attempt to rally for the task ahead. The selfless act of doing more than everyone else actually buoyed his spirits a bit. *And let's see those pussies Jordan works with do this . . .*

At the same time there was no denying his fatigue. His eyes stung, and he had to squint to focus on anything long enough for cognitive thought to take place.

Spud, also showing signs of a long day, got tired of

waiting for the tanker situation to work itself out and started calling the shots from his end. "Hawkeye, one-zero-three's going to return overhead for Texaco. Switching Departure." He switched the frequency before the controller could even think to voice an objection.

Departure quickly revealed itself to be yet another chamber of confusion in the late-night house of horror and sleep deprivation. The air ops officer in the carrier's traffic control center was arguing alternately over the radio with one of the S-3 pilots in a jet spotted just behind catapult one, and face-to-face with the S-3 squadron's rep in the control center.

"Seven-oh-three, are you ready to go flying or not?" the air ops officer asked on Departure.

"Seven-zero-three is the *spare,* not the *go* bird," the Viking pilot responded.

"I know that. Answer the question."

"I have to finish my final checks. It'll be a few minutes."

"Hurry up. We're going to launch you as soon as you're ready."

"One-oh-three's up, looking for 8K give," Spud interjected during the first dead air on the frequency.

"Roger, one-zero-three. We don't have your tanker airborne yet. Hold overhead at angels eight."

The air ops officer shifted his focus back to the lieutenant commander standing behind him. "Tell me again how much gas you've got airborne."

"Not enough to give one-oh-three 8K," the lieutenant commander answered. "I've got 4K available in the off-going tanker up there now, but he's got to cover this recovery." This discussion was distasteful to him. He'd been reared in the S-3 community during the glory days of antisubmarine warfare. The end of the Cold War and a shrinking defense budget slowly shoved ASW to the back burner. Now with only three potentially hostile submarines in the region (Iranian Kilo Class boats that seldom ventured away from their home ports) the S-3's primary utility was that of a carrier-based tanker. The service of providing gas was generally routine and without glory. They didn't make movies about tanker guys, despite the fact that available fuel determined the "how" of carrier aviation: how many, how fast, how high, how far, and how long.

"And I know I'm going to need the recovery gas for the recovery," the air ops officer added. "There's something about the thirteen-hour mark of an air plan. It's the witching hour. We can fly a twelve-hour schedule no problem, but as soon as we go longer than that every pilot in the air wing goes brain dead." He patted his ample belly in a self-satisfied fashion and then ran his fingers through his tight curly hair. The S-3 pilot noted the naval flight officer wings on the air ops officer's chest and the E-2-shaped projection on his belt buckle and wondered what the hell gave the commander any credibility to judge pilot performance. E-2 "moles" like this guy couldn't even see outside as the airplane was brought aboard the carrier.

The air ops officer turned back to study the profusion of information surrounding him.

"What's the divert," the lieutenant commander asked, "and how far away is it?"

"Al Jabar, Kuwait," the air ops officer responded after a few moments of fishing the white letters out of one of his well-stocked data reservoirs. "Right now it's one hundred twenty miles away." Screens and monitors and televisions that accented the otherwise dark room in flickers of blue light surrounded them.

The lieutenant commander took a swig from the styrofoam cup he was holding and observed, "You know, the S-3 was never really meant to be a tanker; it's a sub killer. Our life would be a lot easier right now with big tankers: KC-10s and KC-135s."

"That's true," the air ops officer agreed as he sat back down in his ready room–style chair surrounded by vintage phones and comm boxes, equipment that told the history of the Boat almost as well as anything available in the public affairs officer's files. "But, the Air Force wasn't interested in flying through the night with us, so they're all bedded down in their air-conditioned tents. They consider our little issue with Iran a force protection problem and not a theater concern, and I'm sure they said, 'We're here to support the operations in southern Iraq, not fly over the Gulf.'"

"That reminds me of War College," the lieutenant commander smirked with the tortured memory of one who'd spent some time in the joint arena. "The Air Force guys at school used to proclaim that the Navy caused as much trouble with our presence as we prevented. They claimed that 45 percent of our sorties were overhead."

"Actually, today that number would be a little low . . . by about 55 percent," the air ops officer said with a wry smile in return. He put the red radio receiver back to his ear and refocused his attention to the situation on the flight deck. "Seven-oh-three, how's it going?"

"We're taxiing to the cat now," the pilot answered. "Should be airborne in two minutes."

"One-zero-three, do you copy?"

"One-zero-three copies. Meet you at angels eight."

Two minutes turned into ten, and eventually the S-3 made it into the sky with the eight thousand pounds of gas they intended to pass to Slinger 103. The Viking didn't have the power of the Tomcat, and it was another four minutes before its whiny turbofan motors were able to get the boxy airframe to altitude.

On his left, Punk spotted the tanker's distinctive green flasher stirring the inky murk below him, and he instructed the Viking pilot to pick up an orbit to effect a rendezvous. After another 80 degrees of turn, Punk was positioned on the tanker's left wing, awaiting clearance from the S-3 pilot to plug into the refueling hose that was already streamed to its full forty-foot extension. The signal came: a circular motion with a red-lensed flashlight, and as Spud acknowledged the signal with the same motion of his own flashlight, Punk extended the refueling probe and slid back to maneuver into the drogue.

It had been a week since Punk had tanked at night, and on his first attempt to plug into the basket, he missed completely. He backed away, re-stabilized, and approached again. The second time, he over-finessed the closure, caught one side of the drogue and sent it flinging above them. The assembly flung back and grazed the nose of the Tomcat as Punk was backing out.

"Easy with it," Spud interjected. "No hurry. We've got all the time in the world."

"This is just pissing me off!" Punk yelled over the intercom. "I am definitely not in the mood for this."

Punk parked the jet ten feet behind the basket and made an effort to focus while he waited for the oscillations of the refueling hose to quit. He had startled himself with his anger, and he realized just how tired he was. He kept pushing the image of his dingy-but-soft pillow out of his consciousness.

On the third approach, Spud took a more active role with verbal coaching. "Keep the closure coming," he said over the intercom. "Good . . . keep it coming . . . up and right now, up and right . . . right, right . . . good plug."

Once in the basket with his refueling probe, Punk

drove forward slightly in an effort to get the amber indicator on the tanker's store to turn green, indicating good flow down the line. After ten seconds, the light remained amber. Spud saw the light and confirmed that the value on his fuel totalizer was not increasing.

"One-oh-three's not getting anything, Viking," Spud said on Departure.

"Roger, disconnect and we'll recycle," the S-3 pilot responded. Punk cursed under his breath for the wasted effort of a successful plug as he moved back to the tanker's left side and watched the hose reel in and then run back out. "One-oh-three, cleared to engage."

Following another short jousting match, Punk was in the basket, and this time he was rewarded with a green light on the flow indicator. As Punk flew form on the S-3's left horizontal stabilizer, Spud watched his fuel gauge roll up five hundred pounds, and then stop. The flow light switched back to amber.

What the hell? "Viking, we got a little and then it stopped," Spud said.

"Yeah, go ahead and back out," the S-3 pilot instructed. "Departure, it looks like our package is sour."

That wasn't what the air ops officer needed to hear. The commander wheeled around and glared at the Viking rep as if he'd caused the malfunction. "What's the problem with your air force?"

"Excuse me, sir?" the lieutenant commander asked in return. "What? What did I do?"

"You're the squadron's rep—"

The air ops officer's response was cut off by the sound of the first jet, a Hornet, down on the recovery. Over-propelled by a last-second burst of power commanded by the nugget pilot, the airplane bounced off the flight deck, sailed over the arresting wires, and boltered off the angle deck, trailing a shower of sparks from the tail hook's scraping across the non-skid, like a match struck along the side of a matchbox.

The in-house circuit buzzed a single blast, a signal reserved for the captain's use. "Oh boy, here we go," sighed the air ops officer. "The witching hour." He picked the black receiver out of its brass holder and stammered a "Yessir."

"This can go to hell quick," the captain said. From his chair on the port side of the bridge, five levels above the control center, he attempted to keep his finger on many pulses. He sat leaning heavily on his left elbow with the handset to his ear, alternately focusing out at the flight deck and the hundred points of reflective tape each marking a warm body in the darkness and inside around the handful of computer displays and navigational readouts that surrounded him.

He was the "Boy Captain," so named because he'd been promoted to the rank several years ahead of his peers and because he looked to be about twenty years younger than he actually was. He was average height but had a very muscular build and a head of free-flowing brown hair that he had a habit of balling his fist into when he was stressed.

"I copy that, Captain," the air ops officer replied to the captain's observation. "We've already got our tanker hawking that Hornet off the bolter."

"What's the plan for the Tomcat overhead?"

"We're working that at the moment, sir. We may have to take him this recovery if he can't get gas." The roar of a Hornet snagging one of the arresting wires caused a momentary break in the conversation.

"You'd better talk to the admiral's staff and figure it out. Is my screen correct up here? Do we only have four thousand pounds of available gas in the air right now?"

"That's affirmative, sir."

"How did that happen?"

"One of their jets broke on deck before the launch, and the other one went sour airborne."

"That's not a lot of gas in the air." His right hand worked into his hair for the first time that night.

"No, it's not, sir."

"And we've still got six to recover. What's the divert?"

"Al Jabar."

"Oh, yeah, I see it up here. I'm still getting used to all these computer screens."

The air ops officer forced a laugh in response. "We can't fight technology, Captain."

"Is it open?"

"Excuse me, sir?"

"Is the field at Al Jabar open?"

A shot of adrenaline surged through the air ops officer's portly body. He couldn't remember if they'd coordinated with Air Force personnel at Al Jabar to keep the field open past the normal 2200 closing time. He quickly wrestled with what to tell the captain, knowing that anything other than, "Yessir, I took care of it," was the wrong answer.

"The flag staff wants to know when the Tomcat will be back on station," a lieutenant in another corner of the control center called across the room. "They said the admiral feels vulnerable right now."

"We're in the process of figuring it out, dammit," the air ops officer shot back with his hand over the phone, still unsure of what to say to the captain. "The admiral feels vulnerable?" he mused aloud. "Try doing my job for a while."

"Air ops, did you hear my question?" the captain asked.

"Oh, yessir. Um . . . I'm almost positive we checked

with Al Jabar base ops earlier today, but I'll call them and make sure they're still open."

"Do that," the captain said, and then dropped the connection at his end.

"Sampson!" the air ops officer screamed at one of the enlisted men kibitzing around the lone coffee pot in the space. "It's damage control time. Get on the phone to Al Jabar and tell them we need the field open through the night."

"Again?" the petty officer asked in return.

"Again? What do you mean?"

"Well, sir, I think Furlong called them earlier today. I read it in the log during my turnover." The lanky sailor moved across the space and picked up a light green book with "Official Phone Record" scribbled on the front cover in black marker. "Let's see . . . yeah. Here it is: 'Called Al Jabar base ops to keep field open.'"

"Oh . . ." the commander muttered, angry air completely let out of his balloon. "Ah . . . good job."

"You want me to call them again?"

Another jet slammed into the roof and failed to catch any of the four arresting cables strung across the flight deck. "Jeezus," the air ops officer exclaimed. "Viper rep. What do you want to do with that guy?"

"He had plenty of gas at the ball call," a ruddy-faced Hornet pilot answered, rising from his seat in the rep bleachers at the back of the room. "Let's let him go around and try again."

"Commander, do you want me to call again?" Petty Officer Sampson repeated.

"What?" the air ops officer asked back, trying to focus on the PLAT as if that would cause the pilots to snag a wire. "No. If you say Furlong called, then we should be good-to-go." The petty officer shrugged and returned to the coffee machine to rejoin the muted but lively discussion between several of his peers.

The air ops officer wondered how hard an eight-jet recovery could be as another Hornet successfully engaged a wire. At the same time, a voice boomed over the distress frequency. "Slinger one-zero-three, this is Alpha Bravo. Return to CAP station. One-zero-three, return to CAP station. Alpha Bravo, out."

"Departure, did you hear that Guard transmission?" Spud asked over the radio. "What do you want us to do?"

"Stand . . . by," the air ops officer intoned with a measured two-beat cadence, quickly losing his patience with the competing multi-source concerns. He fought the urge for drink, but at the same time he sensed life had felt easier when he was drinking. How calming it had been to quietly slink to his stateroom and grab a nip off a well-hidden bottle. Rum was his favorite in those days, the days before the butt-biting incident with the American Counsel General's wife in Rhodes, Greece, and the follow-on rehab. What a big deal the Navy had made of the rodeo, and how they had repeatedly told him he'd squandered any chance for command, as if that was the sum total of the tragedy. Now, as part of his seemingly ongoing and endless program of contrition, he held down what many considered to be the most thankless job for a commander on the Boat.

He picked up another handset and pressed two numbers.

"Tactical Force Command," said the voice at the other end, presumably that of the battle watch captain.

"Yeah, this is air ops. Look, right now we don't have the gas in the air for one-zero-three to play in the admiral's game. You're going to have to give me a little time to figure this one out. I mean, the bow is closed now because we're parking the jets from this recovery and I can't shoot another Viking for about twenty minutes or so, if the squadron even has another ready jet—"

"This is the Admiral."

"Say again?"

"I'm the Admiral and this isn't a game. I want one-zero-three back on station, with or without gas. Send the tanker to him if you have to."

"Oh, yes, Admiral," the commander awkwardly returned. "And by 'game,' sir, I meant—" The line went dead.

"Departure, say intentions for one-zero-three," Spud demanded.

"One-zero-three, say your state," the air ops officer commanded with an exasperated heave of his lungs.

"One-zero-three's state is seven-point-five."

"Roger, proceed back to station."

"We can't make it another cycle without more gas."

"I know, I know, I know," the commander said with his head cradled in his left palm, sounding on the frequency every bit as pained as he was beginning to feel. "Proceed to station anyway, by direction of Alpha Bravo. We'll figure it out later."

At that point, Fuzzy put the finishing touches on the air ops officer's headache by getting waved off by the LSOs a quarter-mile from touchdown after throwing a way-below-glide slope approach at them.

"Anybody feel like landing and stopping tonight?" the commander rhetorically asked the gathering of squadron reps before responding to a single buzz on the closed-circuit phone. "Yes, Captain?"

"What's the game plan to get gas to one-zero-three?"

"Well, the only plan I can think of is to launch a mission tanker after this recovery."

"What's his state?"

"He gave us seven-point-five about three minutes ago."

The captain reached into the depths of his former fighter pilot self and calculated how long a Tomcat could stay airborne with seventy-five hundred pounds of gas. "He's probably running about twenty-five hundred pounds per hour a side on the fuel flow at conservative airspeeds. How far away is Al Jabar?"

"Still around a hundred twenty miles."

"So that's about a four thousand pound bingo." The captain gave his hair another tug and then held his fingers up to the small reading light in front of him to check the yield of the harvest. He flittered his fingers and allowed the strands to fall to the deck below his elevated chair. "We've got him for a half-hour at best before we either land him here or send him to Kuwait."

"I can't get any gas airborne in a half hour. Might as well recover him this event."

"I'm not sure if that's going to work for the admiral," the captain said. "Is CAG down there with you?"

"Let me see . . ."

The air ops officer scoured the crowd behind him for the air wing commander, a man currently in pure hell with all the confusion. CAG knew eventually someone would want him to make a decision about something, and he ducked down in his seat on the bleachers and avoided eye contact, hoping somehow the jets would just land and everyone would relax. Nothing in his career had prepared him for nights like these, and he had never sought the challenges they presented.

As a war fighter and tactician he'd been unremarkable, a competent-enough EA-6B Prowler electronic countermeasures officer who'd been a face in the crowd of the four-man jammer. But as an administrator he'd been a standout. Upon completion of his first sea tour, his skipper, a bookish man with an eye for like talent, ushered him to the front door of the Pentagon, and from that day on he'd only emerged on two occasions prior to this duty: once to be a department head for fourteen months in a West Coast Prowler squadron, and once to command an East Coast Prowler squadron for a year. Both jobs were forced on him by his bosses as a way to ensure he didn't squander his gift for instruction-guided facsimile and wreck his chances for flag rank, the attainment of which, cruelly enough, required some experience at sea. He viewed every minute in and around jets as an opportunity to screw something up and get fired for it.

And in spite of his underlying repulsion toward the idea of venturing out, this time he was rewarded for his syntax with command of an air wing. When he was selected, he didn't even realize he was being considered, and before he would accept, he had to be assured he could come back to D.C. the minute his god-awful sea duty was over. He was petitioned by his mentors once again to "check the warrior block," with the guarantee that once he pinned on rear admiral he could carve his own permanent niche in the Pentagon.

"CAG," the air ops officer said, catching his eye with a wave, "the captain would like to speak with you, sir." CAG checked his watch: 0247. *You don't know the answer to the question, whatever it is,* CAG thought. *You're out of your league again.*

He took the receiver from the air ops officer as if he'd been handed a poisonous snake and put it to his ear. "Yes, Captain."

The captain paused long enough for another Hornet to bolter and disappear back into the blackness. "Quite an evening we're having, eh, CAG?"

"Yes," CAG replied simply, his soft face without expression for fear the slightest muscle twitches might cause him to convulse in a spasmodic cry for a return to the natural order. He'd come to dread every interface he was forced to have with the captain; he always walked away from them feeling, accurately enough, like he'd been bullied.

"Have you talked to the admiral recently?" the captain asked. Until the mid-1980s, the air wing commander had worked for the aircraft carrier's commanding officer, but when the warfare commander concept was conceived by the secretary of the Navy in 1985, as a way to make more room at the top for naval aviators, CAG's rank was elevated from commander to captain. Now, instead of one working for the other, they actually competed on equal terms for the battle group commander's professional favor. The concept had also caused the carrier CO's role to become more ship driving and less war fighting—a fact that had not really bothered the captain going into the job but ate at him daily now that he was a witness to CAG's poorly hidden repulsion for the idea of leading sailors and being at sea.

"No, I haven't talked to the admiral. I've been watching this recovery here in the control center."

"I wonder how long he intends to keep up this flying," the captain said. "You can see by the boarding rate that folks are getting tired."

"The admiral told me he's very concerned about the Iranian threat."

"Gimme a break, CAG. If the Iranians really wanted to take us out, I mean to the point of risking a bunch of pilots and jets, we'd be at the bottom right now. I'm more worried about somebody planting themselves on the ramp of my carrier."

"Well, I've done my job. The squadron COs have all

guaranteed me safe flight operations throughout the night."

"Well then," the captain returned with every bit of gorge he felt, "there's absolutely nothing to worry about. What have your trusty COs said about one-zero-three?"

"One-zero-three?"

"I thought you said you were watching the recovery ... anyway, the admiral wants one-zero-three to remain on station and I don't think he's going to have the gas."

"I guess I'll have to talk to the squadron reps here and then maybe go next door and talk to the admiral." It sounded as much a question as a course of action.

"This carrier aviation stuff is really scary, isn't it, CAG?" The line went dead. CAG was unsure where to replace the receiver so he just stood in place with his arms at his side, feigning interest in the tangle of lines and digits surrounding them, until he was finally relieved of the device by the air ops officer, who needed the phone to either yell at, or to get yelled at by, somebody.

Eventually the event's Hornets all managed to get aboard and stay aboard, but not before draining the sole tanker down to a thousand pounds of available give. With Punk's status still in limbo, Fuzzy and the S-3 were the only remaining jets to land this event.

At two miles abeam the port side of the Boat and twelve hundred feet over the water, heading opposite the carrier, Fuzzy fought to get the Tomcat trimmed up before attempting his second pass, but the beast didn't want to cooperate. He mashed the coolie hat on the stick with his thumb—forward and back, left and right—but there was no response.

"We've lost the trim," Fuzzy reported to Turtle. "Break out the emergency checklist, please."

"Maybe we should climb up to altitude and trouble-shoot the problem," Turtle suggested as he went through his nav bag in search of his pocket checklist.

"No, we're fine," Fuzzy replied. "I can control the jet; I'm just wondering if there's anything I'm not thinking about here."

"Do you want to talk to a rep on Departure?"

"No," Fuzzy said. "I'm sick of the skipper hooting on us for whining on the radios. We'll just land this pass, and gripe it when we get down to maintenance control. Besides, I'm too tired to screw around with climbing and descending and talking to reps. Let's just make the pain end."

Ten miles away from and ten thousand feet above Fuzzy and Turtle, the crew of Slinger 103 considered their course of action. Their pace back to station was a slow one, as the thought of betting on the come for potential gas seemed unduly reckless to both officers. Punk looked at his fuel totalizer: sixty-five hundred pounds.

"Spud, the lowest I can set the fuel flow right now and keep flying looks to be about twenty-two hundred pounds per hour per side."

Spud was just about done playing the game this particular night. "Hawkeye, say picture."

"Believe it or not, the picture is clean," the controller replied dryly from the tube of the E-2. "No activity."

"Slinger one-zero-three is switching Departure for a rep." Again, Spud flipped his radio from button one to button fourteen without waiting for a response. "Departure, one-zero-three would like to talk to a rep."

"Roger, one-zero-three. Standby."

Several seconds passed and then Smoke's voice came over the airwaves. "Go ahead, one-zero-three. This is your rep."

Recognizing his roommate's voice, Spud said, "We need a reality check on staying out here, Smoke. Our state is below sixty-five hundred pounds right now and I don't see any gas in sight."

"Roger, concur. Hold on a second." Smoke balanced the receiver on his collarbone and attempted to get the attention of the ever-harried air ops officer. "Hey, Commander . . . excuse me, Commander. What's the plan for one-zero-three?"

The crackle of the controller's voice on the terminal approach frequency, set at a volume higher than that of the other frequencies piped into the center, interrupted the commander's response. He held his hand up in response to Smoke and directed his attention toward the PLAT TV hanging from the overhead to the right side of the displays in front of him.

"One-one-four, on glide slope, slightly right, three-quarters of a mile. Call the ball."

"One-fourteen, Tomcat ball, six-point-zero, no trim," Turtle replied, indicating that Fuzzy could see the glide slope reference on the deck—the "meatball"—and that they had six thousand pounds of gas left in the jet.

"Roger ball, Tomcat," the controlling LSO responded from among the small crowd of LSOs gathered on the platform at the deck's edge on the port side, near the stern. "Copy no trim. Twenty-eight knots of wind down the angle."

Fuzzy concentrated on the three basic parameters of a carrier approach through bleary eyes and with tired limbs: "meatball," (glide slope, high or low), "lineup," (azimuth, left or right), and "angle of attack," (speed, fast or slow).

"To be honest, amigo," the air ops officer said in response to Smoke's question while still watching the

TV, "I don't know what we're going to do with one-zero-three. I do know the admiral is going to freak out if they don't get to station soon. Right now, I've got two more jets to land and this recovery is history, thank God."

"Well, I'll tell you a little secret," Smoke said as he also watched Fuzzy motor down the chute on the PLAT. "If the admiral comes up Guard one more time and orders one-zero-three to station, he's going to have a mutiny from inside that jet on his hands."

Smoke continued to concentrate on the PLAT, and as he noticed the lights of the jet travel above the crosshairs of the target glide slope, he wondered aloud why the LSO was not talking to Fuzzy. "How high is he going to let him get?" Smoke asked the room in general. "You know the guy's tired. Help him out."

Just seconds before 114 was over the ramp, the LSO came on the radio with, "You're fast, don't go high . . . power back on . . . power!"

Then two voices could be heard as the back-up LSO keyed his handset and joined the controlling LSO with a chorus of, "Wave it off! Wave it off!"

It was too late. Numbed by fatigue and fighting with the untrimmed jet, Fuzzy had overcorrected for his situation and pulled the throttles back too far. He saw the wave-off lights flash red and jammed the throttles to full afterburner, but the increased thrust lagged the pull of gravity. The F-14 smashed down on the steel deck. Sparks flew from the base of the right landing gear. The wheel came flying off and careened down the deck like an errant Frisbee on a windy day at the beach. The Tomcat bounced over the arresting wires and continued down the angle and back into the sky. The LSO inconsequentially called "bolter, bolter, bolter" on the radio, as if Fuzzy had some doubt he wasn't going to stop.

The wheel continued down the deck, bounced off a plane captain, breaking three of his ribs, punched a hole in the right main flap of a Hornet parked across catapult two, and disappeared over the port bow and into the water. Bits of composite from the wing blew back across the deck and toward the stern, fouling the landing area.

In the tower, six stories above the flight deck, perched above the action like two crows on a wire, were the air boss and, to his right, his assistant, the mini boss. When the wheel disappeared from view, the air boss peeled the foil from around another antacid and popped it into his mouth while he keyed the microphone to the flight deck P.A. "All right, on the flight deck, combat FOD walk down, I say again, combat FOD walk down. Let's get the junk cleared off the angle so the next guy down doesn't suck something through his intake and ruin a perfectly good motor."

The air boss turned in his elevated chair and said to the mini, "I guess it's our turn to jump into this." He picked up another of the four handsets hung in brass at his knee and said, "One-fourteen, be advised you lost your right wheel."

Smoke attempted to take control of the situation from his position. "I need one-fourteen to come up Departure, and I'm going to need one-zero-three to check him out visually," he said to the air ops officer, who sat frozen staring at the PLAT, seemingly unsure of what action to take. "Get one-zero-three up Departure also."

The air ops officer remained perfectly still. "Hey," Smoke said, reaching out to shake the commander's left upper arm. "We've got to do this quickly."

The commander came alive with a jerk as soon as Smoke touched him. "That's not going to work, goddam it," he shouted. "The admiral has already reamed me once for one-zero-three not being on station."

Smoke hissed something in disgust and motioned toward the bleachers for someone to throw him the portable phone. He caught it and dialed the skipper's stateroom.

The phone rang but was never picked up on the other end. "He's got the damned ringer turned off again," Smoke muttered to himself. He hung up and dialed the ready room.

"VF-104 ready room, Lieutenant j.g. Francis."

"Einstein, this is Smoke down in air ops. I need to talk to the skipper, but he's got the ringer to the phone in his stateroom turned off. Is the XO back in the ready room yet?"

"No, I think he's still turning the jet with Beads while maintenance troubleshoots the fuel leak."

"Okay, I need you to go down and bang on the skipper's door and tell him to come down here immediately."

"Roger." Einstein hung up the phone and raced out of the room without a word to the crew briefing for the 0400 go.

Fuzzy knew he needed some help. He also knew he probably wasn't going to get all the help he needed from his RIO. Turtle was a lieutenant commander and currently VF-104's administrative officer, but this was his first tour in Tomcats, having served previously as a bombardier/navigator flying the now-decommissioned A-6 Intruder. He was a reticent sort with nondescript features and distinguished himself only in the phlegmatic way with which he carried out the business of life.

Fuzzy asked Turtle to switch from Approach to Departure to talk to their rep in air ops, and then keyed his radio to talk to Punk on the squadron's common frequency.

"Punk, where are you?"

"I'm hanging out by the marshal stack, trying to pretend like I'm headed for the CAP station."

"I've got a question for you: Have you ever had a wheel come off when you touched down?"

"No. Why?"

"Because I just did. Do you think you could sneak overhead the ship and look me over?"

"I'm on my way."

Einstein was in the middle of his third series of raps on the skipper's door before the skipper yanked it open and stood in the opening, clad only in his boxers, half-asleep and fully miffed.

"Excuse me, sir," Einstein dutifully started. "I'm sorry to wake you. Smoke has requested your presence in air ops. We have an emergency in progress."

"Do you think leadership just happens?"

"What's that, sir?"

Commander Campbell straightened himself up, and raised his hands to drive his point home in synch with the meter of his speech. "Leadership takes endurance. Endurance requires sleep. Sleep requires—" He was interrupted by the ringing of the phone on the night stand next to the head of his rack. The skipper shut the door, leaving Einstein standing in the passageway and unsure of what to do.

Didn't Smoke say the skipper had the ringer turned off? the young RIO wondered. *He must've clicked it back on before he answered the door to cover his ass.* His head slowly moved toward the closed door as he strained to hear the skipper's side of the conversation, and eventually he had his ear against the sheet metal hatch. The moment he touched the door, one of the Boat's crack two-man security teams came wandering around the corner in the middle of their normal rounds. Einstein had his back to them and didn't hear their approach.

The question, "Can we help you, sir?" asked by the taller and leaner of the two, startled Einstein and caused him to jump back from the door. The two stood shoulder-to-shoulder, doing their best to appear intimidating. They were each dressed in dungarees and a ship's ball cap, and the taller one sported a radio on one hip and a holster on the other.

"Jeez, you guys scared me."

"Why don't you try knocking, sir?"

"I already did. I'm waiting for my CO to get off the phone."

"Does he know you're out here?"

"What?"

"Does your CO know you're out here, in front of his stateroom?"

"Yes, he does."

"Why did he leave you out in the middle of the passageway if he knows you're out here? Why didn't he invite you in?"

"I don't know," Einstein replied, becoming a bit perturbed with the line of questioning from what appeared to him to be nothing more than two nosy enlisted men.

"I know," the other one said, running his thumbs along the inside of his belt line. "The fact is your CO doesn't know you're out here."

"Look, he does know I'm out here."

The door cracked open. "Are you still out here?" the skipper asked angrily. "I've got a meeting with the admiral now. Go back to the ready room." The door slammed shut.

As Einstein turned to head back to the ready room,

the tall petty officer grabbed him by the shoulder. "It's not good to get caught in a lie, is it?"

"What? You heard him. He knew I was out here."

"It sounded to me like he didn't know you were out here." The tall one glanced at his teammate and chuckled. "Look, I can see you're just a jay gee, and you're probably new to this business of being at sea, so I'm going to give you a break." He jiggled his badge and his teammate's badge. "You see these? Carte blanche." His hand moved from his badge to his holster. "We're authorized to use deadly force if required to ensure the security of this ship."

Einstein shrugged and hurried back toward the ready room. He made it across one kneeknocker when the security team leader called after him, "Don't forget, sir. Deadly force."

"You're the senior man available right now from VF-104," CAG said to Smoke. "Come with me to the admiral's cabin."

"Sir, I just got off the phone with the skipper," Smoke protested. "He'll be down here in the control center in a second."

"We don't have a second," CAG returned. "The admiral has summoned me, and I imagine he wants to talk about your jets, and he may want details that I can't provide, not having a Tomcat background. Let's go *now*."

On his way out of the room, Smoke threw a tidbit of advice at the air ops officer: "You'd better think about stripping the wires and rigging the barricade."

The mention of the word "barricade" sent shots of adrenaline through every aviator within earshot. The barricade was the answer to the question of how to make a night carrier landing even more dangerous. Instead of catching an arresting wire, airplanes flew into a net-like device jury-rigged across the landing area, a one-time proposition that didn't allow the luxury of a bolter.

Four thousand feet over the Boat, Punk joined on Fuzzy and pulled up as tight as he could under Slinger 114's damaged right side. Spud shined his flashlight on the area of the main strut.

"Yep, your wheel is definitely gone," Punk said over the squadron's common freq. "And your brake lines are dangling. What are your hydraulic gauges reading?"

As Fuzzy turned his head to look at the hydraulic gauge, the master-caution light flashed as if on Punk's cue, sending blinks of yellow light dancing off of every surface that would host them.

Turtle took notice of the light show from the front cockpit, and asked, "Whaddaya got, Fuzz?"

"Damned if I know. Hold on a sec." Fuzzy looked down at the annunciator panel on his right console for a clue about what had triggered the light and noticed an amber "hyd press" indication. He twisted his head back the other way and looked just beyond his left knee, trying with uncooperative and bloodshot eyes to focus on the twin hydraulic gauges, each no bigger than a quarter. Normally, the two indicator needles would form a straight line displaying that both hydraulic systems were fully charged at three thousand psi. As he studied the gauges now, his heart went to his throat. The left needle was drooping to six o'clock; one of his hydraulic systems, in this case the more important one, which controlled the normal operation of the flight controls, the tail hook, the landing gear, and the wheel brakes, was reading zero psi. The system had lost all of its hydraulic fluid through the busted brake lines.

Like a patient who feels intensified symptoms after the diagnosis is rendered, Fuzzy sensed that the stick was beginning to feel mushy. "Okay, Turtle," he passed over the intercom in a calm voice he hoped would belie the growing intensity of his heartbeat, the noise of which was pounding in his inner ears, "break the pocket checklist out and give me the steps for 'combined hydraulic failure.'"

"I've got you covered, partner," Turtle responded with an excessively chipper tweet, trying his best to sound upbeat and optimistic but lacking the people skills to pull it off. He was the kind of guy who could accurately repeat a funny joke but drain the life out of it with his presentation. In this case he missed the mark of calming the pilot and actually left Fuzzy momentarily wondering whether his RIO fully understood how dire their situation was. "I've been looking at the stub main mount procedures, but I'll turn to the hydraulics section." He slowly flipped through the PCL, and added another lump of coal to Fuzzy's stocking by saying, "Oh, before I forget, if I read the procedure right, it looks like we're going to have to take the barricade."

With that bit of news, Fuzzy promptly placed the contents of his bowels into the seat of his flight suit.

The admiral struggled to grasp the complexities of the situation. His intelligence officer and surface ops officer were telling him to fight the war, his chief of staff and a *lieutenant commander* squadron rep were telling him to land the jets, the captain was on the speakerphone saying from the bridge that his deck crew might have to rig the barricade, whatever that was, and the air wing commander stood apparently deep in thought, but without counsel.

"Are you telling me one of our jets left station without permission?" the surface ops officer indignantly asked Smoke.

"Commander, with all due respect, did you hear me when I said we've got an airborne emergency to deal with? That should trump the threat of an Iranian attack." Smoke turned toward the intelligence officer and asked, "When was the last time we saw them fly at night?"

"When was the last time they flew overhead an aircraft carrier and shot a missile at one of our jets?" the intelligence officer replied. Smoke looked at him like a surgeon who'd located an inoperable cancer, with feelings of both relief at the discovery and frustration with the inability to do anything about it. It was now obvious who was fanning the flames of imminent conflict, but from the admiral's slight nod in response to the commander's retort, it was also obvious that the battle group commander found the hawkish stance sage to the degree it was not readily dismissed.

"We can't have pilots deciding for themselves when to leave station," said the admiral, his back now turned to the small gathering as he blankly stared at the god's-eye view tactical data link display perched on the corner of his desk. He'd set the range scale to cover the top half of the Gulf region, cutting Qatar in half at the bottom left and barely squeezing in Baghdad proper at the top. The only things moving on the display were a few symbols close to the north and east of the ship's symbol. Moving or not, all the symbols presently displayed in the link were blue, indicating they were all friendly.

The chief of staff knew the admiral's sentiments were horrifically foreign to the fighter pilot, who was not young but still unlearned in the realities of staff work, and as Smoke leaned forward to respond, the captain paternally placed his hand across Smoke's chest and began to speak.

"Admiral, this is a safety of flight issue," the chief of staff said pedagogically, hoping a few buzzwords would break through the haze and elicit a proper reaction. He'd endured with the admiral a pre-deployment training track designed to familiarize the future battle group commander with his command's capabilities and his responsibility for their employment, and he knew that the admiral had been trained that the phrase "safety of flight" was a fire alarm best not ignored. "We need to land one-zero-three and then take one-fourteen in the barricade." He moved to the data link screen and scribed an arc around the eastern side of the carrier's symbol. "We've still got two Hornets and a Tomcat up there, not to mention the cruiser under them. That's plenty of firepower to fight the intelligence officer's war." The chief of staff shot a quick look toward Smoke to ensure that the younger aviator had noted that the old eagle still had some fighter pilot left in him.

The admiral worked "safety of flight" through the midterm storage areas of his mind and repeated the three words several times aloud. Naval aviation had seemed so automatic during his days on destroyers and frigates. If you needed a jet for ship's services, you requested one via message and it showed up. He suddenly was overwhelmed by a paralyzing sense that he was out of his element. How could they be five months into the deployment and never have been forced into this sort of situation before? Had they just been lucky or was he in the middle of a once-in-a-career night?

These aviators were such enigmas to a surface war-

rior. They might demonstrate immense talent and pro-
fessionalism one minute and extreme self-servitude or
recklessness the next. Only naval aviators could
squander the public trust courageously earned during
Desert Storm with a three-day drunken binge six
months later at a convention in Las Vegas complete
with seventy-some cases of sexual battery. The rever-
berations of shame and controversy spread beyond
the flyboys and hit the entire Navy, and resentment
from other warfare communities was still strongly felt
years later. But regardless of the assortment of com-
batant ships that comprised it, a carrier battle group
was about carriers, and carriers were about airplanes,
and airplanes needed aviators. Aviators were the
power behind the Navy's strike warfare capability, like
egotistical high-profile quarterbacks nobody cares for
off the field but everybody turns to when the big
games need to be won.

The admiral was reminded of leadership's lonely
burden, of how, in spite of being surrounded by years
of expertise, only he could make the decision. He
thought of the frigate *Stark* getting hit with an Iraqi
air-to-surface missile and the cruiser *Vincennes* inadvertently shooting down an Iranian airliner and reflected on the infamy their commanding officers were
bridled with. He felt ill prepared at that moment to be
in command and wondered if there could ever be a
better time. In a queer juxtaposition that demonstrated to him the irrepressibility and independence of
the mind, he reflected, not on the teachings of Sun Tzu
or Clausewitz, but of his mother telling him, "There's
never a good time to buy a puppy. You just get one and
start taking care of it."

He turned from the screen and passed his eyes
across each officer's face before him, as if tallying an

unspoken vote. He stopped at Smoke and engaged the fighter pilot in a ten-second, resolve-testing staring contest before asking, "If I allow both Tomcats to land, how soon will I have two F-14s back on station?"

"As soon as the next event launches, sir," Smoke answered while simultaneously performing a mental inventory of VF-104's available aircraft to ensure what he'd said was true. One-fourteen was out of the hunt, obviously. The XO's leaky jet, one-oh-six, could probably go either way. That left one-oh-three to be turned around to join the squadron truck, one-oh-five, for the 0400 launch. Then Biff and Bill Thompson would land in one-twelve and they could use that jet with the repaired one-oh-six for the event after that. And those pairings would have to last for the rest of the flight schedule: one-oh-three and one-oh-five relieving one-twelve and one-oh-six relieving one-oh-three and one-oh-five, and so on.

Twenty-seven days without a break was about as long as ten Tomcats went these days. Five of the *Arrowslingers* stable were crowded below in the hangar bay, including Slinger 102, the shot in the squadron's collective foot courtesy of the skipper's insistence the jet was hard down for the phantom electrical short, in spite of the maintainers' assertions to the contrary. The other four awaited parts or technical assistance from civilian experts who would be arriving once the ship pulled into Bahrain in six days.

Bahrain. What would this little crisis do to their port visit? Would it be canceled? Smoke fought the urge to ask the Admiral if they were still on track for some liberty as he picked up the nearest phone and dialed VF-104's maintenance control for an update on the health of their air force.

*   *   *

"Tower, one-fourteen is declaring an emergency," Fuzzy passed on the Approach frequency.

"Yeah, I know, one-fourteen," the air boss replied. "Your wheel is gone. I told you, remember?"

"Well, yessir, but we've also experienced a combined hydraulic failure."

After slamming his fist into the Plexiglas in front of him, the air boss looked over to the mini with disbelief and asked, "Did I hear what I thought I heard? He said 'hydraulic failure,' right?" The mini boss nodded in response.

"Tower copies, one-fourteen. Stand by."

The air boss reached for the tactical circuit phone and pressed two digits.

"Captain . . ."

"Yes, Captain, this is the boss. We're going to have to rig the barricade immediately. I don't know if you caught that last transmission, but one-fourteen has a hydraulic failure along with the missing wheel. We can't wait."

"Did the pilot say whether it was the combined or flight hydraulic system?"

"Combined."

"Ouch, that's the big ticket," said the captain. "I guess we can't afford to attempt to land one-zero-three first, huh?"

"No, we'd better not risk him blowing a tire or somehow clobbering the landing area," the air boss advised. "We'd lose one-fourteen for sure then. We'll probably wind up sending one-zero-three to the divert field."

More hairs dropped to the deck. "Okay, let's keep our fingers crossed. Do what you have to do quickly."

The air boss picked up the flight deck P.A. microphone and bellowed, "All right, let's rig the barricade. I say again, rig the barricade."

At four thousand feet directly over the Boat, Punk dropped his landing gear and flaps to match Fuzzy's configuration and steered his fighter under the other Tomcat in an attempt to see if there was any more damage to the stricken jet. Satisfied one-fourteen's crew was aware of the full extent of their troubles, Punk pulled loosely abeam.

Spud read through the pocket checklist to back Turtle up, quite sure that his fellow department head was behind the situation. "A real quick courtesy heads up, guys," Spud diplomatically said on the squadron's common frequency. "Don't forget to get rid of your external stores. You don't want the barricade to rip a missile off and sling it across the flight deck when you land."

Turtle's reply of "whoops" told Spud his instincts had been dead on. After a few seconds, several million dollars worth of missiles came humbly tumbling off 114 without the designed fire and flash; they simply fell away from the Tomcat like lawn darts, only to splash in the dark sea below. Spud mentally added a Phoenix and two Sparrows to the ordnance tally for the Great Iranian War. What a conflict it had been, and it still wasn't over. If the Iranians only knew how well they were doing now by doing nothing.

On the flight deck, a hundred men crouched shoulder to shoulder, working the wires and nylon straps that formed the barricade. After just more than five minutes, the stanchions were raised and the effort proved to be inadequate. The top wire sagged too far to safely stop a jet's slamming into it at a hundred fifty miles per hour.

The air boss snapped at the sight of the pathetic webbing. "Take that damned thing down and tighten it up!" he screamed over the flight deck P.A. "This ain't a drill, folks. We've got two shipmates in a Tomcat out there whose lives depend on you."

The deck crew rallied, and the second time the barricade was raised into place the top line was nearly straight. Then the deck hands stripped the four arresting wires so they wouldn't get sliced in two by 114's stubbed gear as the jet landed.

"Okay, one-fourteen, we're ready for you down here," the LSO transmitted. "Let me briefly review the barricade procedures with you." His voice was friendly and calming, like that of an airline pilot talking to passengers just after takeoff, or of a cop trying to talk a suicidal person off a ledge. "I'm going to be talking to you more than a normal pass, so don't try to overcorrect. Once you get over the ramp, I'll give you several 'cut' calls. At that point, I want you to shut the engines down completely. It's going to feel unusual because you're used to shoving the throttles forward to military power at touch down, but you need to force yourself to do it."

"Copy," Fuzzy replied mechanically at the break in the LSO's transmission.

"You'll lose the ball at the ramp because of the left barricade stanchion, so don't let that surprise you," the LSO continued. "Just keep listening to my calls."

"Punk, are you going to hang with me until I get aboard?" Fuzzy asked on squadron common, voice thin with the weight of the task just minutes ahead. He'd never really felt scared in the jet like this, not even the first time he landed on a carrier during flight school. Then ignorance had been bliss; now he knew just how hard he was going to have to work to land the jet safely. He thought about the possibility of ejecting, and then thought of how going for a swim might not be all bad in that it would clean the mess out of his flight suit. "Punk . . ."

"I'll be with you, buddy," Punk replied, catching the trepidation in his wingman's voice. "You'll be fine. Regardless of what Biff says, I think you're a great pilot." Fuzzy managed a laugh and was calmed by the fact he could.

"Approach," Spud instructed, "make sure you give one-fourteen enough room to make a lazy turn to the final course."

"Approach copies. One-fourteen, are you ready to commence your approach?"

"One-fourteen's ready," Turtle replied.

"One-zero-three, are you going to remain with one-fourteen throughout the approach?"

"That's affirmative." Spud answered.

"Roger that," the controller returned. "Should the calls be to one-fourteen or one-zero-three?"

"Give them to one-fourteen," Spud commanded.

"Roger," the controller replied as he studied the large circular display in front of him. "One-fourteen pick up a heading of two-seven-five, descend and maintain twelve hundred feet."

"One-fourteen's coming to two-seven-five and descending down to twelve hundred feet," Turtle confirmed.

"Verify dirty," the controller requested.

"One-fourteen has had the gear and flaps down since we lost the wheel," Fuzzy said while he kept one eye on the hydraulic gauges to ensure the second system was holding up. The pilot gingerly moved the stick to bring the jet to the proper course, knowing full well that each command he gave the fighter could be the last. In his mind's eye he saw hydraulic fluid squirting out the brake lines with each deflection of the controls.

The Approach controller vectored one-fourteen

until the jet reached an eight-mile final behind the carrier. Punk flew to the left and above the crippled Tomcat, ready to stay with them and assist if they waved off this pass or to mark their position if they crashed.

Fuzzy concentrated on keeping the jet on the proper glide slope and azimuth with feelings mixed between wanting it all to end and wishing he had more time to prepare for the task now just a couple of miles ahead. He felt a sudden jolt through the stick and reacted with an involuntary gasp over the intercom.

"What's wrong?" Turtle asked.

Fuzzy looked down at the hydraulic gauges and noticed the needle for the second system was starting to twitch slightly. "Nothing . . ." Fuzzy replied.

"One-one-four, three-quarters of a mile," the controller said. "Call the ball."

"One-fourteen, Tomcat, ball, four-point-zero, no trim, no right wheel, no combined hydraulics," Turtle replied.

"Roger ball, Tomcat," the LSO said as he assumed control of the jet from the Approach controller. "Copy, no trim, no right wheel, no combined hydraulics. Twenty-eight knots of wind, straight down the angle deck . . . good start . . . keep it coming . . ."

Fuzzy keyed on each of the LSO's words. He told himself to quit breathing so damned hard. His heartbeat filled his chest. He tried not to look at the barricade but couldn't help but notice its nylon straps flapping wildly in the breeze, highlighted just barely by the dim yellow deck lighting.

"You're a little fast . . . don't go high . . . that's it . . . a little power now . . ."

Just a normal pass, Fuzzy thought, *except I only get one shot.* He realized he was trying to squeeze black juice out of the stick and eased his grip. *Smooth, you idiot.*

"Fly the ball . . . that's it, now . . . cut, cut, cut, cut, cut!"

After a split second of refusal, Fuzzy's left arm yielded and pulled the throttles to the aft limit of the quadrant. The absence of engine noise was eerie as the Tomcat crossed the ramp and landed well short of the barricade. The stubbed right main mount caused the airplane to swerve to the right, and by the time the barricade engulfed it, the jet had yawed 90 degrees to the direction of travel down the angled deck.

Both aviators instinctively ducked as if the canopy wouldn't protect them. The tug of the straps caused the jet to slightly roll up on the left wing, but the forward motion stopped and the fighter fell back on both landing gear and came to a complete halt.

The deck crew worked to clear the spaghetti of nylon from around the canopy so the aviators could open it and egress. Fuzzy slumped over the stick, totally drained and unable to focus on anything, while Turtle looked out at the flurry of arms about them like a child going through a car wash.

After several minutes, the barricade had been cleared away enough that Turtle was able to open the canopy. One of the catapult officers ran up the boarding ladder, slapped Fuzzy on the left shoulder and said, "That was awesome. You're a hero, buddy."

"You might not want to get too close to me," Fuzzy replied as he undid his shoulder fittings. "I shit my pants."

"How far is it to Al Jabar?" Punk asked after he realized he'd lost track of their fuel state during all the excitement with Fuzzy. They were down to forty-one hundred pounds and, depending on the range to the divert, it may have been time to start the bingo profile for Kuwait.

"I was just wondering the same thing, although it's almost a moot point," Spud said. "There's no way the flight deck is going to be ready for us anytime soon." Spud mashed a few keys on the computer panel under his left arm and crosschecked the information on the hand-held GPS strapped to his left thigh. "Al Jabar is a hundred twenty-five miles away."

"Let's go."

Spud switched the radio back to Departure and stated their intentions. "One-oh-three's bingo. Confirm pigeons."

"Stand by for pigeons," the controller responded, referencing the data on one of the screens in front of him. "Primary divert, three-zero-zero for one hundred twenty miles. Check in with Strike once outside of ten miles from Mother."

"Roger."

Punk reviewed the bingo information in the back of his pocket checklist and started the jet on the proper profile. He accelerated to seven-tenths the speed of sound and programmed a climb to thirty-two thousand feet. Twenty-four miles from the field, he'd start an idle descent that was designed to get them on deck with two thousand pounds of gas. And since the wind was about twenty knots less than the one hundred knots he'd entered the bingo table with, they should have even more fuel to spare. All in all, it looked like the whole thing was going to amount to a night with the United States Air Force. Punk was actually looking forward to seeing how the other half lived, plus any time away from the Boat was good time.

Spud checked in with Strike and was greeted by the

battle watch captain, who asked, "One-zero-three, where do you think you're going?"

"One-zero-three's bingo," Spud answered in a cocksure tone, convinced he was dealing with a confused enlisted controller. "We're headed for the divert."

"Negative, your signal is return to Mother."

"Strike," Punk added as he fought off a wave of fatigue brought on by both a post-emergency letdown and the seemingly endless string of idiots trying to make his life more difficult. "Our state is three-point-nine. We are twenty-five miles west of you on a bingo profile."

"One-zero-three, this is Alpha Bravo. I repeat, get back here, immediately." The battle watch captain, another in an apparent monopoly of surface warfare commanders on the staff, put down the radio handset and picked up the phone. "Admiral, I'm going to need a ruling. I'm losing assets faster than I can do anything about it."

After listening to the battle watch captain's update, the admiral hung up and moved across the room toward Smoke. "What is one-zero-three's divert going to do to our ability to put two Tomcats in the air next event, as you promised me?"

"What divert, Admiral?"

"One-zero-three is trying to divert. Fortunately my battle watch captain was heads-up enough to stop him and call him back until we can figure this out. So what are we going to do?"

Smoke knew the admiral wasn't going to be happy with the truth, but he stood ready to give it to him anyway. He had no choice. Executing an *only* course of action didn't require exceptional courage, or intellect, for that matter. He'd just been informed by the maintenance master chief over the phone that 106 was hard down because of the fuel leak, and the jet was going to take at least one shift to fix. VF-104 was down to two jets, 105 and 112, and 112 was already airborne. "We could double-cycle the guy on the CAP station now. What's the tanker situation?"

"I'm asking the questions here, lad," the admiral railed. "We proved last event that we can't depend on tankers to solve the problem. So what are we going to do?"

Smoke looked to the chief of staff for help again, but the captain stood silent, apparently unnerved by the normally composed admiral's sudden loss of temper. CAG, the only other aviator in the room, sat in an overstuffed chair, rocking like an autistic child.

"Admiral, I can only speak for VF-104," Smoke said. "Blame the supply chain, blame the old jets, blame the run of bad luck, but our squadron is almost tapped out. You've got one Tomcat each event, and even that is subject to reduction, quite frankly." He raised his hands emphatically before him, and with a touch of defiance added, "And as far as one-zero-three goes, you'd better let him go to Al Jabar immediately. Our pilots don't cry 'wolf.' If he said he's diverting, he's at bingo state and he doesn't have time to—"

The door to the room slammed open against the bulkhead with the crash of metal on metal as Commander Campbell appeared, face freshly damaged from an attempt at shaving while still half-asleep, and hair forced down with generous amounts of water and gel. "I'm sorry I'm late, Admiral," the skipper said, body English evincing his harried state, but verbal élan intact. "I was looking after another affair."

"Ah, Skipper Campbell," the admiral said. "One of your lieutenant commanders was just telling me how your squadron is unable to support the defense of the

battle group, how you're . . . how did you put it . . .
you're 'tapped out.'"

The skipper shot Smoke a dirty look and obse-
quiously replied, "Admiral, VF-104 is always ready to
support you."

Smoke was in the awkward position of not knowing
what the skipper knew, and there didn't seem to be
any graceful way to clear up the confusion. "Skipper,
are you fully aware of the situation?"

The skipper suppressed his first instinct to dress
down his maintenance officer, and said, "I think
you've been enough help here, Smoke. Go back
down to the squadron's spaces and see about getting
us un-tapped out."

Although the action betrayed his instincts, Smoke
compliantly exited the room without another word. Instead of returning to maintenance control he walked
back into the control center.

"Well, if you give us five minutes, we could launch
another tanker," Smoke heard the air ops officer say
into the phone.

"What's one-oh-three's state?" Smoke asked in a panic
as he rushed across the space toward the commander.

The air ops officer didn't answer and turned his
torso around in his chair, trying his best to ignore the
fighter pilot. Smoke looked at the status board and
saw 3.9 next to 103.

"You cannot be thinking about bringing one-zero-
three back here," Smoke said to the back of the air
ops officer's head. "He's on a bingo profile."

The air ops officer hung up with a smash of the tactical phone against its box and angrily responded,
"Would you please get the hell out of our way here? I
was just on the phone with the battle watch captain—
you know, the admiral's direct representative?"

Smoke trusted that Punk and Spud were doing the right thing, but he wanted to make sure. "Can I talk to one-oh-three?"

"For what?"

Smoke couldn't grasp a legitimate reason, having lost the mental edge needed for rational thought after being run through the flag grinder during the last half hour. "I just want to talk to them!" he screamed.

"No, you can't," the commander replied smugly as he turned his back to pick up the tactical phone once again.

The sounds on Strike of the battle watch captain's repeatedly demanding 103's return filled the control center and caused Smoke to shake with rage. He was convinced now men willing to sacrifice assets and perhaps lives while fighting a pretend war surrounded him. He stood with clenched fists, implicitly begging for someone, anyone, of a higher rank to jump in and stop the madness, but as he scanned the bleachers for an ally with clout, he came up empty.

The battle watch captain transmitted his order to 103 yet another time, and Smoke stormed through the side hatch into the adjacent Tactical Force Command Center. Without hesitation, he relieved the battle watch captain of the UHF handset, said, "Your signal is 'bingo,' Punk," into the mouthpiece and then ripped the radio connection out of the wall, snapping it at the adaptor.

"Sorry, sir. I won't let anybody get killed for this," Smoke declared defiantly. The commander stood completely unnerved by the cool violence with which Smoke executed his act, and did nothing but utter "hey . . ." as the lieutenant commander marched out of the space and back into the control center.

Smoke's reign of terror continued as he walked over

to the air ops officer's position, pushed one of the tabs on the phone cradle, disconnecting the commander, and demanded that somebody call Al Jabar and tell them that 103 was headed their way.

"I was talking to the air boss about launching a tanker, goddam it," the air ops officer said.

"Fuck the tanker," Smoke replied. "We're past that. Let's get them into Kuwait."

"I'm getting sick of you, pal," the air ops officer shot back as he rose to square off with Smoke.

"Look, commander, I'm not looking for a fight," Smoke explained, palms outward in a disarming gesture. "I'm just trying to cut through the bullshit and assist a jet that's dealing with an emergency." The fighter pilot picked up the pocket checklist from where he'd thrown it and said, "A bingo profile is an emergency, sir. That's why it's in this book." He pointed toward the nearest phone. "Now please call Al Jabar and let them know one-zero-three is inbound."

The air ops officer slowly reached for the phone while keeping his eyes on Smoke. He raised the receiver and dialed a series of numbers, and as he waited for an answer at the other end of the line, shook a trembling finger at Smoke and said, "I'm going to do this for you this one time, but not because you told me to."

After the first call on Strike, Spud had simply turned the radio to a different frequency and decided to plead temporary equipment failure in the event it became an issue. The principles of naval aviation were semi-amorphous compared to some other undertakings, but one of the absolutes Spud had learned to cling to while swimming in a sea of gray was when a jet reached bingo state, it assumed a bingo profile without deviation for any reason other than a MiG on its tail.

But now their problem shifted from too much communication to the inability to communicate. First Spud wrestled with the clipped English of a Kuwaiti controller on the country's sole air control frequency. Then, once they were inside forty nautical miles from the field, he switched up Al Jabar's tower frequency to clarify their intentions with an American, but after six attempts to talk to the tower and with no lighting visible to Punk from the direction of the field, it became obvious that there was nobody home at Al Jabar.

"What the hell are you saying?" the air ops officer screamed into the phone. "You're supposed to be open."

"Ah, that's a negative, sir. We've been closed since 2200 local," the Air Force enlisted phone watch replied.

"That's bullshit. We requested that the field remain open throughout the night."

"Whom did you talk to?"

"I don't fuckin' know! I do know that one of my—"

There was a click in the earpiece. "That little shit hung up on me," the air ops officer said as he redialed the phone.

"Al Jabar air operations, Major Holmes."

"Yeah, Major. I'm calling from the aircraft carrier in the Gulf and—"

"Did you just curse at one of my men?"

"Huh?"

"Are you the Navy officer who just called and cursed at one of my men?"

"Yeah, I guess I am . . . look, I apologize. We're kind of stressed out here. Look, major, I need your help right now."

"I can't have the Navy calling at three o'clock in the morning and cursing at my men."

"I said I was sorry!" the commander screamed, veins popping from his forehead and throat. He regained his composure and in a more civil tone repeated, "Look, major, I said I was sorry."

The lieutenant across the control center, who seemed to be in charge of bad news in air ops, shouted, "Strike just relayed from the airborne Hawkeye that the crew in one-zero-three told them they were unable to talk to Al Jabar on any of the published frequencies. They think the field might be closed."

"I know that," the commander returned with his hand over the mouthpiece of the phone. "I'm talking to Al Jabar now trying to get them to open the goddam thing back up."

The commander put the phone back to his ear and tried to calm himself. "Major, again, I apologize for cursing at your man. I meant nothing by it. Now, I have a jet on its way to your field with very little gas."

"What unit do you claim to have talked to here to get approval to keep the field open?" the Air Force major asked.

"My phone log indicates air operations," the commander answered.

"Well, there's your problem," the major said with a chuckle. "Air operations doesn't approve those kinds of requests. They don't have the authority. You needed to talk to the command post."

"So can you open the field for us?"

"No way."

The bad news lieutenant called out once again. "Commander, the captain wants to know why Al Jabar is closed."

The air ops officer winced and dejectedly hung up the phone.

"So, are they going to open the field for us?" Smoke asked.

"No."

"So what are you going to do?"

"Get fired." The commander pushed his way past Smoke and left the space.

"Maybe I could pick up the runway with the landing light if we did a low approach," Punk suggested to Spud over the intercom. "I mean, I can see some lights from the buildings down there, and we know about where the runway is. It might work."

"The only problem with that is we'd have to drop the gear to use the landing light," Spud replied. "We've only got fifteen hundred pounds of gas left as it is. We'd better just stick with the max endurance profile overhead the field and hope the ship works this out quickly."

As Spud finished his sentence, both low-fuel-warning lights illuminated on Punk's advisory panel. "We've only got about twenty minutes of flight time left, Spud," Punk said, "maybe even less than that. This fuel gauge starts to get unreliable below about eight hundred pounds, or so I'm told."

Spud petitioned the E-2, their sole contact due to the distance to the Boat, for help once again on Strike. "Hawkeye, any word on the status of the field opening up?"

"Negative."

Spud ran the situation through in his mind, and reconsidered Punk's idea from a minute ago. "All right, let's drop down to one hundred feet and fly the runway heading and see if we can make anything out. If

not, we'll climb back up, head out to sea and get ready
to punch out."

Punch out? Spud made ejecting sound so matter-
of-fact, such a perfectly normal option. Punk pushed
the nose of the Tomcat below the horizon and started
the descent to a hundred feet.

Smoke asked one of the enlisted men for any of the
numbers to Al Jabar. He was handed the phone log,
and inside the front cover more than a hundred numbers were scrawled with half of them scratched out.
After several lifetimes of running his fingers through the
maze of ink and lead, he located the listing for Al Jabar
air operations.

"It's like I told the other guy," the major said emphatically to Smoke through a filter of static on the
line. "The command post controls when the field is
open, not air operations."

"There's a Tomcat coming to you to land!"

"I can't help you. The colonel's asleep and even then
it would take a half-hour to get the crew out of their
tents to turn the runway lights on. Sorry."

Smoke hung up in a huff and muttered, "Well, jointness is alive and well. Thank you very much, United
States Air Force." He was about to slam the phone log
shut when another listing grabbed his eye: Kuwait International Airport. It was a long shot, but worth a try
at this point. He knew 103 had to be close to flaming
out by now, but Kuwait International was only about
forty nautical miles north of Al Jabar. They might be
able to make it.

It was a commercial number, not a seven-digit military
theater network number like the one for the Air Force
at Al Jabar. Smoke endlessly pressed the digits into the
phone, and wondered how many satellites he was going

to have to hit to complete the call. Although they were only a hundred fifty miles from Kuwait, the carrier's phone system was routed through the communications center in Norfolk, Virginia, so his voice was traveling about ten thousand miles. After listening to several international busy signals, Smoke got a legitimate ring.

"Hello?" a meek voice called from what sounded like deep space.

"Hello, can you hear me?" Smoke heard his voice echo several times as the signal bounced between the earth's surface and the near-reaches of the universe.

"Yes, I can hear you," the voice came back, obviously Arabic, but apparently possessing an adequate command of English.

"Is the . . . is the field open?" The echo was confusing, and Smoke tried to talk without being too distracted by his own voice through the receiver.

"No, the field is closed. We will open tomorrow, eight o'clock."

"I need your help, sir." Smoke slowed his speech as he passed the details of the situation. "I am calling you from an aircraft carrier out in the Gulf off the coast. Do you understand?"

"Yes."

"There is an F-14 . . . Tomcat . . . fighter jet. . . just south of you . . . low . . . on . . . gas. It is an emergency. Do you understand?"

"Yes. Aircraft call sign?"

"Slinger one-zero-three."

"Roger. Zinger one-zero-three."

"No, *Slinger* one-zero-three."

"Singer one-zero-three."

"No, er, whatever; close enough. Could you turn the runway lights on and let . . . him . . . land at Kuwait International."

"Yes. I am the facilities manager."

It seemed too easy. Smoke wasn't convinced that the Arab understood. "I mean right . . . now."

"Yes, I know. I'll turn on the lights. Give me two minutes to call the tower to make sure the runway is clear."

Smoke couldn't believe dealing with a Kuwaiti at a foreign international airport was easier than working with a U.S. Air Force officer, but then again, maybe that wasn't such a big surprise. He felt a bit maudlin bathing in the light of his apparent success, and he closed the conversation with, "God bless Kuwait, and may she enjoy independence forever."

Smoke hung up the phone with a sigh and the hope he'd helped remedy the situation. The battle watch captain burst into air ops accompanied by the same two security force members who had hassled Einstein. As the three moved hurriedly across the space, the battle watch captain pointed a shaky finger at Smoke and said, "Arrest this man for the destruction of government property."

Punk flew around the area of Al Jabar's runway between one and two hundred feet, paralleling its published axis, trying to somehow identify the smooth surface, but there was no discerning the asphalt from the desert. They'd also hoped buzzing the field might alert someone to their presence and cause the runway lights to come on; Punk even dropped the gear briefly and flashed the landing light off and on, but the field remained dark as death save the lighting around the tents and at various spots along the perimeter of the base.

Punk added up the tapes on the fuel gauge: eleven hundred pounds. "This ain't working, Spud," Punk said with resignation. "We're outta here." Punk lifted the nose once again and headed due east.

As they passed through ten thousand feet, communications were reestablished with the E-2 on Strike. " . . . and your steer is Kuwait International."

Spud wasn't sure what he'd heard. "Say again for Slinger one-zero-three."

"Hawkeye says again: your steer is Kuwait International. Initial vector zero-zero-five. They're turning on the lights for you."

Spud punched the coordinates into the system, hooked the symbol with his cursor on the navigation display and passed the bearing to Punk, who confirmed that the heading pointed them toward the bright lights of Kuwait City. He flew to the coast, not too far out of their way, and followed the shoreline for the short trip to the north so that if they flamed out, he'd be able to convert his altitude and last bit of hydraulic control into a heading change over the water, away from the oil fields and populated areas.

Fifteen miles from the field, absent communications with the airport, Punk established the Tomcat on the final portion of the published approach. At ten miles, he dropped the landing gear and flaps. The city was a well-lit, major metropolitan area, but he still didn't have the runway lights in sight.

"This may have been the final insult, my friend," Punk passed over the intercom. "I don't see a field here." He looked at the fuel again: roughly eight hundred pounds, but the gauge had ceased to provide any meaning.

At three miles, he leveled off at one thousand feet. He stayed level and passed over the field, left wing slightly down in another attempt to find a prepared surface.

"Sorry, Spud," Punk offered, banking the jet to the

right, away from the city, as he raised the gear and flaps again. "I'm afraid we're going to get wet."

"Oh, well," Spud responded without emotion. "It's a good thing my survival swim quals are up to date."

Then the runway lights came on at their seven o'clock, about two miles away. Punk looked at the fuel: six hundred pounds. They could make it.

"Gear's coming again," Punk said. He threw the handle down and waited for the jet to slow to two hundred knots so he could lower the flaps. As he fished for the flap handle with his left hand, the right engine's RPM began to decay. "We just lost the right, Spud. Hold on here." At that call, Spud reached between his legs and located the lower ejection handle.

Punk continued to maneuver the jet to a modified downwind position with the remaining good motor. "Come on, baby," he said into his mask. "Hold on . . . hold on, now . . ."

He started the final turn for the runway at five hundred feet, one hundred fifty knots, with 180 degrees of turn to go—180 degrees to safety and another dodged bullet. Punk raced through the landing checklist: "Gear's down, flaps full, spoilers—" He was interrupted by the sickening sound of the left engine dying of fuel starvation. His mind fired through the decision matrix thousands of times in a second and came up with only one result: no options. Too low and too slow to try and maneuver the jet, they were left with a single course of action.

Punk started to say, "eject!" but Spud had already beat him to the draw. Punk's voice on the intercom was drowned out by the explosion of the canopy blowing off and Spud's seat traveling up the back rail. Punk jammed his head back and waited an eternity for his kick in the pants.

Life suddenly seemed surreal. Punk heard the rockets fire. He watched the instrument panel slide away and felt the Gs push him hard into his seat. He studied the Tomcat below him as he tumbled though the night. He wondered why he didn't have a parachute and feared it had failed to open automatically, but then felt the reassuring jolt and knew he was safely earthbound.

Punk watched the jet hit behind him and become a fiery mass. A short time later, the young pilot landed in a heap and rolled on the hard sand just before the near end of the runway. His chute billowed in the wind, and he was pulled through the rough desert until he managed to locate and release his attachments to the risers.

The dust settled and he sat up, taking stock of his condition. Cautiously, he tried to stand. He put weight on his left foot and immediately collapsed in pain. His ankle . . .

He worked to get his gear off, careful to route the straps around his damaged leg, until he saw a black outline of a body moving toward him, silhouetted by the bright glow from the fire at the crash site behind it. "Spud?" he called out, voice slightly cracking as the shock of their ordeal settled on him. It had to be Spud. Who else would have been out there?

The figure answered in some foreign tongue. "Saluba bereesh nonreesh ba!"

Damn, who the hell was it? The intelligence officers had warned the crews that not all the Kuwaiti locals thought of Americans as heroes. "Nonreesh ba. Ba!" the silhouette shouted repeatedly.

"English?" Punk asked as if he was addressing the Frankenstein monster for the first time. "Do you speak English?"

The stranger stood processing the words and then answered, "Why, hell yes, I speak English."

Spud . . . "Damn, you scared the shit out of me, asshole," Punk said as he slapped some of the dust off of himself.

"Now you know how I feel flying with you." Spud raised his flashlight to his face to reveal his smile and said, "Welcome to Kuwait."

FIVE

Trash and Fuzzy pulled another plank off the deck of the shipwrecked dhow, ran it across the sand and over to the bonfire—a blaze now certainly visible from anywhere in the greater capital city area around Manama, if not the entire island nation of Bahrain. What had started as a former Boy Scout skills challenge had grown into a college pep rally–sized inferno that brought half the air wing's officer corps and many of the senior enlisted men to the beach.

The two aviators tossed the rotten timber on the pyre, causing a hail of sparks to shoot skyward and a cheer to erupt from the throng ringed around the heat's edge. After a month at sea, here was a crowd who'd earned a night such as this.

Punk leaned against the three flat boards he'd fashioned into a beach chair and took in the mood surrounding him. Maybe it was the horse pills Fighter Doc had given him for the pain following the ejection; maybe it was the ease with which the beers were going down, but Punk couldn't remember a night as beautiful. He inhaled the fresh salt air pushed by a gentle warm breeze off the Gulf. With relaxed eyes, he followed the path of the fire's embers up toward the heavens and swept the sky and contemplated its vastness. Call it a cop-out, but from where he sat, struggling for small-minded things like promotion seemed foolish when the moon could explode at any moment.

He took another slug of Australian lager and listened to laughter, rich and sincere—laughter threaded through the fabric of hatred they'd been forced to weave by the Machine. They weren't mercenaries. Their actions under the heading of "readiness," even those short of war, like planning the war, were mentally filed into the category of good versus evil, because good versus evil made sense and justified their sacrifices. It had started this time almost a year ago, during their first major training exercise against the notional country, "Purple." The three weeks of conflict based in and around the waters off the coast of North Carolina had spawned a hatred for the people of Purple—not a fill-the-streets passion, but a cold and educated hatred that allowed the aviators to drop bombs without compunction. Since that time, they'd mustered up these same feelings toward Cubans, Tunisians, Libyans, Serbians, Sudanese, Yemenites, Iranians, and Iraqis. War, or posturing for it, required a warrior to wear a war face, and a war face required that a warrior internalize the commitment to war.

Punk dug his heels, the left one covered by a thick wrap of gauze and bandage, into the sand, and he thought about how tired he'd grown of the feeling of hatred. He studied the smiles of the locals who had curiously wandered over—fishermen, most likely from the harbor just beyond the breakwater, dressed in gray robes and black head wraps—working-class types cyni-

cal enough about their own lot not to be offended by
the western decadence of drink. Punk's eyes continued
across the crowd. He paused to absorb the cheerful and
delicate faces of the handful of Gulf Air flight attendants the chiefs had convinced to come out of the expa-
triate watering holes and join the party. The scene gave
him a profound sense of harmony. At the same time, he
felt shallow and duped by those who would have him
believe he was better than the rest of the world by the
sole virtue of his citizenship—those who had him wear
his war face just hours ago.

Earlier that day, the admiral's board participants had
pushed through the door to Flag Briefing and Analysis and into the passageway, unified in their thanks that
the proceeding was behind them. Once through the
hatch, the Boat's boy captain reached across the admiral's JAG and tapped the air wing commander on the
shoulder. "Can I talk to you for a sec?"

CAG nervously jerked around and reluctantly said,
"Sure, I guess . . ."

"Let's go to your stateroom," the captain suggested.

The air wing commander's quarters were only one
kneeknocker down from the entrance to Flag Briefing
and Analysis, so the two were behind the closed stateroom door in short order. CAG didn't bother to sit
down, nor did he extend the offer to the captain. He
simply stood waiting for the abuse he was sure he was
about to receive.

"You mind if I zip into your head and take a whiz?"
the captain asked. "The length of that meeting went
beyond the endurance of my bladder."

CAG gestured toward the bathroom door. "Be my
guest."

A minute later, the captain re-emerged and took a

seat on the couch that lined one wall of the office portion of CAG's stateroom. CAG remained standing until the captain knitted his brow and said, "Why don't you sit down? We need to talk and it might take a little while." CAG stiffly sat in the leather executive chair behind the plain wooden desk.

The moment CAG was fully seated, the captain popped off of the couch and wandered across the room to an adjacent wall adorned with pictures. "Trout fisherman, huh?"

"Not really. I went once with my father-in-law as kind of a favor to my wife."

The captain's gaze walked from frame to frame between brief stops on each photo, and he uttered little laughs or hums as he worked his way around the gallery. "How do you think the admiral's mast went?" he asked from in front of a shot of the air wing commander shaking hands with the current secretary of defense.

"I don't know," CAG said. "It's terrible to see a good officer's career ruined."

"Do you really think so?" the captain asked as he looked with muted disdain at a picture of CAG standing in front of a Prowler with his helmet cradled under his arm like some aviation pioneer.

"Of course," CAG replied.

"I only ask because you didn't seem terribly upset during the hearing," the captain explained, now facing the desk. "In fact, if I remember correctly, when the admiral asked if you had anything to say on behalf of the lieutenant commander, you just shook your head."

"I felt everything had already been said."

"Everything had not already been said, CAG," the captain railed. He ran his hands through his hair several times as he continued, flexing his muscular biceps in the process. "That pilot was one of yours. A man who deserved your protection. And you just let the goddam staff pukes chew him up and spit him out."

"He was guilty of the charges against him, Captain," CAG defended. "I can't help that."

"Fuck that," the captain shot back. "Destruction of government property? What hen house shit. We're going to bring one of the best pilots in this wing down for that?"

"It wasn't my call to make," CAG replied. "It was the admiral's decision."

"It was the admiral's decision because you allowed it to be the admiral's decision," the captain countered. "He's never been in this situation before; he doesn't know the right answer any more than you and I do, but he does know you didn't seem to give two hoots for the guy and he interpreted that to mean the officer deserved to be punished."

"He seemed to listen to you."

"The goddam JAG wanted a court martial. I'm not going to just sit there and let things get that out of control, even if the man doesn't work for me." The captain caught himself, and he decided he'd better sit down. "Look, Mike," the captain continued once he reached the couch again, using CAG's civilian name for dramatic effect, "I know you think the fleet supports the Pentagon, but it's actually the other way around." He paused. "Let me ask you a question: Have you ever had a regular conversation with Smoke? Do you know anything about him?"

"No, not really."

"Then how could you possibly ensure that justice was served during the admiral's mast?"

"I listened to the squadron commanding officer's testimony."

"Campbell? That self-serving sycophant?" The captain let out a sarcastic guffaw. "What do you know about him?" The air wing commander shrugged. "CAG, you're not a Tomcat guy. I am. I've known that asshole for a lot of years and I'll tell you quite candidly it scares the shit out of me that he's made it this far."

"He's the number one skipper in the wing."

"Is that your opinion, or did you have a little help with that one?" The captain emitted another quiet laugh. "I'm sure it was guidance given to you by the same cabal that made you a CAG."

The air wing commander rose in protest. "All right, Captain. I think you've badgered me quite enough for one day. I'm going to have to ask you—"

"I'm not badgering you, goddam it," the captain bellowed. "I'm trying to tell you it's not too late for you to clue into the fact that you're fucking up here!" He got off the couch and calmed himself by wandering back over to the wall of photos. "You know, one of my last jobs before I took this ship was to manage the aviation bonus program. Do you know anything about that?"

"Just what was put out about it in message traffic."

"We were offering lieutenants a bonus of nineteen thousand dollars a year for seven years to stay in the Navy past their first commitment. Nineteen thousand dollars!" The captain turned away from the photos and looked over to CAG. "Do you know what percentage of those officers eligible took advantage of that bonus offer?"

"No."

"Twenty percent. We were offering one hundred and thirty-three thousand dollars to guys to keep flying jets for the Navy and only twenty percent of them decided to go for it. Can you think of anything that might explain that?"

"Not really. One hundred and thirty-three thousand dollars is a lot of money."

"They're not in it for the money," the captain said. "They want to love it. It's why they signed up in the first place. And, goddam it, CAG, we can't sit around and watch a charade like the one that went on today without doing something about it."

"So what do you intend to do?"

"CAG, unfortunately, you and I aren't friends. You have your mafia; we nuclear power aircraft carrier commanding officers have our mafia—a very powerful bunch, I might add. At the end of the day, we're all in the same Navy, and eventually the word gets passed."

"'The word gets passed . . . ' What is that, some kind of a threat?" the air wing commander shot back.

"No, but this is: You've got two more guys coming up for a board as a result of our little problem the other night. You're going to let me help you resolve that one."

"I am? What if I don't?"

"Well, then I'll have to talk to my chief engineer and make sure you never have another hot shower on this ship again." The captain flashed an evil smile. "Remember that old Beltway saying: 'Access is power.'" He moved a few steps and opened the door to the stateroom. "This is not about me against you, CAG. This is about doing what's right. I would hope you'd flag me the same way if I got out of the box."

Spud and Smoke arrived on the beach from their traditional first-night-in-port formal dinner, Spud armed with a box of Cuban cigars he'd purchased in town and a bottle of eighteen-year-old scotch he'd smuggled from his stateroom. They were both over-dressed for this setting: jackets and ties and stylish long overcoats, but the look gave them an aura of timeless cool, like Cagney or Bogart. They took up positions either side of Punk and sat on the sand with legs crossed Indian-style.

"You guys look like a couple of tools with those suits," Trash said as he poked at the fire with a large stick. Spud studied himself with a mock expression of concern and then looked over at Smoke. Smoke reached over to his roommate, adjusted Spud's tie in a doting manner, and said, "I wouldn't worry about fashion input from a man who, given the choice, would just as soon walk around nude."

"Well, you're not writhing in pain," Spud said to Punk. "You must be on the mend."

Punk fished into his pocket, pulled out a prescription bottle half filled with largish, oblong pills, and said, "Better living through chemistry," with a wry smile.

Spud grabbed the bottle from his pilot and pretended to read the label in an officious monotone: "Do not take with alcohol." He handed the pills back and said, "Well, since you're already mixing your magics, you'd better have a swig of this." Spud cracked open the scotch and passed it to Punk, giving him the hobo's honor of first draw.

The scotch burned pleasantly. Punk felt the sensation reach his septum and scatter up under his rib cage. He caught his breath and passed the bottle back to Spud with a shake of his head and a choked thanks.

Spud prepped several cigars and passed them around. He'd taken up cigars as a way to quit his pack-a-day cigarette habit, and had become quite the aficionado in the process, ready at any time to edify those nearby about the art of dark smoke.

Punk only smoked when he had a drink in the other

hand, and, as Spud often pointed out, when somebody else was buying the cigars, and he found his most recent gift to be the perfect complement to the scotch. With the first puff, his equilibrium continued to erode, and he sensed with his waning senses that the night was beginning to have all the elements of the kind salty cruise vets recounted with beery guffaws around the back bars of officers clubs in the states.

"Cubans," Spud said proudly through a cloud of thick smoke. "They're legal here." He held the cigar in front of his face and studied it. "Just look at how tight that ash is. Total quality." He returned the fat cylinder of tobacco between his lips and continued to speak with a movie gangster's annunciation. "Now why are these illegal in the states? Goddam politics, that's why. We cut off our national nose to spite our face."

"Man, that's deep," Smoke said with a hoist of his beer can.

"Yes, I know much, including a good cigar, and a good cigar is worth dying for," Spud said. He held the cigar at arm's length as he fashioned a tribute: "God bless Cuba. This flavor transcends politics. If you can't believe in this kind of hand-wrapped masterpiece, then what can you believe in?"

Spud wheeled around and faced the crowd around the bonfire, and screamed, "Viva Cuba!" to which only the Bahraini fishermen responded with ignorant but polite smiles and waves.

Eventually, the fire collapsed into the sand and began to crackle down to a mere flicker of its former conflagration, and as the blaze died off, so did the crowd. The chiefs announced they were headed back to one of the hotels to close down the disco, and much to the disappointment of the officers, they took the flight attendants with them. Soon only the Cheesequarters residents and Smoke and Spud were left on the beach, all seated comfortably around what remained of the fire.

"So what happened?" Punk asked Smoke at the point the silence among the gathering had become tiresome.

"The chiefs took the girls," Smoke replied.

"I noticed, but that's not what I'm asking about," Punk said. "What happened today at your little get-together?"

Smoke chuckled and then sat silently for a few moments contemplating the day's events before answering. "It was your standard admiral's mast, I guess."

"What's standard?" Punk asked. "I've never been to admiral's mast."

"Not yet," Spud added. "I believe we're next on the docket."

"We're going to admiral's mast?" Punk returned.

"Maybe," Spud said.

"I don't think there's any 'maybe' about it," Smoke said. "If I heard the innuendos during my session correctly, you guys will be getting an audience very soon."

"Why?" Punk asked with disbelief. "I understand we have to go through the standard squadron-level evaluation board just because we crashed an airplane. But why would the admiral want to take us to mast?"

"You can't be that naive, Punk," Biff said. "You know damn well why."

"No, I don't," Punk shot back defiantly. "Maybe I'm the last guy in the Navy who clings to the concept of justice."

"I'm afraid you cling to a different concept than justice," Biff said as he shook the dregs from his oversized can of beer into the sand.

"Back to the original question," Trash said. "Smoke, what happened at mast?"

"Well, my brothers, I won't bore you with the details," Smoke said. "Let me just say a punitive letter is better than no mail at all."

"A punitive letter?" Punk repeated. "That's a career ender, isn't it?"

"So I hear," Smoke replied with a long draw on his cigar.

"Unbelievable," Biff said. "They should give you a medal for ripping that phone out of the wall."

"Damn right," Spud said, leaning behind Punk to smack Smoke on the shoulder.

"So didn't anybody stick up for you at mast?" Punk asked.

Smoke considered the question while carving figures in the sand with his index finger. "Well, actually, the air ops officer wrote a nice statement. He put in some things about my actions saving lives and such, but unfortunately, any clout he once had has been severely reduced by the fact he's been fired from the air ops job for his lack of quality assurance on the divert."

"And he was your only ally in there?" Punk asked.

"No," Smoke said. "The captain of the ship was a big help. In fact, he kept me out of a court-martial."

A chorus came back with "court-martial?"

"Yeah," Smoke said. "The battle watch captain had convinced the admiral's JAG that my actions constituted a court-martial offense. The two of them had the charge sheet written up and everything. The boy captain convinced the admiral they were overreacting." He stopped speaking and gazed deeply into the fire.

"What about the skipper and CAG?" Punk asked. Smoke's deadpan expression in response told them what they already knew to be the answer.

The gathering sat in uncomfortable silence for a time as each officer worked the situation through his military mind. After a few minutes, Punk looked at Smoke and Spud on either side of him and broke the quiet with, "Why did you guys stay in the Navy?" Both of the lieutenant commanders shrugged, but neither answered. "Smoke," Punk prodded, "why did you stay in?"

The more-senior pilot stroked his mustache and thought about the question. "I've been in the Navy fourteen years," he started, but then stopped suddenly to reshape his presentation. "I went to school at Embry-Riddle for one reason: I wanted to be an airline pilot. I'll never forget the time I walked into Orlando International Airport for the first flight of my life. I was nine, traveling by myself, and going to see my grandparents in St. Louis. My parents left me with one of the stewardesses and she took me through the boarding gate and onto the plane, got me all strapped in, and made sure I was comfortable. I was pretty nervous, as any young kid who'd never flown before would be, and I'm sure it showed on my face. After we got airborne, the co-pilot came back and asked me if I wanted to see the cockpit." Smoke spread his hands dreamily in front of him. "I walked through that door and into another world—my world. The jet was an old 727 so it had panels and gauges everywhere. There was that cool hum of electricity and the whoosh of air in the place. I shook hands with the flight engineer and the pilot, and then the pilot asked me if I wanted to hear what the controllers sounded like on the radio. He turned on the speaker and let me listen while he explained what was going on.

"And then they moved me forward, right against the throttle quadrant, so I could see out the front, and the pilot pointed out a few landmarks and—something that I thought was exceptionally cool—other airplanes flying around the skies with us. I stayed up there until we started the final approach."

"So what happened to your dream of flying with the airlines?" Biff asked.

"Money happened," Smoke said. "Or didn't happen, to be exact. I saw how expensive the private route was going to be as I worked through high school to get my pilot's license. At Embry-Riddle, my favorite instructor schooled me on the advantages of military aviation as a stepping-stone toward the airlines. It may not have been the quickest way, but it seemed more dignified. So, that's how I showed up for Aviation Officer Candidate School in Pensacola."

"What was the commitment back then?" Punk asked.

"Five years after winging," Smoke said. "So, all told, I could've been back on the streets after seven years. I had 1,500 flight hours and the airlines were definitely hiring."

"So, I'll ask again," Biff said satirically, "what . . . happened . . . to . . . flying . . . with . . . the . . . airlines?"

"Well, my original five-year commitment ended during my first shore tour while I was out in Miramar flying with the West Coast Tomcat training squadron as an instructor. My first fleet flight-lead was a guy named Bam Bam Bergeron, and he'd gotten out as soon as he could and was hired right away by one of the major airlines. He'd been a big influence on me, so I made it a point to keep in touch with him. I arranged to meet with him to discuss the airline life in detail while I was home one Thanksgiving. We met in the same Orlando Airport I'd stepped into as a nine-year-old." Smoke shook his plastic cup in Spud's direction.

Spud took the hint and filled it to a polite level with scotch.

"Bam Bam took me into this executive lounge," Smoke continued. "The place was huge, very opulent. And we're sitting there with our designer coffees and he's telling me about how he only works half the month and how he plays golf wherever he goes and how he's moved up to A-scale with his salary . . . and I didn't hear a word of it."

"Why not?" Biff asked with disbelief. "That stuff sounds pretty good."

"His hat," Smoke responded. "In spite of all he was saying, all I could see was that his hat didn't fit right. He was sitting in the lounge in his cheesy airline outfit with this stupid bus driver's cap perched on the top of his used-car-salesman hairdo. He looked like a cartoon character. And the sad part was he wasn't trying to be funny; he was trying to impress me. I called the Bureau of Naval Personnel that following Monday and got orders to my second squadron sea tour." Smoke sat still and considered that crossroads for a short time. Even in light of the day's proceedings, the memory brought a placid smile to his angular face.

"So, why did you stay in, Spud?" Biff asked. Always one with a sense for theater, Spud took the floor, tossed the balance of his first stogie into the embers, and waited for the imaginary stagehands to rearrange the set for his soliloquy. He reached into his coat with one hand and produced another cigar. He found the nipper in the deep recesses of the other pocket and began to work on the tip of the cigar with a pediatrician's concern.

Spud brought the cigar to life with his torch and took several healthy puffs to ensure it was fully lit before he spoke. "My situation is different than Smoke's.

In fact, as I look at the faces around this fire, I'm sure my situation is much different than any of you guys." Spud rose, stretched, and began to walk a slow circle behind the group at the fire's edge. "I enlisted in the Navy not because of patriotism, but, to be completely honest, because of something somewhere between civil disobedience and cowardice." Punk smiled at Spud's philosophical air. "You see, gentlemen," Spud continued, "we had this little thing called the Vietnam Conflict going on when I was a younger man. Vietnam forced a guy to figure out pretty quickly where he stood, and it was a lot more complicated than simply being for or against the war. I wasn't chicken-shit enough to dodge the draft and I wasn't opposed to the war enough to go to jail over it. So, in the most clinical terms, I joined the Navy because I was apathetic.

"But that's not what kept me in the Navy all these years. The Navy gave me all the time I needed to grow up, like a parent with unlimited patience. The Navy sent me to college, gave me a place to get married, and delivered my kids. The Navy let me make a living flying jets. The Navy let me make a living defending the right thing to do after Vietnam. So, now you're inferring I should forget all of that because of a few losers in our current chain of command? I don't think so. When you look at the circumstances that led me here, I'm pretty lucky. Every day hasn't been a day at the beach, but what in life is?" Spud made a slow pirouette with both arms extended, faced the water, and said, "Look. Today is a day at the beach. Tomorrow can be a day at the beach, and the day after that, too. So what are you complaining about?"

"I don't remember us complaining, really," Punk said defensively. "We just asked a question."

Spud continued his stroll behind the group. "I've

come to understand that the Navy is like a cloud across the sky. At a glance, it looks like it's a certain shape, but glance again and it's something different." He worked the air above his head into invisible billows with both hands, cigar in one and plastic cup of scotch in the other. "Now at some point you may look up and say, 'That's an ugly cloud,' but if you give it a few minutes, its shape changes to something that appeals to you. People join the Navy; people leave the Navy. Maybe, as you look at the Navy right now, you see an ugly cloud. That's fine. As long as you realize the Navy *is* the lofty ideals and mottoes it claims to be. But, the Navy is also people—everyday human beings with all the faults and foibles that man has possessed since the dawn of time." Spud stopped pacing and faced the fire. "However, the faults of people do not bring down the nobility and accomplishments of the institution. It's like Biff always says: 'the bar lives here.'" Spud pantomimed the existence of a bar over his head the same way Biff did every time he used that expression. "And that bar was placed by the achievements and sacrifices of great men. I was apathetic once, but I grew up. You can judge a cloud, but don't hate the sky."

Spud plucked the scotch bottle out of the sand at his feet, and seeing it empty, said, "Enough bullshit. Let's go relieve the chiefs of those flight attendants."

The lobby of the Empire Hotel was deserted as the aviators pushed their way though the massive glass revolving door at the hotel's main entrance. The lack of activity caused the group to pause in the middle of the immense space and collectively wonder if they'd come to the right place. While Trash and Biff wandered off to the front desk to inquire about the location of the discotheque the chiefs had claimed to be headed for, the others plopped into the leather couches strategically placed about. Einstein sat at an adjacent grand piano and began to play. A beautifully haunting progression of notes filled the cavernous room and caused all conversations to come to a halt. He continued with growing intensity but then stopped suddenly, a bit embarrassed by the attention. His squadronmates were so stunned by the spontaneous demonstration of talent that they didn't respond at all until Spud said, "All right, Ein-steinway." With that cue, the gathering, including two elderly Arabic men who'd wandered in, gave the performance a healthy round of applause.

"The club's around back," Trash said as he and Biff returned from the front desk. "The guy said we could get there quickest by going down that hallway over there."

"We'd better hurry though," Biff added as he looked at his watch. "The place is only open for another hour." With a new sense of earnestness, the group moved toward the disco.

Punk told the others to go ahead, and with the aid of a cane, hobbled in the opposite direction to empty his bladder. On his way back to join them, he passed an Irish pub among the line of shops just down the corridor from the lobby. He stopped to read the menu posted next to the entrance, and as he turned to continue toward the club, three figures at the bar inside the pub caught his eye, as he had obviously caught theirs: the skipper and the Pats sat rigidly in their stools, stares fixed on him. There was no way to gracefully move along now, so Punk breezed into the pub and prepared to greet the ugly clouds with the hope that they'd somehow change into something more appealing.

"We saw your buddies blow by out front a few minutes ago," Commander Campbell said with a wave of his hand as Punk approached. "They went down that way."

"Yeah, thanks, skipper," Punk returned. "I'll catch them in a minute. Can I get anybody a beer?"

"We don't drink," the Pats cried out in simultaneous sanctimony, both seemingly irritated by the intrusion on their quality time with the boss.

"I'll take one," the skipper replied before shifting his attention to the bartender. "Another of those dark ones on tap, please." He looked back to Punk. "Try one; they're really tasty."

"Make it two," Punk called out as he hung his cane on the edge of the bar and slid onto a stool next to the skipper. "You guys been here all night?"

"No," the skipper said. "I had to go to one of those CO dinners with the admiral and the local muckety-mucks, and on my way back to the ship, I decided to stop for a night cap." The skipper didn't provide any information on how he hooked up with the intelligence team, and Punk thought it better not to ask. Without passing judgment on the Pats, it struck Punk as somewhat pathetic that the commanding officer of a fighter squadron could only find two of his most junior charges, and non-aviators at that, to accompany him on liberty.

The two pints of dark beer were placed before them, and the four sat in awkward silence as Punk and the skipper took alternating sips from their respective glasses. Finally, the skipper asked, "So where have you guys been?"

"We had a little party on the beach next to the causeway leading into town," Punk said. "There was a big crowd at one point and a bonfire, too. You should've come out." Punk's inner voice flagged the last sentence's disingenuous air even before he was finished delivering it.

"I didn't get an invitation," the skipper replied.

"I don't believe any were handed out, skipper," Punk said. "It was kind of a spontaneous happening, although the XO must've received the word 'cause he was there for a little while."

"Okay, then *I* didn't receive the word." Commander Campbell turned to the Pats and asked curtly, "Could you two excuse us for a few minutes?" The ensigns contorted their faces in confusion but compliantly gathered their Cokes and small bowls of peanuts and moved from the bar to one of the round tables a few feet away. Both shot Punk angry glances during the short trip.

The skipper slowly rubbed both hands against his face and let his arms fall to the bar. He didn't look at Punk, but straight ahead at the line of bottles that decorated the shelf behind the bartender. "Do you think I took this job to be an asshole?"

"Excuse me, sir?"

Commander Campbell shifted on his stool to face Punk. "Do you think my main goal once I assumed command was to be an asshole, you know, a flaming jerk despised by all under me?"

Punk felt his face blanch as the skipper locked it with his gray eyes. Senses dulled from smoke and drink, the lieutenant could only stammer a weak "no, sir" in response.

The skipper took a healthy slug from his glass before returning his attention to Punk. "I am loved, goddam it. You walk into any O-Club in the country—or the world, for that matter—and say the name 'Soup Campbell' and people will be buying you beers for the rest of the night. I don't even bring my wallet when I take a jet on the road." He finished his drink and signaled the bartender for a refill with one hand while pointing at Punk's glass with the other. "You ready for another?"

"No, sir. I'm fine right now, thanks."

"You know, I was just like you when I was a lieutenant: opinionated, a good stick, popular with the other guys. But now I'm in a position of responsibility and leadership; last time I checked, leadership wasn't a popularity contest."

"Is it the opposite of a popularity contest?" Punk's normal threshold of decorum, however porous, had completely eroded by this point in the evening. "I mean, not that I'm directing this at you personally, skipper, but isn't there something good about being likable as a leader?"

"I'm not sure you guys understand the pressures on a CO. I'm responsible for every little issue even remotely associated with VF-104. The admiral and CAG are on my ass all the time. Nope, it is certainly no popularity contest."

The skipper took a big gulp of his newly delivered beer and wiped the foam from his lips with the sleeve of his pinpoint oxford shirt. He let out a muffled burp and continued, "Not that I want to be hated, either . . ." The commander paused as something caught his eye toward the floor. He reached into the back pocket of his pleated silk trousers, removed a cotton handkerchief, and began gently wiping the toes of his Italian loafers. Punk noted that, unlike some of the career officers in ill-fitting and dated mufti he'd come across on liberty over the few years he'd been at sea, Commander Campbell cut a fashionable figure in civilian attire. "In fact, since it's just you and me talking here, why don't you tell me what I should do."

"What you should do?"

"Yeah. You're the Speaker of the Cheesequarters House. Wrecked jet notwithstanding, you've got the world by the balls. What should I do? How can I fix my program?"

"You're serious."

"Yeah, I'm serious. You're half shit-faced; I'm half shit-faced. That makes us even. Tell me the truth. Trust me, I can take it, lieutenant."

Punk paused and searched deeply into the skipper's expression for a valid read on whether the Old Man really wanted to hear his opinion. His mind went to Spud's telling him one boring night in the airplane a few weeks ago about how idealistic it was to think that the skipper—or any leader cut from the same cloth, for that matter—would change his style based on feedback from his subordinates. But Spud wasn't here now, and he couldn't see the receptive look on the CO's face. And as the freshly validated Speaker of the Cheesequarters House, Punk would be negligent in his responsibilities to the squadron's junior officer corps if he completely shied away from this opportunity.

"All right," Punk started. "But, in spite of the fact, as you've said, we're both half shit-faced and that should be a license to steal because anything I say can't be taken seriously, I still have to work for you for a while." He raised a finger pedagogically. "I won't get into details. Instead, I'll give you the benefit of my Naval Academy education."

Commander Campbell rolled his eyes. "You know I don't put too much stock in you Boat Schoolers and your education."

"Stick with me, skipper." Punk finished his beer with a dramatic toss of his head and then wiped his mouth in the same manner as the CO had moments before. "One: loyalty is a two-way street."

"What are these . . . Kung Fu riddles?" the skipper asked. "Okay, loyalty is a two-way street. I agree. When was I ever disloyal?"

"Why would you automatically assume I was referring to you?" Punk returned serenely. He was starting to enjoy this. "Plus, I said I wasn't getting into details." He raised a second finger. "Two: a man is never so right as when he admits he's wrong."

"I agree with that too, Confucius. So what do those sayings have to do with me?"

"Nothing, I guess."

"Because if you're talking about my little incident a few days ago, there's a big difference between being wrong and having bad luck."

"Okay."

"A shitty controller in an E-2 and a stick with an electrical short are bad luck."

"Fine."

"Don't 'fine' me, you smug little bastard." The skipper suddenly got up and threw some local paper currency on the bar in a huff. "Oh, you guys have got it all figured out don't you, so damned smart about everything. I know what you talk about in your staterooms and at your beach parties." He leaned over his stool toward Punk and extended both hands emphatically. "You're married to truth? I'll give you truth. I make one mistake, there are eight other squadron commanding officers waiting to take my place at the top of the food chain. That's all it takes, one mistake. One mistake and I'm done. One mistake and I don't have a prayer of making captain."

Commander Campbell took a few steps toward the door before he turned back and said, "We'll see how willing you are to admit you're wrong at your board in a few days." And then he walked out. The Pats missed his exit until he was clear of the darkish pub and into the well-lit hallway; but once they noticed, they scurried after him.

Punk sat with a fresh draft, stunned by the pace at which the skipper's congeniality had disappeared, but also feeling a bit guilty for flushing him out of the pub. In spite of the still-growing laundry list of misuses of power during his time in command, Soup probably deserved a few hours away from his professional persona just like the rest of the fleet. Although the lieutenant was deftly sucked into the discussion by the skipper, he cursed himself for attempting to dance around a topic he should've avoided altogether. Spud was right again. *Think what you will about the man, but respect his office.*

Even as he felt the peace of that guidance, he fought his acceptance of it. Blind allegiance to a billet seemed like such a company-man cop-out. What about truth? Did Punk invent this concept? He could've sworn there was some promise of it in the Navy's catalogs, billboards, and commercials. Where did truth fit into the balance of idealism and human frailty? Was it professionally immature to think truth mattered? And to what truth did the skipper subscribe with his thinly veiled comment about the upcoming board?

Punk listened to the titters of a group of Japanese women down the bar from him and continued to nurse his beer until a rush of people through the entrance to the pub broke his solitude. A handful of the squadron's senior enlisted guys stumbled toward him with Chief Wixler in the lead.

The chief fell against the bar, and his recoil off of it caused a chain reaction collision with the four drunks behind him. He steadied himself and slapped his palms loudly on the bar while screaming for service like a Wild West outlaw in a saloon. Punk kept his back to the group, hoping they'd be accommodated and move along without taking notice of him. His plan worked: they didn't notice him. Unfortunately, they did notice the group of Orientals.

"Well, well," Chief Wixler said with a drunken, greasy leer, "konnichiwa, ladies." The chief pushed his way past Punk unawares and nestled up to the nearest girl, throwing his arm around her and putting his face uncomfortably close to hers. "Do you speak any English? How you say, 'sit on my face?'" Punk could see from her expression that, although the woman forced a smile, she was not enjoying the company.

"Hey, chief," Punk interrupted, hoping that his mere presence might police the situation, "how's it going?"

"Oh, look, fellahs," Chief Wixler mocked. "It's my buddy, Big Watch Boy." He let the girl go and moved to Punk, looking back toward the women as he patronizingly massaged the lieutenant's shoulders. "You know what they say about these pilots, ladies: 'Big watches, little dicks.'" The maintainers broke into raucous laughter.

Punk feared the worst. The chief's company was already embarrassing; he wanted to keep it from becoming criminal. As Chief Wixler continued with his campy massage, Punk checked the bartender's expression. The bartender, a dark, burly guy who looked like he could more than hold his own in a scuffle, nodded slightly as he ran a towel around the bottom of a beer mug.

Punk took firm hold of the chief's hands and stood and faced him, crossing the chief's arms in the process. Punk had no desire to fight the enlisted man, but he was fairly sure he could take him if it came to that. The chief had a few inches and a dozen pounds on Punk, but Punk was in much better shape and less inebriated. He took a deep breath, calmed himself and said, "Wix, I think you guys should head on back to the ship."

Chief Wixler ripped his hands out of Punk's grip and responded, "The hell you say, lieutenant. I've been in this business a lot longer than your young ass. While you were crapping your diaper, I was in the P.I. banging three chicks at once." He pushed past Punk once again, and this time grabbed the girl more forcibly. "And tonight I'm interested in feasting on some sushi."

Punk pulled the chief away from her, looked him squarely in the face, and said, "This is bullshit, chief. You're smarter than this. I'm going to ask you one more time: Please leave and go back to the Boat." The chief relaxed as if he'd been beaten, took one step away, and then attempted a roundhouse to Punk's jaw. Punk saw it coming and used the chief's own momentum to push him across a nearby table—the same table the Pats had occupied twenty minutes earlier. The chief flipped over the table, clearing it of half-full Coke bottles in the process, and landed on the floor with an ugly thud. Punk's attention was diverted by the screams of the women as they ran out of the pub, but, as he turned, he sensed the other four enlisted men were moving on him. He grabbed his cane and, pointing it at them, shouted, "No chance, men. No fucking chance! Unless every last one of you wants to spend the night in the brig and stand tall before the skipper first thing in the morning, you'd goddam better get out of here." The group of four assessed Punk's rage (and the fact that the bartender had vaulted from behind the bar at the first sign of a fight and now stood behind the lieutenant with a cricket bat in his hands), polled each other's body language, and then reluctantly shuffled toward the door.

Punk called after them: "Hey, you're forgetting something." He pointed behind the table at Chief Wixler's writhing form. "Take him with you."

The chiefs attended to their fallen comrade and then ignominiously continued out of the pub. Punk watched with regret as the group headed for the exit. "Hold it, guys," he said across the bar. "You're a mess. You'll never get by the shore patrol or the officer of the watch." Walking over to them, the lieutenant reached into his back pocket, withdrew his wallet and pulled out several bills. "Here. Get yourself a room at the hotel. Let Wix sleep it off for a few hours. Those of you with duty tomorrow can still make it back for muster in the morning, no problem."

The nearest man took the bills with contrite thanks as the light of the lieutenant's altruism shone brightly on them. They gathered their burden again and moved toward the lobby. Halfway out, Chief Wixler lifted his head from between them and slurred back threateningly, "This ain't over between you and me, lieutenant."

Before Punk could think to open his mouth, the quartet of chiefs sang: "Shut up, Wix."

Once the rabble cleared the pub, the bartender gave Punk a well done and a slap on the back before returning behind the bar. "We close in a few minutes," the man said. "Last call's on me."

Punk thanked him as he brushed himself off and retook his place. He hooked his cane on the bar's edge once again and sat wondering what the hell else the night had in store for him. Another mob passed through the door—this time a friendlier group: the *Ar-*

rowslingers' finest with the flight attendants in drunken tow.

"Where have you been, asshole?" Spud asked, splitting off from the rest of the group headed for the mini dance floor as he approached the bar. "We were worried you'd been carted into the desert or something."

"Well, first I ran into the skipper in here," Punk answered as he stood and met Spud halfway.

"The skipper?"

"Yeah. We had a little discussion going and then he lost it on me and split with the Pats."

Spud narrowed his eyes knowingly. "You tried to fix him, didn't you?" Punk averted his eyes. "Goddam it, how many times have I told you not to try and fix him?"

"He gave me an opening . . ."

"Ah, bullshit. If he wants the truth, he'll talk to himself." Spud pulled out a cigar and started prepping it at the bar. "So how long ago did he leave?"

"I dunno," Punk said. "It seems like a couple of hours, but it was probably only thirty minutes or so."

"All right, everybody," Spud announced to the group as the music stopped and the lights brightened. "We're taking this circus upstairs."

"Where are you going?" Punk asked.

"The girls all have suites in this hotel, my friend. Rally, for the night is still young."

Punk panicked. He had to make the phone call to Jordan before he went upstairs to any parties. Once sucked into such a vortex, he'd never reach a phone. "What room are you going to be in?"

"I'm not sure." Spud called out to one of the girls: "Hey, Maggie. What's your room number?"

"Fourteen oh five," the woman replied. "Are you lads ready to go up?"

"What else?" Spud said. "This place is done. Let's go."

"Spud, I've gotta make a quick phone call," Punk said. "I'll catch you guys in the room."

"Who are you calling?"

"Jordan, my girlfriend."

"You've got all these gorgeous flowers of the Thames blooming right here, and you're calling back to the States?" Spud stuck his cigar between his teeth and grabbed Punk's face with both hands like an Italian uncle. "You're single, my stupid-ass nose gunner. Sing-gull."

"Right, right," Punk returned with a wave of his hand. "I know. It's still something I have to do."

Punk was out-of-phase with the crowd once again as he made his way along the hallway, across the lobby, and on toward the bank of phone booths while the rest of the group headed for the elevator and the fourteenth floor. He climbed into the first empty stall and pulled the door shut. A fluorescent light above him flickered to life as he fell back on the small bench that ran the length of one side of the booth, lifted the receiver, and began to dial the long series of numbers that he hoped would connect him with Jordan.

He listened to the ring through the earpiece as his eyes darted nervously around the walls. Between the third and fourth buzz, he noticed a line of black marker scrawled in Arabic followed by a six-digit number, and he wondered if it was one of those "for a good time call . . ." messages.

Five rings. Damn it, still not home. His luck with catching her had not been good lately. He'd tried her from the Boat following the ejection but had missed her both at home and at work. In fact, as he thought about it, his luck with catching her seemed to have gotten progressively worse over the course of this deployment.

Her answering machine clicked in, and as he listened to her recorded voice, he was about to hang up when he thought better of it and decided to leave a message.

"Jordan, it's me. We're here in Bahrain for a few days and I wanted to check in and basically just hear your voice." He paused for a second and gathered his thoughts. Like most of the civilized world, he found talking to a machine awkward. "I assume you received my e-mail about the mishap. I hope it explained everything and reassured you that I'm all right. I tried to call you but didn't have any luck. I know my voice message was short but you understand how much—"

Jordan's voice suddenly materialized on the other end of the line. "Rick, I'm here," she said breathlessly. "I just got back from my run."

"Oh . . . well, hello!"

"Hello," she returned with less enthusiasm. "How are you?"

"I'm fine, I guess."

There was a short pause. Depending on how deep they were willing to delve across the thousands of miles that separated them, they either had a lot to talk about or only a few pleasantries to exchange. Jordan broke the silence with, "How's your ankle?"

"It still hurts a little bit, but Doc gave me some pills for the pain, so it's not unbearable. I'm walking with a cane."

"A cane?" she said with a laugh. "I just don't see you with a cane."

"Well, I've got one." They both emitted a few chuckles, but as they died away, so did the conversation. Never one with the patience to work to a point, Punk grew frustrated with the stillness between them and cut right to the heart of it. "It feels strange talking to you," he said.

She waited for a time and then responded, "It's been a long cruise."

"It's almost over."

"Is it?"

"Well, yeah," he said, surprised by her comeback. "We'll be home in less than a month."

"Then what?"

"What do you mean: 'Then what?'"

"I mean, then what will you do after that?"

"I dunno," he said. "Enjoy being home for a while."

"Until you go out again," she shot back. "Rick, I don't think I can do this year after year."

"Do what?"

"Sit here and pine away while you save the world. I'm not sure I can take it."

"Who says I'm ever going on cruise again? I'm rolling to shore duty soon, for one thing. I can also drop my letter anytime. I've served my required time. I could get out of the Navy nine months from now if I wanted to."

"But will you?" she asked. "Will you get out?"

"Well, the way things are going . . ." He sensed the need for a redirect. "What's this about? The ejection?"

He heard her release a long breath. "Not entirely, but it has caused me to think. You know the first word I got after the crash?" she asked, intensity growing through her voice. "It wasn't your message or your e-mail. The skipper's wife called me at work and said that they weren't sure if you were dead or not, but I should brace myself for the worst, just in case." Jordan began to break down. "I'm too young to be a widow." Punk wasn't sure what to say to calm her. He felt as many light years as miles away from her.

"I tried to reach you at work," he offered. "I called as soon as the helicopter dropped us back aboard, but you were out."

"That's not the point," she railed through the tears before stopping short. "Look," she continued with a more steady voice, "I've got to get ready to go out. Allison owes me a dinner so she's taking me to La Playa. Why don't you call again later?"

"There's an eight-hour difference between here and there, remember?" Punk explained with a measure of irritation in return. "It's two fifteen in the morning where I am."

"Well, then that proves it," she said with all composure apparently regained. "You really are far away." Following one more awkward pause she said, "I've got to go."

Punk attempted to wedge in an "I love you" before she hung up, but the line went dead mid-statement. He was stunned. It had not been the phone call he'd hoped to have, nor the one he'd needed. He sat in the booth for several minutes with the receiver still to his head, listening to the static caused by worlds drifting apart.

On the elevator ride to the fourteenth floor he thought of Jordan at dinner with Allison—Allison, the gorgeous gold digger, the original material girl, the part-time model who'd been impressed by young fighter pilots up to the point she'd discovered how relatively little money they made in the seven-digit cosmos of the bull market. Punk could hear her counsel to Jordan, replete with references to opportunity lost and the natural order. And at La Playa, no less—the overpriced hangout of the nouveau riche, the perfect venue for Allison's pitch. He felt the adrenaline course through his veins, and held his hands up and watched them shake involuntarily. The phone call had ruined a good drunk. He felt sober, and now he definitely didn't want to feel sober.

Fortunately, the inhabitants of his current destination frowned on sobriety. As he entered Room 1405, he was welcomed by two cans of lager and the same number of the largest breasts he'd ever seen unholstered. "Don't mind her," another of the British girls advised as Punk tried to avoid staring. "She loves showing off her boobs—loses her top at the drop of a hat." In a funk because of the phone conversation and not quite ready for the leap to light speed, Punk politely smiled so as not to offend the effort and continued across the room. Another of the girls walked topless out of an adjacent room and then another. Even in his foul mood, he appreciated that this was liberty they'd talk about for years to come. The renaissance was upon them.

Punk spotted Spud, with jacket removed and tie loosened, seated on a coffee table holding court with two of the girls on a couch in front of him. From another room a female voice squealed loudly with delight.

"Now ladies," Spud instructed as Punk took up a position on the coffee table next to him, "this is what I was talking about." He put his arm around Punk's neck. "This guy is a rock star, but he's a reluctant rock star, like those guys in those political bands. He's not satisfied with a good time; he's got to find meaning in everything." The girls looked at Punk with expressions of pity. A bottle shattered in the kitchenette.

A hard rock song came on and the volume was raised a few notches. Spud studied his pilot and then leaned over and spoke directly into his ear. "Bad phone call, huh?"

"No . . . well, yeah," Punk allowed.

Spud gave the lieutenant a couple of fatherly taps on the back. "I see you're holding two beers."

"Uh huh."

"Drink them . . . quickly," Spud advised.

Trash entered the room completely nude. He walked over to Punk, Spud, and the two now-tittering British flight attendants, and portraying disgust, asked, "What's with all the clothes? I thought you guys were cruise party veterans."

Smoke, with dress code relaxed to the same degree as Spud, poked his head out of the bedroom and called over to them: "Could you guys give us a hand in here for a sec?" With Trash in trail, Spud and Punk excused themselves from the two girls. They entered the bedroom and saw Einstein face down on the bed with Monk attending to him. "Help me turn him over," Monk pleaded as he tried to corral one of the young backseater's uncooperative arms. "Somebody get me a couple of cold washcloths, stat."

"What does 'stat' mean?" Trash asked.

"It means . . ." Monk torqued around to face Trash, and seeing his roommate nude, contorted his face in pure disgust. "For crying out loud, Trash. Why are you naked?"

Trash threw his hands up and appealed to the military mind. "What does it say about our war fighting capability when a guy can't nude-up at a squadron function?"

"Whatever," Monk returned while looking the other way with his hands fashioned as blinders around either side of his face. "'Stat' means hurry. Don't you watch those medical shows?"

"Sure," Trash replied as he walked toward the bathroom. "Human anatomy, mostly . . ."

Once a few of them managed to roll Einstein over onto his back, they could see that his face below his nose and most of his chest were covered with vomit.

"Oh, very nice," Smoke said with a grimace.

"He's not dead is he?" Fuzzy asked as he entered the bedroom and closed the door behind him. "Is he breathing?"

Monk held his breath and leaned in close. After a few seconds he moved away and, with a whoosh of an exhale, rendered his diagnosis: "Yeah, he's breathing."

"I knew he shouldn't have done those gin shooters at the disco," Fuzzy said. "I warned him, but you know how there's no telling a new guy anything."

"How many did he have?" Spud asked.

"Well, I stopped at four . . ." Fuzzy replied.

Trash hurled the wet washcloths from across the room and they hit the back of Monk's balding head with a comic splat. Unmoved, Monk removed them from his head and shoulders and began to gently swipe Einstein's face. With the first cold touch, Einstein's eyes shot open, and, startled by the group around him, especially Trash, he wrestled with Monk in an attempt to sit up.

"Ahhh!" Einstein screamed through the jetsam in and around his mouth. "Why is he naked?"

"If I knew the answer to that," Monk replied through clenched teeth as he tried to hold the young officer down, "I'd be a psychiatrist instead of a fighter pilot."

Einstein continued to flail for a bit until he was overcome by another wave of nausea. The gathered all saw the surge coming, and the new RIO was quickly roused off the bed and guided into the bathroom. All the aviators left him to his business except for the attending physician, "Florence Nighten-Monk," as Spud referred to him, who stayed in the bathroom to ensure Einstein didn't drown in the toilet.

"Look at that," Spud said, pointing toward the

soiled bedspread. "Somebody had better clean this place up. If those British chicks see this mess, they're liable to put their clothes back on."

That thought scared Trash more than anything else, and he quickly gathered up the bedspread and threw it out the nearest window. A handful of them stuck their heads through the opening and watched the king-sized cover hurtle earthward and drape itself over one of the trees near the pool. Trash pulled his head back inside, looked at Spud and reported, "Sir, mess cleaned, sir!"

Punk heard the shower come on followed by a scream as he left the bedroom and hobbled back through the main room toward the kitchenette to get another beer. Along the way, he passed Biff sprawled over a chair, flaked out and snoring, and Scooter in deep embrace with one of the girls Spud had been talking to minutes earlier.

As Punk took a bottle out of the refrigerator and fished the counter for an opener, he felt his ankle begin to hurt again. He pulled out his pill bottle and poured eight hundred milligrams worth of transitory peace into his palm. He stuck the pill under his tongue and continued to hunt for the opener, eventually finding it and using it to pry open the bottle. With a healthy swig, he washed down the painkiller. Punk leaned against the sink, surveyed the unfolding insanity before him, and waited for numbness to come.

Jordan doesn't want to pine away . . . His thoughts were interrupted by a loud knock on the front door. He was tempted to ignore it, but based on the lack of a reaction by anyone else in the room and the persistence of the banging, he elected to look through the peephole to find out who was behind the noise. Punk peered through the small, fish-eye glass and saw a bearded, dark-skinned man in a suit holding a walkie-talkie. The lieutenant put on his most compliant face and cracked the door just wide enough to be diplomatic.

"What can I do for you this evening, sir?"

"I am Kamil, the assistant hotel manager," the short Arab said in a high-pitched staccato. "We have had many complaints of the noise and carryings-on in this room." The man worked to see beyond Punk, but the pilot blocked his view. "I must ask you to keep quiet or all guests will have to leave."

"That's entirely fair, sir," Punk said as he started to shut the door.

"This is my only warning," the man cautioned.

"I'm sure we understand completely," Punk replied. "You'll have no trouble from us. We're *Americans*." He closed the door and, through the peephole, watched the Arab walk away.

Punk turned from the door, walked across the room, and took a seat on one of the couches away from most of the activity. He watched the circus around him and, in his pensive state, wrestled with how to characterize the scene. Something bumped the couch from behind. He peered over the back of it and was greeted by Weezer's hair-covered buttocks. Punk was about to douse him with a beer when he noticed a girl's face across Weezer's shoulder. Her eyes were shut, and she appeared otherwise happy with her situation, so Punk quietly slinked away and took up a station on the other side of the room.

He slouched in a chair and felt the pill he'd just swallowed disburse its cool salvation, starting with his extremities and slowly working inward toward his torso. He took another gulp of beer, and felt his heart pound, but at the same time, he noticed he was graying out. His mind gave orders, but his flesh ignored them

in the name of the more pressing issues of re-
generation. The evening was finally taking its toll with
an abrupt pace. The last thing Punk saw before he
passed out with a crooked smile was one of the girls
hauling Scooter's pants down while another slathered
him with a light brown goo that he guessed was peanut
butter.

Punk was awakened by the report of a pistol. He shot
up from his supine position on the chair and tried to
assess where the distinct *pop* had originated. It was a
sound like no other, one he'd first heard up-close during plebe summer training at Annapolis. He wondered
how long he'd slept and noted 9:01 on a nearby digital
clock.

While still clearing the cobwebs left from a hard
slumber, he traced the commotion to the television.
Through bleary eyes, he could just make out the scene.
The footage began with a handful of men in blue wind-
breakers—United Nations inspectors—and twice as
many military troops handing documents back and
forth while huddled at a large iron gate in front of a
nondescript warehouse. A discussion turned into an
argument. The senior military figure, evidenced by his
beret, pushed the documents into the chest of the man
in a windbreaker in front of him. In return, the man in
the windbreaker, a large man who stood a full six
inches taller than anyone around him, shoved the papers back into the chest of the military man, a blow
that caused the mustachioed soldier to fall back
against the troops behind him. The soldier threw the
documents into the air and rushed the tall man.
Framed by documents descending like mammoth
snowflakes, a melee ensued, punctuated by the gun-
shot. And then the crowd scattered, revealing the tall

man crumpling to the ground. The video clip was repeated over and over in an endless loop.

Punk concentrated on the commentary: " . . . and we're not sure who fired the shot, but one could naturally assume it was one of the Iraqi troops. Again, U.N. Inspector James Gleason has been shot and killed during a routine site visit. We're standing by for reaction from the White House."

Spud came out of the bedroom, as groomed and pressed as an acolyte. The lieutenant commander stood before his hung-over pilot and delivered a short message: "Liberty's over."

SIX

"Don't you ever get sick of this movie?" Punk asked Spud from behind the duty desk in the ready room, a room lighted only by the light flickering on the screen.

"Don't you guys ever get sick of asking me if I ever get sick of this movie?" Spud asked back sardonically. "*Cheers for Reggie* is, quite frankly, a cinematic achievement nonpareil. Each time I watch it, I see something different or something I'd never noticed before: some twist in the plot, something in a character's voice inflection, something in a scene's setting. It's pure magic."

"Spud, *Cheers for Reggie* is a sophomoric B-comedy about a guy losing his virginity to a whore."

"I see . . . and basketball is nothing but guys throwing a ball through a hoop."

"That's a terrible analogy."

"And how did this so-called B-comedy get to be a cult classic?"

"What cult? You?"

"Since when did you turn so sour on *Cheers for Reggie*? If my memory serves me correctly, last time we

watched it you were repeating the script line for line."
Spud paused and exaggeratedly scratched his chin in
thought. "So what's different now? Gee, maybe it's the
fact you've been the squadron duty officer for almost
two weeks straight, and here it is: eleven P.M., the end of
another long flying day? I think you're getting a little
punchy."

"I'm not punchy," Punk returned. "I'm just sick of sitting here watching other guys go flying."

"That's why we call the duty desk 'the healing chair,'"
Spud said. "Guys tend to get better a lot faster when
they're faced with the prospect of having the duty day
in and day out."

"Look, Spud," Punk replied with irritation in his
voice, "I'm med down because of my ankle, and I'm
awaiting the final recommendation from the chain of
command on our board. That's it. No more and no less."

"You could save the chain of command a lot of trouble and just turn in your wings now," Spud suggested.

Punk looked down his nose at the gold-plated device
pinned above the left pocket of his working khakis and
quipped, "No, I'll let the write-ups take care of that." He
raised his head and asked, "How long until this is resolved for good? It seems like it's been hanging over
our heads for months now."

"Well, we just gave our testimony a couple of weeks
ago and the board's report is already on the streets,"
Spud said. "Trust me, that's quick. I believe they received some executive-level guidance on resolving this
one in a hurry because of this pending war we've got
here. That's also what kept us from going to admiral's
mast. We don't have an unlimited supply of aviators out
here, and the admiral needs us flying. Thank your lucky
stars, boy. You picked the perfect time to crash."

"I feel great now," Punk said. "Thanks . . ."

"Have you seen the skipper's endorsement?"

"No," Punk answered. "It's not out yet, is it?"

"No," Spud said, "but Turtle gave me a draft copy . . ."

"Well, damn, Spud. Let me see it."

"Not until the movie's over."

"You forget that I have control of the VCR here at the duty desk," Punk said. "I can end your bliss in short order."

"All right, all right. Here." Spud removed some papers from the stack on his lap and spun them the short distance to the desk; in spite of the poor lighting, Punk managed to catch the sheets between his palms. The lieutenant illuminated the desk's sole fluorescent bulb, centered the pages under it, and began to read with the same feeling he used to get before opening his report card back in grade school.

He skimmed over the report, through the statistics and basic narrative of the mishap, until he got to Findings. At that point, he carefully studied each word.

"Aircrew error—Aircrew failed to manage fuel during cycle, forcing a high-risk bingo profile—Rejected. Do not concur." The skipper's endorsement would either concur or not concur with the board's assessment of each factor that may have led to the crash. In this case, the CO didn't agree with the board's finding.

Punk read on: "Although a bingo field, Al Jabar, Kuwait, was briefed, it was also common knowledge within the air wing that the field was not always a reliable alternate. This should have caused the crew to raise their fuel ladder by a safe margin above normal." *What? What the hell was that supposed to mean?*

With a quickened pulse, he continued to take in the text: "Aircrew error—Aircrew failed to keep the ship informed of their intentions—Rejected. Do not concur. While the crew claims to have transmitted bingo inten-

tions prior to beginning their profile, they were not understood by those in positions to effect solutions." *Excuse me? In light of the fact that Fuzzy had just taken the
barricade and all hell was breaking loose on the flight
deck, I thought we made our intentions very clear. And
what "solutions" are we talking about here?*

"Supervisory error—" *Good. Let's blame somebody
else for a while.* "The air operations officer did not ensure the briefed bingo field was open during extended
flight operations—Accepted. Concur." *Sure, no harm
piling on the guy near death.*

Punk skipped to the end of the report, the Commanding Officer's Comments section: "This unfortu-
nate mishap re-emphasizes the need for tactical crews
to be prepared to make the correct decision in high-
pressure situations. Not only did this crew wait too
long to confess their fuel state, they also allowed themselves to be put into a box. Naval aviation is full of
gray areas, and in cases such as this one, only the crew
can make the right call. This is part of the responsibility that comes with strapping into an aircraft."

Punk rearranged the sheets and handed them back to
Spud. "You've read this?"

"Of course," Spud replied.

"And?"

Like doctor to patient, Spud studied his pilot for a
few seconds. "You've got that look again."

"What look?"

"*Your* look ... the one you get when you're convinced
you can fix the world."

"I'm not trying to fix the world," Punk countered. "I
would like to fly again."

"And you will," Spud said assuredly. He lowered his
right arm and pointed his index finger at Punk. "The
race doesn't always go to the swift."

"What the hell does that mean? You sound like the skipper's endorsement."

Smoke burst through the front door to the ready room followed by the other three members of his event all fresh from the last scheduled flight of the day and still in full gear. Much to Spud's dismay, Punk brought the house lights back on, while Smoke placed his pistol, two full cartridges, and blood chit on the duty desk.

"The natives are restless," Smoke said.

"What natives?" Punk asked.

"Those natives," Smoke returned, gesturing out the door to the great beyond. "The Iraqis. Their ground radars were tracking us all night long."

"Any shots back at them?" Spud asked.

"Yeah, one of our Prowlers shot a HARM," Smoke said, referring to the electronic jamming aircraft's high-speed anti-radiation missile. He arced a parabolic shape with his hand. "That's the first one I've seen fired—actually saw it hit the ground. It was very cool; although, to be honest, I'm not sure we'd met the rules of engagement criteria."

"What's to meet?" Scooter said as he pressed behind Smoke to return his pistol, cartridges, and blood chit to Punk. "They lock you up; you shoot back at them."

"There's more to it than that and, as the mission commander, I need to ensure that the Prowler had all of the steps in the matrix suitcased."

"The ROE is so complicated, I'm not sure it can be suitcased," Scooter added. "Just shoot the damned missiles. Otherwise, the flight is boring as hell."

"Well, Lord knows we're here to keep you entertained, Scooter," Spud said. "You'd better suitcase it before you go lobbing ordnance downrange. We're claiming the high ground, and if you're going to be aggressive, you'd better be right."

"Where's the skipper?" Smoke asked. "We need to make him smart on this thing before CAG and the admiral grab him."

"He's in his stateroom," Punk replied. "How much flight time are you logging?"

"Three-point-two hours of quality night time."

"Three-point-two," Punk repeated as he scribbled the digits down on his tracking sheet. "Gas burned?"

"Sixteen thousand pounds plus ten thousand from the KC-135."

"Other comments? Any bandit activity?"

"Not a single Iraqi airplane flying anywhere." Smoke looked toward the large television in the corner of the ready room. "Anything on the news about the situation here?"

"I dunno," Punk replied. "I've been a prisoner of *Cheers for Reggie* for the last ninety minutes."

"All right, all right," Spud said as he rose out of the skipper's chair. "Turn it off. It's almost over anyway." He strolled down the center aisle of the ready room, detouring toward the coffee machine to charge his spill-proof plastic mug. As he snapped the lid back on top of the container and stepped through the doorway, he called back toward the duty desk: "I'm headed for CVIC. If we're lobbing HARMs, I'd better get down to the mission planning cell and see how my team is doing on tomorrow's flights. I might not be able to fly right now, but I can still throw in my two cents."

Punk switched the view through the ceiling-mounted projector from *Cheers for Reggie*'s final scene to the twenty-four-hour international news. They jumped into the middle of the day's World Cup soccer highlights, but a few seconds later, a "breaking news" graphic flashed on the screen, followed by a report about the attack on the Iraqi radar site.

"About an hour ago, American warplanes attacked an Iraqi radar site fifty miles southwest of Baghdad," the white-haired anchorman said.

"Not 'warplanes,'" Smoke said to the screen. "War . . . *plane.*"

"Spokesmen at the Pentagon stated that the American crews were simply reacting to hostile actions by the Iraqis," the anchor continued. "The Iraqi foreign ministry responded that the American attack was blind and unwarranted aggression."

"Now I feel like my life has meaning again," Smoke said as he unzipped his G-suit from around his legs and waist and slung it over the back of his ready room chair. "Reporters are back in Baghdad, therefore Baghdad is the news. We might just get our war after all."

A female correspondent came on the screen, looking earnestly into the camera next to the dark streets of the Iraqi capital. In the background, the illuminated spires of a mosque framed both sides of her rain-soaked head. The wind occasionally flapped the hood of her jacket across her forehead and right eye as she spoke, but she took no notice. "Iraqi leadership has taken a hard line following this latest series of attacks on their radar facilities. The Iraqi foreign minister told reporters here that Iraq will no longer tolerate what he referred to as 'U.S.–led insults to Iraq,' and he vowed that Iraq would never back down from their demands for the removal of all U.N. inspection teams and a lifting of economic sanctions."

The view shifted to a clip of the foreign minister, garbed in olive drab tinged with regalia, speaking before a cluster of microphones in a bleakly appointed room. "The international community demands justice," the Iraqi said through his close-cropped beard. "The United States cannot use the mask of the U.N. and assign false blame for the death of James Gleason to forward its selfish desires."

The scene went back to the reporter in Baghdad. "The foreign minister went on to say that Iraq intended to defy all of the provisions of the U.N. agreement against them, including the agreement against flying in the no-fly zone and moving troops and equipment into southern Iraq. In the latest game of cat-and-mouse between the United States and Iraq, Iraq just might be the cat."

"Iraq just might be the cat," Smoke mocked. "Well, bitch, that cat took a big-ass missile down the throat a little while ago."

"If she wasn't such a fox, I might really have a problem with her," Scooter said. "I'll bet she'd keep the ol' bunker nice and warm once the bombs started hitting."

"All right, guys, we're late for our debrief," Smoke said to the other aviators from his event. "Let's get down to the Prowler ready room and piece this thing back together."

The front door flung open, and the Pats rushed in, breathless from their sprint from CVIC but committed to the delivery of their news, nonetheless: "Some of our jets just attacked a radar site," one of them cried.

"No kidding?" Smoke deadpanned. "How do you know?"

"We just saw a report on the news down in CVIC."

As Smoke started his group on the journey to the Prowler ready room, he thought aloud, "We don't need all those complicated and expensive intelligence systems down in CVIC, do we? We just need cable TV."

Punk organized the day's flight operations summary sheet while half-listening to the increasingly heated discussion on the talk show that had followed the news report. Within minutes, the exchange between the State

Department spokesman in the New York studio with the host and the mercurial foreign minister beaming in from Baghdad was compelling enough to eclipse the aviators' interest in other activities around the ready room. The first two rows of chairs were soon filled with officers hoping to witness an old fashioned tele-fracas.

"So what are we doing in Iraq, Kevin?" the host asked the State Department spokesman. "Do we have a goal there?"

"Our only desire in the region is to carry out the will of the United Nations," the spokesman said. "I'm not sure where the foreign minister comes up with these accusations about America's selfish desires in Iraq. The United States is—"

"The United States is only interested in the domination of the entire Middle East," the foreign minister interrupted from ten thousand miles away. "That's why a man like James Gleason is made into a so-called inspector."

"What do you mean, 'a man like James Gleason,' Mr. Foreign Minister?" the host asked.

"Please," the foreign minister returned. "James Gleason, the former member of your Marine Corps, the war criminal from the Desert War of the Martyrs, created confrontations wherever he went in the Middle East. His mission wasn't to ensure compliance with U.N. charters. It was to harass the peace-loving peoples of Iraq."

"So that justifies murder?" the spokesman asked.

"It wasn't murder," the Iraqi replied. "It was self-defense. Watch the tape carefully." With that, the foreign minister pulled the small monitor out of his left ear and walked out of the view of the camera.

The host, skilled in dealing with the sudden and unplanned loss of a guest, used the opportunity to segue to two other pundits he had waiting in the satellite-facilitated wings. "Gentlemen, is there any merit to the foreign minister's assertions about self-defense in this case? Paul, let's hear from you first."

"Jeezus, is that guy fat enough?" Trash observed mockingly from the skipper's chair. "He makes Biff look thin." Biff replied with silence and the flash of a single digit.

"I don't think his claim can be dismissed out of hand," the burly, bearded newspaperman said from a studio near Capitol Hill. "If you look closely at the tape, you can see some things that potentially shift the blame for the shooting."

"Why don't we run that tape?" the host suggested to his production crew. Within seconds, the tape was running on screen, the same tape that had awakened Punk in Bahrain, the tape that the entire television-viewing world had been subjected to countless times during the last two weeks.

"Okay, slow the speed down," the newspaperman requested. "There, now look at that. Gleason pushes the guard over and then pulls his arm back like he's going to throw a punch. At the same time, he reaches inside of his jacket with his other hand."

"What's the implication, Paul?" the managing editor asked from his magazine's West Coast bureau in Sherman Oaks, California, as his head and upper torso took the screen from the well-worn tape of the shooting. "Are you saying that James Gleason was about to pull a gun?"

"Well, I think . . ."

"By the agreement, the weapons inspection teams are not allowed to be armed at any time."

"I know that, Ben. That doesn't mean they aren't armed."

"You've always gotta have your conspiracy, don't

you? And who says he was reaching for anything? It looks to me like his arm simply got caught inside of his windbreaker as he was trying to catch his balance."

"Gentlemen, we have ten seconds left," the host announced. "Last question. War: yes or no?"

"If we don't take strong action soon, our status as a leader in the post–Cold War world will be jeopardized," the editor said.

"You know, not only am I tired of that argument," the newspaperman replied, "the president is tired of that argument, most of Congress is tired of that argument, and the international community is tired of that argument. The U.S. policy in Iraq is confusing and pointless. We don't have cause to go to war right now. We're supposed to be a world leader; let's set the right example."

"That guy has always been a fucking communist," Biff muttered.

"All right," the host said. "Before we go to a commercial break, let me tell you that we would like to hear from our viewers on the following: should the United Nations take military action against Iraq? Let us know where you stand on this issue by dialing one of the two numbers on your screen. The phone lines are now open. We'll be back with lots more, so stay tuned."

"Punk, throw me the phone," Biff said. "I want to vote for a war."

"You're serious . . ."

"Damn right, I'm serious. Throw me the phone."

Punk tossed the portable receiver to Biff and advised, "You can't dial outside the Boat from here."

"Watch and learn," Biff replied as he dialed four digits and brought the device to his head. "Hello, is this the comm center? To whom am I speaking? Petty Officer Bryant, this is Lieutenant Bartlett down in the *Arrowslingers'* ready room. How are you tonight? That's real good. Look, I need to get an outside line from this phone. Could you help me with that? No way, huh? That's too bad because it's a very urgent call. How 'bout if I throw in a couple of squadron patches for the effort? Closer? How 'bout a VF-104 ball cap, too? Okay, then. Thanks, Petty Officer Bryant." Biff pressed the phone off and shot Punk a self-satisfied grin. "Never say die, my friend. I'll have an outside line in two minutes."

Two minutes later, Biff dialed in his vote of support for a war against Iraq.

The midnight bell sounded and Pavlov's aviators made their way to Wardroom One for midrats, the fourth meal of the day for some, the third meal for most. Midrats took its name from midnight rations, an old surface Navy tradition of feeding the crewmembers before they assumed the watch through the middle of the night. But, with the advent of the aircraft carrier and the special breed who populated the passageways just below the flight deck, midrats took the form of an end-of-the-day social, a chance for aircrews to unwind over a slider (the at-sea term for a hamburger) or a bowl of cereal and relate the day's tales to each other.

Punk was not among them. He still had some paperwork to finish before he could turn the watch over to the enlisted man who would guard the phone for a few hours while the lame lieutenant got some sleep before starting the duty process all over again the following day. Punk re-figured the day's sortie count, flight hours, and fuel usage and, once satisfied with his addition, headed out of the ready room for the skipper's stateroom. Before he left, he re-read the CO's endorsement one more time.

Punk found the skipper's stateroom cold and antiseptic, especially compared to the Cheesequarters. No carpet, no posters, no huge stereo speakers on the floor, no personal touch. Unlike the junior officers, who treated their staterooms as places to get away from the Boat's atmosphere, the skipper was satisfied having his stateroom look like a ship, not a den.

"What's on your mind?" asked Commander Campbell without looking up from the paperwork he was working on. He was still dressed in his flight suit, but he'd unzipped it to the waist and drawn the sleeves around the front of him like the belt of a bathrobe. Punk noticed that the Blue Angels T-shirt he wore was creased down the center of each sleeve, indicating it was probably brand new, and he wondered how many of those the skipper had gone through over the years.

"I've got the recap for you to sign," Punk said.

"Oh, that's right. You're the duty officer for life." The skipper took the sheets from Punk and gestured for the lieutenant to sit down in the only other chair in the room. "How did we finish up?"

"Real strong," Punk said. "We missed that one sortie early on, but that was it."

"Who's on the first Alert 15 shift tonight?"

"Monk and Weezer," Punk replied. "They're sitting in the ready room in their flight gear."

"And the Alert 5?"

"Beads and the XO are in the jet spotted on cat three."

"Okay." The skipper changed the subject. "You heard that a Prowler shot a HARM?"

"Yessir."

"This could get hot quick."

"I think it could," Punk agreed. "The topic is sure dominating the news."

"So how's the ankle?"

"The ankle? Better, I guess. I don't need the cane anymore, and Doc thinks I'll be ready to fly in about a week." Punk looked away from the skipper and down to the floor in front of where he was seated. "I'm not sure my ankle is the problem."

"The mishap report?" the skipper asked. Punk nodded. "Well, I wouldn't get too balled up over that thing."

"Why not?"

"Because when it's all said and done, you'll still be flying the Tomcat."

"What will I have to endure between now and then?" Punk pressed.

"Endure?"

"What sort of second guessing? What kind of assaults on my competence?"

"I think you're overreacting, Punk," the skipper said. "Nobody's going to assault you. The system is just going to run the facts to ground and see what needs to be done to prevent this sort of thing in the future." The commander pushed his chair away from the desk and swiveled toward the younger pilot. "I've never taken the time to tell you, but I'm actually damn proud of the judgment you showed that night."

Punk rose out of his chair and moved toward the closed stateroom door. He turned and faced back in the skipper's direction. "Please, skipper, don't B.S. me."

"I'm not," the CO countered. "I really am proud of you."

"That's not what your endorsement said . . ." The words just shot out. Now there they were, adrift between them like floating mines between two ships.

"My endorsement's not even on the streets yet," the skipper said. "How do you know what's in it?"

"Never mind that, skipper. I read your statements, and they didn't mention anything about your pride in me."

Commander Campbell exploded. "Sit down and shut up, lieutenant," he shouted, rising out of his chair. "Christ, you guys are whiners." He paused for a time to rein in his temper and retook his seat. "Every time you and I get into a discussion you go angry young man on me." The skipper slid his chair back to his desk and began shuffling papers. "You're so damned idealistic all the time, Punk. You're getting too senior for that shit. I'm sorry if my endorsement hurt your feelings, but—"

"It didn't hurt my feelings, sir; it was a lie."

"NO," the skipper railed with a slam of his fist against the top of his desk. He checked himself again. "No," he repeated calmly. "It's not a lie. It's an interpretation that the chain of command can live with."

"They can't live with the truth?"

"You mean your concept of the truth?"

"No sir, I mean the real truth."

"What's the real truth?"

"Well, we were overextended due to a misguided priority, and we diverted to a field that we were told was the primary divert, but was, in fact, closed."

"So," the skipper said, "you want me to tell the battle group commander that his priorities are misguided?"

"Only if you're interested in forwarding the truth ... sir."

The phone rang, and the skipper silenced Punk with a wave and lifted the receiver. "Campbell . . . yes, Rex . . . yeah . . . yeah . . . when? That soon, huh? All right, I copy. In fact, I think I have the perfect candidate right in front of me." The skipper hung up and gave Punk a sleazy smile. "Are you sick of standing the duty?"

"Yes sir, definitely. Why?"

"Because you get to go to Saudi Arabia as part of a planning team with the air wing staff. The joint task force needs some help putting the war together."

"When do we leave?"

"Early tomorrow."

"How long will we be gone?"

"Three or four days."

Punk winced. There were worse deals than standing the duty. One of them was a multi-service strike planning mission. He'd received the dubious nod twice before: once during a stateside exercise and once at the beginning of his first deployment to the Med. Both experiences had been frustrating and painful. He uttered an unintelligible noise of disenchantment, excused himself from his audience, and opened the stateroom door to exit.

The skipper stopped him in the doorway. "I probably won't see you before you fly off. Remember, you're on the side of the United States Navy and carrier warfare. Make sure you don't let the Air Force take all the primo targets, and get us some air-to-air missions."

"If my previous experiences are any indication, skipper, I won't have any say over that stuff," Punk observed. "I'll be doing grunt work instead."

"Whatever, you can still influence the process." Punk nodded and turned to go. He pulled the door along behind him and before it was fully shut, the commander threw out: "And stop worrying about the mishap report."

Punk reversed himself and swung the door back open. "Sorry, skipper, but I can't leave until I figure this out. Not to whine again or anything, but *my* concept of truth doesn't speak to you at all?"

"I might ask you the same question," the skipper returned. "As I said, you're going to keep your wings and fly again. Nobody's attacking you beyond the mishap. Your reputation is safe."

"My reputation . . ."

"Believe me, that's the most important element," the commander said. "Both your peer group and mine respect what has to be done here. Success for you is keeping your wings; success for me is protecting the dignity of my superiors." The skipper's voice turned ethereal and his gaze lifted to the pipes that lined the ceiling of his stateroom. "You guard your reputation for years and then one thing destroys it . . ." He paused momentarily and then looked back at Punk. "Think what you will of me. Quite frankly, that doesn't matter. I'm the number one commanding officer in the eyes of my boss, and I've worked hard to orchestrate that, goddam it. I'll go into the next promotion board with good paper, but now I've got another problem. You know damned well that the rumors about this Iranian F-4 thing are spreading like wildfire up and down the flight line back home, and not just among the junior officers. Like I told you in Bahrain, that's all it takes. All anybody on the board has to do is mention it in casual conversation—'hey, did you hear about Soup and the F-4?'—and I'm fucking toast." The commander paused again, turned back to his desk, and mindlessly shuffled some papers.

Punk cleared his throat. "So, skipper, the write-up?" he prodded. "We'll just keep the boss happy? Is that what it's about?"

"I'm satisfied with the truth of my endorsement. That's not conniving; that's good business. It's just like the civilian world. A happy admiral is like a happy CEO, and when the CEO is happy, the whole company is happy." The skipper smiled at the intuitiveness of his concept.

"Just like the civilian world," Punk repeated mechanically.

"That's right." The commander's smile widened.

Punk shook his head and walked out.

"You know what I'm sick of?" Rex asked the seven other officers seated at one of the circular tables in Wardroom One. "I'm sick of getting crayon renderings from my three-year-old that depict a happy family without a father."

"I'm sick of trying to figure out why my fiancée isn't home when I call," Trash said.

"I'm sick of shitting in a crowd," Scooter said.

"I'm sick of this strike planning trip that I haven't even started yet," Punk said. "Rex, what's the itinerary for this thing?"

"The COD launches at 0800," the air wing operations officer answered, referring to the carrier onboard delivery airplane that did double duty as a cargo plane and a transport, "so be in the transport office by 0700. We'll land at Manama Airport about forty minutes after that."

"Manama? I thought we were going to Saudi Arabia."

"We are, after a night in Bahrain. We have to get our marching orders from the Fifth Fleet staff before we do battle with the Air Force in Riyadh."

Punk got up from the table without finishing his slider and hobbled back to the ready room to tell Biff that he needed to find a new duty officer for the following day. He passed through the back door and happened upon the mail clerk with a large stack of letters under one arm and two boxes under the other. Punk relieved him of half of his letter burden and began rifling envelopes into the appropriate slots. When he was down to five, he shuffled through them and, seeing none addressed to him, swapped his handful with the balance of the clerk's stack. The lieutenant madly flipped through the new bunch until he came across a letter from Jordan. He set it aside with a sigh of relief that he hadn't been shut out and finished aiding the clerk with his duties.

Punk sat in his ready room chair and opened the letter with anticipation. Letters had almost become extinct with the proliferation of electronic media, and as Punk removed the pages from the envelope, he considered the tragedy of their loss. All an e-mail had over a letter was the speed of its arrival. There was something about the touch of her stationery and the curves of the handwritten lines of ink on the page that made her letters seem more intimate than the by-products of digital transmission. He brought the paper to his nose. After months of breathing jet exhaust, the faint trace of her fragrance reminded him of better days. He began to read.

Dear Rick,

 I'm sorry it has taken me so long to write. I'd claim I've been very busy at work, but that's not the reason for my delay. I haven't quite known what to say to you lately, and our last phone call obviously didn't help the situation. As I said, this has been a long cruise.

 I have to be honest with you, Rick. You deserve that from me. I know your life on the carrier is far from enjoyable, but I have been miserable during the last five months. I can't do this year in and year out. I don't want you to make any career choices because of me, and at the same time, I'm afraid of what you might choose if I forced you to.

*I don't have the endurance you give me credit for,
and frankly, I wouldn't want it if I could get it. Life
is too short. I don't want to wish away half a year
at a time for the next twenty years of my life.*

*I know this isn't what you want to hear in the
middle of what has got to be a very stressful time
for you, but I felt I had to tell you what I'm feeling. I don't want to forget this emptiness, and I
know I would if I waited until you got home to
talk about it.*

*This isn't easy. I've cherished our times together
and don't regret a minute of it. But the time has
come for me to think about me.*

Let me call you when you get home,

Jordan

Punk sat motionless for a time, staring blankly at the
letter. Her sentiments weren't exactly a surprise but, at
the same time, seeing them in writing had a finality he
wasn't prepared for. Had he already experienced her
final kiss? He had spent so many hours thinking of her.
With a few sentences it all seemed a waste.

He checked the postmark and felt a fool for the day-
dreams he'd allowed himself to have over the last five
days. He read the letter one more time and then wadded
it up and chucked it into the trashcan next to the coffee
machine. His first instinct was to fire a stinging e-mail
back to her, one that pointed out her poor timing and
myopic point of view, but as he stood at the keyboard in
the back of the ready room, the words wouldn't come.
Who could blame her for running from this warped way
of life? He stared at his reflection in the computer
screen against the backdrop of the e-mail display. She
wasn't going to be there when he got home.

Punk left the ready room and headed down the passageway toward the Cheesequarters, still looking for Biff.

The only things the battle watch captain could make out as he entered the stateroom were the red digits showing 3:07 on the clock next to the admiral's rack. The commander carefully made his way across the space as he aimed his penlight at the head of the bed. He slowly reached out and gently tried to shake his boss awake.

"Admiral . . . sir, we think the strikes have started . . . Admiral . . ."

The battle group commander quickly sat up and revealed his bare chest. The watch captain feared the old man might have elected to sleep in the nude, so he directed his light on the opposite corner of the room.

"Strikes have started?" the admiral asked as he clicked on the fluorescent light above the headboard. "What are you talking about?"

"We just saw a news report on the television in the command center. The reporter said she heard explosions."

"Explosions? What kind of explosions?"

"What kind? I don't know, sir. Big ones, I guess."

"Get Fifth Fleet on the line."

The commander scanned through the directory taped to the wall until he found the listing for the Fifth Fleet duty officer. He grabbed the receiver off the cradle of the most complicated-looking of the four phones on the admiral's desk and dialed the number.

The admiral rustled out of bed and padded across the floor toward him. With the receiver against his head, the watch captain shot a quick glance over his shoulder and was relieved to see the admiral was, in fact, wearing boxer shorts.

"Is anybody picking up?" the admiral asked as he put

his glasses on and attempted to pat down his sleep-mangled hair.

"No, sir," the watch captain replied.

"Here, give me that." The admiral relieved his staffer of the phone and hung up. He immediately picked it back up and began punching in another series of numbers.

As the battle group commander stood impatiently waiting for the fleet commander to answer his home line, the watch captain said, "Admiral, if I may say so, I always knew the Air Force would pull something like this . . . you know . . . try to start the war without us. I worked with—"

Another commander burst into the stateroom. "It was an industrial fire!"

"What?" the admiral asked, still waiting for the three-star to answer the phone.

"The explosion wasn't us," the commander explained. "They just had another report on the news that said it was some combustible liquids going off inside a burning warehouse."

"Hullo?" a gravelly voice uttered through the earpiece. Without a word, the admiral slammed the phone back onto its cradle.

SEVEN

"I'm kinda confused, Rex," Punk said over the din of turboprops, a sound that didn't lend itself to easy conversation between those seated in the temporary accommodations slung along the sides of the C-130's cargo bay. He took another disbelieving look at the paper that the air wing operations officer had handed him after their transport lifted out of Manama and headed toward Al Kharj, Saudi Arabia.

"There is guilt to be assigned in this case," the air wing commander had written, "but it should not be on the shoulders of the men who were in the aircraft. Both aviators met or exceeded every reasonable expectation of professional conduct in what turned out to be a nowin situation. The responsibility for the loss of this F-14 lies with the senior officers in the chain of command, myself included. Officers in command are paid to make better decisions than those made in this instance. Any attempt by senior leadership to explain away or shift blame for what happened would be unprofessional and recklessly negligent. Our war fighters are precious resources who deserve better support than these two were offered on the night of the mishap. I recommend both the pilot and radar intercept officer be returned to flight status immediately and that their records be expunged of any negative characterizations associated with this event."

"This doesn't sound like CAG," Punk said.

Rex, whose seemingly constant intake of food belied the anorexic appearance that earned him his call sign, finished the last bite of spaghetti and meat sauce he had been spooning out of the dark green meals-ready-to-eat (MRE) bag in his lap and returned, "There's a good reason for that." He folded the bag and put it aside before fishing another out of the cardboard MRE box. "CAG didn't write it."

"CAG didn't write it? Who did then?"

Rex ripped the thick plastic bag open and popped a cookie into his mouth. He shook his curly-haired head and put his index finger to his thin lips. "I've said too much."

"Oh, c'mon," Punk implored. "You can't just drop a bomb like that and walk away."

"If I tell you," Rex said with a waggle of the same finger, "you can't tell anybody else."

Punk raised his right hand. "I swear."

"I'm serious, Punk," Rex said. "This information is not for public consumption."

"All right, I won't," Punk promised. "Who wrote it?"

"I work for CAG, and I'd like to make commander some day."

"I said all right. Who . . . wrote . . . it?"

"The captain of the ship."

"The captain of the ship?" Punk couldn't make the connection. "Why would he write CAG's endorsement? I don't think I've ever even seen the two of them together."

"Well, they're not exactly close buddies," Rex said. "And I don't think they will be anytime soon."

One of the C-130's crew chiefs, an Air Force tech sergeant, walked over with one side of his headset slid in front of his ear and addressed Rex. "Sir, you can eat as many of those MREs as you'd like. We're sick of 'em."

"Thanks," Rex returned. "They're not bad."

"Did you check the preparation date on the box?" the crew chief asked. "It's on the bottom."

Rex flipped the box over and read the date. The result turned his stomach. "This was made during Desert Storm."

"That's right," the sergeant replied. "They tell us that MREs don't have an expiration date, but there's something gross about eating food that's been sitting around for that long." The crew chief opened a large trash bag in front of him. "I have to be good and hungry before I'll eat 'em."

"Yeah," Rex returned, with an expression that evinced a sudden loss of appetite. "I see what you mean." He gathered the spent food bags and the balance of untouched goods in the MRE and held them over the sergeant's trash bag.

"Ah-ah. Save the gum," the sergeant recommended. "It's crucial if you want to get that taste out of your mouth."

Rex rooted out the four-stick, olive-drab-wrapped pack of gum before dropping the box into the garbage bag. He immediately opened a piece and began smacking away as he continued to solve the mystery of the endorsement's author for Punk. "After Smoke's board, CAG and the captain went sidebar in CAG's stateroom," Rex said. "I happened to be a fly on the wall, so to speak, and I can tell you, the discussion wasn't pretty."

"What did they say?"

"Let's just say the captain may have started CAG down a different path of sorts. He's seemed like a new man since we left Bahrain. For example, the other day the battle watch captain was trying to blow him some grief about the air plan, and CAG fired back at him like I've never seen. It was awesome."

"There's hope for us all," Punk said.

"Again," Rex proclaimed, "you can't pass this information along. No kissing the captain's ass. No posturing around CAG. I just thought you deserved to know. The captain went to the mat for you guys, and CAG was a big enough man to yield when he needed to."

"I must admit I'm still a little confused by the whole thing, Rex," Punk said. "But, the secret's safe with me." He extended his hand and they shook on it.

Rex fashioned his flight jacket into a pillow and leaned away from Punk to get some sleep. Punk slouched in the nylon-webbed seat and looked around the cargo bay at the seven other members of the air wing planning team, all of who apparently had taken advantage of the extra night of liberty in Manama. The only person not sleeping was the team's intelligence representative, the Ensign Holly half of the Pats, who sat reading *The Bear Lives: A Modern Look at the Russian Threat,* androgynous as ever in the brand new flight suit she'd drawn for the trip from the squadron supply clerk.

The Air Force transport continued to climb, and the cargo bay grew colder. Punk pulled the zipper of his flight jacket to its upper limit, shoved his hands into its pockets and thought about the day before in Manama.

Six hours of meetings with the Fifth Fleet staff gave the team no more direction than a simple "be sure and tell us what goes on in Saudi Arabia" would have and, by the end of the session, Punk was of a mind to spend some time by himself. While the rest of the team went to an American franchise bar for dinner, Punk ventured into the capital.

Sunset mixed with the sand in the air and gave the city a muddy hue. As the light faded, Punk walked the streets. The town was a pleasant variation on the theme of a metropolis built in a desert. He was reminded of Tucson, except with fewer pedestrians and uniformly nicer cars. There was traffic but no congestion.

The underlying press of government-sanctioned morality dominated the mood. As he'd been instructed during the cultural training they'd received before their first passage through the Suez Canal, he avoided staring at a group of women wrapped from head to toe in black robes. The other people he passed were neither friendly nor cold.

He crossed an intersection and came to the gates of a dramatically lit mosque, wondering if the local children dreaded attending services as he had dreaded Sunday school. He imagined them gleefully running back through the gates following their forced march, soccer balls in hand.

The scene had an Old World permanence about it that hinted he might outlast the challenges before him. But that glimmer of optimism was quickly replaced by the desire for his life with Jordan to begin again. He fought the need to call her with every phone booth he passed. Each time his resolve weakened a little more, but he managed to keep suppressing the instinct and continue on.

Punk moved down the wide sidewalk by the main drag, the four-lane that eventually became the causeway by the beach where they'd made the bonfire. He remembered how the boys had covered the streets as if they were their own that night, coming from the waterfront and storming back downtown, and he noted with growing melancholy how different and gray the place looked now. The road show had moved on.

He cut down a side street and wound up among the stalls of an alley market—not a gussied-up tourist stop but a place where commerce went on much as it had for centuries. Punk squeezed through the crowd while listening to the heated Arabic of the traders. The air teemed with the varied redolence of Middle Eastern life; the inviting scent of spices gave way to the stench of dung followed by the provocative odor of hookah smoke. The intoxicating smoke yielded to the warm smell of food as he came upon a dilapidated kiosk. He adventurously ate a lamb wrap with curd sauce and washed it down with a tepid cup of orange milky liquid he guessed was tea.

In time he came upon the Empire Hotel. He made his way to the pub and took up a position at the bar very near where he'd been seated the last time he'd patronized the establishment. The place was empty. Punk recognized the bartender and was pleasantly surprised when, without being asked, the man drew a dark beer and placed it before him. "You're alone," the big man said with an accent that Punk couldn't place.

"Yes," Punk replied as he studied the man's face. He had smooth brown skin and jet-black hair slicked straight back across the top of his big head. His hands looked as big as bear paws as he alternated a towel between them while he methodically wiped the top of the bar.

"The girls are gone now," the bartender said. "Some flew to Frankfurt, some to Singapore. They won't be back for a few days."

"Oh," Punk returned with forced cool, trying to downplay the man's perception regarding his presence.

"You're going to Saudi Arabia," the man observed. Punk didn't respond, and as he wrestled with the classification issues, the bartender reached over, patted his hand, and said, "Relax, my friend. It's no secret what the American military does here." He took Punk's glass away and topped it off as he continued to speak. "When you are here in large numbers, the carrier is in port. When you are here by yourselves, you are on your way to Saudi Arabia." He replaced the glass on the bar and leaned over toward the pilot. "You know, the Iraqis are sleeping now. You can relax, too, you Americans."

Punk sat in awkward silence for the few minutes it took to finish his beer, and then he passed a quick thanks and walked out of the pub. He sat in the lobby for twenty minutes watching the elevator doors open, hoping one of the British girls would stroll back into his life if only for some light conversation over dinner and a few drinks. He was rewarded for his efforts with nothing but a parade of somber locals.

The C-130 touched the runway and jarred everyone in the cargo bay awake. Punk glanced at his watch and figured he'd managed just over an hour of sleep, although he didn't know exactly when he'd drifted off. Never good at sleeping while traveling, he was thankful for the gift of rest, however brief.

The crew chief dropped the loading ramp below the tail of the plane as they taxied toward the transient line. Punk joined the others craning around to get a view of Saudi Arabia's topography out the back of the transport. As he had expected, there didn't seem to be much to see, just sand-covered, wind-blown flatness.

Once the last of the four propellers stopped spinning, the crew chief instructed the passengers to grab their bags and move to the terminal for processing. On the way down the transport's ramp, the sergeant took Rex by the elbow. Once they reached the tarmac, he guided him a few steps opposite the direction of the line of new arrivals.

"Sir," the sergeant said, voice wavering slightly due to the delicacy of the matter. "The Saudi locals are going to search everybody's bags in the terminal. They're looking for two things: booze and porn. We've got a little amnesty bag set up in the back of the plane if you need it."

"Thanks, sergeant," Rex replied. "I can vouch for all the members of my group. We're clean."

"You're sure, sir? No harm, no foul here."

"I'm sure."

"It's very embarrassing to get caught by the Saudis. They make a big deal out of it. I'm just asking because . . ."

"Yes, sergeant?"

"Because you kinda look like a porn reader, sir. I'm not saying you are one, but you look like one. Me and the rest of the boys on the crew have gotten good at spotting them, and our efforts have saved the United States of America a lot of bad face time, if you catch my drift, sir."

"I look like a porn reader?" Rex asked with concern. "What the hell does a porn reader look like?"

"It's more than physical appearance, sir," the sergeant replied. "It's the whole package . . . like an aura, I guess. Anyway, the hair on the back of my neck stood up when I saw you, so I thought I'd check it out. I apologize, sir, if my instincts betrayed me."

"I'm afraid they did," Rex confirmed. "Now if you'll excuse me, sergeant, I'll rejoin the others."

"Roger that, sir," the sergeant said. "Look, we'll probably be the crew who takes you back once you're done here. I'll hook you up with a couple of choice offerings from the amnesty box on the other end, just so there's no hard feelings." The sergeant gave Rex a pawnbroker's wink and walked back up the ramp into the transport.

Rex considered his aura as he moved toward the terminal, which was nothing more than a small open-air hangar that housed several lines of tables placed end-to-end. A man dressed in a white robe and red-checked Arab headdress motioned for Rex to put his two bags on the table between them, and as Rex complied, the Saudi called one of his co-workers over. They huddled with their backs to him, looking over their shoulders occasionally, and Rex suddenly feared, as a vampire might fear in a crowd of mortals, that he *was* radiating some immoral vibe. The huddle broke and each man took to one of Rex's bags with an intensity that he was certain they hadn't demonstrated with the luggage of those who'd preceded him in the line. The inspectors left no piece of clothing or toiletry untouched during the search, looking up from their duties only to read Rex's eyes. The American stood wearing his best poker face, afraid that a magazine might materialize as the Arabs' hands tilled through his belongings. The locals finished the search without incident, and Rex breathed a suppressed sigh of relief as the inspectors halfheartedly resecured what they'd opened.

"Navy personnel over here," someone shouted. "Navy personnel over here." The eight of them, already road weary from the less-than-comfortable flight in the C-130, migrated to a heavyset gent dressed in civilian clothes and awaited further instructions.

"What's wrong with this picture?" the man asked as he tugged on his flannel shirt. "I'm in civvies, you're in flight suits. We're about to drive a hundred miles across the Saudi Arabia countryside, and we're going to do our best to not stick out. You need to look like me for the trip to Riyadh, so get changed." He pointed to a group of tents about a quarter-mile away. "There are heads over there you can use. Once you're finished, come back here, and we'll climb into the vans and get going."

Twenty minutes later, the team was reassembled. "I'm Porky, Lieutenant, United States Navy." Porky gestured toward another stranger standing across from him. "That's Beatnik, Captain of Marines. We're your hosts for this part of the trip. Who's the senior man here?" Rex raised his arm. "You're with me, sir. I'll take three more; the other four pile in with Beatnik. The general expects us at Escavah Village in two hours, so let's rock." He took a few steps toward his van and then stopped himself. "Oh, sir," he said to Rex, "I understood from the manifest you had a female in your group." He panned the team. "I don't see one here. Did she not make it?"

"Yeah," Rex returned with a cagey grin as he gestured toward Holly. "She's right there."

Porky started to contort his face in disbelief, but he politely caught himself as he fished around inside a green helmet bag. "You need to wear this once we clear the perimeter of the compound," he said to the young intelligence officer. "The Saudis get real offended if they see a female without one of these on." He removed a black veil from the bag and handed it to Holly. "It loops around your ears like a robber's mask."

Holly held the veil between her thumb and forefinger as if she'd just been given a dead rat. "I'm not wearing this," she said.

"C'mon, Holly," Rex implored, "don't make trouble here. Just wear the mask."

"No." She handed it back to Porky. "That thing's an insult."

"You're not in Kansas anymore, Holly," Porky said. "You know what they do to Saudi women who refuse to cover their faces?"

"I don't care," Holly declared defiantly.

"They behead them."

Holly paused for a few seconds and weighed her personal convictions against life without a head. "All right," she said disdainfully as she took the veil back from Porky, "I'll wear it . . . but under protest."

"Good choice," Porky said. "Now let's go." He climbed into the driver's seat of the closest van, a dark blue Ford Econoline, while Rex took the shotgun position next to him. Punk and Holly were joined in the back seats by Sticky, the electronic warfare rep for the team. Beatnik manned the far van, a maroon twin of the other vehicle, accompanied by Hoot, the E-2 rep; Bird, the Hornet rep; Gozer, the air wing strike operations officer; and Dancer, the combat search and rescue expert.

The two vans snaked slowly along a bumpy dirt road for just over a mile. At that point, the drivers stopped at a Quonset hut and instructed their passengers to disembark. A team of helmeted sentries dressed in desert cammies emerged from the hut, wrapped in Kevlar body armor and armed with rifles. One of them held a long pole with a mirror attached to the end of it. Another led a large German shepherd by a leash.

The security detail painstakingly went over one van and then the other. Once convinced that neither vehicle was venturing off the base with a bomb strapped to it, and that none of the occupants was a terrorist, the head sentry allowed the party to get back into the vans and drive away.

After another slow, bumpy mile they came to a four-lane divided highway, which Porky turned onto, immediately accelerating the van to a cool hundred-mile-per-hour pace with Beatnik four car lengths in disciplined trail.

"Ah, the open road," Porky remarked with satisfaction.

"Not much out here is there?" Punk observed.

"Nope," Porky replied. "We'll pass though one small town along the way, but the rest of the trip is just like what you're looking at right here. Nothing like it—miles of highway and no traffic at all. I'm spoiled now; I'll never be able to drive in the States without losing my mind again."

"How long have you been here?" Punk asked.

"Seven months; I've got five to go."

"Is this all you do?"

"Officially, I am the Fifth Fleet Naval Liaison at Al Kharj," Porky said. "But, yeah, this is all I do. I'm like a fireman—lots of down time until the alarm goes off. Beatnik and I just hang out in our tent, play cards, go to the gym and work out, and wait for a call that a group needs to get to Escavah Village. We just got the word on you guys this morning, which is actually the most heads-up the knuckleheads at Fifth Fleet have given us in months."

"What is this Escavah Village you keep talking about?" Rex asked. "Is that Riyadh?"

"Escavah Village is on the outskirts of Riyadh. Like Al Kharj, it's in the middle of nowhere, which is where the force protection boys like our bases to be. The Saudis originally built the village to lure Bedouin tribes out of the desert and into the factories, but the nomads didn't go for it. So when Joint Task Force Southwest Asia was looking for a more permanent home after the Gulf War, the Saudis ushered the contract signers to Escavah."

"So where were you before this good deal?" Punk asked.

"I'm not sure I should answer that until I get to know you better," Porky said mysteriously. "Excuse me for overreacting, but I'm getting kind of tired of being judged out of context by people." He drummed on the steering wheel for a few seconds. "So, let me ask you something."

"Shoot," Rex returned.

"Do you think farts are funny?"

"Ah, sure," Rex offered congenially, without fully considering the question. "I mean . . ."

"What kind of fart?" Punk asked.

"Just farts in general," Porky replied.

"Because there's a big difference in the various presentations . . ."

"Okay," Porky allowed, "I'll take that as a yes." He looked in the rear view mirror. "And you two?"

"I guess . . ." Sticky said reluctantly, as if he'd sacrificed all self-respect by answering the question.

"I'm not playing this stupid game," Holly groused, veil flapping with the consonants.

"I'll take that as a yes, too," Porky said. "You see, in the last few months I've done a lot of soul searching here—there's something about the desert that clears your head and lets you think straight. I've organized life's lessons into a list of maxims. Maxim number two is never trust anyone who doesn't think farts are funny." He reached into the console between the front seats, removed a pair of wraparound-mirrored sunglasses, and slipped them onto his face. "Fart haters are a strange breed, all right—repressed and whatnot. And they judge . . . they do judge."

"What's Maxim Number One?" Rex asked.

"I don't have a Number One," Porky replied. "Deciding on a paramount maxim felt a lot like the sort of pressure that landed me over here, and I'm trying to unload that. Anyway, to answer your original question, I used to fly Hornets."

"*Used* to fly Hornets?" Punk asked.

"Yeah . . ."

"Hold it," Rex interjected. "You're Hornet Porky!"

"In the flesh . . ."

"You haven't heard of this guy, Punk?" Rex asked over his shoulder.

"No," Punk returned. "Should I have?"

"Porky's the guy who . . ." Rex stopped himself. "It's your story, Porky. Why don't you tell it?"

"There's not much to tell, really," Porky reminisced. "I almost killed the President of the United States."

"Oh, I *did* hear about that," Punk admitted. "Weren't you doing an air show or something?"

"Yeah," Porky recalled, "the president and his wife came out to the boat for a few hours during an exercise off the coast of Florida. I was the show's live ordnance bombing demonstration with four thousand-pounders strapped to my jet. I don't know how much you guys know about the Hornet, but it has this great feature where the pilot can manually enter a range for weapons impact from a point designated through the heads-up display. It's great for close air support missions where your target is usually called by the forward air controller in reference to something else more visually significant. So, for the air show, once I started my final bomb run, I was going to designate the ship and then have the bombs hit two thousand meters abeam, far enough away to be safe, but close enough for the onlookers to feel the boom. Unfortunately, when I entered the digits for the impact range from the ship I left out one of the zeros." He humbly threw his hands up. "As you might expect, at only two hundred meters away, the explosion threw some shrapnel across the flight deck. Luckily, the secret service had enough time to cover the president, but one small chunk of steel ripped a sleeve of the leather flight jacket the first lady was wearing, a gift from the secretary of the Navy, who'd been standing directly to her right as the bombs went off. I was on my way over here a week later."

"Did they take your wings?" Punk asked.

"Yeah," Porky replied with resignation. "I might have gotten away with it had the VIP been an ambassador or a state senator or something, but not the president."

"Politics . . ." Rex decreed in sum.

Without warning to the passengers, the lead van left the smooth asphalt of the highway and took off into the untamed desert, followed closely by the second vehicle. Summarily shaken from slumber, Rex feared their driver had also fallen asleep, but a check on Porky, followed by a look out the front windshield and down the barely defined dirt road they were now plying, assured him that their fallen angel of a tour guide was in control.

A mile down the road they came to another checkpoint, a bigger and more permanent building than the Quonset hut at Al Kharj. Again the passengers were directed to get out of the vans, but this time they were led to a bench and made to sit down. Sentries drove the vans into twin bays that resembled automotive service garages, complete with lifts. Once both vans were within the confines of the building, the doors to the bays were lowered, shielding the inspection procedure from any onlookers.

"Boy," Punk said, "these guys are hard core."

"Who are they afraid of?" Dancer asked. "The Saudis are on our side, right?"

"Don't forget that the barracks in Dharahan was blown up a few years ago," Porky said. "That's what drove us to Al Kharj. Dharahan was a relatively nice place, just across the causeway from Manama, but as you've seen, the Air Force's primary airfield is now in the middle of nowhere." Careful not to upset the sentries by rising off the bench, Porky stretched his arms and legs in front of him while remaining seated. "Our popularity here has waned in the years since Desert Storm. In fact, you'll discover when you start strike planning today that the Air Force's greatest fear is that the Saudis won't let them launch strike missions against Iraq from Saudi soil. That makes all those jets you saw lined up along the flight lines at Al Kharj worthless."

"You mean we risked American lives and spent a shitload of tax dollars here protecting their sovereignty not that long ago, and now we can't even launch from their country?" Sticky asked.

"Don't try to figure it out," Porky warned. "It's the Middle East."

The small auditorium's complement of officers created a wave of desert camouflage fatigues and khaki flight suits as they rose out of their seats upon the general's arrival through the main entrance at the back of the room. Although Rex had wanted to swing by the supply tent and attempt to use a single flight jacket to barter for eight sets of I-was-there desert cammies complete with floppy hats and suede boots, the multi-step check-in process through security and the lodging office had barely afforded the team enough time to jump back into their flight suits and make it to the kick off. As a result, the air wing team stood in olive green, a stain on the gathering's sand-colored quilt.

The general strode down the center aisle followed by his aide, who separated from the procession once his boss successfully climbed the five steps leading to the stage. The general grumbled "carry on" and made his way to the podium as the audience took their seats. He grimaced and shielded his eyes against the lights with one hand while tapping the microphone twice with the other.

"Welcome to Escavah Village," he started, "home of the Joint Task Force Southwest Asia. I'm the commander of JTF-SWA"—*jay tee eff swah*—"Major General Frank Bullock, United States Air Force, but that's the last time you'll hear me mention my service." He hit the podium with his fist and a squeal pierced through the speakers until he steadied the microphone. Punk sensed the crowd wanted to laugh but chose not to. "This is a joint task force. Joint. Not an Air Force task force. Not a Navy task force. Not a Marine Corps task force. I don't care what service you're in. In the next few days, you are going to work long hours planning a war that we could be asked to fight very soon. My guidance to you is simple: Choose the best weapon for the job. Don't worry about politics; don't worry about news coverage. Worry about your bombs on the right target; worry about getting home safely; worry about winning.

"Now before you break up into your strike planning teams, let me see a show of hands. How many of you have flown combat sorties before?" Roughly two dozen of the two hundred officers in the room raised their hands. "Okay, not that many; just as I suspected." The auditorium darkened, and the general was bathed in the stark white light of a single spotlight for a short time, silver hair appearing bright white in the view from the seats, and the lines on his face accentuated by wide shadows. Punk furtively glanced to either side of him at the faces of his teammates to gauge their reactions to the drama. All sat transfixed by the glow, so he joined them.

"I'd like to tell you a story," the general said. "It's a story about a pilot's first look into the face of war." He grabbed the microphone from its stand on the podium and began working the stage like the star of a one-man Broadway show. "This exposure came relatively late in the officer's life: He was a full colonel. And as he stepped for his first combat sortie, he was sure twenty-one years of preparing for war had, in fact, prepared him for what he was to experience. In fact, the colonel was pleasantly surprised when he didn't feel nervous as he launched out of the coastal air base in Saudi Arabia. The event seemed just like an exercise, and you know we military professionals like to say our exercises are just like the real thing. He attributed his lack of nervousness to good training and blessed the American taxpayer for the dollars wisely invested in him over the course of his career.

"The rendezvous and tanking went like clockwork. He had three fully-mission-capable F-16s on his wing and all the SAM suppression and fighter cover a mission commander could ask for as the division pushed out to the north. He felt alive and cocky and thanked God and the President for the opportunity to do their bidding.

"Their targets were the hangars at the south end of the airfield at Tallil, an area that hadn't seen much action the first day of the war because the coalition's focus had been on Baghdad. As the flight got deeper into Iraq, they heard the AWACS and Eagles calling out MiGs. *MiGs!* the pilot thought. *There really is a war going on here.* And then their radar warning gear started singing angry songs and SAMs started coming up at them. They were suddenly four sorcerer's apprentices: every missile they defeated was replaced by two more and then four more and so on until the sky was striped near solid with brilliant white plumes. Dash Four in the division, a young first lieutenant, wound up at the top of his third evasive maneuver too slow to do anything but watch the missile with his name on it guide toward him. His last words over the radio were: 'I love you, Gloria . . . '." The general paused to allow the quote to echo through the room.

"The colonel looked to his right and saw the first lieutenant's jet explode. He wanted to stop the game, to hit Restart and try again, but as he watched the fireball that used to be an F-16 tumble toward Iraq, he understood for good that death in combat was irreversible. And the missiles kept coming.

"The colonel fought to keep airspeed on the jet as he dueled with another SAM. He heard 'Devil Two's hit, ejecting!' on the radio and saw a chute open below him. Between jinks he wondered if the pilot would be taken as a POW or shot in his straps before he hit the ground. He wanted to call 'mission abort,' but he was already at the roll-in point, so he made his bombing run. His mind was Jello now, and he couldn't recall flipping any switches, but the bombs came off. He looked back over his shoulder as he pulled up and saw the explosions erupt on their mark, but he didn't feel the elation he'd expected. The charm of war was gone. And to make it home, the two remaining Falcons still had to fly back through the same SAM envelopes they'd just gone through.

"Well, the colonel made it back to his base in Saudi Arabia. And as he walked back to the hangar to debrief, the exhaustion of post-mission let-down hit him and he forgot about the glory of bombs on target and MiG kills and hoped tomorrow he could have a day off to pray for a speedy end to the war."

The general moved back to the podium and slipped the microphone into its stand. "Gentlemen, I was that colonel." He paused and grimaced slightly as if the memory tortured him. "War is no joke. Plan well." With that, the room came to attention again, and the general stepped back down from the stage and marched out the main door.

The walls were closing in on them now. "Can you escort the B-52s or not?" Rhino the F-117 pilot asked gruffly, patience threadbare from twelve straight hours of strike planning.

"Where do they need us?" Punk asked as he mindlessly smoothed the front of the new desert cammies Rex had obtained for him and slowly moved to the closest of the six large charts mounted on the walls of the planning room.

"From the Straits of Hormuz, here," Rhino said while scribing the heavy bombers' route with his index finger on the chart, "to their cruise missile launch point up here in the northern part of the Gulf."

Punk wearily squinted at the master time line scrawled in dry erase marker on the board against the adjacent wall. "What's the window?"

Rhino checked one sheet among the pile of mission planning documents strewn about the conference tables. "Eighteen hundred zulu to twenty-two hundred zulu."

"Goddam it," Punk snapped. "That totally screws up Strike Package Delta."

"What's Strike Package Delta?" Rhino asked.

"Four Tomcats against a missile storage facility at Al Damin Nahya."

"What kind of bombs?"

"Precision guided. GBU-12s."

Rhino pulled out a spreadsheet labeled "Asset Apportionment," and ran his finger down one of the columns. "We can assign that target to a division of F-15Es out of Al Kharj."

"We're undoing work we've already done here, Rhino," Punk entreated. "Why don't we let the F-15Es escort the B-52s?"

"F-15Es don't do defensive counter-air missions," Rhino answered.

"Why not?"

"Because they're not designed for them and the crews don't train for them."

"Where are all the F-15Cs?"

Rhino checked his sheet again. "In offensive counter-air missions up north."

"Why don't they come south?"

"Because they're up north looking for MiGs," Rhino countered. "You remember what the general said: 'Choose the best weapon for the job.'"

"If we're so concerned about the best weapon for the job," Punk asked, voice growing in volume as he spoke, "why do we have B-52s flying all the way from a small island in the middle of the Indian Ocean to launch a few cruise missiles when we can fire all the cruise missiles we need from ships in the Gulf?"

"That's kind of a parochial attitude don't you think?"

"Parochial? That's a—"

"Hey, you two," the team leader, a Marine Harrier pilot, shouted across the room, "knock it off! Take a break. Go get some fresh air."

Punk and Rhino looked at each other like two rough-housing brothers who'd been ordered outside of the house by their father. They sheepishly shuffled out of the room, down several hallways, past the cipher-locked steel main door, by the guard shack and badge issue station, and through the barb-wire-trimmed fence that surrounded the world-within-a-world that was the Planning and Targeting Cell at JTF-SWA.

The two pilots walked onto the compound's dusty

main street. Punk stretched out his arms and yawned. "I wonder where one goes for a pick-me-up around here?"

"I dunno," Rhino replied, directing his attention to a group of enlisted airmen who happened by. "Excuse me, guys, is there a central hooch here?"

"Yeah," one of them replied. "The Thirsty Camel. Down that way, on the right. You can't miss it."

"Thanks," Rhino said, and they started down the road.

"Don't get your hopes up too high," the airman called back to them. "This is a Condition One post."

"Condition One?" Punk asked.

"No alcohol," Rhino explained before re-addressing the airman. "Got it. Thanks again."

As they continued down the street, Punk considered his new boots and noticed with pleasure an absence of pain from his ankle. "Man, these things are comfortable," he observed, looking down toward his moving feet highlighted by the stadium lighting that washed over the entire base, leaving no shadows in which saboteurs could hide.

"Yeah, they are, aren't they?" Rhino agreed. "That's the Army's contribution to Goldwater-Nichols."

"Ah, yes," Punk mused, "jointness: the military's forced march of cooperation. What's the Air Force's contribution again?"

"Strategic airlift and tankers," Rhino answered matter-of-factly, ignoring Punk's attempted dig, "and everything else associated with power projection from the air, of course, except tactical reconnaissance and electronic warfare, the two missions the Navy now owns thanks to a few bad decisions some of our generals made in the eighties."

"Hey, that reminds me," Punk returned, "did you guys figure out how the Serbians were able to shoot down that F-117? Stealth technology hasn't been exploited, has it? That would be ugly since we've put so many of the taxpayers' eggs in that basket."

"You're worried about taxpayers' eggs? How much does an aircraft carrier cost again?"

"How much did we have to throw at Arab royal families to base you guys in this region? A carrier battle group goes wherever it wants for free, and it's a stand-alone unit once it gets there."

"So what was that divert to Al Jabar you were telling me about?" Rhino countered. "When's the last time an Air Force pilot tried to divert to an aircraft carrier?"

Punk started a line about the spindly struts and dental floss tailhooks on delicate Air Force jets but ran out of momentum halfway through it. The two officers silently strode the rest of the short distance to the Thirsty Camel. Rhino tugged on the front door's old refrigerator latch and they entered the pre-fab shed that stood in stark architectural contrast to the rest of Escavah Village's neat clusters of identical one-story brown buildings.

The shed was roomier than it appeared from the outside. The decor featured a sports theme with appointments that would make any stateside establishment proud. The walls were punctuated with memorabilia, including a number of autographed jerseys displayed in ornate frames. In one corner, two airmen played a mini-basketball free throw game. Punk's eyes were drawn to the bank of four wide-screen televisions, each tuned to a different event. *Say what you will about the Air Force,* thought Punk, *they know how to relax.*

"How 'bout a near beer?" Rhino asked. "A Condition One favorite."

"Sounds good," Punk replied.

"I've got the first round," Rhino said as he moved toward the refreshment counter. "Why don't you go grab us a couple of those chairs over by the TVs?"

Punk stepped across the room, tossed his floppy desert hat onto the seat of one of the overstuffed chairs and took his place in another. He shifted his attention between the four professional football games on the screens before him and looked at his watch. *They're all live . . .*

"This is an impressive set up," Punk commented as Rhino handed him a can of alcohol-free beer and took the adjacent seat. "A lot of places back home would kill for this sort of coverage."

"We have one just like this at Al Jabar," Rhino said. "Ours is called the 'Sandshaker.' They're shipped as a single unit—lock, stock, and barrel. Size is only limited by the width of a C-5's cargo bay." He gestured over his shoulder. "Did you see the satellite dish farm on the right as you cleared security at the main gate? Only half of those are used for military purposes. The others are for sports and movie reception."

"Man," Punk sighed and leaned back in his chair. "I could get used to this."

"This . . ." Rhino returned with a sweep of his arm about the room, "is killing retention in the Air Force."

"What?" Punk asked with knitted brow. "Lazy Boys and live sports coverage?"

"No," Rhino said. "The desert . . ."

"What's wrong with the desert? It beats life on the Boat."

"The Boat is no surprise to you," Rhino tried to explain as he lowered the volume of the televisions with the four remotes mounted on the big plywood coffee table in front of them. "You knew it was part of the deal when you joined the Navy. The desert has become the Air Force's culture, but none of us signed up for it. It's like a breach of contract. Now we're here all the time."

"Where did you think you were going to go?" Punk asked.

"Germany, Thailand, Korea . . . places like that, places with character."

"Didn't I read they just shortened the length of your deployments?"

"They did," Rhino confirmed. "They shortened them from ninety to forty-five days to stop the complaining, but that was just smoke and mirrors. What the secretary of defense forgot with his concept of rightsizing is that, when you do the same with less, those left in the military wind up doing more. So now we're over here twice as often. It's actually more of a hassle to do the shorter ones. And we seem to be doing fewer and fewer things of any importance each year we're here. I'm not against doing my duty, but any idiot can see there's no mission, or at least not one that requires the level of effort we've put into this region since Desert Storm. I mean, just look at this drill we're doing now. You think we're ever going to execute this thing?"

"Maybe . . ."

"No way. This is just part of the entire harassment package, nothing more. And we've still got another whole day of strike planning left."

"So are you getting out?"

"Damn right, ten months and counting. How 'bout you?"

"I'm seriously considering it," Punk replied. "And being in the great outdoors the last couple of days makes me realize how unnatural it is living on a boat for six months at a time. It confines the spirit."

"I visited a boat a few years back," Rhino said. "I thought it was great. Clean sheets, hot running water, real ice cream with every meal, no need to walk through the wind and the cold to take a piss . . ."

"Your runway doesn't move."

"Your runway moves to scenic European ports."

"You can go for long runs in the desert."

"You don't have to go for long runs in the desert."

"We fly jets older than most of the lieutenants in the squadron."

"We only fly at night."

"My girlfriend broke up with me."

"My wife divorced me."

"All right," Punk admitted, "You win. Your life sucks worse than mine. I'd get out in a heartbeat if I were you, too."

Rhino smiled contentedly and then considered his victory. "Wait," he said. "My life really isn't *that* bad . . ."

EIGHT

"SAM trap . . ." Holly said softly as she compared the satellite image in one hand, a list of coordinates in the other, and the replay of the tactical picture over southern Iraq on the computer screen in front of her. "It's a SAM trap," she shouted. "Steven, check this out."

He rushed from his target folder–laden desk and looked at the display over his female doppelgänger's shoulder. "What are you talking about?"

"Watch . . ." She let the file run. "This happened a few hours ago when some Air Force F-15s were working the offensive counter-air stations just south of the thirty-third parallel. Take a look at the pattern these MiG-23s fly."

Steven keenly studied the view. "They came south of thirty-three . . ."

"Yeah," Holly confirmed, "but we already knew that. Look at this . . ." With a keystroke, she halted the motion of the symbols on the screen. "See where they start turning north?" She ran the cursor over the position and pointed to the corresponding coordinates displayed in the data box at the bottom of the screen while simultaneously running her finger across one of the papers on her desk. "According to the latest imagery, there's an SA-6 site there." She craned around to face Steven. "This is not like the other feints we've occasionally seen them perform to probe our reaction. This is a SAM trap."

"Did the Eagles get any shots off?" he asked.

"No, the Iraqis timed their moves perfectly. They know what they're doing here."

Steven peered at the screen again. "Hold it . . . Where did those MiGs originate?"

Holly pointed to a spot just south of Baghdad. "Al Sharat Air Base."

Steven hurried back to his desk and dug a sheet out of a messy stack towering over the rest of the clutter. He read the page for a short time and then carried it over to Holly. "This is the latest air order of battle from national sources," Steven said as he threw the paper down on her desk. "There are no MiG-23s at Al Sharat anymore; those are either MiG-25s or 29s."

"That's even worse," Holly pronounced as she looked at her watch. "Who's the lead for the next Southern Watch mission?"

"Smoke," Steven replied. "He's briefing a reconnaissance package down in our ready room right now."

They grabbed what evidence they could and rushed out of CVIC.

Smoke moved to the easel adjacent to the podium at the front of the ready room and ran his hand along a line of thin red tape on the large chart. "This is a TARPS mission," he said, referring to the Tactical Airborne Reconnaissance Pod System, a device that housed three types of cameras and was strapped to the bottom of the Tomcat specifically for photo missions. "The two TARPS birds, with Biff in the lead jet and Scooter on his wing, will start here, just north of Kuwait. They'll take it north until they fly right against the thirty-third parallel, work their way to the east past Al Kut to the Iranian border, and then come south along the Shat al Arab to Al Basrah, and then back out feet wet. They'll be flying at ten thousand feet for the entire run to get the tasked resolution.

"The fighter package, led by me, is a mixed division with two Tomcats and two Hornets. We'll fly in front of and above the TARPS birds." Smoke pointed at the closed circuit television set that had hosted their intelligence brief minutes before. "Now, you heard that MiGs are flying today, which is consistent with some of the rhetoric we've listened to in recent days on the news about increased Iraqi resistance to the no-fly zone and other bullshit like that. The fighters really need to be heads-up. Remember the rules of engagement; no hot-dogging, but if a shot opportunity presents itself, take advantage of it.

"Finally, the interdiction package will be led by Punk, whom we're proud to welcome back to the land of the living as he embarks on his first flight into Iraq since his mishap." Smoke led the other aviators in a short, polite round of applause, and Punk acknowledged the recognition with a papal wave. "Punk has another LANTIRN-equipped Tomcat and two Prowlers with him, and that package is ready to take out any pop-up SAM activity with precision-guided bombs or HARM missiles." Smoke gestured toward the two RIOs in Punk's element. "Spud and Einstein, just as the fighter package needs to suitcase the ROE, you two own the burden of ensuring you bomb the right target if it comes to that." Both RIOs nodded confidently. Smoke scanned across the two Prowler crews. "Quite honestly, your business is a complete mystery to me. Do the right thing."

Smoke moved back behind the podium. "Okay, that's the overview. Why don't we break into elements and brief our particulars in the smaller groups? Also, review the search and rescue procedures. Are there any final questions before—"

The Pats tripped through the front door of the ready room with the grace of two foals on ice. "SAM trap," Holly shouted at Smoke as she worked to catch her breath.

"What?"

"Your intelligence brief . . . is not complete," Steven explained, as winded as his co-worker. "We know . . . some things you . . . you need to know."

Smoke studied them suspiciously but yielded to their intensity. "All right, let's not break up just yet. Our intel team has something to add." With some reluctance, he handed the floor to the Pats and took a seat in the front row.

Holly composed herself behind the podium for a few seconds and then began speaking. "One of the things our photo interpreters will be looking for in the TARPS images you get this flight is the location of SA-6 sites," Holly said. "Unlike the larger surface-to-air missile systems like the SA-2 or SA-3, the SA-6 is mobile. The Iraqis have been slowly moving these systems south since James Gleason was shot, and we're having a tough time keeping track of where they are.

"As you heard during the televised brief from CVIC, the Iraqi Air Force is active today." Holly moved to the chart. "This morning some Iraqi fighters came below the thirty-third parallel, which is something we've seen before, albeit not very often. But what we haven't seen before today is the jets flying through a SAM envelope as they made their way back north.

"Now we know that the Iraqis subscribe to classic Soviet doctrine and have the connectivity to de-conflict airplanes and SAMs, but we also suspect their leadership is willing to risk one of their own jets to shoot down one of ours. They will fire at you even with a MiG in the same envelope."

With a motion from Holly, Steven took the stage. "Remember the SA-6 can be fired optically and, if it is, you may not get any indications on your radar warning receivers. As briefed, the weather is clear, so you'll be able to see the ground, but they'll also be able to see you."

The Pats looked at each other and exchanged shrugs. "That's it . . . good luck," Holly said. They made for the exit, fearing the perception that they'd taken up too much valuable brief time.

"Hey, you guys," Smoke said, stopping them in the doorway. "Thanks." They responded with impassive nods but were both smiling as they left the room.

"Okay," Smoke said, "I know Southern Watch events have become routine, even boring for us in the four months we've been flying here. I also know we've all grown frustrated lately with wondering if the president is going to show the Iraqis how this game's played and call on us to fight the war Punk and the gang cooked up when they were in Saudi Arabia." He poked a thumb over his shoulder toward the door. "You've heard the evidence. Put your game face on because Punk's war might start today."

Punk mustered his element at the back of the ready room. His group consisted of Spud and him in the lead jet, Monk and Einstein on his wing, and the two Prowler crews. In the lead Prowler was one of the only two female pilots in the air wing, and her presence in the brief, despite the recent push for gender integration by the system, was still a bit unusual for those who'd been in the business longer than three years. After reviewing the navigation plan and the ROE, he dismissed the Prowler flyers back to their ready room to perform a last-minute update to their mission computers.

As the jammer crews excused themselves past the legs of the fighter guys, Punk couldn't help but notice that Einstein was fairly beaming. "First flight without the skipper?" he asked.

"Yeah," Einstein effused back. "He has a flight physical this morning down in medical, and Weezer has the duty, so Biff stuck us together."

"Beautiful," Punk returned. "This is going to be a good hop. All right, let's go through some of the details. Monk, don't worry about rendezvousing overhead the Boat. I'll see you on the tanker or, if I miss you there, I'll see you at the push point."

He shuffled through the handful of kneeboard cards perched on his left knee. "Break out the navigation plan and your tactical charts. Now, as you look at the TARPS birds' route of flight, you can see that they won't fly through any known SAM envelopes. But remember, as the Pats said, the SA-6 is a mobile system. That's why we're flying these recon missions twice a day.

"So once we get feet dry, Monk, I want you to kick out into defensive combat spread. And, at that point, I want all eyes out of the cockpit and looking at the ground for SAM launches. You own the area under us and we own the same scan under you. The gouge Steven gave us about the absence of radar warnings is crucial. For all of our fancy equipment, the SAM that'll get you is the one you don't see with your eyes.

"If we do get an indication on our warning systems, call it out to the entire flight over the AWACS frequency. Be concise but clear." Punk motioned toward his RIO. "Spud, why don't you talk about LANTIRN pod switchology?"

"Okay, remember we have two Prowlers with us," Spud said, "and if we satisfy the ROE for engagement, they'll probably be the first ones to take action with their HARM missiles. But, if we get into a real slugfest and the Prowlers run out of missiles, then it'll be up to us to kill the sites with precision-guided bombs." Spud rose and studied a copy of the ordnance plan on the wall next to them before re-taking his seat. "We've got two thousand-pounders each. That's a good punch. Drop one at a time.

"Because we'll be reacting to a pop-up threat, you won't be able to cue the pod using coordinates. This is where the RIO makes his money in the air-to-ground arena. Einstein, if you see a SAM launch, you've got to quickly call Monk's eyes onto it, and, if he doesn't get a tally in short order, then you have to make him into a voice-activated auto pilot and get the jet pointed at the site. Once that's done, bore sight the pod down the nose of the jet, go to the lowest magnification, and look for the plume. When you've got it, increase the magnification, verify the target, get a contrast lock, and drop a bomb on those naughty Iraqis. Oh, and Monk, keep sight of the missile after launch, and, if it's tracking on you, forget about guiding the bomb and dodge the missile."

"Speaking of dodging missiles," Punk said, "when you preflight your jet, take a good look at your chaff bucket and note the mix of chaff and flares. We've got a limited number of rounds to use, and they're crucial when you're trying to defeat a SAM, so don't waste them. Okay, let's—"

The back door to the ready room slammed open and Commander Campbell rushed by on his way to the duty desk. Punk perfunctorily paged through the briefing guide while he kept one eye on the skipper's gesturing between Weezer and the flight schedule board behind the desk. It didn't feel right. Punk looked to the front corner of the ready room and saw that the CO's sudden presence was not lost on Smoke either.

After all of twenty seconds, Commander Campbell pushed away from the desk and strode a deliberate stride to Punk's group. He stared at Monk and bluntly declared, "You're out."

Monk, looking like a little leaguer pulled by the coach just before walking to the plate in a bases loaded situation, shot a pleading glance to Punk and slowly rose out of his chair.

"Skipper," Punk interjected while he motioned for Monk to keep his seat. "What are you doing?"

"I'm going flying."

"I thought you had a flight physical."

"It's over. I'm healthy as a horse and ready to kill."

"You've missed most of the brief," Punk pointed out.

"Was he here?" the commander asked as he gave Einstein a chummy pat on the shoulder. "My RIO's got the brief." He then pointed toward Punk. "Plus, you're the flight lead. I'll just follow you." The skipper fixed his eyes on Monk and called him out with several jerks of both thumbs. "See ya . . ."

"What's going on?" Smoke asked as he neared the discussion from behind the skipper.

"The skipper's taking Monk's spot on this hop," Punk answered matter-of-factly.

"Skipper," Smoke advised, "I'm not sure this is appropriate."

Commander Campbell did not turn around to face Smoke. He grinned demonically and thought out loud, "You know, this is really my fault. Over the months we've been together, I guess I've created the illusion of a democracy. It's a failing of mine we'll just have to overcome." The skipper forced a chuckle before whirling around and engaging Smoke with a scowl. "Now get this, my friend," he railed. "I'm going flying on this event. When and if you ever get to be a commanding officer, doubtful as that might be with a punitive letter in your record, you can make the rulings. For now, get out of my face and go finish your brief!" He glared at Monk, who was still seated and very much surprised by the turn of events. "Are you still here?"

"Again, skipper," Smoke implored, "this is not . . ."

"MiGs are flying, goddam it," the skipper bellowed before the mission commander could finish his appeal. "Now let's get out there and bag some."

The players in the drama remained in place, including Monk, who was pushed back into his chair by Punk every time he attempted to stand. Finally, Smoke looked at his watch. "All right, we've got five minutes until we man up. Get the skipper up to speed, and let's fucking do it." Smoke started for the front of the room and then turned and addressed the CO. "Skipper, I'm the mission commander for this event. Punk is your flight lead. You're a wingman. Are we clear with our roles, sir?"

"Whatever," the commander returned, downplaying the ire that surrounded him. "Monk, may I please have my seat?" Monk pushed by without a word, balling up his kneeboard card that outlined the mission and angrily throwing it into the CONFIDENTIAL BURN trash bag next to the safe at the back of the ready room. He pulled the back door open to walk out, and the skipper called to him. "Don't get mad. You can have my night hop tonight."

Punk used the balance of available time to focus the skipper as much as possible on the mission at hand. At every turn the CO preemptively returned an "okay, okay" as if insulted by the details Punk provided. After a few fruitless minutes, they broke and fanned out into their own final preparations before the trip to the flight deck.

Punk made it a point to go in a direction opposite the skipper. Commander Campbell headed to the front of the ready room and the duty desk to draw his blood chit and pistol, so Punk went to the back and mindlessly rinsed his coffee mug in the sink.

At the other end of the ready room, Smoke took Einstein aside. "You've learned by burning since you arrived a few weeks ago," he admitted to the receptive young RIO. "But I'm afraid today is going to be an exceptional challenge. I want you to focus on two ideas this flight. First, be respectful, but don't let yourself be bullied. Second, although you don't have any flight controls in the rear cockpit, you have to take control of the airplane from the moment the engines come on line as if you did." The lieutenant commander grasped the young officer by the shoulders and shook him gently. "I know both of those things are easier said than done, but the success of this mission may depend on them."

"Sure, Smoke," Einstein replied resolutely in spite of his disappointment.

"Don't get too down over this," Smoke said as he released Einstein and gave him one last pat on the

back. "These things have a way of working themselves out."

As always, the final point of congregation for the
aircrew before stepping onto the flight deck was the
paraloft, a space not much bigger than a large broom
closet. The paraloft functioned as an office for the
parachute riggers, who kept the aviators' gear in
working order, and a last stage dressing room for the
aviators. Eventually, all twelve of the Tomcat crews
were in the crowded room trying not to punch or
kick each other while working bodies into harnesses,
zipping into G-suits, slipping kneeboard cards into
nav bags, placing helmets on heads, and holstering
pistols.

Punk was wary of the skipper's intensity, and he
stole glances at him through the crowd as they each
made ready to go flying. The lieutenant pulled the
webbing of his harness snug across his chest and then
picked up his 9-millimeter pistol from the shelf where
he'd momentarily placed it and worked it into its inte-
grated holster. After he snapped the top flap across
the weapon, he looked up and noticed the skipper was
going through the same routine, but with a significant
twist. Instead of storing the 10-round clip separate
from the pistol as Punk—and all of the other aviators
in the room—had, the skipper slammed it home
through the grip and then allowed the slide to translate forward.

"Skipper," Punk called earnestly across the contor-
tion of bodies that separated them. "You know you
just chambered a round . . ."

"No, I didn't," the skipper insisted.

"Yes, you did," Punk returned as he moved toward
him.

And he watched with disbelief as the CO leveled the

pistol at an empty corner of the otherwise packed room, said, "If it was loaded, I couldn't do this," and pulled the trigger.

The report was deafening and the bullet careened off the steel deck and two bulkheads before embedding itself in the shell of Monk's helmet, which was sitting in the line of helmets on the rack.

A wisp of smoke trailed from the tip of the barrel as Commander Campbell calmly removed the clip and split his focus between it and the gun in his other hand. "Weezer must've issued me a faulty weapon," he declared.

"What the fuck?" Punk yelled. "You could've killed somebody."

"Ah, bullshit," the skipper replied. "I had the gun aimed over in this corner."

"Is anybody hit?" Smoke asked as he straightened his survival vest and retrieved his helmet from across the floor.

"Nobody's hit, damn it," the skipper declared as he scanned the line of aviators on the floor before him. "You guys get up."

"You're the safety officer, Spud," Smoke pointed out. "What do we do now?"

"I think you have to fill out an accidental discharge form, skipper," Spud said before he looked to one of the stunned parariggers. "Call the ordnance shop, Petty Officer Smith."

"Don't call anybody," the skipper said as he pushed his way toward the door. "We'll worry about the goddam paperwork later. Shit happens. It's time to go flying." The CO slapped the magazine back into the butt and re-holstered the pistol before he grabbed his helmet and walked out.

"Okay, so a shot was fired," Spud mused once the

commander was out of the room. "We are in a war zone, you know."

One by one the rest of the aviators got off the floor, inspected themselves for bullet holes, and then filed out of the paraloft toward the flight deck.

Smoke grabbed Einstein one more time as he started to walk out. "Remember what I said." Einstein didn't reply but continued out the door.

"Look at the bright side, sir," said Petty Officer Smith, the senior-most rigger. "The flight can only get better from here."

The day was clear and bright as the aviators entered the outside world. Punk looked at the sunny sky and glassy blue water and almost forgot that the skipper had just tried to kill them. As he negotiated the last set of steps to the flight deck, he caught sight of something else that shifted his thoughts: another aircraft carrier steamed next to the Boat, about half a mile away on a parallel course.

"Now that's a beautiful sight," Punk commented to Spud two steps ahead of him.

"Ah yes, the Other Boat," Spud observed as he stopped and admired the scene. "It's always good to lay eyes on your relief."

"Man," Punk reflected with a sigh, "the skipper's endorsement, our relief on station . . . I've been missing a lot lately. I almost forgot we exit the Gulf tomorrow."

"Yep," Spud returned. "This is our last Southern Watch flight right here, my most trusted nose gunner, our last chance for glory. After today, the Other Boat owns the war. In fact, I'll bet Rex is in CAG Ops right now turning the plan over to the other air wing staff."

"*My* plan?" Punk asked. "Well, I'm glad we busted

our asses for two days so the other guys could just walk in and take advantage of our efforts."

Spud looked back as he stepped onto the flight deck and ducked under a missile-laden Hornet's wing. "Timing is everything in this business."

Through a shroud of steam from catapult three's track, Punk watched the skipper coax his fighter into the sky and then level off at five hundred feet and rage toward the horizon. A moment later, the downward movement of the three-panel jet blast deflector, raised when a jet was at full power on the catapult to keep the push of exhaust from blowing everything behind it over the side, turned Punk's attention to the steam-obscured taxi director's signals, and the pilot slowly urged the big fighter forward and gingerly split the catapult track with the twin nose wheels.

Two enlisted men, wearing the white jerseys and float coats signifying they were troubleshooters, emerged from the cloud, reached for the silver probe that extended from the nose of the F-14, and then separated down either side, tapping and shaking their way over the jet as Punk inched forward. He lost sight of them as they passed outside of the intakes and continued aft on their last-chance inspection toward the exhaust nozzles.

On the director's signals, Punk spread the wings for takeoff and then "knelt" the Tomcat by compressing the nose strut, which gave the fighter the appearance of a rail dragster and allowed the jet's launch bar to eventually mate with the catapult's shuttle, a joining of airplane and carrier metals that effected flying speed for the jet by the end of the stroke.

The yellow-shirted director flashed the sign for the pilot to drop the wing flaps, but then immediately

countered the move with two closed fists, the signal to
stop everything. Punk and Spud both watched the director gesture behind and underneath them, presumably to the troubleshooters. He extended his left palm,
petitioning the deck crew for an explanation across
the world of engine noise, while he kept the other fist
balled in Punk's direction. Then he followed with an
alternating thumbs up and down, a signal that suggested there was some doubt whether the jet was
ready to go flying.

"Oh, fuck," Punk passed over the intercom, "don't
tell me we're down."

"It certainly looks like that's a possibility," Spud
replied. "Don't freak out, yet. Let's see what they've
come up with."

One of the troubleshooters emerged out of the
shadows of the right wing and waved at the cockpit
until he was sure he had Punk's attention. He pointed
under the jet, worked both hands in opposing half circles, and then motioned an angry slash with his right
arm; then he mouthed "the . . . tire . . . is . . . cut" and
gave Punk a thumbs down.

"Damn it," Punk responded, "we must've sliced it on
one of the arresting wires on the way to the cat."

Spud looked at his watch. "It's still early in the
launch. If they sideline us quickly, maybe the air-
framers can swap another tire on there."

"That's a long shot," Punk figured as he followed
the director's signals to sweep the wings back and
extend the nose strut so they could clear the catapult
for the jets behind them. "It would take a varsity effort
by the maintenance crew." Punk looked over his left
shoulder at the spare Hornet parked behind catapult
four. The Tomcat's status had not been lost on the F-18
pilot or his ground crew, and they all gesticulated

toward the nearest director to indicate their jet was in full working order should a substitution be required.

Punk and Spud were sidelined just aft of the carrier's island, facing the fantail on the right half of the landing area. The director passed control of the jet to the plane captain, who signaled for Punk to secure the right engine.

Punk pulled the right throttle fully aft and watched the corresponding gauges wind down. As he looked back through the canopy toward the plane captain, he noticed Chief Wixler rushing toward them, pushing an aircraft jack—a man-sized tripod on wheels—in front of him, accompanied by two green-shirted maintainers.

The chief blew by the plane captain and disappeared under the wing. Punk and Spud felt a series of lurches as the jet was raised slightly on the right side. Chief Wixler sprinted off again and returned half a minute later rolling a wheel. A yellow shirt walked up to the plane captain, and Punk saw him give the young sailor an angry indication that they only had two minutes until their Tomcat would be ruled down and shelved for this launch.

Punk adjusted his mirror in an attempt to see what was going on around the right main landing gear, but he only managed an occasional glimpse of an arm or a leg as the maintainers shuttled tools back and forth between the toolbox and the wheel assembly. Then the yellow shirt reappeared, pointed to his watch, and gave the plane captain two thumbs down.

The plane captain flashed Punk a fist and ran under the wing. Seconds later, an enraged Chief Wixler emerged and squared off toe-to-toe with the yellow shirt as a major league baseball manager might confront an umpire during an argument.

"Spud, are you watching this?" Punk asked over the intercom. "Wix is some kinda fired up."

"Yeah," the lieutenant commander replied, "I've never seen this sort of intensity from him."

The two deck hands continued flailing, each matching the emotional ante of the other until Chief Wixler tapped his watch and forcefully flashed the director two fingers. The yellow shirt repeated the signal back to the chief and followed with a conditional thumbs up before crossing his arms expectantly and focusing clearly on his watch. The chief sprinted back under the wing and disappeared from the aviators' view again.

"It looks like Wix bought us a couple of minutes," Spud said.

As Smoke's jet moved across the jet blast deflector to prepare for launch, Punk looked across the landing area at the spare Hornet and confirmed it was still chained to the deck awaiting a final ruling.

"Are you guys going to make it, Punk?" Smoke asked over the squadron common frequency as he moved onto the catapult.

"I'm not sure," Punk replied. "The chief is giving it a Herculean effort, I'll tell you that."

The skipper suddenly transmitted on the frequency from overhead the carrier: "Smoke, pass to the spare Hornet that Soup will take the lead if Punk goes down."

Punk looked over his right shoulder to Smoke, who had his hands raised above the canopy rail along with Gucci while the ordnance team armed their missiles. Smoke noticed Punk facing his way, and he tapped his right index finger against the side of his helmet and then signaled "three" four times to him. Once the ordies cleared away with all the arming pins in hand, both pilots switched their radios to "quad three" for an unofficial discussion.

"You'd better be fixed, Punk," Smoke demanded. "There is no way in hell I'm allowing the CO to lead the interdiction element unbriefed. That's just plain stupid."

"How did you plan on stopping him?" Punk asked. "It's his world, remember? We're just living in it."

"This pinball machine is ready to tilt, damn it," Smoke said. "I'm ready to cancel this whole shooting match and then run up to CAG and tell him . . ."

Punk stopped listening as his jet ratcheted back down and Chief Wixler came into view, sweat-drenched and covered with grease. The chief gave Punk an emphatic thumbs up and then spun on his heel and gave the same sign to the yellow shirt.

"Smoke, we're up," Punk passed on quad three as soon as he could get a word in edgewise around the lieutenant commander's ongoing diatribe. "I'm switching my radio back to squadron common."

"Oh . . . good," Smoke replied. "Disregard my last then . . ."

The plane captain passed control of the jet back to the director, and, as Punk started to taxi forward to take his place back in the line for catapult three, he made it a point to catch Chief Wixler's eye. The lieutenant rendered the chief his best salute, at which point the chief came to attention and solemnly returned the gesture.

In-flight refueling during a normal Operation Southern Watch mission was as difficult as any other phase of the flight, not necessarily because of the skill required for the pilot to plug the tanker with the jet's probe, but because of the confusion and danger that surrounded getting into and out of the flow of the tanker pattern. Even during the daytime, the sheer number of airplanes on and around the tanker made tanking far from routine, and like the California rule that stated to cars on the on-ramps—"You ain't shit until you're on the freeway"—the pattern didn't yield to planes not yet within it.

Spud painted Punk a radar picture, and Punk compared it to his view through the canopy as he tried to figure out which of the two groups of specks across the sky to join on. He quickly glanced at the kneeboard strapped to his left thigh, and, after reviewing the briefed altitude for their tanker, continued his climb to twenty-five thousand feet while crossing his fingers for the blessing of a KC-10.

Air Force tankers came in two models: KC-10 and KC-135. The KC-10 was the preferred platform from a Navy carrier pilot's point of view because it was designed from inception to accommodate both Navy and Air Force aircraft: It had both a boom for Air Force jets and a hose and basket for Navy and Marine Corps jets.

The Navy had always designed its aerial refueling apparatus with the receiver as the male in the union with the tanker. The Air Force, mostly concerned with tanking strategic bombers and other larger, less nimble aircraft than tactical fighters, elected to make the tanker male. So, in order to make the KC-135 work for Navy aircraft, a hose with a basket on the end of it had to be attached to the end of the boom, a rig that appeared and acted every bit the afterthought its utility was.

Spud bore sighted the LANTIRN pod in the air-to-air mode and sweetened the view with his thumb on one of the system controller tabs on his left console and reluctantly pronounced, "KC-135 . . ."

Damned Murphy's Law. All things being equal,

Punk would've preferred the docility of the KC-10's friendly refueling rig as he continued to chip away at the rust formed by nearly a month out of the cockpit, but there was nothing he could do about it now. He determined to put on the good face and try to keep from ripping the probe off of his jet in the process.

Punk joined the gaggle as Dash-Eight on the tanker's left wing, and after playing crack-the-whip for a time with the line of jets to the right of him, he established himself on Dash-Seven, Biff's TARPS bird. Once the oscillations settled down, he was able to take a couple of glances at the Hornet plugged into the hose and noticed that the two Prowlers on the right wing were now banking away from the pack and steering to the push point ten miles to the north.

One by one the procession through the basket continued. Gassed-up flight leads waited on the tanker's right wing for wingmen, and then the two-jet sections departed for the push point. Because Punk and Spud were the last crew off the deck, they were last to tank, and, although the skipper was only two jets in front of them, he didn't wait after he'd received his gas, but immediately headed to the rendezvous.

The whoosh of the probe in the air stream flashed Punk momentarily back to the night of the mishap, and he realized he hadn't attempted to tank since then. But like an avid golfer surprised by the fluidity of his swing after a long winter layoff, Punk slipped the Tomcat's probe into the tanker's rigid basket on his first attempt. Once he saw he was mated he almost relaxed, until the growing bend in the hose caused by the Tomcat's creeping forward on the tanker reminded him that the ad hoc male-to-female rig of the KC-135 didn't allow the same amount of movement between parties that the take-up reels of the KC-10 and S-3 did.

He focused on the joint between the boom and the hose and flew formation on it in an effort to preserve the shape of the hose he'd managed at the moment.

While staying in the basket was a white knuckler, the KC-135 showed mercy to Navy pilots by pumping fuel at an extraordinary rate. Punk continued to stare just below the apex of the canopy bow on his forward windscreen to the point on the refueling rig where metal boom turned to rubber hose as Spud watched his totalizer roll up. Within two minutes they'd received the four thousand pounds of JP-5 jet fuel they were due. As Spud passed "that's it" over the intercom, Punk eased back and uncoupled from the basket. After a quick pause on the right wing and a wave to the tanker's copilot, they were headed for the push point.

Spud checked his watch and cross-referenced some of the chicken scratch on the top card of those clamped to the kneeboard strapped around his right thigh: ten minutes until the package was supposed to start the route. Plenty of time. He switched his radar to the Pulse mode with a mash of his right index finger against the appropriate button and studied the pepper specks on the scope, watching their drift across the screen. After a few seconds of observation, he elected to lock up the left-most of the blips and reasoned, based on relative position to the rest of the radar contacts, it had to be the skipper or one of the Prowlers.

Punk sighted through the diamond on his HUD created by Spud's radar lock and saw that his trusty RIO had, in fact, locked one of the Prowlers. He slid his Tomcat onto the bearing line and closed with his element at a quick-but-controlled rate until he'd positioned his jet Blue Angel close to the skipper's left wing. Commander Campbell, who'd assumed the interim lead of the two jammers, either didn't notice or refused to acknowledge Punk on his wing, and although Einstein looked over at them, the CO stared straight ahead as the four jets flew above but in synch with the rest of the package as they continued to circle the push point.

"He's fucking with us," Punk commented to Spud on the intercom. "He knows we're here. He just doesn't want to give up the lead."

"What, one murder attempt and you think the guy's got it out for you?" Spud cracked as he checked his watch again. "We've got just over six minutes until we press out. Humor him for a bit."

Spud used the time to groom the LANTIRN pod. LANTIRN, short for Low Altitude Navigation Targeting InfraRed at Night, was a precision attack system developed for the Air Force twenty years earlier and used on F-16s. The Navy's use of the pod on Tomcats came out of the requirement for another precision strike platform following the retirement of the slow-but-venerable A-6 Intruder and a casual conversation between two lieutenants and a contractor at an officers' club bar. A year and a half later, the F-14 community was given a new lease on life in the form of the LANTIRN pod, and strike planning doors that had been slammed in the face of fighter crews only able to counter air-to-air threats were reopened with gusto. In fact, because the workload was shared between two aviators compared to the Hornet's one, and because the resolution of the RIO's ten-inch-by-ten-inch display allowed the Tomcat to pick out tough targets and was very TV news friendly, the F-14 had actually superseded the Hornet as the Navy's precision attack platform of choice.

Spud double-checked the coordinates he'd entered into the system and watched the view blur from side to side as he commanded the gimballed infrared lens from waypoint to waypoint. He walked through all of the pod's modes and magnifications and made sure the laser was ready to fire.

Smoke's voice cracked over the strike common frequency. "Smoke's up . . ."

"Biff's up . . ."

"Soup's up," the skipper passed before correcting himself with a laugh. "Sorry, force of habit." He looked to his left and gave Punk the lead with a toss of his left hand.

Punk assumed the lead with a signal of his own and said "Punk's up" on the radio before pushing his jet into the lead position.

"Kick AWACS control frequency on primary radios," Gucci called over strike common from the cockpit behind Smoke's.

The AWACS frequency greeted them with a series of emphatic transmissions between one of the controllers in the AWACS jet and the F-15s leaving their counter-air stations and returning to Al Kharj.

"Titan shows two groups fifty-five miles north of you, loitering above the thirty-third parallel."

"Roger, Titan. Watch those groups. Eagle flight is southbound, out of gas, and returning to base."

"Titan, the photo package is checking in as fragged," Gucci said, indicating they were at full tasked strength.

"Roger, photo," the controller returned. "Say call sign of your counter-air package."

"Diamond," Gucci answered.

"Copy, Diamond," the AWACS said. "We have MiG activity at this time; standby for picture: two groups, bearing three-five-five, twenty miles north of the no-fly zone."

"Roger," Gucci said as he and the rest of the flight torqued their radars to the aforementioned piece of sky, in spite of the excessive range to the contacts in question. "We're still feet wet, Titan. We haven't pushed yet."

"Copy, recommend you push now," the controller replied.

"Kodak is detaching," Bill Thompson called from Biff's backseat as the two TARPS F-14s started a slow descent to ten thousand feet for their photo run.

"Verify combat checks complete," Smoke commanded. "Check mission recorders running, weapons armed, and radar warning receivers on."

"Biff flight copies . . ."

"Punk flight copies . . ."

"Pushing now," Smoke passed, and the ten Navy jets began to trade the blue Gulf under them for the parched desert of Southern Iraq. As Smoke started a climb to the high twenties, Punk mirrored Biff in his descent, remaining a few thousand feet above him so that he wouldn't have to crane his head around excessively to keep both the reconnaissance airplanes and the ground in sight. In spite of the excitement on the radio, Punk reminded himself his job was to look for SAMs, not MiGs.

As the package proceeded, things were quieter than the initial scenario had suggested they might be. The airplanes' radar warning receivers were silent, and the cadence of the AWACS controller's calls slowed to a near halt as the MiGs well north of them ran out of gas and returned to their bases.

But it was hard to be angered by the ennui of another routine Southern Watch event on a gorgeous day like the one that surrounded them. The sky turned a deeper shade of blue as they worked their way north. Punk marveled at the visibility and tried to make out Baghdad in the far distance. Fully-mission-capable jets, great weather, MiGs teasing them just above thirty-three . . . It was a good day to be flying. And tomorrow they were headed home.

"Kodak's headed south," Bill Thompson said as the TARPS jets passed Al Kut and neared the Iranian border. "Titan, verify picture clear north . . ."

"That's affirm—" The controller cut himself short as several new symbols popped up on his scope. "Negative, negative. New picture: two groups, north-south split, climbing through angels seven, headed two-four-zero, bearing zero-zero-two from Diamond, range sixty-five miles."

"Roger, looking," Gucci replied.

"The second wave must've just launched," Smoke said to the rest of his element on their discrete frequency.

"Two's clean," Turtle called from behind Fuzzy.

"Brick's clean," the Hornet pilot returned.

"Bird's clean," the other Hornet pilot passed.

In Operation Southern Watch, the thirty-third parallel defined the northern end of the playing field. Any Iraqi military jets that flew south of it were considered free game by their mere presence. Conversely, American fighters had to remain south of the thirty-third parallel. These simple rules made a fighter pilot's job a lot harder than it otherwise would have been. Spud had summed up the challenge after their first ROE brief months ago with, "If you're going to shoot a burglar, you'd better make sure he falls in your house."

"We're getting too close to the thirty-third to run a good intercept," Smoke said. "Let's bring it south and start again." Without waiting for a response, he banked the jet sharply to the left and tugged the stick back until he had five Gs on the aircraft. "Titan," he said into his oxygen mask as he tensed the muscles in his stomach and legs in an attempt to keep blood flowing to his brain, "Diamond is nose cold."

"Roger, bogeys are now level angels two-five, headed two-seven-zero."

"They're paralleling the upper limit of the no-fly zone," Smoke said to Gucci over the intercom. "Where are we relative to the known SA-6s?"

Gucci hopped the cursor on his tactical display over several different symbols and then replied, "The closest one bears three-zero-zero for thirty-five miles."

"Diamond, let's float it west," Smoke said over their discrete freq. "I've got a feeling these guys might make a move south." He started the nose to the right across the horizon, followed dutifully by his three wingmen. "Titan, Diamond is coming nose hot to the northwest."

"Roger, Diamond. Picture now: two groups, east west split, heading two-zero-zero, bearing three-five-zero at sixty-three miles. Titan shows their speed accelerating through 700 knots."

"Seven hundred knots?" Smoke mused over the intercom.

"Foxbats," Gucci returned. "They're going too fast to be MiG-29s. They've gotta be Foxbats."

The MiG-25 Foxbat had been introduced by the Soviet Union early in the Cold War. It was designed as a supersonic interceptor, ready to defend the homeland by shooting down strategic bombers, spy planes, and even low-flying satellites. The Foxbat wasn't very maneuverable for a jet fighter, but it was fast—over two Mach's worth, and the concern for aviators in an Operation Southern Watch scenario was that, due to the geographic constraints of the no-fly zone, a Foxbat could rage south, stirring shit up for a short time, and then exit untouched because of its speed. In this type of arena, success for the Americans against a MiG-25 would depend heavily on the proper use of geometry. Smoke understood that fact, and now it was his job to mentally wrestle with the angles.

"Biff, call your posit," he said over the AWACS frequency, focusing himself on his primary mission of protecting the reconnaissance birds.

"Biff's approaching Point Six, southbound."

Gucci read his pilot's mind and passed, "That puts them fifty miles east of us," over the intercom. "They still have five points to hit, about a hundred twenty miles 'til feet wet."

"Bogey's now crossing the line," the AWACS controller reported. "Titan shows two groups now, lead-trail turning left through one-seven-zero."

"Diamond's committing," Smoke replied. "Titan, call our bearing and range to bogeys."

"Bogeys now bear three-five-five for fifty-five miles."

"Diamond is contact your call, Titan," Gucci said as a group of Doppler mode symbols materialized on his tactical display. "Showing two groups, five-mile lead-trail, lead group three-five-three for fifty-one miles, angels two-five. They appear to be in a right-hand turn."

"That's your bogey," the controller replied. "Showing lead group turning through west at this time."

"What's the range to the nearest SAM site?" Smoke asked his RIO.

"Twenty miles," Gucci answered.

"Diamonds, let's bring it nose cold to the right,"

Smoke commanded on the discrete frequency before telling the AWACS, "Diamond flight is turning back to the southeast, Titan."

"Roger," the controller said. "The bogeys are still in a right-hand turn."

"I want to redefine the engagement zone," Smoke explained to his wingmen on the discrete freq. "This may take a little patience."

In the skipper's jet, Einstein was getting an earful. The CO, driving away from the action with the interdiction package covering the TARPS birds nearing the final leg of their photo run, only heard the fact that Smoke was turning away from the bogeys. "I knew that guy was weak," he shot over the intercom. "Nobody's going to shoot anything down by running away."

Although Einstein understood Smoke's methodology as he referenced the symbols on his own tactical display, he elected to remain silent in the face of the commander's tirade. *You have the stick and throttle,* he thought to himself repeatedly. *You have the stick and throttle . . .*

The Diamond element did the crab dance with the Iraqis bracketing the thirty-third parallel for two more rotations, and Smoke noticed that the MiGs came a little more to the east with each pass. As he turned the element away for the third time, he commented to Gucci that he thought they'd be able to commit missiles the next time around as the SAM site wouldn't be a factor. *Wait 'em out,* he thought. *Let them get sloppy . . .*

As soon as he heard Smoke turn away for the third time, the skipper snapped. Without a word to his flight lead or his RIO, he threw the stick against his right thigh and started a hard turn to the northwest.

The unexpected maneuver caused Einstein to bang

his head against the left side of the canopy, and as he worked to gather his wits, he asked the skipper, "Where are we going?"

"To kill some MiGs," the commander shouted. "Somebody's gotta do it."

"Where the fuck is he off to?" Spud asked over the intercom.

Punk checked his mirrors to see which direction Spud was looking and then joined him in watching down their wing line as the skipper's jet drove away.

"Skipper, what are you doing?" Punk asked on the discrete frequency. There was no reply. "Iron Two, state your intentions."

Commander Campbell sensed his RIO was about to key the mike to answer Punk's question, so he said over the intercom, "Stay off the radio. Let's focus on the MiGs."

"But skipper," Einstein explained, "we're configured as a bomber. We don't have any long-range missiles on board."

"We have a Sparrow and two Sidewinders," the skipper countered. "They'll work fine. Now get me a radar picture."

You have the stick and throttle; you have the stick and throttle . . . "Skipper, this isn't our mission. Let's bring the jet back to the left and rejoin Punk."

Again the CO didn't respond. He pushed the throttles forward and accelerated the jet through mach one. "Titan," he said on the AWACS frequency, "bogey dope for Iron Two."

The request threw the controller off a bit. "Ah . . . standby Iron Two." He checked the call signs on the Air Tasking Order to verify which symbol on his display was "Iron," ran his palm across the trackball in front of him for a few seconds, and passed the information. "Lead group currently fifteen miles north of the no-fly zone, in a right-hand turn through zero-two-zero, bearing three-four-five from you at seventy-three miles."

"Perfect," the skipper thought aloud over the intercom. "These guys won't even know what hit 'em."

You have the stick and throttle; you have the stick and throttle . . . "Skipper, again, this is a bad idea. We need to come hard left now and get back with our element."

"Einstein," the skipper said, "The flight controls are in my cockpit. Now shut up and get me a lock so I can shoot something down."

As Smoke started to bring the fighter element nose hot to the threat again, he saw the skipper's jet scream down his right side. "You have got to be shitting me," he railed over the intercom. "Even the skipper can't be this out to lunch."

"Smoke, are you tally the rogue Tomcat?" Brick asked from one of the Hornets.

"That's affirmative," Smoke replied before keying the other radio. "Iron Two, is that you?" There was no response. "Iron Two, retire to the southeast, now. You're fouling the lane of fire for the Diamond package."

Einstein desperately petitioned the commanding officer. "Skipper, we're in the way here."

The skipper ignored all around him except the AWACS controller. "Titan, continue bogey dope for Iron Two."

"Iron Two," the controller replied, "Showing a single group now, three-five-zero, fifty miles, heading one-seven-zero. Crossing into the no-fly zone at this time."

In the Current Operations Cell of JTF-SWA, General Bullock scratched his head and asked the room, "What is Iron Two's mission?"

"Interdiction, general. He's supposed to be escorting the TARPS package," a captain seated in front of one of the myriad of displays around the room replied.

"So what is he doing over there?" the general asked, pointing toward the real-time tactical display that dominated the far wall of the cell.

"Kodak abort!" Smoke ordered over the AWACS freq. "Kodak abort! Iron lead, snap to SAM Site Bravo!"

The TARPS birds immediately climbed and accelerated south to the exit point as Punk picked up a hard turn toward the northwest with the two Prowlers in tow.

"Skipper, we just caused the photo mission to abort," Einstein explained in earnest.

"We didn't cause anything," the skipper shot back at his young RIO. "We are doing the job somebody else failed to do."

Einstein jabbed his cursor into one of the symbols on his display and called up the range to it. "We're going to fly over a SAM site. This could be the SAM trap Holly was talking about."

"SAM trap? Bullshit. Do you hear anything? Our warning gear is silent." The skipper glanced down at his repeat of Einstein's scope. "Now call that contact."

With some reluctance, Einstein keyed the radio. "Iron Two, contact, single group, three-four-zero for thirty-one miles."

"That's your bogeys," the AWACS replied.

"I have Sparrow selected," the skipper methodically passed over the intercom, as much thinking aloud as coordinating with his backseater. "I'll take the shot as soon as he gets inside of max range."

Einstein both watched the range readout on his scope and scanned the ground for SAM launches. He heard the skipper call "Fox One," and then felt the missile leave the airplane accompanied by a quick roar from the weapon's rocket motor. *This just might work,* he thought as he monitored his tactical display.

But then the closure between the would-be foes decreased. With growing concern, Einstein watched the numbers on his readout count down through the four hundreds. He crosschecked the evidence with the symbol on his tactical display and confirmed the bogey was in a hard right-hand turn. "They're beaming us," he shouted at the skipper. The Tomcat's radar broke its Doppler lock as the two jets ceased to close, and the Sparrow lost its guidance information and flew benignly over Iraq.

"All right . . ." the skipper concluded, "we'll just have to use our Sidewinders."

"Iron Two get out of there," an anonymous voice called over the AWACS frequency.

"Titan shows group passing through west toward north," the AWACS controller passed, confirming Einstein's analysis. "Recommend dropping them, Iron Two. They'll be north of the no-fly zone in five miles."

"Skipper, get out of there."

And then the trap was sprung. Iron Two's radar warning gear tittered a few times and the corresponding display on the right side of the instrument console in each cockpit blinked with an inconclusive indication. Moments later, the blare in their helmets was almost unbearable, and both aviators watched their displays saturate solid red with input.

The skipper reefed the jet into a series of opposing hard turns while Einstein instinctively began dispensing chaff from the buckets near the base of the tail hook by tweaking the coolie hats above the rear cockpit glare shield as he desperately searched the ground under them for a SAM launch—although he wasn't really sure what one looked like.

Ten miles in trail, Smoke was the first to see the series of plumes form on the desert below. "SAMs in the air," he cried over the AWACS freq. "SAMs in the air."

Both Prowlers turned their jammers on and ripple fired their complement of HARM missiles at the guilty site from sixty miles away, but they provided no sanctuary for the skipper and Einstein now. The aviators in Iron Two were alone in their fight against the salvo of SAMs streaking toward them.

Einstein caught sight of the launches just after Smoke called them over the air. "Tally launch, three o'clock low," the young RIO shot over the intercom. "Do you see it?"

"Negative, negative!" the skipper returned between nervous huffs into his mask as he continued to twist the jet in an attempt to shake the track the Iraqis had on them. "Keep the calls coming."

"I see two now," Einstein reported. "First one is definitely tracking on us. Roll right and pull hard!"

The skipper complied with Einstein's commands, and as the nose fell through the horizon and toward the desert, he looked through his right quarter panel and saw the streaks across the sky snaking toward them. "I've got 'em," the skipper said over the intercom. "Keep the chaff coming."

"It's coming," Einstein returned. "It's coming."

The skipper held the first missile down his wing line until he couldn't stand it anymore, and then he pulled back on the stick for all he was worth. The missile swung wide and streaked by them without exploding. "That's one down . . ." the CO declared as their jet passed through the missile's smoke trail. The skipper kept his eyes out of the cockpit and focused on the second missile. *Speed is life, speed is life.* The stick felt soft and unresponsive as he worked to beat the next SAM as effectively as he had the first. "What's our airspeed?" he demanded from Einstein.

Einstein had to force himself to look away from the smooth white arc etching across the blue sky and come inside to his gauges. "Eighty knots."

The skipper tried to dump the nose and regain some energy, but as he watched the missile make its final ghastly angular correction and scribe the curve of the grim reaper's scythe toward them, he knew he didn't have time for that luxury. He commanded the last-ditch pull, but the jet had nothing to offer.

Smoke watched the explosion in front of him with detached disbelief until the scream of his own warning gear snapped him back to reality. The Iraqis weren't out of SAMs yet. As he started a turn back toward the southeast, he noticed two parachutes above the flaming fighter falling to the arid land below. "Mayday. Mayday," he shouted on the radio. "Titan, Iron Two is hit. Diamond lead sees two good chutes."

"Roger, Titan copies. Zeus do you copy?"

"Zeus copies," the general at JTF-SWA replied stoically. "We're launching the Sandy package now."

Spud had locked the SAM site with the LANTIRN pod following the first launch, and as he watched the view to see if any more missiles were being loosed, he saw the HARMs hit in a series of four explosions. "Good hits on the site," he passed over the frequency. "Good hits on the site."

With Spud's call, the electronic countermeasures officers in the twin backseats of each Prowler turned off the jamming pods slung under the wings and listened to the airwaves for a time. The silence that greeted them seconded Spud's motion.

"Iron Lead is assuming rescue mission coordinator," Punk called over the AWACS frequency. "Cover us, Smoke."

"Roger that," Smoke replied as he rolled his flight out headed one-six-zero and worked away from the thirty-third parallel to get some fighting room. "Call your posit."

"We're fifteen miles southeast of SAM site Bravo," Punk said. "I've got both chutes in sight. We'll follow them down and establish an orbit overhead." He keyed the other radio to talk with the lead Prowler on his wing. "Bambi, do either of you have any more HARMs?"

"That's a negative, Punk," Bambi replied. "We can stick around and keep jamming down the threat axis for a while. That'll keep the SAM operators guessing."

"Appreciate it," Punk returned. "Iron flight switch secondary radios to primary distress frequency."

The controller's voice came over the AWACS frequency: "Titan shows bogey group headed south back across the line."

"Bogey dope for Diamond," Gucci requested.

"Diamond, bogeys now three-four-three, thirty-six miles, angels two-five. Appear to be hot for you."

"The MiG drivers probably think we're confused," Smoke commented to Gucci. "They're trying to cherry pick us for a quick kill or two." The pilot stoked his fighter's afterburners, snapped the jet into a 90-degree right angle of bank, and pulled into a seven-G turn. "Fight's on . . . gentlemen," he grunted over the discrete frequency to the Tomcat and two Hornets on his wing. "Fight's . . . on."

Just as the admiral and CAG sat down to an executive lunch in the flag mess, one of the staff commanders, a surface warfare officer who was currently standing the duty as battle watch captain, came storming in with a disturbing bit of news: "Admiral, one of our jets has been shot down over Iraq."

Both admiral and CAG rose out of their chairs. "Shot down?" the admiral parroted. "Oh, my God . . . How?"

"We think it was a surface-to-air missile," the battle watch captain answered. "We're getting the information secondhand."

"Who was it?" CAG asked.

"We don't know, sir."

"What type of airplane?"

"We don't know that either, CAG. As I said, we're getting our information secondhand."

"Were there any survivors?" the Admiral queried.

"We think so," the commander answered. "JTF-SWA just called and said they were launching the search and rescue package, including the helicopter out of Camp Doha in Kuwait. They wouldn't do that without an indication of survivors."

"Good," CAG said.

"Well, it may not be good," the commander replied.

"Why not?"

"They're using one of our helicopters."

"So?" CAG asked. "Two of our HH-60s are under the tactical control of JTF-SWA." The air wing commander turned to the Admiral and explained, "They do a two-helo detachment to Camp Doha every two weeks for four days. It's a multi-service rotation. You may remember you were briefed on this contingency as soon as we arrived in the Gulf."

The battle watch captain walked around CAG and faced the admiral directly. "Sir, this is a very important asset to the battle group. We can't afford to lose it."

"Lose it?" the admiral echoed.

"A search and rescue mission into Iraq can be very risky," the commander opined.

"It *is* risky," CAG said from behind the commander. "That's what those guys do."

Unmoved, the battle watch captain continued his counsel: "Sir, we're talking about one of the platforms we use to get you to the other ships in the battle group . . ."

"What are you suggesting, commander?" CAG asked acerbically, "that we attempt to stop the helicopter from launching out of Kuwait?"

"CAG," the commander patronizingly intoned over his shoulder, "I'm trying to unemotionally advise the admiral on all of his options here."

"We may have American aviators on the ground in Iraq," CAG railed. "This is an emotional situation." For once, the spirit behind the instructions that outlined his responsibilities was revealed to him as his first response. This gut impulse surprised him as much as those around him, but he embraced the resolve he suddenly felt. "Yes," he repeated more calmly, "this is an emotional situation. There are no options here, commander. This is why we have contingency plans."

"There's a big difference between having a plan and actually executing it," the commander countered. "Whoever thought somebody would actually get shot down? We have to—"

The admiral silenced his battle watch captain with a gesture and then pointed him toward the door. The commander looked as if he wanted to say something, but took the hint and hurried out of the mess.

"Let's get our shipmates back," the battle group commander declared to the rest of the officers in the room.

*   *   *

Einstein came to at eight thousand feet over the Iraqi desert. Knocked unconscious by the SAM's explosion, he wasn't sure how he'd come to be floating gently through the air, but his first impulse was to look above him and make sure he had a good parachute.

He scanned the sky above and Earth below. He felt the wind through his hair and realized he'd lost his helmet at some point during the ejection. He could hear the jets flying around him. He saw another parachute, certainly the skipper's, a good distance away, and he tried waving to see if he could get a response, but there was none.

The scene seemed surreal, even peaceful, until he remembered that he was coming down over hostile territory. He was suddenly gripped with fear. What would they do to him? Where would he be taken? The young RIO thought about something he'd read, a revelation that had gone through Medal of Honor winner James B. Stockdale's mind as he descended into North Vietnam where he was a POW for seven years: "I am leaving the world of technology and entering the world of Epictetus."

He again looked down at the ground and tried to assess whether one area was less inhabited than another, remembering what the SEALs had said during their combat search and rescue brief a few months ago: "Go west and south." He grabbed the risers and did his best to steer toward lighter patches of desert, away from rivers and buildings. He wasn't sure of the wind direction, but he seemed to be drifting west.

Einstein thought about something else the SEALs had said: "Your survival radio is your lifeline. Without it we won't find you." He let go of the risers and carefully unzipped the right front pocket of his survival vest. He found the thin nylon cord that ran between the radio and the vest and ensured it was attached at both ends. Then he pulled the radio out of its pouch, turned it on, selected the frequency option labeled "243.0 MHz," and attempted to talk to the skipper. "Iron Two Pilot, this is Iron Two RIO; do you read me?" He put the small speaker to his ear and waited for a response. "Iron Two Pilot, this is Iron Two RIO; how do you read, over?" Nothing. His despair grew as he was now certain he would fall into Iraqi hands.

"Iron Two RIO, this is Iron One. How do you read?" *Spud's voice.* "Iron One, Iron Two RIO has you loud and clear. How me?"

"Einstein, we have you weak but readable. Hang in there. We'll be covering you until the CSAR package gets here."

"Roger, Spud. Any suggestions on what I should do?"

"Well, it looks like you're floating away from civilization, which is good. Keep going the way you're headed. When you hit the ground, quickly find a place to hide."

"Roger . . ."

"I'm going to stay off the radio now, and I recommend you do the same until you get situated in a safe place. The Iraqis may be monitoring this freq. Stick with CSAR procedures and you should be out of there within the hour."

"Copy that," Einstein replied with poorly concealed trepidation. "Hope I see you soon."

"You will, buddy."

As the four jets came nose-on to the bogeys, Turtle was the first aviator with an accurate radar picture. "Diamond Two showing single group, three-four-two for thirty-four miles, angels twenty-five. I'm breaking out four of them."

"Titan shows that group as your bogeys."

"Can I shoot?" Fuzzy asked Smoke over the discrete frequency.

"Shoot! Shoot!" Smoke cried in return.

A few seconds later, a Phoenix missile came off Fuzzy's jet with a burst of flame followed by a thick smoke trail as the weapon climbed with the enthusiasm of a blood hound latched to a scent in the breeze. Turtle marveled at the sight, watching the deadly rocket scream higher and higher until it reached its apex and started back downhill. Just as it seemed the missile might hang forever in the sky, it hit its mark and transformed itself and the better part of the lead Foxbat into a ball of fragments and flame. No chute emerged from the falling wreckage.

"Splash One! Splash One!" Fuzzy called. The Hornets sorted around the fireball and each fired an AM-RAAM. The missiles came off more aggressively than the graceful Phoenix, and they flew faster, straighter lines to their targets. The hapless Iraqi wingmen had attempted to turn their Foxbats away from the attack after their lead exploded before their eyes, but no amount of expendables or Doppler shift was going to defeat the AMRAAMs now. The two missiles hit almost simultaneously and twin fireballs bracketed the dissipating remnants of the first explosion. Like the Phoenix, each AMRAAM had aimed for the centroid of the radar return instead of the MiG's heat source, and both destroyed their prey as unmercifully.

"You guys stay level," Smoke commanded as he pulled into the vertical. "Dash Four is mine." Smoke climbed to slightly higher than thirty thousand feet, then rolled the jet onto its back and pulled the nose to the horizon. "I still don't have a tally, Gucci. What's the range to this guy?"

"Twelve miles. Look slightly left and five degrees low. He's fast as hell. I'm showing 1,300 knots of closure."

"That's not going to matter," the pilot assured. "We'll convert this altitude advantage into speed and angles." Smoke kept the jet inverted for a few seconds and scoured the sky against the sandy backdrop beneath them. "I'm tally. He's merging with our wingmen."

"Mark the bandit down my right wing," Fuzzy reported. "It's a Foxbat. Do you have him, Smoke?"

"That's a roger. I'm overhead pulling for a shot," Smoke returned. "Stay offensive on him, but give me a few seconds . . ."

Smoke came through 90 degrees nose low and tracked in phase with the MiG as he closed for the kill. He selected Sidewinder and listened for the distinctive tone the weapon gave off when it had acquired a heat source. He guessed the Foxbat had to be in full afterburner, with the pilot now fully immersed in the attempt to run away, and he anticipated the Sidewinder would have no trouble acquiring the MiG's red-hot engines.

But the missile was silent. "Two miles, Smoke," Gucci prodded from the backseat. "Take the shot."

"I can't get a tone," Smoke replied. "There's no way he's in afterburner."

And then the Foxbat's pilot did the most unlikely thing. He pulled hard into Smoke and Gucci, and in the blink of an eye, Diamond One overshot the bogey's flight path. "This guy's no idiot," Smoke commented to Gucci through the G forces as he worked to get the Tomcat's nose headed the other direction. "He had us in sight the entire time, lured us into the overshoot."

As soon as he saw Smoke fly beyond the MiG, the lead Hornet pilot, who'd maintained an offensive position in the rear quarter of the Foxbat, pulled for a shot of his own. Brick's missile tone was suspect, but he knew he'd probably never get another opportunity like this. Once Diamond One cleared his windscreen, he pulled the trigger. The Sidewinder came off with a roar and immediately corkscrewed in the wrong direction. He winced behind his mask and visor and feebly uttered, "Heads up . . ." over the radio.

Smoke continued to bring his nose to bear on the Iraqi and was surprised to see a missile sail a few hundred feet in front of him. "Cease fire back there, goddam it," he screamed over the discrete frequency. "I'm engaged!" He pulled the stick into his lap and, before looking back to his left at the Foxbat, shot a quick glance inside the cockpit to make sure he hadn't pegged the angle of attack. The Tomcat didn't fly for very long that way, and the airframe didn't give the pilot any seat-of-the-pants indication when it was about to depart controlled flight. One second the pilot had absolute dominion over his killing machine, and the next he was no more than a passenger on a roller coaster taking the big plunge—and a falling roller coaster could easily be shot by opposing pilots still in control of their aircraft.

The engagement quickly became a slow-speed affair, which surprised Smoke because he'd always been briefed that the Foxbat was not capable of fighting at slow speeds. The Iraqi maneuvered with aplomb, and the two pilots matched each other in an airborne dance contest where the winner would be the guy who was able to stop his down-range travel better than his opponent. They floated relative to each other like two leaves in the autumn breeze, and from the rest of the Diamonds' vantage points, the scene was ghostly still.

The MiG was making a respectable showing, and Smoke was reminded of the etiquette between the great aces of World War I following a well-fought engagement, of flowing scarves and salutes between cockpits, as he mirrored the nose-high attitude of the Foxbat with his jet and passed close enough several times during their fight to see the color of the other pilot's white helmet. Smoke never feared he would lose, but he hoped winning would not come with the price of killing his adversary. He felt unjust in punishing a good pilot for his country's aircraft procurement failings.

Finally, the MiG would fly no longer. Smoke saw the Foxbat shudder slightly, and then snap roll to the right and drop like a rock. The lieutenant commander anticipated the MiG's fall from grace, and booted his rudder full in the direction of the enemy jet until the Foxbat filled the view through the front of his canopy. At that point, the lieutenant commander selected Guns, let the sight walk behind the Iraqi's canopy, and pulled the trigger. The nose cannon cooked off a hundred rounds, every fifth bullet a tracer, and the American pilot watched with cold satisfaction as the bulk of the ammo hit the enemy jet on the left wing and fuselage. The dotted line of hits joined with a number of angry flashes, and flames quickly engulfed the rear half of the MiG. Smoke was pleased to see the ejection seat fire, and shortly after, a parachute open.

"Splash Four!" Smoke called to the AWACS. "Titan, call our picture."

"Titan shows picture clear. No other air activity at this time."

"Roger, we copy that. Diamond flight is out of gas and heading back to the Boat."

"Good show, Diamond," the controller returned. "Good show."

The young enlisted man walked back into the *Arrowslingers'* paraloft after eating lunch on the mess deck five stories below. "I don't know about you, Smitty," he sighed, "but I am really sick of corn dogs."

"I know the feeling, son," Parachute Rigger First Class Smith replied. "What's that you've got there?"

The airman looked at the object in his right hand as if it surprised him. "Oh," he said, "I stopped by the electronic repair shop to bullshit with my man MacAffee for a while, and he gave me back this radio that we'd given their shop last night for a routine inspection." The sailor walked over to the squadron flight schedule and ran his finger along the list of pilots for the day. "I think it belongs to the skipper . . . where's his name? Okay, here it is. He's flying tonight. I'll stick this back into his survival vest."

"Don't bother," Smitty said to his junior co-worker with dismay. "The skipper's airborne. He jumped into the second event at the last minute. In fact, he was a regular pain in the ass about it. He was so fired up about going flying, he accidentally shot his pistol in here."

"You're shitting me."

"No. It scared the fuck outta me. The gun fired, and officers were diving all over the place. The bullet bounced around a few times and lodged in one of the helmets."

"Was anybody killed?"

"You think you would've gone this long on this boat without hearing about somebody's getting killed? You know that gouge hound MacAffee would've told you about it. No, nobody was killed." The petty officer motioned to the worktable in front of him. "Just put the radio down here. We'll replace it in the skipper's gear when he gets back."

"Do you think he'll notice?" the youngster asked innocently enough.

The petty officer shook his head and responded dryly, "Only if he gets shot down . . ."

Commander Campbell hit the ground first, coming down in the western outskirts of the city of An Najaf. No locals were there to greet him, but he knew his descent had not gone unnoticed by the residents or the military authorities in the city. They were all certainly headed his way in good numbers. He unfastened the fittings to the risers, rolled his parachute into a ball, and stuffed it deep into the nearest thicket of brush. Once he was certain the bright orange-and-white cloth was concealed, he disconnected the seat pan from the lower straps of his harness and cracked it open. He quickly assessed what he might need and what he could discard, keeping the bag of water, the space blanket, the packet of hard candy, and the small first-aid kit. He then closed the seat pan back up and tossed it into the bush with the parachute. He looked back to the city and, seeing no activity, took off into the desert to the west.

Although he felt the desire to sprint, the skipper paced himself with an athletic jog, figuring he'd ultimately be able to go farther in less time at the more moderate pace. The commander was in good physical shape, and he ran for a while, stopping only occasionally to look over his shoulder back toward the town.

After covering two miles, he started to make out a line of camels on the western horizon ahead of him. Reasoning that the animals had nomads handling them and wanting to avoid human contact, he jumped into a nearby dry gully and waited for the train to pass. His breathing slowly quieted from the runner's huff he'd maintained during the first part of his evasion, and, once it did, he was able to hear jets overhead. For the first time since he'd hit the ground, he thought to try and communicate his status over his survival radio.

The skipper reached for the right-hand pouch on his vest and pulled the zipper back. A wave of shock hit him when he discovered that the radio was not where it should have been. He reeled in the nylon security cord like an angler who feared he'd just been robbed of his prized lure and was hit with another burst of nauseating adrenaline once he reached the bitter end. The skipper maniacally slapped at himself hoping the radio might have been placed in another of the many pockets that adorned his flight gear, but he came up empty. He fell to the bottom of the gully in a heap of anger and frustration and punched and kicked the dirt, threw his helmet, and cursed at the top of his lungs. He screamed of conspiracy and envy and of the weak-minded sons of bitches surrounding him at every turn. He was the victim of professional negligence and there would be courts-martial upon his return—courts-martial and then public hangings.

The skipper continued his tirade until fatigue overwhelmed him. He flopped chest-down on the side of the gully and started to look to the eastern horizon but was instead greeted by a pair of legs just inches in front of him. The commander screamed in horror and recoiled back into the center of the gully.

He tripped as he fell and, after a backward somersault, wound up with his spine against the other side of the ditch. He threw his hands up in surrender, squinted through the cloud of dust to assess his captor, and was relieved to discover a lone boy looking down on him. The skipper laughed boldly and dropped his hands. "Go away," the commander directed with several outward casts of his knuckles. "Shoo . . ."

The boy stood with the moderate breeze flapping his white robe and black vest, holding a shepherd's staff nearly twice his height. "I said get out of here," the skipper shouted. The boy remained frozen, but not because of fear. The little Arab's eyes held no emotion as they continued to lock the downed American pilot. *This kid can't be alone,* the skipper thought. *He's too calm.*

The commander reached for his pistol and began to turn when the lights went out.

"Iron One, this is Iron Two RIO . . . How do you read? Iron One, this is Iron Two RIO . . . How do you read?" The transmission was barely audible to the crew in the F-14 leveled at ten thousand feet to avoid drawing any small arms or shoulder-fired SAM fire until it might become absolutely necessary to effect a rescue.

"Einstein . . . Einstein, is that you?" Spud asked in return. "Are you all right?" The aviators had lost sight of both chutes at some point in their descent, and had waited eagerly to hear from one or both of the crews on the ground.

"Yeah, I'm fine," the RIO replied, again very quietly. "I see some vehicles coming toward me."

"What's your position?" Spud asked. "Give us a range and bearing from SAM Site Bravo."

Einstein studied the hand-held global positioning system he'd fished out of his vest and fought a paralyzing sense of frustration. Goddam the skipper for being such an idiot. He wouldn't listen, would he? And now look at the mess they were in. "I don't have that information," Einstein dejectedly passed into his radio. "I don't know the lat and long for SAM Site Bravo. It was written on my kneeboard card but I lost it during the ejection."

"All right. Hold on." Spud keyed the intercom. "What do you think, Punk?"

"The SEALs can home in on his radio," Punk replied. "Maybe we'll just have to wait for them to show up in the helicopter."

"I think they're coming for me," Einstein called, even quieter than before. "I see some trucks headed my direction."

"Are you hidden?" Spud asked.

"I think so, but maybe not well enough. There's really no good place to hide around here. They're headed right for me now, about half a mile away, maybe less than that."

"Stay low," Spud commanded, "but try and see if there are any landmarks you could call out to us. We don't see you or the trucks."

Einstein scanned the entire horizon surrounding him. "Like I said, there's nothing here but sand and rock and bushes, Spud. I don't know what to tell you."

"Shoot a flare," Spud ordered over the radio.

"That'll give his position away," Punk returned on the intercom.

"They already know where he is, but we don't," Spud explained before keying the distress frequency again. "Einstein, shoot a flare—now."

Einstein dug through his vest and found a flare. He stepped a few feet from the two clumps of bushes he'd crawled between, held the flare away from his face, and fired. It took off with a resonant thump and arced brightly across the sky. Once sure the flare had worked, he jumped back under cover.

"I've got it," Spud said. "Down the canopy rail at ten o'clock."

"I'm tally, I'm tally," Punk said. "Einstein, where are the trucks from you?"

The young RIO held his pocket compass at eye level and took a reading. "Zero-two-zero . . . They bear zero-two-zero from me . . . Half a mile away at the most."

Punk spied a column of dust. "Spud, can you get the pod on them?"

"Can you read a book through a straw?" the lieutenant commander replied. "I'm trying. Bring 'em to the nose."

Punk buried the nose and pointed the jet toward the column. "Look for the dust trail they're kicking up . . ."

"There we go . . . got 'em," Spud said. "I'm breaking out some trucks and some armored personnel carriers. It looks like four total."

"Einstein, keep your head down," Punk called as he put the jet into a climbing right-hand turn now that Spud had acquired the targets. The LANTIRN pod's gimballed lens would now automatically track the target, regardless of the F-14's heading, as long as Punk didn't blank out the pod's view with the fuselage, which, with the pod mounted under the right wing, was why he chose a right-hand turn.

He looked at his altimeter: eight thousand feet, lower than they should have been to remain out of the reach of anti-aircraft fire. He kept climbing. The pilot looked at his repeat of Spud's display and saw they had a bead on one of the Iraqi vehicles. Punk depressed a button near his thumb on the stick, releasing one of the two thousand-pound bombs strapped to the Tomcat.

Spud waited until he felt the thump of the bomb clearing the airplane and then fired the laser while holding the crosshairs over one of the personnel carriers. He eagerly watched the display for impact. "This is either going to scare the shit out of the rest of them, or really piss them off."

"I'm banking on the first option," Punk replied.

The weapon hit and the resultant violence was vividly captured in their view through the LANTIRN pod. Spud decreased the magnification by one click, and the crew observed the remaining vehicles scatter in all directions.

"That was awesome, but close," Einstein called over the radio. "Don't drop anything west of your last hit or you'll take me out, too."

The vehicles continued to drive away from the flaming wreckage for a while, but eventually all turned back toward Einstein. "These guys don't learn very quickly," Punk commented as he rolled toward them for the second time.

"No, they don't," Spud agreed as he walked the pod's crosshairs from a truck to the remaining personnel carrier. "Hopefully our bluff will stick with our last bomb." With that, Punk punched off the final thousand-pound precision-guided bomb. Again, they concentrated on their screens as two guys plopped on their couches at home might concentrate on an exciting football game on TV.

The personnel carrier swerved at the last instant, and the second bomb hit long. The explosion caused the vehicles to disperse as they had following the first hit, but again they weathered the attack and returned to their quest for Einstein.

"I was afraid it would come to this," Punk said.

"Hold on," Spud said over the intercom before keying the radio. "Titan, any word from the Sandy package?"

"Negative. They haven't checked in yet."

Spud knew what was on his pilot's mind. He glanced down at his display and saw that Punk had switched his weapons toggle to Guns. The RIO cursed his luck as he realized the lieutenant in front of him was taking a crucial step toward becoming either the bravest or the dumbest nose gunner he'd ever been paired with.

Without another word between them, Punk rolled in on the vehicles more aggressively than he had the first two runs. While he sighted through his HUD and waited for his in-range cue, he noticed small bursts of light from the ground, like flashbulbs going off.

"They've jumped out of the trucks and they're shooting at you," Einstein reported from the bushes.

Punk responded by pulling the trigger on his stick, and he watched the tracers streak toward the ground but had to pull up before they hit their marks. As he jinked the nose back above the horizon, the jet bottomed out at fifteen hundred feet. He rolled quickly to the left and tried to assess the damage he'd been able to inflict with his strafing run.

Einstein came on the air again with, "SAM in the air."

Spud had already caught sight of the shoulder-fired missile's distinctive spring-shaped smoke trail, and as Punk pulled the throttles back to cool the engines, the RIO twisted one of the switches on his right console four times, which caused an equal number of flares to fire out of the same buckets that housed the bundles of chaff used to confuse radar operators. Shoulder-fired SAMs were heat-seekers and the flares were designed to give the missiles something hotter than the jet's motors to seek. This time the SAM took the bait and exploded harmlessly behind them as they climbed for a second strafing run.

"Where the hell is the CSAR package?" Punk asked. "We've only got three or four more bursts from the gun and then we're done."

"Titan, we can't hold the locals off the survivor much longer," Spud reported over the AWACS frequency.

"Roger. I still have no comms with Sandy," the Air Force controller replied before changing the subject. "Iron One, I showed you momentarily below the minimum authorized altitude. You're reminded that aircraft are not allowed below ten thousand feet without a waiver from Zeus."

"We need the waiver," Spud instructed.

"Titan copies. We'll coordinate clearance with Zeus. Remain above ten thousand feet until further notice."

"Roger . . ." Spud replied without any intention of complying with the guidance.

"Spud," Punk shot over the intercom, "we can't strafe from ten thousand feet, and we don't have time to sit up here and wait for this administrative horse shit to happen. The gomers will be on Einstein any second now."

"I concur," Spud returned. "But if we wreck the car, dad will really be pissed."

"I never liked dad," Punk said as he rolled in and executed another strafing run, and this time as he pulled out, several Iraqi bullets struck the canopy just behind his seat. Spud jerked his head below the canopy rail and shouted "fuck!" over the intercom as bits of Plexiglas flew into his cockpit, but he immediately rose back up and scoured the ground for SAMs.

"Are you hit?" Punk asked as he continued the climb and surveyed the damage behind him.

"No, I'm fine," Spud replied. "They might have our number."

"That's true," Punk said, "but they're not going to get Einstein on my watch." Accompanied by the discussion between the AWACS controller and the watch officer in the JTF-SWA command center about whether or not the Tomcat should be allowed below ten thousand feet, Spud attempted to dig his fingernails into the thick plastic glare shield above his instrument panel as Punk white-knuckled the controls and rolled in for a third strafing run.

The first thing Commander Campbell noticed when he regained consciousness was a terrible stench. He opened his eyes and saw that he'd been lashed across the back of a camel. He tried to move but couldn't, and soon the camel's heave as it walked coupled with the discomfort of the bindings and the pressure on his ribs caused him to feel motion sick. "Hey," he cried, "get me down."

The animal was halted and several nomads came into view, all apparently startled by the fact the commander had spoken. The little boy from the gully struck several blows to the skipper's neck and shoulders with his shepherd's stick and an older nomad flashed the skipper's pistol while shouting at him in Arabic. The skipper pleaded for the boy to stop the beating, but that just seemed to further enrage them.

Just as the commander was sure he was going to vomit, a military truck raced up and came to a stop in a cloud of dust. The skipper heard their approach, and he lifted his head in time to see several helmeted figures dressed in olive drab and armed with rifles jump out of the back of the truck. Half of them brusquely herded the nomads into a group, and the other half gathered around the left side of the camel where the skipper's head hung toward the ground.

The skipper felt the rope around the belly of the beast slacken, and, with ankles and wrists still bound, he was lowered to the dirt and stretched flat on his back. He wasn't sure what to expect as the soldiers removed his boots and socks, but their intent was quickly made clear with the hellish sting of a rifle butt across the bottom of his feet.

The commander could hear laughter over his screams as strikes landed. He lost count of the hits and felt himself detach. He heard somebody wailing even louder than he was, and he looked over and saw another American flyer being beaten, and as their eyes met, he realized he was looking at himself. Then he saw himself begin to heave.

The taste in his mouth ended his out-of-body experience, and he fought to turn over against those who held him down. His tormentors took note of his gags and stopped their assault. They continued to laugh as he rolled onto his stomach and yielded to the angry waves of nausea.

Once the convulsions ceased, the skipper twisted onto his back and tried to reach to the small pocket on the left biceps of his flight suit. "Blood chit," he shouted at them as he jerked his thumbs toward the pocket as far as his bound wrists would allow. "Blood chit. Money."

Two of them pinned him again, and an Iraqi officer, distinguishable by his black beret, leaned across the skipper, unzipped the pocket, and removed the blood chit. The Iraqi officer read it, chuckled, and then read it aloud. The entire group laughed boisterously. The

Iraqi officer wadded the tear-proof paper in the skipper's face, screamed something at him in Arabic, and then slapped him twice. The officer shouted some orders at the men and then climbed back into the cab of the truck on the passenger's side. The skipper was blindfolded and thrown between the troop benches that ran the length of either side of the bed. The soldiers climbed in around him and took turns kicking him as the truck began to move.

After twenty minutes of bouncing across the desert, the soldiers grew tired of their prey. The skipper lay dazed and bruised along the bed, still as death for fear that any movement might cause the soldiers to recommence the beatings. The truck stopped and the soldiers got out, leaving the skipper alone in the back. He listened intently to the shuffling of boots and the clicking of rifles as the officer barked orders at the men, and in his mind's eye he saw them lining up into a firing squad.

Then hands were on him again, and he was slid along the bed and propped up onto his feet on the dry plain behind the truck. The blindfold was removed along with the bindings on his ankles and wrists. Before him stood a tall man in a uniform similar to the rest, but with more sparkle to it.

"Commander Campbell, welcome to Iraq," the man said in perfect English. The skipper wondered how the Iraqi knew his name and rank, but then saw that he was holding the leather nametag from his flight suit. "I am Colonel Nabbah."

The colonel gestured to the boots that had newly been placed at the skipper's feet. "I believe these are yours. Please put them back on." The skipper sat on the dirt and gingerly worked his boots over his sore feet. "I apologize for the overzealous conduct of my countrymen. I'm afraid they are a bit excited after today's battle."

Once the skipper finished tying his boots, the colonel guided him into the back seat of a large Mercedes staff car idling nearby and then walked around the rear bumper and joined him from the opposite side. As soon as the colonel shut his door, the car sped off. The skipper fought the urge to ask where they were going, figuring that he was in the middle of a "soft sell" routine. He had been schooled on this insidious technique during his SERE (Survival, Evasion, Resistance, and Escape) training right after flight school, and he knew that it was as dangerous as torture in its ability to effect the flow of classified information.

"You must be thirsty," Colonel Nabbah said as he reached into a canvas bag between them and removed a liter of bottled water. "Please . . ."

The skipper accepted the offer with a nod and took a healthy series of draws on the plastic container. The cool water felt good as it streamed through his dry mouth and throat. "Where are you from?" the colonel asked. The commander didn't answer but stared blankly at the back of the driver's head directly in front of him. The Iraqi laughed to himself. "You don't feel like talking?"

"I *won't* talk," the skipper muttered, as much convincing himself of his resolve as responding to the colonel's question.

"That's fine," the colonel replied. "We really don't need you to talk . . . not right now, anyway. The fact that you're in our hands provides the nation of Iraq everything it needs. Plus, I'm sure your co-pilot will tell us everything we want to know."

Einstein. "Did you capture him?" the skipper blurted almost involuntarily.

The colonel smiled as he reached into the bag again and withdrew a bottle of water for himself. "See? You do like to talk." He took a swig from the bottle. "Don't you want to know where we're going?" The skipper attempted a return to his original silent tack, this time staring into the desert through his window. "I'm sure you do," the Iraqi continued. "We're going to drive above the thirty-third parallel and then get into a helicopter and fly the rest of the way to Baghdad." The colonel reached over and calmly grasped the skipper's right forearm. "Have you ever been to Baghdad?" The Iraqi's touch startled the commander, and he nervously twisted his head away from the window and found himself gripped by his captor's confident expression. The colonel laughed again and said, "No, of course not. Americans don't visit Baghdad. They drop bombs on it."

That's because Baghdad's not a very nice place, the skipper thought, but dared not say. At the same time, the idea of going to Baghdad horrified him, and the very sound of the word caused him to realize what shock had prevented thus far: He was in for the trial of his life. He tried to strengthen his resolve by remembering the Code of Conduct: *I am an American fighting man . . .*

They rode silently for a time until Colonel Nabbah lit a cigarette and started another monologue. "You know, I lived in New York City for three years." This time, although startled by the break in the quiet, the skipper forced himself to do nothing but gaze out the window as the Iraqi spoke. "I attended Columbia University until I was called back by the Revolution." The colonel took a long drag on his cigarette and smiled. "I learned much from your country, much more than you'll ever know."

*   *   *

Punk only got half a burst from the gun on his third strafing run, and as soon as the firing stopped he pulled out of the 30-degree dive while Spud threw the expendables switch twice as many times as there were flares remaining to obey his command. "We've got nothing left," the pilot said dejectedly over the intercom. "Einstein's as good as captured if the rescue package doesn't get here in the next minute or so."

"We've still got the drop tanks," Spud quipped. "We could drop those on 'em."

Punk considered the idea. "That'll work, Spud. Set up the switches to jettison the tanks."

"I was kidding . . . It was a joke, get it?"

"No, it's our last chance," Punk countered. "They'll see them come off the jet and they'll have to honor them."

"I think they know you're out of bullets," Einstein shouted over the distress frequency. "They're all out of the trucks now firing up at you."

"Ah, shit . . . All right," Spud said with resignation to his pilot. "One more run. Maybe we'll even hit something. Even an empty drop tank can do some damage."

Punk rolled in one last time and this time as he established the jet in the dive twice as many white flashes as before greeted him. "This is going to be ugly . . ." he thought aloud.

"Iron One, pull off high and right," a voice called over the distress frequency. "Survivor, stay put until further notice." As Punk started to raise the nose, he looked over his left shoulder to the southwest and saw one A-10 diving toward the Iraqis and then another plunging toward the desert, 45 degrees off the

strike axis of the first jet. Punk leveled the F-14 and
started an orbit overhead to watch the Air Force jets
execute their attack.

The A-10s each shot several missiles on the way
down while simultaneously firing their 30-millimeter
Gatling guns. Punk looked to the ground around the
vehicles and saw the incendiary bullets stir the dirt like
schools of fish disturb the surface of a lake, and then
the Maverick air-to-surface missiles exploded with
deadly accuracy. Once the blasts settled, all that remained mobile was a lone truck limping toward the
east, finished off in short order by a follow-on fusillade
from the lead Warthog. The scene was disquieting and
exhilarating at the same time.

"Sandy Three, the zone is secure," the A-10 lead
called to the HH-60 crew who trailed him by ten miles.
"We'll be flying low cover."

"Sandy Three copies," the helicopter pilot replied.
The Navy lieutenant turned to the SEAL team leader,
another Navy lieutenant, behind him and asked, "Are
you ready?"

The SEAL responded with a thumbs up and then
turned to his team as he slammed the magazine into
his M-4 rifle. "Load 'em up, gentlemen; load 'em up."

Einstein heard the distinctive sound of the helicopter's rotors as it approached. The young RIO mentally reviewed the pickup procedures and tried to
recall the information he'd put on his ISOPREP card,
personal information that the rescue crew would use
to quiz him to ensure the enemy wasn't luring them
into a trap. *My first dog was a beagle named Sparky,* he
recalled repeatedly, fearing he might choke in the heat
of the rescue and cause the team to retire without him.
My first dog was a beagle named Sparky.

The helicopter pilot directed Iron Two RIO to pop

a smoke near his position to show the SEAL team exactly where he was and to allow the pilots to assess the direction of the wind for the landing. The HH-60 set down about fifty yards from Einstein, and at that point, the RIO emerged from the bushes with his hands in the air. Once he caught sight of the SEALs running for him, he fell to his knees and waited for their instructions.

Einstein was suddenly jumped from behind. His right arm was twisted painfully behind him, and he felt the blade of a knife at his throat. His assailant coolly uttered, "Who won the college world series last year?" into his right ear.

"What?"

"Who won the college world series last year? Your life may depend on the answer . . ."

Einstein gulped and replied, "I don't know."

"Okay, then what was the name of your first dog?"

"Sparky," Einstein shouted. He was hoisted to his feet and hurried to the helicopter. Once past the chaos of the rotor-generated wind blast, the RIO was pushed through the crew door in a heap, and the SEALs piled in behind him. As they lifted off, the door gunner put a few rounds from his mini-gun into the wreckage of the vehicles for good measure. The HH-60 raced south just a few feet off the ground with the two A-10s in company above it.

"Iron Two RIO aboard Sandy Three," the helicopter pilot relayed over the AWACS frequency. Cheers erupted in the Current Operations Cell at JTF-SWA and were soon followed by more from Flag Briefing and Analysis aboard the Boat. At the same time, the next Southern Watch event began to check in with the AWACS to continue the search for Commander Campbell.

Twenty-five minutes later, the HH-60 touched down at Camp Doha, Kuwait. Just over two hundred fifty miles to the north, two burly guards were escorting the skipper from Colonel Nabbah's staff car to a Russian-made transport helicopter for the final leg to Baghdad.

NINE

"I can't believe we're just sitting here," Biff said to the rest of the officers gathered around the circle in the middle of the Cheesequarters.

"Believe it," Trash advised. "Congress is full of weak tits. This country used to protect its own—even assholes like the skipper."

"It's not Congress. It's the United Nations," Monk said. "There's no support in the U.N. for punitive strikes against Iraq. Our coalition, if you can call it that, is falling apart. It seems like the international community is starting to listen to Iraq's side of the argument."

"You think too much, Monk," Trash said. "Sometimes in life you should just react. Don't you ever wanna smash some joker in the face when he pisses you off?"

"Last time I checked, assault was a crime, Trash," Monk replied.

"See?" Trash said. "That's exactly what I'm talking about. That's why you're bald. Your hair got bored with hanging out with you."

"I'm with Biff and Trash," Fuzzy said. "It's time to fish

or cut bait. If we're not going to head home, then let's kick some ass. We've flown less since we got extended here in the Gulf than we did before this crisis, if you can call it that."

Biff pointed to the television above Fuzzy's head. "Look, the skipper's on the news again. Turn it up." Fuzzy tapped the volume button a few times and then flipped his seat around to face the screen along with the other six officers in the room.

Although they'd seen the tape many times in the last five days, the footage still captivated them. The skipper entered the stark white room from the right and was escorted to a chair behind a wooden table on which sat a single microphone. Once he was seated, the camera zoomed in on his upper torso and head. His face was bruised below both eyes, and his thick hair was a wild mess. His flight suit had been stripped of patches, and he wore it zipped fully up to his neck. The commander didn't look at the camera but stared at the floor in front of him. He squinted as a spotlight was turned on and shifted toward his face, causing a dance of shadows on the wall behind him, and then he nervously shot a look off to his right, apparently listening to someone off camera. The skipper nodded compliantly and began to speak in a plodding monotone.

"I am Commander Alexander Campbell, United States Navy." The skipper paused and coughed twice. "I was patrolling the no-fly zone over Southern Iraq when I was shot down by a surface-to-air missile." He let out another cough, this time a single, drawn-out hack. "I do not have any comment on my situation." Another long, single cough. "I would just like to tell my family that I am fine and that, God willing, I will see them soon." The segment ended as it had each of the hundreds of times it was previously televised with the skipper offering a halfhearted wave and rising from his chair.

"That's a bad cough the skipper's got there," Fuzzy observed. "Einstein, was he sick the day you got bagged?"

"No . . ." The wheels were already turning in the young RIO's head. "Remember some of the tricks the POWs used during Vietnam? One of them blinked 'torture' in Morse code while he was being filmed by an East German propaganda team." Einstein grabbed a small notebook from his desk and began to scribble on one of the sheets of paper inside of it. "Maybe that wasn't just a random cough . . . Maybe he was trying to relay a message."

"What are you talking about?" Trash asked as he stood and adjusted the terrycloth towel around his waist.

"Look at this." Einstein held his notebook up and pointed to what he'd written on the paper. "He coughed twice, and then once, and then once—dot-dot, dash, dash. In Morse code that's 'ITT.'"

"And . . ." Trash returned impatiently.

"The ITT Building," Einstein explained. "That's our code name for their communications headquarters in downtown Baghdad. It's on our target list for the contingency strikes. The Iraqis are probably holding the skipper there." He slammed the notebook shut and stood up. "We need to find the Pats."

"Einstein, you're a genius," Monk proclaimed.

"That's how I got my call sign . . ." the young RIO returned with a cocksure smile.

In Punk's mind, the anticlimax of their status was bad theater. Entertainment demanded a sense of timing, and that sense was apparently missing among those in the chain of command above him, right up to the president. The actors are supposed to be out of sight once the final curtain falls, not left hanging around in the footlights at the front of the stage. Now the lieutenant sat in CVIC, surrounded by charts, calculators, laptop computers, time lines, and dozens of Styrofoam cups half full of cold coffee. He watched a repeat of the video teleconference that included the admiral in Flag Briefing and Analysis, and listened to General Bullock at JTF-SWA size up the situation.

Punk wondered how he had ever been roped into the sorry world of macro-level strike planning, remembering what he had come to realize a long time ago: Navy status quos were easily established and hard to change once created. He'd stumbled onto the last strike planning team, so naturally he'd be part of any follow-on strike planning teams. A sticky booger he couldn't flick off his finger.

The general attempted to explain the big picture to folks he sensed had long since grown weary of their task, and as he spoke, his voice carried a message of resignation despite his earnest pitch regarding the importance of their undertaking. Words like "readiness" and "freedom" and "flexibility" failed to hide the fact that the general had become a cheerleader on the sidelines of a game that was already over. But he kept cheering all the same . . .

The Navy's role had originally called for the Boat to simply hand their part of the plan over to the Other Boat and then start the trip back to the United States. That plan was changed once the skipper and Einstein were shot down. The Boat was "extended indefinitely" in the Arabian Gulf by the president, and the National Security Council ordered the Joint Chiefs of Staff who ordered the commander in chief of the U.S. Central Command who ordered the commander of Joint Task Force–Southwest Asia to be ready to execute strikes

against Iraq utilizing both carriers as well as all the Air
Force and Marine Corps air assets in the region. Those
orders meant that the plan Punk had helped create in
Riyadh was old news and that a new plan had to be developed.

There wasn't time for another three-day trip to
Saudi Arabia, so all joint coordination between Es-
kavah Village and the rest of the commands around
the region was performed over secure phones and
other classified electronic systems, including video
teleconferencing for the flag officers. The Navy's target assignments and strike chronology came over the
wires in CVIC, and the intel geeks retrieved them one
by one out of the printers and ran them to the planning teams like newsmen with a hot scoop.

As painful as the planning process in Saudi Arabia
had been, Punk quickly discovered distance planning was worse. Confusing changes arrived without
explanation, and their incorporation was left to
those on the receiving end. The planners' frustration
grew exponentially as, each time they thought they'd
finally solved the puzzle, another change arrived that
scrambled the pieces again. And, on top of everything else, the goddam news on the TV in the corner
of the room kept reporting that nobody supported a
war.

Then the news covered U.N. Secretary General
Olaf Svarsbrooder's trip to Baghdad and the
progress of his peace plan. There was also a story
about how the king of Saudi Arabia had told the U.S.
secretary of state that if the Air Force launched
strikes from Saudi soil they would have to land somewhere else. The Bahrainis were saying the same thing.
Punk cursed at the soon-to-be-outdated joint coordination spreadsheet he'd just figured out covering the

table before him as the secure phone rang, and General Bullock walked off camera. Those gathered braced for the next surge of pain.

A few minutes later, the general reappeared and said, "It looks like this is a Navy-only war, gentlemen. Standby for some changes."

"Some changes?" Punk called out irreverently from where he sat. "Dropping the Air Force from the plan is a lot more than 'some changes.'" He left his chair and walked across the room to where Rex was seated. "I want to go on record as saying this sucks."

"The line for that sentiment forms to the rear, shipmate," Rex replied.

"So are we taking the same target list and splitting it between the two air wings now, or what?"

"That's a likely possibility."

"So much for a three-day war." Punk picked up Rex's copy of the target list and brushed a finger down the length of it. "It'll take us twice as long to get through this list without the Air Force."

"Uh-huh . . ."

"Tankers?"

"If you mean Air Force tankers the answer is probably no. Those that aren't stationed at Al Kharj are based in Bahrain. If you mean S-3s then the answer is yes."

"I don't mean S-3s," Punk shot back with all of the frustration he felt. "We've got targets around Baghdad. How are we supposed to go that far without heavy tankers?" The pilot let out an exasperated pshaw. "The skipper doesn't have to worry about fratricide while he's camped out in the ITT building. We can't even get there now." Rex started to reply but caught sight of the other admiral on the VTC screen and moved closer to the monitor.

"What's the allowable risk?" the other admiral asked into the little camera inches in front of his face.

"I believe it's low," the admiral replied into his own lens.

"Well," the other admiral followed hyperbolically, "I guess that rules out one-way missions." Beyond that realization, they still had a lot of work to do. In many ways, despite the hours they'd spent planning thus far, they hadn't even started planning yet. Home—that carrot that had been cruelly dangled before their collective face—remained a long way off—almost as far away as the war they were now wrestling with. Punk quietly cursed his miserable life, rolled up the sleeves of his flight suit, and made ready to continue their work, knowing that he'd now lost what was left of the idealism that might have made the task a bit easier.

But just as the rising tide of crises threatened to flow over all their hastily placed sandbags of accommodation, an angel of mercy in the form of a female correspondent beamed from the TV in CVIC and shored up their defenses once and for all. Following a breaking news graphic, she appeared from the streets of Baghdad.

"We have just learned from both Iraqi and United Nations spokespersons that U.N. Secretary General Olaf Svarsbrooder has brokered an end to the standoff between the United Nations and Iraq. Here is a statement Mr. Svarsbrooder made just minutes ago."

The scene shifted to a microphone-covered podium in a dark-paneled room. Behind the podium stood a diminutive man whose head barely crested into view. He spoke the King's English, but with a distinct Scandinavian accent as he delivered his message. "I am pleased to announce the terms of the agreement between the United Nations and the nation of Iraq. After much deliberation, Iraq has agreed to remove all troops and weapons from south of the thirty-third parallel in accordance with the original U.N. mandate. Iraq has also agreed to release the American pilot, Commander Campbell, to U.N. officials. In return, the United Nations will review the terms of the sanctions against Iraq and the conduct of weapons inspections. I thank all negotiators involved in the peace process for averting a greater crisis and ask the world to appreciate the utility of the United Nations in these sorts of situations. Thank you, and God bless."

Punk and Rex sat motionless, numb from the emotional Ping-Pong game they'd played over the last week. They both stared blankly at the reams of strike planning documents that surrounded them, afraid to acknowledge the latest turn of events for fear that it was nothing but another cruel joke.

A minute later, Spud walked into CVIC and tried to break them out of their ugly spell. "I just ran into the admiral's air ops officer, boys." He swept his thin arm over the table in front of them. "Give all this shit to the Other Boat. The governor has called. We've been granted a reprieve." The two strike planning team members still didn't respond. "Didn't you hear me?" Spud asked the pair of frozen forms. "We're headed home."

With that, Punk slowly raised his arm and Rex met him in a fatigued but heartfelt high five.

Although the Boat had only traveled part of the way back to Norfolk and there were many waters left to navigate, the captain was as ready to unwind as anybody else on the carrier. He ruled that their Suez Canal transit would be a celebration complete with a basketball tournament, live music from the ship's bands, karate and judo demonstrations, a talent contest, and, most important, a massive barbecue that featured all the steak the crew could eat. Upbeat moods stirred the air, and every conversation was put in terms relating to the end of cruise: two more pizza days. Four more laundry days. No more haircuts.

The Egyptian natives on the canal's western bank whistled and waved their arms as the carrier glided by. The circus had arrived in their town, if only for a few minutes. Towering ten stories high and packed with airplanes, bombs, and missiles, the Boat was an impressive demonstration of military might, but the impression left with the locals was more comprehensive than that. For all its difference from average American society, at times like this, the Boat was in many ways a perfect microcosm of it, like a traveling exposition of Americana.

A few of the sailors tossed their ball caps ashore, causing grown men to scurry like fans after a foul ball. The locals also received an unexpected souvenir, as the quarterback for one of the teams playing touch football near the stern overthrew his receiver and sent the pigskin bouncing down the flight deck and into the drink. Two boys in a rowboat were on the ball within seconds. "We'll probably see those two kicking field goals in the NFL in a few years," one of the sailors cracked to his teammates.

Spud and Punk used the occasion, as they had during the southbound transit, to chip the rust off of their golf swings by setting up a driving range between the airplanes parked on the starboard side near the stern. While preparing for the cruise, Spud had packed an Astroturf mat, complete with tee, and a laundry bag full of golf balls specifically for use during the Suez Canal transits.

Punk watched one of Spud's shots land between two tank hulks half-buried in the sands of the Sinai Peninsula and pondered the setting's history. "Why would anyone want to die over this? There's nothing here."

Spud held his follow-through and admired his handiwork as the next ball drew over the canal's bank. "Land is its own reward, I guess. I know I've had some hellacious arguments with my neighbor over the property line."

Punk chuckled and then stared blankly into the desert. Spud hit perfect shot after perfect shot until he noticed the silence next to him. He made a half turn on the mat, waved his hand, and said, "Hello? Earth to Punk . . ."

Punk spoke without turning his gaze from the Sinai. "I was just wondering if we really did anything."

Spud shrugged. "I dunno. We did our thing; now the Other Boat is doing their thing. It's their problem now." He stopped and turned completely around to face his pilot. "Why do you even worry about that? You'd better concentrate your energies on the important stuff like praying that the sun continues to set in front of the bow for the rest of this cruise. Remember it only takes ten minutes to turn the carrier around. One call from the Pentagon and we're back in the Gulf faster than you can say, 'Oh, shit.'"

The lieutenant commander reached down and plucked another ball out of the mesh bag and placed it on the rubber tee. He took his stance, waggled a few times, and then drew the four hundred dollar club smoothly back. As his hands came back down, the pass through the ball looked as technically sound as the thirty-odd that had preceded it, but this time the white sphere sliced wildly to the right and flew an awkward path until it hit the canal with a sorry splash.

"You're fucking me up here with all your heavy-duty meaning-of-life stuff, nose gunner boy," Spud said with disgust as he reached back into the mesh bag.

He regained his composure and was about to take the driver back again when Scooter scrambled out of the catwalk a dozen yards away and called over to them: "Hey, you guys, the skipper's homecoming will be on TV in a few minutes." Spud and Punk grabbed the few clubs they'd brought up from their staterooms and handed the driving range over to a couple of enlisted men who had been admiring Spud's form and asking him for swing tips. "Remember, boys," Spud passed as he headed for the ready room, "you can worry about a lot of different things with a golf swing, but in the end, it's all about keeping your head still." He relayed one more bit of advice before he got out of earshot: "Don't hit any Egyptians with a golf ball. We just got out of one international crisis, and we don't need another one."

The two aviators entered the ready room through the back door, tucked their clubs next to the sink, and moved to their chairs. The room was packed, as all of the squadron officers and senior enlisted men had come to see the latest, and perhaps final, chapter of the Commander Campbell saga unfold on the big screen.

"This homecoming is kind of a dubious occasion for the skipper, don't you think?" Biff asked Punk in the chair next to him.

"I guess," Punk replied. "I wouldn't want the world to know the circumstances that got me shot down. I'd slip out the back door of the transport, get into the minivan, and wait for the public to worry about something else."

In the front row, Spud asked Smoke about the intel debrief that had followed the fateful flight and how he'd characterized the skipper's actions. "You didn't pull any punches did you?"

"Trust me, Spud," Smoke said, "the chain of events spoke for itself. I told them the cold facts, and I imagine the rest will just follow the natural order of things." Smoke shot a furtive look down the row to the squadron's operations officer across the aisle from them. "I kinda feel sorry for Beads ... you know, latching onto a falling star," he whispered. "He invested a lot of pain and effort in his bright future only to have his sea daddy commit professional suicide."

"That's the risk you run playing that game," Spud stated. "Although what do I know? I'm a terminal lieutenant commander."

"Maybe ... but you've still got your pride."

"Oh? Can I send my kids to college with that?"

The news came out of a commercial and an expectant hush fell over the crowd. "Commander Alexander Campbell's long journey from the skies over Iraq to a cell in Baghdad to a hospital in Germany and then back to the United States is almost over," the anchorman said. "We now go to Andrews Air Force Base just outside Washington, D.C."

"It's a beautiful, clear, crisp winter day here at Andrews Air Force Base," the reporter observed. "The jet transport arrived from Wiesbaden, Germany, a few minutes ago, and we expect Commander Campbell to come out any second now. I'd like the cameraman to pan around and show the viewers just how big the crowd is here. Several thousand people have come out to welcome the commander home and—oh, I see the transport's door has just opened. Let's watch and listen to this poignant scene ..."

The skipper emerged from the cabin resplendent in his service dress blues, and the crowd let out a cheer.

Hundreds of balloons were released along with a covey of white doves. The Marine Corps Band began to play "Anchors Aweigh." The commander looked a little dazed as he stepped off the boarding ladder and limply shook hands with a silver-haired man who appeared very happy to see him.

"Damn," Punk exclaimed. "It's the fucking president."

The president guided the skipper into the loving arms of the long-suffering Mrs. Soup Campbell and their two teenaged daughters, and the camera focused on the family's tearful group hug.

The president moved the few steps to a podium and began to address the throng. "Today is a great day," he said, voice echoing dramatically through the public address system. "Today is a day where America shows the world what it's made of—what *we're* made of. Commander Campbell is a perfect example of that." The president paused with a broad smile until the round of enthusiastic applause and cheers died down. "Our freedom doesn't come easy. It's a gift given to us by people like the man standing next to me. So please join me in welcoming home a patriot for whom sacrifice is a way of life: Commander Alexander Campbell."

Another roar erupted from the crowd as the president threw his arms around the skipper in an exuberant bear hug. He pushed away, held the commander at arms' length, and studied him with his pat expression of national gratitude. The skipper wiped tears from his eyes. The president yielded the podium with a gesture and took a half-step back.

"Wow . . ." the skipper said emotionally as he leaned over the microphone. "I certainly didn't expect this sort of reception."

"I'll bet you didn't," Smoke muttered from across the planet as the thousands of well-wishers on the screen let out another cheer.

The skipper stood silently for a few moments, unsure of what to say, and just before the mood shifted from uplifting to awkward, he lamely offered, "God bless America!" The crowd erupted again, and the band took the CO's cue and began to play "God Bless America." The president ushered the Campbells the short distance to the limo and gave one last wave to the supporters before climbing in behind the family. The camera followed the official procession away from the flight line through a sea of arms, heads, balloons, banners, and doves.

"Oh my God," Spud announced in a state of wide-eyed denial. "Soup Campbell is an American hero."

Epilogue

Although it was still spring on the calendar, summer had come early to Virginia Beach, and a slight breeze blowing across the runways and through the open doors of the hangar was the only thing that kept the heat of early evening from dominating the awards ceremony. The large audience fanned themselves with their programs and shifted in their seats to stay cool as the Chief of Naval Operations made his way across the dais down the line of officers facing him at rigid attention dressed in their choker whites. Smoke, Spud, Turtle, Fuzzy, Gucci, Brick, and Bird stood wearing their new medals, highlighted by the orange glow of the setting sun as it disappeared behind the tree line across the field. The four-star moved in front of Punk, and the adjutant at the foot of the stage read the lieutenant's citation to the crowd:

The President of the United States takes great pride in awarding the Distinguished Flying Cross with Combat V to Lieutenant Richard J. Reichert,

United States Navy, for services as set forth in the following citation:

As the pilot of an F-14 Tomcat, Lieutenant Reichert demonstrated extreme courage and aviation prowess after his wingman was shot down during an Operation Southern Watch mission over Southern Iraq. With the help of his radar intercept officer, Lieutenant Commander O'Leary, and with little regard for his own safety, Lieutenant Reichert executed numerous bombing runs on Iraqi positions, neutralizing assets that threatened the capture of Lieutenant (junior grade) Paul Francis, one of two downed American airmen. Once he had expended all of his bombs, Lieutenant Reichert continued to pin the enemy down with strafing runs employing the Tomcat's gun. Even as enemy fire intensified, Lieutenant Reichert made multiple attacks, keeping the Iraqis from capturing Lieutenant (junior grade) Francis and effecting his eventual rescue by a Joint Task Force–Southwest Asia Combat Search and Rescue Team. Lieutenant Reichert's selfless dedication to duty reflected great credit upon himself, and his actions were in keeping with the highest traditions of the United States Naval Service.

The crowd applauded enthusiastically as the CNO pinned the medal to Punk's chest. The two of them shook, held the pose for the official photographer, and then shook some more as the admiral gave the lieutenant some heartfelt words of praise. The CNO then moved to the podium.

"This is just incredible," the admiral gushed. "How about one more round of applause for these brave men before you?" The gathering complied with the CNO's request and offered another round of applause. "I'll match these officers against any who've come before them. I mean that. Now before we end the ceremony, I have some special news." The admiral studied the line of officers on the stage. "Would Lieutenant Commander Stackhouse and Lieutenant Commander O'Leary please step forward?"

Spud and Smoke glanced at each other out of the corners of their eyes, exchanged subtle shrugs, and then simultaneously paced off a step. "I'm fresh from Washington where the command screen board finished up earlier this afternoon," the admiral continued. "I have in my hands the results of this board." He held several sheets of paper above his head. "I ordered the president of the board not to release these results until I returned from this ceremony because I wanted to make sure you good folks were the first to get the news." With a sly smile and a scan across the rows of people before him, the four-star paused to heighten the drama of the moment, like a celebrity presenter might do at the Academy Awards. "I'm pleased to announce Lieutenant Commander 'Smoke' Stackhouse and Lieutenant Commander 'Spud' O'Leary have been selected for squadron command. Congratulations, gentlemen." The crowd roared as Smoke and Spud's expressions of disbelief changed to irrepressible grins. The two carrier roommates shook hands, and although that display didn't fully capture the feelings between them, they left it at that.

Biff pushed away from the main bar at the officers club and waded through the mass of guests at the reception until he reached the more relaxed atmosphere of the back bar. He pulled up a chair and joined Punk seated at one of the quiet tables in the comfortable room. The big pilot reached into a back pocket of his tight white trousers and removed a folded sheet of paper, which he fanned in front of him like a small flag. "I got it."

"What?"

"My acceptance letter. I've been hired."

"Which airline?"

"Delta."

"Damn right, boy. Congratulations." Punk rose and shook Biff's hand across the table.

"Are you here alone?" Biff asked.

"I guess," Punk replied. "So much for my celebration."

"I wouldn't worry about that," Biff advised with a hearty laugh. "You can always take the CNO to dinner. Plus, there are plenty of boomerang girls left around this reception." The big pilot tossed his head slightly to the left a couple of times and continued to speak in a theatrical whisper. "In fact, don't look now, but I think your single status has been noticed."

Punk nonchalantly worked his scan across the room behind him and, in the process, awkwardly locked eyes with a high-speed blond leaning against the bar. "Goddam it, Biff," he said as he faced his squadronmate once again. "Don't do that."

"I told you not to look," Biff chided. "Man, I wish I was single again, not to mention a war hero."

"No, you don't; trust me. It's a long, cold journey out of the apartment once the panting stops."

Biff peeled the label from his beer bottle and pasted it on the surface of the table. "Pardon my curiosity, but have you heard from Jordan?"

"No," Punk returned. "To be honest I was halfway hoping she'd show up here since the ceremony had such a big build up on the local news and in the papers."

"Why don't you call her?"

"Because in her last letter she wrote that she'd call *me*." Punk's bold face failed to introduce the minor detail that he'd reached for the phone to call her countless times but something had always gone off in his head and kept him from going through with it.

"I've heard about you fighter pilots and your pride," Biff cracked before he took another swig and changed the subject. "So, Punk, you and I haven't talked about it lately. What's in your future?"

"What do you mean?"

"Are you going to stay in or get out?" The big man flapped his acceptance letter in front of him again. "The industry is looking for pilots like you read about, and I know some people to talk to now . . ."

"I appreciate that," Punk said.

Biff leaned in closer. "There are more of him out there, you know."

"Him?"

"You know damn well who I mean," Biff answered as he pointed to the far wall. "Him. Them. They're out there—more Soups waiting to make your life a living hell. He's not alone in this business. Just look at Beads."

"That's harsh, Biff," Punk said. "Beads wasn't that bad."

"You didn't work for him like I did. He's shown all the traits so far. He just needs the power." Biff rose from his chair. "Think about it. You're coming up for orders later this year. Now is the perfect time to make the move."

"I'll think about it, trust me," Punk replied. "I'm not interested in making my life any more painful than it has to be."

"Don't be."

"I won't."

"You shouldn't."

"I won't."

"All right." Biff folded the letter and returned it to his pocket as he stood up. "I've gotta find the wife. She doesn't really care for the club too much. She's probably standing by the front desk ready to go. Plus, we've got a sitter on the meter for seven dollars an hour. Can you believe that? Seven dollars an hour? That's really what we should do, Punk: Let's all get out of the Navy and become baby-sitters." He offered a small wave and moved out of the back bar and back into the crowd at the reception.

"Why isn't the game on TV?" Scooter cried from an adjacent table. "Reggie," he called to the bartender. "Can we get the game on?"

"Which one?" the old fixture asked back.

"The NBA finals, what else? Tonight's the deciding game."

"All right, all right," the white-haired curmudgeon mumbled as he fumbled with the remote he'd long ago ruled that only he could touch. "What channel?"

"Seven, I think."

The bartender walked the channels down from 13 and, when he passed through 8, Punk noticed something. "Hold it, Reggie," he called across the room. "Go back a few."

"Why?" Scooter protested as Reggie began climbing back through the channels.

"I thought I saw something," Punk explained while concentrating on the television. "Okay. Hold it there . . ." Commander Campbell appeared on the big screen before them dressed in his summer whites. The uniform's black shoulder boards with three gold stripes on each were well defined against the crisp whiteness of the certified Navy twill, and his shiny Wings of Gold and four rows of ribbons over the left breast pocket were highlighted by the studio's lighting. He was in the middle of a description of the events that led to his capture.

"I noticed my radio was missing, and I knew I was in trouble. I had no way to communicate with American forces. I had to dig in and get tough."

"What did you feel at that point?" the host asked. "Desperation? Fear? What goes through your mind?"

The skipper drew a deep breath and gazed above the host into the lights as if searching for inspiration. "All those things; all those things. But in the end, when every source of solace is shredded to bits, a man has to keep his head. He has to look down the barrel of a tough situation and say to himself: 'I'm going to beat this.'"

The host looked at the CO as if he were the wisest man he'd ever had on his show, nodded as one nods when offered truths from the mouths of great figures, and effused, "Yes . . ." before snapping himself out of the trance. "Let's go to the phones. Robert from Indigo, go ahead with your question for Commander Campbell . . ."

"Yeah . . . hello," the telephone-modulated voice said. "This is Robert from Indigo . . . hello?"

"Yes, Robert, we've got you," the host said. "Go ahead with your question."

"Yes, thank you. First off, I'd like to say I'm a big fan of your show. I watch every night."

"Thank you, sir. Your question, please."

"Before I ask my question, I'd like to tell Commander Campbell that I've seen him speak on TV several different times, and I want to say that he's given me new hope in the American way. I served in the Army for a few years, and since then I had become convinced that this country couldn't produce heroes any more. I now know that I was wrong."

Soup responded with a blush and a shy smile. "Actually,

I'm no different than any other hardworking member of the military out there serving the nation every day."

"I hope that's not true," Punk muttered.

"I was wondering . . . do you have any political aspirations?" the caller asked. "I'll hang up to hear the answer. Thank you both."

"That's a good question, commander," the host observed. "What's in your future? The country could always use another good leader."

"Well," the skipper replied as he smoothed the front of his thick hair, now more brown than gray. "I've got a lot more work left to do in the Navy. I've recently been selected for promotion to captain, and I've been told I should expect to be assigned as an air wing commander soon."

"Excuse me for my lack of military knowledge, but those are both good things, right?"

"Very good . . . very good."

"All right, folks, the book is called *Flight to Glory,* and we're dedicating the full hour to the author, Commander Alexander Campbell. We'll be right back with more insights from this modern-day American hero, and we'll be taking a lot more of your calls after this break, so stay tuned."

"I'm going to be sick," Scooter screamed. "I swear I'm going to lose my lunch on your table if you don't turn away from this, Reggie." He shouted over to Punk, "Can we watch the game now, or are you going to keep scratching your fingernails on the chalkboard here?"

Punk got up from the table. "Turn to the game, Reggie. I'm sorry we had to see that." He shuffled by the bar, through the smoked glass doors into the night and strolled across the expansive wooden deck until he bellied up to the rail ringing the edge of it on the far side.

With a sigh, he leaned against his elbows and looked down at the medal on his chest. He dropped one hand and fingered the bronze-colored propeller dangling from the red, white, and blue ribbon.

"Anybody need a fresh beer out here?" the executive officer asked, surprising Punk as he stepped across the deck. "Mind if I join you?"

"No, not at all, XO," Punk said as he waved him in.

"Beautiful night, isn't it?" the XO said as he handed Punk one of the two bottles he had threaded between his fingers.

"Sure is," Punk said with a nod of thanks as he twisted the cap off the bottle. "Even the commanders might go flying on a night like this."

The commander chuckled. "This has been quite a day, hasn't it?"

"Yes it has," Punk agreed. "Quite a day to go along with quite a year." He took a swig and looked over at the commander. "I don't know how you did it."

"Did what?"

"Stayed sane . . . you know . . . through all of it. You and Soup are such different types of people."

"Maybe," the commander allowed, "but he was the commanding officer, and I was the executive officer. That fact was—and remains—clearly defined. Trust me, two guys trying to be CO at the same time would've been worse."

"But how does he get away with it?"

"What?"

"*It* . . . the whole bogus program of his," Punk said. "You saw him on TV. He's been selected for captain, and he's going to be a CAG. He's still the commanding officer of this squadron and he hasn't even been here for three months. And now he's out there being an American icon and pushing his book, fer crissake."

"That's true. He will be a CAG. And when he holds that position, those below him will be his subordinates. And all the while, the Navy will keep going to sea. As for his fifteen minutes of fame, you have to understand that the public's perception of our business is important. As ironic as it might be, Soup's helping with that, and the Navy is naturally going to reward him for his efforts. Now, I've got my own opinion about the ethics of that situation, but that's the way it is. If it means that Congress is willing to fund our follow-on aircraft programs because they think Soup Campbell is a great American, then I'll live with it."

"He caused some good men to drop letters of resignation."

"That ebbs and flows," the XO said just before he lifted the bottle to his lips and took a healthy slug. "I'm not sure a guy like Biff would've stayed in regardless of who his commanding officer was." The XO allowed a short silence to hang between them. "Did I ever tell you my Leak Johnson story?"

"No sir. I don't think so."

"Leak Johnson was my first commanding officer. Actually, his call sign at the time was Tiny because he was a bit overweight. This guy was a real hateful bastard and was unanimously disliked by the boys in the ready room, but he did a masterful job of looking good to those above him in the chain of command. He was on his way and we were all convinced the system was flawed. He made captain, and because he had an engineering master's degree as well as a great record, he was put into the pipeline for command of a nuclear powered aircraft carrier. Now, if you get command of a nuke boat, chances are you're going to be selected for admiral. Admiral Johnson. We couldn't believe it. We all drafted our letters of resignation on principle alone."

The commander turned and took in the three-quarter moon shrouded by stars. "And then it happened."

"What?"

"It turns out he had trouble relating to his teenage son, who was a bright kid, but kind of a nerd and a real military buff. Well, Leak used to try and make points with the boy by telling him secret information: capabilities, numbers . . . the whole shooting match. So this kid was bragging to his friends at a Chess Club meeting about all the stuff he knows, and one of the teachers, a chief's wife, happened to hear. She knew the information sounded a bit too detailed, so she told the chief about it, and he then told the Naval Criminal Investigative Service. Long story short, Leak was yanked out of his training track overnight and forced to retire that same year."

"So, as far as Skipper Campbell goes . . ."

"Justice will be served before it's all over," the XO insisted. "He'll pull his own Leak Johnson stunt. Maybe he'll be somebody's chief of staff and get nailed by a female government service worker for sexual harassment or something. I don't know. I do know good leaders breed more good leaders, and if the system's lucky, bad leaders just breed angry junior officers who vow never to be like their bosses once they get in the same positions."

A car squealed its tires in the parking lot, and they both laughed. "So, what about you?"

The lieutenant raised his eyebrows and shrugged.

"Look, Punk, I'm not going to bullshit you. You're a good officer, and good officers will always have options. The CNO told me he wants to step up the date for the change of command, so that means I'll be the skipper sooner than expected. I'll need good officers to help run the squadron. Spud and Smoke will need good officers in the future." He patted Punk on the back. "Oh, one more thing. Soup doesn't have a Distinguished Flying Cross." The commander smiled as he moved away. "Enjoy the rest of your night."

Punk was left alone on the deck, and he stared into the night. He caught sight of the lights of an airliner and watched it scribe a predictable path across the star-dotted blackness—headed south, he figured, maybe toward the Virgin Islands or some other exotic destination. He considered life as an airline pilot and thought about what Biff would be getting into. Punk wondered what Jordan's reaction would be if he called her with the news that he'd dropped his letter of resignation and been hired by a major airline. Would a message of affluence and stability cause her to change her mind? Did he want her to change her mind?

Then the nearby roar of a fighter going into afterburner as it started its takeoff roll grew louder. Punk craned his head around until he caught sight of it. The thunder vibrated through him as the Tomcat passed over the club and pulled into a steep climb. He watched the jet scream upward, seemingly unbounded by gravity, and he knew the pilot under the canopy was looking down with the same feeling of superiority he'd possessed from that vantage point just yesterday. Punk followed the fighter until it disappeared from view.

The sound died off, and Spud appeared through the glass door, well into the celebration of his selection for squadron command. "I heard you were moping around out here," he called across the deck to his pilot. "Are you coming in?"

"Yeah," Punk replied. "I guess I am."

The electrifying fiction debut of
A MILITARY WRITER WHO "TRANSPORTS
READERS INTO THE COCKPIT."
—San Diego Union–Tribune

Robert Gandt

WITH HOSTILE INTENT

**A novel of modern-day dogfights
by a former Navy pilot**

"A RED-HOT AERIAL SHOOT-EM-UP...
for anyone who is, was, or wants to be part of the
glorious adventure that is naval aviation. Gandt makes
me wish I were doing it all over again."
—Stephen Coonts

"A GREAT JOB! The suspense builds, the
characters are believable, and the combat scenes are
excellent." —Dale Brown

AVAILABLE FROM SIGNET
0-451-20486-7

To order call: 1-800-788-6262

PENGUIN PUTNAM INC.
Online

Your Internet gateway to a virtual environment with
hundreds of entertaining and enlightening books
from Penguin Putnam Inc.

*While you're there, get the latest buzz on
the best authors and books around—*

Tom Clancy, Patricia Cornwell, W.E.B. Griffin,
Nora Roberts, William Gibson, Robin Cook,
Brian Jacques, Catherine Coulter, Stephen King,
Ken Follett, Terry McMillan, and many more!

**Penguin Putnam Online is located at
http://www.penguinputnam.com**

PENGUIN PUTNAM NEWS

Every month you'll get an inside look at our upcoming books and new features on our site. This is an
ongoing effort to provide you with the most
up-to-date information about
our books and authors.

Subscribe to Penguin Putnam News at
http://www.penguinputnam.com/newsletters